Mrs. Hudson in New York

Barry S Brown

Paperback ISBN978-1-78092-788-6
ePub ISBN978-1-78092-789-3
PDF ISBN978-1-78092-790-9

Published in the UK by MX Publishing
335 Princess Park Manor, Royal Drive,
London, N11 3GX
www.mxpublishing.co.uk
Cover design by www.staunch.com

Disclaimer

This is a work of fiction, and while real people and historic events are liberally sprinkled throughout the story, the situations described, and the parts played by the story's characters are drawn entirely from the author's fevered brow.

To Peter Mark Roget, about whose work Stephen King has written:

"Any word you have to hunt for in a thesaurus is the wrong word."

If true, there follows a host of wrong words.

Acknowledgements

Although liberties are taken with a reporting of some facilities of the original Waldorf Hotel in the interest of story-telling, the occasional accuracies in its description are a tribute to the assistance of Erin Allsop, archivist for the Waldorf-Astoria Hotel.

I am also indebted to Dr. Jeffrey Warhaftig for providing understanding of certain non-lethal effects of gunshots.

1.
Voyage to America

At precisely four o'clock, Mrs. Hudson entered the sitting room Holmes and Watson shared, set down her tray of tea and scones, poured out a cup for each man, and announced she would be leaving for New York City at the end of the week. She then proceeded to answer the question they shared before either man could pose it.

"I've gotten a letter from my cousin, Edna. She's the one with the daughter in service in America." Seeing their blank expressions, she explained, "Caroline. You met 'er when she was a maid to Mr. Junius Morgan, the American who was livin' in Knightsbridge. It was Mr. Junius' wish Caroline be kept on after 'e passed which is 'ow a place came to be made for 'er on the staff of Mr. Junius' son, Mr. J Pierpont Morgan. In fact, she 'as now become Mrs. Morgan's lady's maid." Mrs. Hudson took a sip of tea and made a face that had nothing to do with her tea. "Of course, that means she'll be livin' in America for a time."

While Holmes covered the corner of a scone with a generous dollop of strawberry jam, Watson screwed his face into a frown of recognition. "I do remember Caroline. If I'm not mistaken she came to Baker Street on one of her days out, probably five or six years ago. I remember her as a very attractive young lady with quite a mass of dark curly hair. But why is it so urgent for you to go see her? She's not in any trouble I trust."

"Quite the contrary, Doctor. My cousin writes that she's engaged and is to marry 'er young man the week after next. My cousin can't travel what with 'er own man bein' off 'is feet. Besides which, it bein' April, the season is just startin' in Brighton where they 'ave their pie shop. She's asked me to represent the family for 'er. Which I plan to do, and of course Edna will want a full report about Caroline's young man."

1

Holmes looked up from his pastry long enough to register his puzzlement. "If this Caroline is about to be married, isn't it a little late to be looking over her young man?

"Indeed it is, Mr. 'Olmes, but Edna's a worrier—that side of the family always 'as been."

Watson looked to Mrs. Hudson with a well-arched eyebrow. "Is there something about the young man your cousin finds worrying, Mrs. Hudson?"

"I won't say worryin' exactly, Doctor. I'd say more like confusin'. It's about the way 'e makes 'is livin'. Caroline writes that 'is job is doin' somethin' called baseball. 'E's what's called a pitcher, and the people 'e works for are called the Brooklyn Bridegrooms. Which all sounds strange enough, but it turns out 'e only works at that job six months of the year. My cousin doesn't see 'ow 'e can support a wife and family workin' six months a year at whatever it is a pitcher does. Of course, my cousin's been sellin' meat and fish pies in Brighton for fifteen years, almost entirely durin' the season, which you know is no more than six months long, but there'd be no good pointin' that out to Edna. Like I say, she's a worrier."

Holmes took a sip of tea to wash down a second bite of his scone, and looking to the cuffs of his dressing gown, he off-handedly elaborated a plan that was to change their lives in ways none of them could have imagined. "If you are determined to make a transatlantic voyage, Mrs. Hudson, I propose that Watson and I accompany you."

Watson clapped his hands. "Holmes, that's inspired. We have nothing on currently, and if you could stand the company, Mrs. Hudson, the truth is we could all do with some time away. And I must admit I, for one, am anxious to see this metropolis some say rivals London."

Mrs. Hudson made a small smile which she withdrew as quickly as she became aware of its appearance. She told Holmes and Watson that the arrangements they proposed would be "very agreeable." She informed them that she planned to sail from

Liverpool on the SS Teutonic in five days although she hadn't purchased her ticket yet. She made clear she would be traveling second cabin, although they should not feel they had to. There was, as it turned out, little danger of their feeling any such pressure. Instead, Holmes and Watson tried to argue Mrs. Hudson into accepting more luxurious accommodations, only to fail as they had failed many times before in encouraging Mrs. Hudson to, as she described it, "throw money around." It was agreed finally Watson would purchase tickets for the cabin assignments each preferred.

Watson also made arrangements for their stay at the newly opened Waldorf Hotel. He took the precaution of keeping from her both its cost, and its description as "the natural abode of fashion and wealth." He reserved connecting rooms for himself and Holmes, thinking to make it easy to share a pipe with his friend at the end of the day. He reserved a parlor suite for Mrs. Hudson, informing her it was the only accommodation remaining. He was certain Mrs. Hudson saw through his small lie, but chose to say nothing about the modest bit of luxury he insisted foisting on her.

Holmes and Watson purchased luggage appropriate to their travel: a steamer trunk to make certain of room for clothes, toiletries and Holmes' disguises "for whatever contingency might arise," and two large Gladstone bags, the one to supplement the portmanteau Watson would be carrying, the other to substitute for Mrs. Hudson's brightly flowered carpetbag if she proved amenable to an exchange. The two men believed they already possessed clothing appropriate to an ocean voyage and their stay in New York, and set about trying to convince Mrs. Hudson she did not. She yielded finally to an argument that the widow's weeds she wore daily might not set a desirable tone for the wedding.

Having agreed to the need for a change in outfits, Mrs. Hudson made her selections from the shelves of ready-made dresses, a convenience unknown thirteen years earlier when

Mrs. Hudson last added to her wardrobe. She selected traveling suits of russet brown and turquoise blue, and two silk dresses, one purple with a plain skirt and the other olive green with a flounced skirt, both of them high-necked and floor length. Mrs. Hudson decided her blue-ribboned hat would be adequate for her travels, and her rather drab shoes would be hidden from view and didn't need replacing. She decided, as well, the additions to her wardrobe and the prospect of a transatlantic voyage required explanation to Tobias.

She had been Tobias' wife for 29 years and his widow for twelve. And throughout the twelve she had visited his grave in St. Marylebone cemetery once a fortnight to share her news and describe the challenges brought to 221B Baker Street. She was convinced the success of that agency was his doing, and she reminded him of it at each visit. She had called him her "uncommon common constable," as every night after clearing the dinner dishes, she and Tobias would select a crime report from the *Evening Standard*, and together the two of them would puzzle out what was known, identify what still needed to be determined, and develop strategies that would lead to revealing the individual or individuals responsible for the crime. He would bring to bear his years of experience with the Metropolitan Police, she would share ideas developed from study in the Reading Room of the British Museum. Murders were their particular interest, and she taught herself about poisons, falls, stabbings and shootings. She learned from Tobias what to search out at crime scenes, and how to interrogate witnesses and suspects. All the while she honed skills in observation at the greengrocer, on the horse car, or simply while out for a walk. She catalogued facial expression, hands, walk, dress and carriage; then calculated how they all came together to reveal a person's history and character.

After the terrible shock of Tobias' death, she decided there could be only one fitting testament to his memory, and only one initiative capable of filling the days and hours without him. She would organize a consulting detective agency that would put her skills and Tobias' teachings to proper use. The house she and Tobias had leased at 221B provided the perfect opportunity. Knowing it would be impossible for a woman to be taken seriously—especially one of some years and possessed of an unyielding Cockney accent—she advertised "rooms to let, good location, applicants should possess an inquiring mind and curiosity about human behavior."

Sherlock Holmes stood above all applicants both literally and figuratively. He was more than six foot, spoke with the precise diction of a Cambridge graduate, and claimed knowledge of chemistry, boxing and dueling. His high forehead suggested intelligence; his haughty self-confidence seemed to assure it. Those characteristics were certain to impress the carriage trade Mrs. Hudson hoped to attract. The proficiency he claimed with pistol and his fists would impress the toughs he was bound to encounter. The friend who accompanied him, Dr. John Watson, possessed a rock-hard steadiness that impressed Mrs. Hudson. With their selection as her colleagues, the consulting detective agency was founded.

Under her guidance, Holmes and Watson would carry out the legwork of investigation; from their findings as painstakingly recorded by Watson, she would take the lead in identifying the who, how and why of the crime, which Holmes would report to the client and authorities as his discovery. And now, in 1894, twelve years and many investigations later, they had become the leading consulting detective agency in London—if not the world—attracting clients ranging from kings and queens to dustmen and chars.

She replaced the wilted violets in the urn at Tobias' headstone with the bunch of fresh flowers she had purchased for a penny from the blind lady at the cemetery gate; then studied the grass for stray leaves or twigs. She removed the few she found before bringing Tobias up to date on her activities.

"You're goin' to think me a fancy lady, but I need to tell you what I've been doin'." With that, she reminded him of her cousin's daughter, Caroline, recalling to him he had known her as a child. She described her forthcoming voyage to America, explaining its necessity in light of her cousin's request. She then took a deep breath and told him about the new clothes she had bought.

"It's for the weddin' and New York, Tobias. I need to 'ave clothes that won't embarrass Caroline. I think you'd approve, Tobias; I know you'd understand." She spoke the first somewhat doubtfully, the second with greater confidence.

"There's somethin' more I want you to know. It's about Mr. 'Olmes and Dr. Watson. I been tellin' you all along 'ow they're shapin' up real fine. Well, there was somethin' else that 'appened, Tobias—somethin' beyond just them shapin' up. Mr. 'Olmes allowed that both 'im and Dr. Watson wanted to travel with me. There was talk about takin' a little vacation and wantin' to see New York, but they were tryin' just a little too 'ard to make it all sound the most ordinary thing. And the truth of it is, I'll be glad for the company. There's now been three good men in my life, Tobias, even if there's just one I can tell about it."

Her eyes downcast, she alternated speaking to the mound beneath which Tobias lay, and the marker that described him as "beloved husband" and "member of the London constabulary". "The men will be traveling first cabin which is alright for them, but I told them I was wantin' second cabin. That will be luxury enough for me, Tobias. I don't want to be gettin' ahead of myself."

The difficult portion of her report concluded, Mrs. Hudson settled back to tell of life at 221B. She described at length the resolution of the case of the watchmaker with the missing thumb, whose beginnings she had shared at her last visit. She told Tobias how the direction of the stab wound had played such a key role in resolving the case, and how he had long ago alerted her to the importance of such detail. When she was done, she smoothed an unruffled place below the urn and flowers, told him again how much he was missed, put two fingers first to her lips, then to the top of the gravestone, and whispered her good-bye.

By the time of sailing, Mrs. Hudson's new outfits had been folded carefully into the oversized floral carpetbag Mrs. Hudson wouldn't think of leaving behind. She steadfastly refused the pleas of her colleagues to reveal the bag's contents, and continued to wear her accustomed black shapeless dress until she felt "the time was ripe" to do otherwise, and she couldn't tell them when that would be. They spent a night in Liverpool before boarding the SS Teutonic of the White Star Line late the next afternoon. Holmes and Watson made their way to the first cabin staterooms, and Mrs. Hudson sought out her cabin one deck below. They agreed to meet after lunch the next day on the first cabin promenade deck.

Mrs. Hudson found her stateroom cramped, but adequate. A wardrobe stood by the door; beyond it a cushioned bench extended the length of one side of her cabin while a writing table and bed extended the length of the other. A thin red carpet ran down the room's center leading to a basin with hand towels on its either side, two shelves for toiletries above the basin, and a glass above the shelves that caused her to greet herself each time she entered the room. She put her clothes and carpetbag in the wardrobe, and readied herself for dinner. Too tired to change into any of her outfits, she elected to postpone her transformation yet another day.

The dining room was not at all what Mrs. Hudson expected. Rows of white-clothed tables gave it an institutional look and the combination of dark paneled walls and dim lighting seemed to encourage subdued conversation and a decorous approach to taking one's meals. Without hesitation, Mrs. Hudson selected a seat in the row nearest the door. It would afford her a rapid and relatively unobtrusive exit if the evening progressed as she expected it to.

Over soup, the English couple next to her asked about her family, and did their best to look sympathetic when her words confirmed the widowed status her dress already made clear. They clucked their disappointment on learning she was childless to boot. The American couple across the table asked about her home in London, and Mrs. Hudson explained she was a landlady with lodgings in Baker Street. She did not reveal the names of her lodgers, believing to do so would raise a host of questions better left unexplored. There was some discussion about sights in the area; the American couple employed a range of superlatives to describe their visit to Madame Tussaud's just down Baker Street from where she lived. When the last of the tableaus from the Chamber of Horrors had been described in all its gory detail, Mrs. Hudson admitted she had never been to Madame Tussaud's, reporting it as being entirely too terrifying for her taste. That led to a turn in the conversation to the quality of the dinner, and a cataloging of the ship's features, with many of the evening's earlier superlatives sprinkled throughout the new discussion.

Mrs. Hudson added little to that conversation as well, not sharing her neighbors' enthusiasm for either the food or the ship. Her silence encouraged the two couples to turn finally to a topic that made no demand on her for participation. They entered into a spirited competition over family achievements that continued through courses of fish and meat with no clear victor even as dessert was served. Each couple described the fortunate marriages and extraordinary accomplishments of their children, and the near mythic abilities of their grandchildren. When Mrs. Hudson excused herself shortly after finishing an apple tart and tea, she received polite smiles and perfunctory wishes for a pleasant evening. She took a short walk along the second cabin promenade deck, and quite unexpectedly found herself fondly recalling the banter that accompanied an evening meal with Mr.

Holmes and Dr. Watson. She returned to her cabin, pulled from her carpetbag the two books she had borrowed from the Library of the British Museum, *Finger Prints,* and its sequel, *Decipherment of Blurred Finger Prints*, both of them authored by Francis Galton, and both of them certain, in her judgment, to alter the course of criminal investigation. Nonetheless, she found it necessary to re-read sentence after sentence as her mind wandered from the Baker Street she knew to the New York she had yet to see, and back again. Finally, she put the book aside and turned down her light, only to sleep fitfully until nearly three, after which she didn't sleep at all.

Yielding to the inevitable, she pushed herself from bed, dressed, and made her way to the ship's library where she thought she might search out books about baseball, a subject she had found absent from the shelves of the British Museum Library. She carried the Galton book she had been reading in case, as she feared, the library was limited to popular works of the day. She found the ship's central staircase and climbed the four flights to the main deck, then pressed open the heavy paneled door beneath the sign, "Ship's Library."

The room was a good deal larger than she expected, and appeared as much concerned with a display of elegance as of literature which she did expect. Along all four walls, book shelves competed for space with panels containing fleur-de-lis designs embroidered on blue satin backgrounds. Richly carved oak columns supported wooden beams at the room's center, holding in place a frosted glass ceiling which would, in a few hours time, admit sufficient light to make unnecessary the electric lanterns that now kept the room illuminated. Swivel chairs were set out along the walls and throughout the room, some next to small writing tables, some arranged around a large square table beneath the glass ceiling. Mrs. Hudson was surprised to find the room well lit by the artificial light, but even more surprised to find she was not alone. A figure half hidden behind a distant column called to her.

"Are you unable to resist the siren call of literature or simply unable to sleep?"

The voice was genial, and its owner was wearing a sly grin. He was in his late 50's with an unkempt mop of gray hair, hooded eyes that seemed to regard her with some amusement, and a great brush of moustache that hung well past the corners of his mouth. From his accent and easy informality Mrs. Hudson knew him to be American.

"I'm afraid it's more my 'avin' trouble sleepin' although I do enjoy a good book."

"Well, so do I, but I find so few of them. Allow me to introduce myself. My name is Snodgrass. Thomas Jefferson Snodgrass."

There was a good natured self-confidence to his shambling gait as he came forward to greet her. He extended a hand in greeting the way Americans did as though intent on making an instant friend. Taking his hand, she noted the indentation to the tip of his right index finger and inside of his thumb from long-time use of a pen or pencil, revealing writing as his likely profession. His pale complexion indicated his travels involved activity that kept him indoors, marking his trip abroad as involving business rather than pleasure. His well-matched clothes together with their rumpled look suggested supervision of his wardrobe in preparation for the trip but not during the trip, and that in turn suggested a wife who had remained at home. She took note as well of the sheets of paper and three books on the table he had left. He had come to gather information for his writing and had come at night to avoid being disturbed.

"I'm Mrs. 'Udson."

"Well, Mrs. Hudson, what kind of a book is it you're looking for?"

"I was 'opin' to find somethin' about your American game of baseball."

Shaggy eyebrows pressed their way into Snodgrass' forehead. "Forgive me, Mrs. Hudson, but I can't help wondering what an English lady like yourself could want with a book about baseball."

Mrs. Hudson smiled in recognition of his understandable confusion. "I'm sailin' to New York to attend the weddin' of my cousin's daughter. She's marryin' someone who works at baseball for some people that call themselves the Brooklyn Bridegrooms, and I'm lookin' to learn what I can about the boy's job.

Snodgrass let out a laugh he tried to disguise as a cough too late to fool Mrs. Hudson. "And you probably want to be assured he can support the young lady. That's easy, Mrs. Hudson. If he's good at the sport, he can provide for her quite well. However, learning about baseball can take some doing although I believe I can at least get you started. I've seen baseball played in places as remote as the Sandwich Islands, and have even written about baseball in a little book of mine."

"Would I know the book?"

"I suppose you might. It's called *A Connecticut Yankee in King Arthur's Court.* My publisher tells me it sold fairly well in England in spite of its discussion of baseball."

This time there was no hiding his grin and Mrs. Hudson looked at him dumbfounded for just a moment. "Mr. Snodgrass, indeed. You're Mr. Samuel Clemens, which is to say, Mr. Mark Twain, the writer. You do, indeed, have quite a following in England. In fact, you're nearly as popular as Mr. Charles Dickens." And now there was no hiding the grin on Mrs. Hudson's face.

The unmasked Samuel Clemens roared with laughter. "You must grant me, Mrs. Hudson, your Mr. Dickens has the advantage of having died recently, a condition my creditors have expressly forbidden to me." Still laughing, he took Mrs. Hudson's arm and guided her to a chair at one of the small tables before seating himself opposite. "Let me tell you something of the game of baseball." With that, Clemens explained the roles of the nine men on the field, and of the rules regarding balls and strikes, hits and outs, and innings. He asked to call the daughter of Mrs. Hudson's cousin her niece, explaining it was less cumbersome then calling her the daughter of her cousin each time he referred to her. On learning that the young woman's fiancé was a pitcher, he described the central importance of that player, and his role in making the batter miss the ball or hit it to one of the fielders to make an out.

Mrs. Hudson nodded repeatedly, raised questions occasionally, and made notes on the paper Clemens generously provided. She wondered at last about the name, Brooklyn Bridegrooms, given to the "nine" which he said a baseball team was sometimes called.

Clemens explained that, when they were first organized, the team from Brooklyn had a number of men who were about to be married. He explained that other teams in their league had equally colorful names including Beaneaters, Spiders, Giants and Pirates. He asked her the name of the pitcher she would be meeting, and when he learned it was William Wilson, he inhaled a noisy breath and informed her that the young man went by the name Brakeman Wilson, was a very successful pitcher, and could provide for her niece quite handsomely.

The library they began to jointly explore was far better stocked and far better organized than Mrs. Hudson had anticipated. They found the section marked "Sports—American" and a shelf that held *Spalding's Official Baseball Guide 1889*, which Clemens explained would contain the rules of baseball, but be a little out of date, while the up-to-date April, 1894 issue of *The Sporting News* they also located, would tell her about teams and players.

She thanked him and stacked the book and the journal on top of the work by Francis Galton she had set on a table. Taking note of the third piece of reading matter, Clemens asked why she had brought a book to the library.

"I wasn't sure what I might find 'ere, so I brought somethin' to read in case there turned out to be nothin' but entertainments."

Mrs. Hudson instantly reddened and tried to make amends. "Not that there's a thing in the world wrong with writin' entertainments which bring pleasure to so many and are sometimes very instructive. I just meant I was plannin' on some other kind of readin'."

Grinning broadly, Clemens waved away her concern and took the book in question from her. When he looked up from its cover, the great writer was nearly at a loss for words. "You have an interest in Galton's work, Mrs. Hudson?" The response was a cautious nod. "May I ask why you would be studying fingerprints?"

Mrs. Hudson had not expected anyone to be in the library at three in the morning, or anyone familiar with the writings of Francis Galton to be there at any hour. She decided to provide Clemens a small measure of truth supplemented by a large portion of fancy.

"I do have an interest, Mr. Clemens. I should explain I run a lodgin' 'ouse in London, and my two lodgers are Mr. Sherlock 'Olmes and Dr. John Watson. You may 'ave 'eard of them."

Samuel Clemens' widened eyes made clear he had.

"Well, with all that goes on at Baker Street, I've developed an interest in learnin' about crime and the way crimes get solved."

"And what do you think of Professor Galton's ideas?"

She was wary about the conversation, but too tired to be as guarded as she might have been another time. "I'll tell you the truth, Mr. Clemens, I think Mr. Galton is writin' about the future of police work. I believe we're lookin' at what could be one of the most important ways to get at guilt or innocence that's ever been found."

Clemens peered intently at Mrs. Hudson. He was no less stunned at discovering their common interest than was Mrs. Hudson. Perhaps more so. It was plainly intriguing to find someone who read Francis Galton for pleasure. For that someone to be in widow's weeds and speak a slightly fractured Queen's English strained credulity.

"Mrs. Hudson, I am plainly astonished, while also being in complete agreement with you. I must tell you I have only just finished writing a little book I call *Pudd'nhead Wilson—Those Extraordinary Twins*, in which I use Professor Galton's contribution in much the way you suggest. That is, I use fingerprint evidence to establish identities. You're the first person I've met who doesn't find my ideas fanciful, if not outrageous. The book won't be out until June although it's currently appearing in sections in an American magazine, *The Century*. When the book is available, I will be certain to send you a signed copy if you'll give me your address. Please share it with your boarders, and ask them to recommend it to their friends and colleagues—provided, of course they find it a suitable entertainment," he added with a chuckle.

"I should really like to continue our conversation about fingerprints and the investigation of crime, but it is getting late—or I suppose some might say early—and I suspect both of us need our rest. I know I do. I wonder if you would agree to resuming our talk at a later time."

Mrs. Hudson allowed that she would be delighted to resume their talk, and they arranged to meet at eight-thirty the following evening on the second cabin promenade deck at the stern of the ship. They reasoned the hour and the remote location would make it easier for Clemens to go unrecognized. As a further precaution, he was again to become Mr. Snodgrass if anyone joined them. The author never asked to meet Holmes lest Mrs. Hudson think he had an ulterior motive in wanting to see her, and Mrs. Hudson never offered to introduce them lest Clemens transfer his attention to her famous colleague.

While Mrs. Hudson carefully selected a seat affording easy egress from the second cabin dining saloon, Holmes and Watson, anticipating no comparable difficulties, chose seats near the center of one of the several tables that ran nearly the length of their cavernous dining saloon. A high-domed roof and stained glass windows gave the room a cathedral-like quality, while the images of frolicking mermaids, sea nymphs and bearded mermen carved into the room's oak paneling promised attention to secular pleasures. White jacketed waiters ladled asparagus soup with well practiced efficiency, and the room became a buzz of introductions and a sea of polite smiles of acknowledgement.

Holmes and Watson nodded greetings to the strangers around them with every intention of having them remain strangers. It was not to be. The well-jeweled middle-aged matron to Holmes' right introduced herself as Mrs. Sylvan Westermore, and nodding to the slender, bald man to her right, completed the family portrait with the introduction of Mr. Westermore. She went on to explain they were returning to Minneapolis, Minnesota from their third trip to the continent, then paused to allow her fellow diner to share a comparable revelation. Holmes gave Mrs. Westermore a thin smile before making the obligatory response.

"I'm delighted to make your acquaintance, Mrs. Westermore. I am Sherlock Holmes."

At that moment the man sitting across from Watson came bolt upright from where he had been hovering over his soup, and laid his spoon aside as though needing both hands free for whatever crisis had been wakened. He looked hard at Holmes, his eyes narrowing in disbelief.

"Are you *the* Sherlock Holmes?" At that point all within earshot turned their attention to Holmes and his inquisitor. Mr. Westermore leaned far back to get beyond his wife's formidable presence and have a better view of the man who might be an imposter.

"I know of no other."

Holmes' response appeared to reassure all at the table except the questioner who continued to look to Holmes as though he was certain to pocket the silverware if his eyes strayed. "I must talk to you. Not here, not now. After dinner on the promenade deck." With that, the man turned back to the asparagus soup, and did not speak another word for the remainder of dinner; instead, scowling at each succeeding course set before him as though he suspected one of them contained poison, but couldn't guess which.

Mrs. Westermore, having no idea who Sherlock Holmes was or why anyone might pretend to be him, described her tour of the continent, her home in Minneapolis, and her four children and three grandchildren. Holmes found he had to do nothing more than grunt admiration, surprise, pleasure, or disappointment depending on her words and her accompanying facial expression. He did wonder if there was really a place with the improbably alliterative name, Minneapolis, Minnesota, but decided its invention required an imagination exceeding that possessed by Mrs. Westermore. Watson exchanged small pleasantries with the white haired banker on his left and the honeymoon couple across from him, all of whom did recognize the name Sherlock Holmes, and asked reverential questions about the conduct of criminal investigation.

The dinner proceeded from soup to croquettes of salmon followed by roast beef a la russe, mutton chops with Londonderry sauce, and roast capon. Dessert consisted of crème of apricots, ice cream, pastry and fruit. Each course was accompanied by an appropriate white wine or claret, and the dessert selection by Madeira. There was some complaint about the near absence of fish, but in the main the passengers expressed satisfaction with their dinner while they lingered over American coffee or English tea.

When Holmes had drunk the last of his coffee—his choice reflecting an effort to Americanize his diet while still at sea—he nodded to Watson his readiness to leave. The two men pushed back their chairs, tendered their good wishes to those around them, and left the room closely followed by their self-selected companion. He caught up to them as they approached the ship's center staircase, producing his card while slightly inclining his head and shoulders, then jerking back as if catching himself before bowing.

"I am Dr. Hollander, Dr. Bernard Hollander of the British Hospital for Mental Disorders and Brain Diseases. You may have seen a paper of mine, Dr. Watson, 'Positive Philosophy of the Mind,' or perhaps you're familiar with the *Phrenological Record*, a journal I have the privilege to edit."

Dr. Hollander waited hopefully, but received no support from Watson.

"No matter. The point is I am a student of the human mind." As they arrived at the promenade deck he looked from Holmes to Watson to make certain the significance of his statement was appreciated. "I am engaged in developing a methodology for measuring the parts of the skull. When my work is complete, I will publish a listing of the measurements I have made of the heads of different kinds of deviates. I feel certain that my findings will add an entirely new element to the work of criminal investigation. I am already finding a considerable expression of interest from professionals in many countries in addition to our own. Indeed, my travels in America will involve an extensive lecture tour as well as demonstrations at several hospitals and medical schools."

Hollander pulled out a cigarette case, and offered its contents to Holmes and Watson, each of whom declined in as much as both were looking forward to sharing a pipe as soon as they could escape Dr. Hollander. They stopped for a moment while Hollander lit a cigarette behind hands cupped against the ocean breeze. "I was hoping we might join forces since the three of us are men of science and share an interest in the workings of the criminal mind."

17

Watson's grimace was concealed by the night and Holmes' snigger by the sound of the ocean. "I am aware that phrenology has a number of adherents in the medical community," Watson seemed at pains to choose his words carefully, "and that our Queen had a phrenologist read her children's heads. However, I'm afraid I've never felt comfortable with the idea of there being distinct areas of mental organ locations—as I believe they're described."

Holmes' words were spoken neither softly nor with an excess of care. "Dr. Hollander, you raise a medical theory with which I've had no experience and so can add nothing to the conversation. Besides which, it's been a rather exhausting day for both Dr. Watson and myself, and I mean to have an early evening as I suspect Watson may want as well."

"I understand completely, Mr. Holmes, Dr. Watson. The first day out can be very taxing. I must apologize for the enthusiasm I feel for my work. Perhaps we can meet tomorrow and I can convince you of the potential phrenology holds for your own activities. Shall we say after breakfast about ten in the smoking saloon?"

Holmes and Watson agreed to an appointment they could find no way of refusing, holding fast to the hope that a way might appear with the dawning of a new day.

By the time Mrs. Hudson woke, the Teutonic had put into port in Queenstown on the Irish coast and departed, taking on goods and passengers before resuming its seven day journey to New York. She decided this would be a good time to introduce the russet-brown traveling suit she had purchased. She felt certain of an enthusiastic response from her colleagues, although they weren't the ones she sought to impress.

Having slept through breakfast, she took an early lunch allowing her to eat without having to pretend sociability with diners who began to fill the room as she was leaving. She made her way to the first cabin promenade deck to meet with Holmes and Watson as had been agreed, and was met at the top of the stairs by a deck steward who wondered if he could help her. His intent, as Mrs. Hudson recognized, was to protect the first cabin passengers from suffering the indignity of contact with second cabin undesirables, or worse. She thanked him for his concern, and made clear she had no need of his assistance. The steward's plastic smile and curt nod suggested he would have been pleased to pitch the small woman over the promenade deck railing, if he could be assured the resulting splash would not disturb his first cabin passengers.

The stand-off was resolved by a hearty voice familiar to the second cabin passenger. "So good of you to join us, Mrs. Hudson." The owner of the voice looked down his aquiline nose at the deck steward. "Is there some sort of problem here?"

The smile disappeared and the nod he gave Holmes was far from curt. "Not at all, sir. I was just asking madam if I could provide any assistance."

"In fact, you can. We'll be wanting three deck chairs and blankets." With that, Holmes turned from the steward with a flourish that suggested he had already wasted too much time addressing him. "May I say, Mrs. Hudson, how delighted I am with your outfit."

"Indeed, Mrs. Hudson, this is a most agreeable surprise," Watson added.

She smiled her thanks, and became aware she was blushing like a schoolgirl.

The three members of the consulting detective agency moved to occupy the chairs the deck steward was setting out for them. They accepted the blankets he offered and wrapping them over their legs, they looked every bit the seasoned transatlantic travelers.

"And 'ow 'ave your travels been to 'ere?" Mrs. Hudson asked.

Watson looked up and down the deck before responding for the two of them. "We've run into one small problem, Mrs. Hudson. A Dr. Bernard Hollander discovered Holmes and is determined to convince us of the contribution phrenology can make to our investigations. He was with us last night and again this morning. He would be with us now if we hadn't claimed a prior commitment. I'm afraid unless we stay in our staterooms—which I for one am close to choosing—we will be playing a game of hide and seek with Dr. Hollander for the rest of the voyage. But I trust your experience has been more pleasant, Mrs. Hudson."

"It 'as been, Doctor. It's been very pleasant to 'ere. I've 'appened on a gentleman who is very interested in crime investigation, and is quite well informed, besides bein' able to tell me a good deal about baseball. We'll be talkin' some more, and I'm thinkin' it's likely to make for a pleasant voyage."

"Don't tell me you've found yourself a beau, Mrs. Hudson," Holmes asked with a sly grin. "I should have known your outfit wouldn't be for us alone—if it's for us at all."

"There's nothin' of the kind, Mr. 'Olmes. My gentleman is a 'appily married man who simply shares some of my interests. Besides, I'd be afraid my Tobias would come out of the grave if I was to take up with anybody new."

Holmes smiled puckishly to Watson leading the Doctor to change the subject before Holmes could pursue it further. "Voyages are designed to promote the development of new friendships, and I'm sure I speak for Holmes in saying we're pleased you met someone interesting. For now, I wonder if we might continue our conversation in the smoking saloon where Holmes and I can have a pipe, and we might see about getting you a cup of tea, Mrs. Hudson, if you're not averse to being our prior commitment should the need arise."

For the next six days, their voyage followed a predictable pattern. Holmes and Watson spent their days and nights avoiding Dr. Hollander with only partial success; Mrs.

20

Hudson spent her evenings in conversation with Samuel Clemens moving from the study of fingerprints to a more detailed review of the rules and conduct of the game of baseball, then to a description of Clemens' European lecture tour and his impressions of the places he'd visited, while Mrs. Hudson waved off any discussion of her own activities as "nothin' more than tendin' to my men." Clemens professed disbelief that her life was as limited as she claimed, but did not pursue the subject. By the time they docked in New York, Mrs. Hudson had mixed feelings about leaving her new friend, while Holmes and Watson anxiously awaited the opportunity to disembark.

They retrieved their luggage and joined the line at the carriage stand, waiting a coach to take them to the Waldorf Hotel. Watson puzzled over the American coins he had gotten in exchange for pounds on board the Teutonic before calling over a newsboy and purchasing a *New York Tribune*. All three glanced at the paper's front page and issued a collective gasp. The banner headline read: "Bridegroom Pitcher Sought in Attempt on JP Morgan's Life—Financier Wounded, Aide Killed." Beneath that, a headline in smaller print read: "Mrs. Morgan's Maid Interrogated."

2.
The Waldorf and the Tombs

The paper passed from hand to hand and each read the first several paragraphs of the lengthy article.

"An attempt was made on the life of the financier, JP Morgan, at 9:30AM yesterday morning. His long-time aide, Conrad Wagner, was fatally shot when he came between the gunman and Mr. Morgan. The renowned banking executive was struck by a bullet which lodged below his left shoulder. An operation performed later that morning by Dr. A.B. Brown was successful in removing the bullet which miraculously struck no bone or large blood vessel. Mr. Morgan is now resting peacefully at home. Mr. Morgan was fired on as he arrived to attend a breakfast celebration for his daughter, Juliet, who had become the bride of Mr. William Pierson Hamilton the evening before.

This was the second attempt on Mr. Morgan's life within the month. The first took place at the Metropolitan Club when a single shot was fired wildly in his direction. Mr. Morgan stated a refusal to be cowed by the gunman's action, and insisted he planned no change to his schedule after a brief period of recuperation. On the morning of the latest attempt, Mr. Morgan had gone to his office to prepare for the market opening, as was his accustomed routine, before returning home for the breakfast celebration. Guests and onlookers were witness to the frightful scene and the shooter escaped in the ensuing confusion.

Mr. Morgan's assailant has been identified as William Wilson and his whereabouts are now being sought by both the New York City Police, and staff of the Pinkerton Detective Agency whose services have been retained by JP Morgan & Company. Mr. Wilson was reported to have been visiting his fiancée, Caroline Littleberry, who formerly served as Mrs. Morgan's lady's maid. Mr. Wilson is better known to patrons of the sport of baseball as Brakeman Wilson, a pitcher for the Brooklyn Bridegrooms nine. Mr. Wilson is said to have ties to radical elements seeking to disrupt the operations of railroads in which Mr. Morgan has significant financial interest. Mr. Wilson is known to favor the union of railroad workers and to support the Chicago firebrand, Eugene Debs, in that endeavor. Mr. Wilson earlier participated in the Players League, a short-lived renegade organization of baseball players.

Mr. Wilson also appears to have anarchist sympathies. A large body of literature supporting that radical cause was found in his apartment by police investigators. He is thought to have used his relationship with Miss Littleberry to put himself in close proximity to Mr. Morgan in association with a well conceived assassination plot. Miss Littleberry, who was described by police as quite distraught, was detained for questioning and released. The authorities did not disclose what they learned from Miss Littleberry, but reported she has been asked to remain in the City of Brooklyn where she is now residing. The police in Brooklyn are cooperating closely with those in New York City."

The remainder of the story contained the surgeon's assurance of a full and speedy recovery, as well as a statement from the injured man's son, J. Pierpont Morgan, Junior, expressing the family's appreciation for the swift action of the New York City police, and for the work of Dr. Brown. There was also a report of interviews with Mr. Morgan's banking colleagues, all of whom wished for his speedy recovery. There was a description of what little was known about Conrad

23

Wagner and a summary of Brakeman Wilson's baseball career. Nothing further was reported about Caroline Littleberry.

The three detectives were unnerved for only a moment. By the time they boarded their carriage, each had traded the role of carefree tourist for the more familiar one of determined investigator, and together, they were steeled for the chase.

The Waldorf Hotel had opened just one year earlier. William Waldorf Astor had razed the mansion he inherited at the corner of Fifth Avenue and 34th Street, and replaced it with a luxury hotel designed to drive from her home next door his imperious aunt, Caroline Schermerhorn Astor, the widely acknowledged doyenne of New York society. With that impediment removed, he planned to install Mrs. William Waldorf Astor in his aunt's place. Within a year, the crowds, noise and traffic created by the Waldorf Hotel had achieved a part of his objective. Caroline Astor had been forced to move. She relocated a mere twenty streets uptown in a French chateau built for her across from the decade old Central Park. Once established in her new home, she resumed her role as hostess to New York's aristocracy. William Astor gave up the effort to supplant his aunt and moved to England in hopes that being unknown there, he might gain greater acceptance. The hotel bearing his name added significantly to his already considerable fortune by becoming the gathering spot for the rich and famous he had hoped his home would welcome. Eventually, Caroline's son, John Jacob Astor IV, would build a hotel on the site she vacated and join both the new structure and the family's name to the Waldorf Hotel, but that was three years away.

On this day, the three detectives took uncharacteristically little note of the tasteful excess of their surroundings as they left their bags in the custody of a uniformed young man who was disappointed to learn he would not be carrying those bags to the guests' rooms, would not have opportunity to describe the luxurious features of their rooms, and would not thereby receive the monetary reward that routinely followed his combination of physical labor and oratory. He nonetheless smiled a recommendation of the English Rose Room for a light lunch in response to their question and the accent in which it was spoken.

Watson stopped to purchase two afternoon papers, the *Evening World* and *Evening Sun*, just delivered to the hotel. Both carried the same lead story; the *World* headline read: "Morgan Assailant Captured, Admits Nothing;" the *Sun's* stated: "Morgan Attacker's Getaway Foiled." Unspecified persons from the Pinkerton Detective Agency were said to have joined forces with Captain Vocci and members of the New York City Police to capture Wilson at the ferry station in New Jersey before he could reach his objective, the Pennsylvania Railroad Station. Wilson's ultimate destination, if it was known, was not stated. Both papers reported Wilson was arrested after minimal resistance and was being detained at a place called the Tombs, which it became clear was the city's detention facilities. The reports went on to describe the state of Morgan's recovery—one extolled the financier's "stoicism," the other his "courage"—and both detailed ongoing efforts to locate the relatives of Conrad Wagner who were believed to be in western Pennsylvania or Ohio.

Mrs. Hudson looked around to the tables that had been empty when they first arrived, and nodded her approval at finding them still empty. "I'm thinkin' we need to see Miss Littleberry and Mr. Wilson as soon as we can to get their sides of the story." Watson had already withdrawn the pencil and accounts book he used for taking notes during the group's investigations. He observed that Mrs. Hudson was no longer calling her relative by her Christian name, but said nothing.

"Mr. 'Olmes, Doctor, it would be best for you to go to this Tombs place to talk to the people there and to Mr. Wilson. I'm thinkin' when you tell the officials who you are and why you're there, they'll do what they can to be 'elpful. My cousin wrote to 'er daughter we were all to be at the weddin' so I'm sure Mr. Wilson will know who you are as well."

"Meanwhile, I'll go to Mr. Morgan's 'ome. One of the servants there is bound to know where Miss Littleberry 'as gone, and I'll go look for 'er wherever she is in this 'ere Brooklyn." Mrs. Hudson waited as the waitress poured tea for all of them with a devotion to the task she would have appreciated at any other time. After the waitress had removed the teapot and an ingratiating smile from their presence, Mrs. Hudson resumed giving direction to the afternoon's activities.

Fifteen minutes later they had developed sets of questions for the police, William Wilson, JP Morgan's service staff, and Caroline Littleberry; and had agreed to meet again at half six in the hotel's reception. The doorman at the Waldorf signaled for two hansoms, asking the guests their destinations before helping each into a cab. His eyebrows rose for an instant on learning the small, middle-aged woman in the inexpensive turquoise traveling suit was going to the Morgan mansion; his eyebrows rose still higher on learning the destination of the two English gentlemen. They remained at full mast as he stared after the coach he had directed to the Tombs.

Mrs. Hudson was distressed to find the carriage ride from the Waldorf Hotel to the Morgan home covered a distance of only four streets and not as many minutes, but would nonetheless cost fifty cents. It was sufficiently exorbitant that she pocketed the full fifty cents change from the silver dollar she handed the driver, ignoring his repeated throat clearings and intense stare. She waited outside the ivy-covered brownstone until the hansom was well down Madison Avenue, then turned past the entrance on 36th Street following the carriage path that ran behind the house. A wall of neatly trimmed and tightly packed evergreens, twelve feet high and at least three feet thick, paralleled the path forming a blind that hid from view the coach-house and stable on its other side. Mrs. Hudson followed the path as far as the steps leading down to the door through which the Morgan staff would enter and depart the Morgan home. Several yards beyond she could see the three steps leading up to the family's back entrance, through which Morgan would have been carried on the morning of the attack.

A footman of at most sixteen years answered her knock at the staff entrance. His collar was undone, his tie hung down his chest and she could smell tobacco on his breath. His age and deportment indicated he was new to his position; Mrs. Hudson doubted he would grow much older in it. His struggle with the trappings of service was complicated by a demoralizing bout of homesickness. A much crumpled envelope protruding from a pants pocket would have come from family living too far away to provide the comfort of occasional visits. The crumpling suggested the letter had been read often, and his keeping it with him indicated how much he missed the people who had sent it. For now, however, the footman had another problem. His deeply furrowed brow reflected his confusion about the diminutive woman who was unknown to him, and looked not unlike his own mother if only she owned such fine clothes.

"May I help you, madam?"

"You may indeed, thank you. Miss Littleberry may 'ave spoken of me. I am Mrs. 'Udson. I've come all the way from London, England to attend the weddin' of Miss Littleberry. Now, I learn there's been this terrible shootin' that 'as changed everything, and I need to see the 'ousekeeper to find out where things stand with the girl."

Mrs. Hudson watched the furrows deepen with her every statement. She recognized it would be necessary to help him deal with this upheaval to his routine.

"May I come in, Mr. …?" Her voice rose in pitch as it trailed off.

"My name is Charles, ma'am, and, yes, won't you please come in while I go find Mrs. Sowder. You might have a seat in

Mrs. Sowder's parlor seeing as how you've come about Miss Littleberry, I'm sure she won't mind."

Mrs. Hudson was led to a small, but comfortable room that held the housekeeper's maple desk and a matching secretary's chair, as well as a thinly cushioned easy chair also of maple into which she eased herself. She smiled Charles out of the room and waited the arrival of Mrs. Sowder. The wait was brief.

After hearing the reason for her visitor's call, Mrs. Sowder was determined to make short work of Mrs. Hudson. The unrest created by Miss Littleberry and her fiance still hung over her household, and she had no intention of allowing this woman to irritate wounds not yet healed—regardless of her own feelings for the former lady's maid. She crossed the threshold of her parlor and strode to the room's center. "I'm Mrs. Sowder, the housekeeper. I understand you have some relationship to Miss Littleberry."

Mrs. Hudson stood to meet the housekeeper, but the two women never got within five feet of each other. "That's correct, Mrs. Sowder. I'm Mrs. 'Udson, and as I was tellin' Charles, I've come from London for the weddin', Miss Littleberry bein' my cousin's only daughter. I know there's to be no weddin' on account of the tragedy that's occurred to this 'ouse and family. And I know you've got a terrible lot to do, so I don't want to take any more of your time than is absolutely necessary. But you see, after comin' all this way I've no idea where the girl 'as gotten to. I understand she's lost 'er position, but was wonderin' if she left an address with you. The girl could likely do with seein' a familiar face from 'ome. Besides which, 'er mother will be worried sick if I don't get word to 'er, and there's nothin' to tell until I talk to the girl."

In spite of her intention, Mrs. Sowder found herself softening toward the woman with the strange way of speaking, who showed a concern for Miss Littleberry she privately shared.

"Perhaps you'll take a cup of tea with me in the servants' hall and I'll tell you what I know about Miss Littleberry."

Charles watched the two women leave, his confusion undiminished, but his responsibility at a welcome end. With no one to see, he lit another cigarette, took the letter from his pocket, and stepped outside where he could spend a few welcome minutes with them both.

Mrs. Sowder took a seat at the foot of the table, the same one she occupied every night when staff assembled for dinner. She poured a cup of tea for Mrs. Hudson and coffee for herself, explaining somewhat sheepishly that the tea was a result of Miss Littleberry's influence.

"I'm sincerely sorry for your situation, Mrs. Hudson." She added milk to her coffee, and raised the small pitcher to Mrs. Hudson who smiled refusal. "I can tell you the whole staff was shocked by what happened. Miss Littleberry introduced her young man to all of us a few months ago and he made a very favorable impression. A little quiet maybe, but that was only natural for someone meeting a houseful of strangers. Nobody could have suspected he'd be part of anything so terrible. Besides which, there's not a person here who would have had anything unpleasant to say about Miss Littleberry—or does now, come to that. Which I can't say was true for the woman she replaced." Mrs. Sowder sniffed her dissatisfaction with the unnamed miscreant and sipped her coffee.

"You may not know it, Mrs. Hudson, but there's those who become the maid to the lady of the house, and right away put on airs forgetting where they came from. Miss Littleberry was nothing like that. I can tell you it's hard for anyone here to believe Miss Littleberry had any part in the terrible goings-on."

There was another sniff and another sip. It was apparent to Mrs. Hudson that Mrs. Sowder counted herself among the unbelievers.

"It's good to 'ear that, Mrs. Sowder. Caroline was raised in a God fearin' 'ome and was always a good and proper girl. I can tell you that learnin' of 'er good reputation will be a comfort to 'er mother and father." Mrs. Hudson fingered the rim of her cup before raising her question. "Is it certain that she and 'er fiancé were both involved in this awful thing?"

Mrs. Sowder leaned back in her chair and took a long breath as she considered her response. She had her own ideas about all that had happened that morning, but hesitated to share them with this woman no matter how well meaning she appeared.

"The police are sure the boy's involved. He did run off after the master was shot, and I hear he had a gun. Besides which, the newspapers are full of talk about him being a radical and wanting to make war on the railroads, which is anyway what Mr. Sachs says is what's in the papers. Mr. Sachs is our butler, and in his own way is quite an educated man. He says there's some who believe our Miss Littleberry had to know what was going on, and there's others believe she was just being used by her boy friend. Mr. Sachs says there's reason on both sides. Which I guess is the case, but like I was saying there's none here will say a bad word about Miss Littleberry, and that includes Mr. Sachs. Anyway, all I know for sure is that the police questioned Miss Littleberry and let her go, so I'm thinking the police don't think Miss Littleberry is mixed up in all that happened. Still and all, the master didn't feel it wise for Miss Littleberry to stay on, what with the reporters being everywhere—the master tries to avoid the newspaper people— and the disruption it was making for the household, which I'm sure you can understand."

Mrs. Hudson didn't understand and wasn't certain the housekeeper did either, but there was no point in pursuing that course. "I wonder, Mrs. Sowder, were you outside the morning the shooting took place?"

"Just for a moment or two, and before all the excitement. There was too much to do getting ready for Miss Juliet's party."

"What about Caroline and 'er beau? 'Ow did they 'appen to be outside when Mr. Morgan arrived?"

"Well, that was nothing out of the ordinary, Mrs. Hudson. Mr. Wilson would often come by mornings when his baseball team was in town. And Miss Littleberry reported directly to my lady so she could sort of go her own way after she attended to Mrs. Morgan. On that pa'ticular morning, Mr. Wilson had to wait in servants' hall quite a while before Miss Littleberry finished attending to my lady. Mr. Wilson had made such a good impression on all of us that Mr. Sachs let him wait for Miss Littleberry, although it was really quite inconvenient what with all that was going on. I can tell you that Franklin didn't get any such consideration when he came by earlier that same morning." A look came over Mrs. Sowder's face as though she'd inadvertently swallowed something distasteful. "Mr. Sachs put him in his place right enough."

Mrs. Hudson tried to make her question sound as nothing more than idle curiosity. "And who is this Franklin?"

"A bad one, Mrs. Hudson. He was an under-footman here. In fact, it's Charles who replaced him. That was after Mr. Sachs caught him out, red-handed as it were, when he tried pocketing some of the silver he was supposed to be polishing— not the best silver of course which Mr. Sachs wouldn't trust to anyone but himself. Well, when Mr. Sachs reported it to Mr. Morgan, Franklin was sacked on the spot. And here he comes bold as brass the morning of Miss Juliet's reception, all gussied up like some swell, with a story about how he always liked Miss Juliet, and was only there to pay his respects when she and Mr. Hamilton arrived—like he had any respects to pay. I was afraid Mr. Sachs was going to burst a blood vessel—I swear I was. He practically threw Franklin out bodily. And it was just as well Franklin was gone by the time Mr. Wilson came. The two of them never got along. I thought that maybe Franklin had made a play for Miss Littleberry. I wouldn't put anything past him."

31

"Anyway, when Miss Littleberry came downstairs, she and Mr. Wilson went outside where they could be alone. And of course, with the two of them keeping company, we gave them their privacy. Not that there was a great deal of privacy to be had. James—he's first footman—said the newspaper people were out there carrying those cameras they have, hoping to get a picture of the master when he arrived. Most of them knew from before that the master liked to avoid the crowds at the front entrance by going around to the back of the house. We knew there'd be a crowd, there always is when people learn about a party at the house, and the breakfast party was in all the papers. You'd be amazed how many turn out to get a look at people they read about, and see what fancy clothes they're wearing. I can tell you it's not how I'd spend my free morning. Anyway, by the time Miss Littleberry and Mr. Wilson got out, most all the guests had arrived, but there was still a crowd waiting to see the master and the family coach. A lot of them followed the newspaper people around to the back, thinking they must know something—which of course they did. And then all the rest went around back after they saw where Mr. Morgan's coach was headed. Besides which, it wasn't just the newspaper people and the nosey-parkers who went out back, some of the guests went outside to welcome the master as well. Anyway, Mr. Ferguson, our coachman, said he and James had a time shooing everyone away from his path."

Mrs. Sowder looked to the coffee pot, but decided against a second cup, thinking she needed to get back to work. Her recitation of the events had, however, stimulated a desire to share other tidbits she had no one else to tell. No longer hesitant, she reasoned she could share them safely with this woman who would be across the ocean in a week or so.

"I will say, Mrs. Hudson, there were two people in that crowd I never would have expected to see. One was this Franklin I've already told you about. Except what I didn't see was that Franklin's friends arrived as well, and according to James they were some pretty rough looking customers."

"The other was Mr. McIlvaine, who we all knew had proposed to Miss Juliet and been turned down. It was said the master did not approve of the marriage. When Mr. McIlvaine came to the front door it was left to Mr. Morgan, Junior, Miss Juliet's brother, to tell him to leave the same way he came in, which is how Mr. Morgan, Junior put it to him according to Polly—she's our parlor maid—who said she was near enough to hear the whole thing, and see most of it. Mr. McIlvaine said he'd only come to offer congratulations and show there's no hard feelings, but Mr. Jack told him it wasn't fitting."

Her revelations exhausted, Mrs. Sowder pushed away from the table, signaling the conversation was at an end. She gave Mrs. Hudson a small smile, and said she hoped some of what she'd told her would be a help with Miss Littleberry's mother and father.

"I thank you for your kindness, Mrs. Sowder. You've been most gracious with your time. I'll now be wantin' to find my cousin's daughter, and I'd be much obliged if you could give me an address for her."

"I can, Mrs. Hudson. She's staying with a lady friend in Brooklyn. If you'll give me just a moment, I'll get you that address. I suggest you don't plan on seeing her before three. I went to see her on my day out and found she's down at the jail every day until two when visiting hours are over, and then she's got at least an hour's trip from downtown to her apartment in Brooklyn."

"Thank you, Mrs. Sowder, I'll remember that. I wonder, too, if you 'ave the address of that Franklin chap as well. I know someone who will want to 'ave a chat with the young man about what 'e might 'ave seen that terrible morning."

"I do have it, Mrs. Hudson, but I'd tell your friend to watch himself with that one. He's a bad egg as Mr. Sachs would say."

Mrs. Hudson was not about to spend another fifty cents for a five minute ride. She ignored the two hansoms that passed her as she waited for a break in the traffic on Madison Avenue. When she started across the street she caught sight of a man in a dark frock coat and soft homburg crossing Madison from the other corner. She proceeded west along 36th Street to Fifth Avenue, stopping once when apparently overcome by the need to study the wares in a tobacconist's shop window. Reflected in the store's angled window she could see that the man in the dark frock coat was still behind her and had stopped to light a cigarette. She stepped away from the shop, snapped her fingers suddenly, and giving her head a vigorous shake as if responding to a sudden thought, turned on her heel to retrace her steps on 36th Street, passing as she did the cigarette smoker. She took careful measure of the man as she went by him. He was in his early 40's, a little below middle height, powerfully built, heavy browed, clean-shaven and a private detective. She judged his profession not only from his uncommon interest in her, but from his too frequent exhaling of smoke from a cigarette without a significant amount of inhaling, identifying him as a man who was not a smoker, but was intent on appearing to be a smoker. The stick he carried was thicker than the usual walking stick suggesting that it had another use more in line with the bulge below the left shoulder of his tightly buttoned coat. Since the detective had started following her after she left the Morgan mansion, it was clear to Mrs. Hudson he was one of the Pinkertons described in the newspaper as having been retained by JP Morgan and Company.

Mrs. Hudson came again to the corner of 36th and Fifth, and this time headed downtown over Fifth, still within sight of her long-range companion. She walked past the Waldorf, having decided to enter the first hotel she found beyond her own to confuse the Pinkerton about where she was staying. At 30th and Fifth she came to the white-stone Holland House and allowed the uniformed doorman to open its door for her entrance. She smiled a greeting to the clerk who beamed a welcome in return, not daring to risk ignorance of a guest's identity, and entered the elevator of a somber young operator who closed the door's gate with a white-gloved flourish. He steered the two of them to the eighth floor as Mrs. Hudson requested. She was certain the detective would arrive in time to take note of the progress of the arrow through the half-moon of numbered floors that was mounted above the elevator in the lobby.

The operator called out her floor in a tone suggesting he had made the trip many times before without once finding the scenery inspiring. Mrs. Hudson stepped briskly from the elevator as though certain of her destination until she heard the car start its descent whereupon she doubled back to seat herself on the chaise beside the elevator. She felt certain the detective would satisfy himself with having learned her floor, and only later attempt to coax a room number from the registration clerk for a woman meeting her description. After a suitable period, she again summoned the elevator, reacquainting herself with its morose operator and his unenthusiastic announcement of her destination. She exited the building to the nodding approval of the registration clerk, and the good wishes for a pleasant evening from the uniformed doorman. She turned in the direction of the Waldorf Hotel with the Pinkerton man nowhere in sight.

Their carriage took Holmes and Watson past the half-block brownstones housing many of the four hundred who eagerly accepted invitations to Caroline Astor's parties, then past the shops of merchants whose livelihoods depended on the residents of those brownstones. As they neared downtown, shops catering to the very rich gave way to shops catering to the merely well to do, and finally to department stores that carried a variety of goods appropriate to both clienteles. Beyond the shops, they came on low office buildings housing those tasked with managing much of the city's commerce and providing nearly all of its governance. Now, horse-cars and the newly installed cable cars became common, and hansom cabs all but disappeared from the roadways.

The driver crossed to Broadway, turning onto White where it met Centre Street, stopping his cab before a broad expanse of dark stone stairs leading to a portico extending well past the four striated columns at its front. The Tombs, as the building was universally known, bore striking resemblance to the final resting place of Egyptian royals, a resemblance it owed to the architect's success in duplicating the mausoleum he found pictured in a book detailing its author's travels through Egypt. It was an achievement little appreciated by those confined behind the walls of his artfully constructed burial chamber.

The building held within it the city's Police Court and Court of Special Sessions as well as its jail. A single police sergeant sat behind a desk strategically located between arriving visitors and the doors to the courtrooms. Since it was mid-afternoon and the business of both courts had concluded hours earlier, the sergeant waited patiently for them to come near enough to avoid having to raise his voice before delivering the short speech that was his standard greeting to those arriving after hours. "The courts are closed for the day. You'll have to come back tomorrow. Courts open at ten."

Holmes spoke in a tone calculated to make him appear unaware of the sergeant's cavalier dismissal. "Good afternoon. I am Sherlock Holmes and this is my colleague, Dr. John Watson. You may have heard of us."

The sergeant came to attention without leaving his seat and stared wide-eyed at his two visitors. "Mr. Holmes, Dr. Watson, I am of course familiar with your work. I doubt there's a police officer in New York who is not familiar with your work. It's a pure honor to welcome you to the detention facilities of the City of New York. Were you wanting a tour of the building?"

36

"That's most kind of you, Officer, and very inviting, but Dr. Watson and I are here on business." With that, Holmes recounted their association with Mrs. Hudson, Mrs. Hudson's association with Caroline Littleberry, and Caroline Littleberry's association with William Wilson. It turned out that William Wilson was better known to the sergeant as Brakeman Wilson and that he was quite familiar with the ballplayer, identifying himself as a fan of what he called "the grand game." He was familiar as well with Caroline Littleberry, whom he reported seeing first thing in the morning every visitors' day and last thing in the afternoon.

"We wondered if a police officer familiar with the case might be available," Holmes asked. "Our housekeeper will want to report the situation to her cousin who will be quite anxious to learn the facts about her daughter. I'm sure you understand, Constable …?" Holmes allowed his voice to ascend before breaking it off mid-question.

"Norbert, sir. *Sergeant* Norbert," the officer said as he came out from behind the desk. He was a short, burly man, now brimming with the spirit of cooperation. "You should know, sir, this is not strictly speaking a police station. We do have a small detachment that works with the courts, and I'd be pleased to introduce you to our captain who may be able to help you." Receiving a judicious nod from Holmes, he led them through the door whose beveled glass top contained the words "POLICE COURT STAFF." Without relaxing his pace or acknowledging the two female typists and several male officers whose desks he passed, he proceeded grim-faced to a far back corner of the room, and an office consisting of three walls of plasterboard joined to one masonry wall. The three makeshift walls stopped well short of the ceiling. One of them contained the only door in the otherwise open area, and the sergeant rapped soundly on it. He received a gruff, "Enter," from its other side, and the three men found themselves facing the bald head of a figure bent low over a closely typed sheet of paper.

The figure did not take his eyes from the paper which did not deter the sergeant from introducing the two men to his superior. "Captain Chamberlain, allow me to introduce Mr. Sherlock Holmes and Dr. John Watson who are here visiting us from the other side. They have an interest in the Brakeman Wilson case."

The head came up instantly; the Captain looked to each man with a fierce squint that he settled finally on Holmes. "Are you *the* Sherlock Holmes?"

Faced with the same question he had received from Dr. Hollander, he gave the same reply. "I know of no other."

A broad smile broke across Sergeant Norbert's face. Having seen what he had come to see, he cleared his throat and expressed the need to return to his station. His leaving drew a disinterested wave from the Captain whose eyes never left the face of his visitor.

Chamberlain stood, smiling welcome to men whose accomplishments were well known to him. He was a large man, nearly as tall as Holmes, but with broader shoulders and a deeper chest. A thin fringe of gray hair ran along the back of his head and contrasted with neatly trimmed moustaches that remained jet black. He leaned across the small desk to shake hands with each of his guests and waved them to the only two chairs in the office other than his own, grimacing embarrassment at the inadequacy of the accommodations he had to offer.

"We're honored by your presence, gentlemen. Your many accomplishments are well known in this country. But I don't understand. Why in the world would you be interested in Brakeman Wilson?"

Holmes reprised the tangle of relationships he had provided the sergeant a little while earlier. "Because of the effect it is having on my housekeeper, I'd like to learn all I can about the investigation and arrest of Mr. Wilson."

Chamberlain shrugged his response. "I'll try to help you with that, Mr. Holmes—at least I'll tell you as much as I know about it." He leaned back in his chair after first scraping a pencil from his desk that he proceeded to twirl between the thumb and index finger of each hand. "I must tell you, Mr. Holmes, if you're thinking there's some way to get Wilson out of this, I'm afraid it's just not in the cards. Not even for you, sir."

Seized by a sudden thought, Chamberlain tossed the pencil back onto his desk. "Since it's you, Mr. Holmes ...." Without finishing his sentence, he went to the door, opened it wide, and called to an unseen aide to bring him the file on William Wilson.

"You're welcome to read the case file, Mr. Holmes, but I'll need you to study it in my office." He took up the pencil and again began to rotate it between his fingers. Holmes and Watson each chose a wall to occupy their attention while they waited the aide's appearance.

After a short time, there was a soft knock at the door to which Chamberlain barked an invitation to enter. A slim young woman in a starched blouse with expression to match deposited a thick folder on Chamberlain's desk, looking neither to the Captain or his visitors. She hesitated a moment at the desk until Chamberlain simultaneously thanked and dismissed her.

With the door closed behind her, Chamberlain enumerated the litany of incriminating evidence in the files he invited Holmes to leaf through. "You'll first of all see where Mr. Morgan and a whole lot of other people say they saw Wilson with a gun in his hand right after the shots were fired. Not only did he have a gun, but he takes off right after the shooting like only someone with something to hide would do. Then, when we catch up with him, it turns out there are two cartridges missing from his revolver—the same number and the same caliber as were fired that morning."

"Did anyone see Wilson fire at Morgan?"

Watson's question led Chamberlain to gnaw on his lower lip for a moment.

"The truth is nobody did. But that's hardly unusual. Everybody's focused on Mr. Morgan's carriage and working to get the best view, when all of a sudden something happens someplace they're not looking, so of course nobody can tell you exactly what happened. Plus the day was against us, Mr. Holmes. Usually, you'd get some little bit of smoke—which is about all there is with these new Colts—but it was one of those windy days left over from March and nobody saw any smoke either. Not that any of it really matters, not with him the only one holding a gun and the only one running off."

"And it's not like it's hard to find a motive for him taking a shot at Mr. Morgan." Putting his pencil aside, Captain Chamberlain leaned in closer to Holmes, prepared to shatter any hope the famous detective might harbor of proving the New York Police Department in error. "Brakeman Wilson has been a troublemaker all his life." The Captain winked a confidence to Holmes.

"You know he gets his name Brakeman from the time he worked the railroad yards. We know he was an organizer for the union, and that he spoke against Mr. Morgan, saying he was getting blood money from bankrolling the railroads. According to our sources, he got started in his radical ways after a friend of his was killed when he got caught between cars in a switching yard. Anyway, even after he started playing baseball he kept right on agitating. You know it was just four years ago he joined what they called the Players League, which was nothing but an outlaw league of ballplayers who didn't like working for their National League owners. It only lasted a year, and then the players come back begging for their old jobs. But even that didn't stop Wilson. He was giving speeches in Union Square calling for a workers' revolution right up to the time he tried to kill Mr. Morgan."

40

"Tell me, Mr. Chamberlain, how does Miss Littleberry fit into all this?" Holmes asked.

"Well, I'll tell you, Mr. Holmes, there's been two ways of looking at that. Some thought at first that Miss Littleberry was in on it with him. But after they took her down for questioning it looked more like Miss Littleberry was simply a naïve young woman taken in by Wilson. She's English, you know." Holmes didn't understand the significance of her place of birth, but decided against interrupting the Captain's flow of ideas. "She didn't seem to know a thing about the shooting, but she did say that Wilson bought a revolver about the time he started seeing her."

Chamberlain paused, eyeing Holmes critically, and leading both Holmes and Watson to wonder whether their English origins led him to see them, too, as unable to appreciate the situation he was describing. In fact, that was precisely the Captain's thinking.

"I'm not sure you're in a position to understand about things over here, Mr. Holmes. I mean with you coming from England and all. You see, in our country, Mr. Morgan is a very important man. If anything happened to him—anything at all serious—it would bring on exactly the kind of crisis these people are looking for. And it's not like they haven't tried this kind of thing before. A year ago they went after Mr. Andrew Carnegie. They didn't get to him, but they got to his assistant, Mr. Henry Frick, and they pretty near killed him." Chamberlain's pencil twirling picked up speed. "I'm telling you, Mr. Holmes, it's dangerous times in this country. You know we have what they're calling a 'panic' that's got men being thrown out of work and families going hungry. And there's no end to it in sight. Right now, there are men marching to Washington from all over the country—men who fought in our Civil War—coming to demand jobs that just don't exist. Besides which, you got coal miners and railroad workers ready to go out on strike to force the owners to give them more money. And if they get away with it, it'll be anarchy, Mr. Holmes. Workers all over will think they can get together and do the same thing. You can see why business owners are going out and hiring their own private police—which is what these Pinkertons are. I don't like that part of it, Mr. Holmes—none of us do—but I can see why they do it. And I don't mind telling you it's keeping us real police on our toes. Which is why, when we catch one of these radicals red-handed, it's important to make sure he gets everything coming to him. That's the only thing that'll make the others sit up and take notice."

"Are you're certain he's a violent radical, Captain?" Holmes' question was put softly to make his questioning of Chamberlain's judgment sound more tactful than it was.

Chamberlain sat silent for the moment, and Watson thought the questioning might not have sounded quite as tactful as Holmes intended. But the Captain was only considering how best to make clear the accuracy of his characterization of Wilson. He pulled back the folder Holmes had been leafing through, withdrew a thick envelope at its back and hunted for the paper he found particularly damning. Finding it, he pushed back the folder with one hand and slapped the seditious document down in front of Holmes with the other.

"Look at this, Mr. Holmes. There's a whole lot more like it in the envelope, but this one should be enough to convince you about Wilson. You don't have to read the whole thing. Just the part Wilson's underlined. You might read it out loud so Dr. Watson can get some idea of Wilson's thinking."

Trying to sound as perturbed as Chamberlain thought he should, Holmes read aloud from the pamphlet he'd been handed. "Today, we have patriots who urge us to sacrifice in the name of God and country. But what did they do when their country called? They did what the rich have always done. They bought their way out of trouble by paying to send the poor to fight their battles. Morgan, Rockefeller, Carnegie, Gould, Armour, Fiske, Pullman and others of the privileged class paid for substitutes to fight, and yes to die for them when their country called. Even President Cleveland, who is in their pocket if not in their pay, hired a substitute to do his fighting for him in the War Between the States. But of all these, only Morgan reaped huge profits selling defective rifles to the Union Army and endangering the lives of the poor men sent to fight the war he avoided. These are not men to be tolerated by a nation wanting to call itself just. These are men to be rooted out, and their stolen gains returned to the people who labored to produce their wealth."

Chamberlain nodded his satisfaction with Holmes' recitation. "And like I was trying to tell you that's just one of the pamphlets that was found on Wilson's nightstand—his bedtime reading you might say. If that's still not enough for you, Mr. Holmes, we have reason to believe this was not the first time Wilson tried to assassinate Mr. Morgan." Chamberlain paused, whether to catch his breath or for dramatic effect was unclear, but for an instant the only sound came from Watson's pencil capturing the last of the Captain's allegations.

"It happened at the Metropolitan Club a month ago. And it was just the same as happened at the house. Mr. Morgan was getting out of his carriage when a shot was fired, this one from Central Park across from the Club. That time the shot went wild and no one was hit. It was a Saturday morning and between the streets being empty at that hour, and all the bushes and trees in the Park to hide behind, nobody saw who did it. But we know Wilson could easily have gotten Mr. Morgan's schedule for visiting his club from Miss Littleberry, and from all we've learned Mr. Morgan is very regular about his schedule."

Holmes grunted acknowledgment of Chamberlain's comment before skipping to something else in the folder that had caught his eye.

"What is this entry about questioning a Mr. Archibald McLeod? There's a notation that McLeod may be linked to Wilson, but underneath someone has written, 'NO association'

43

with the 'no' in capital letters. Can you tell me who this McLeod is, Captain?"

Chamberlain blanched. "I'd appreciate your not mentioning that to anyone, Mr. Holmes. The girl was supposed to remove it. We learned that Mr. McLeod was in town and it was just good police work to check on him. He was president of the Philadelphia and Reading Railroad until Mr. Morgan had him replaced as a condition for putting up the money to bail out the railroad, and we thought—just for a minute—that he might be holding a grudge. We found out Mr. McLeod did call Mr. Morgan several times from the Waldorf Hotel where he's staying, but he never did get in touch with Mr. Morgan. He told us he wasn't at the Morgans' that morning, and with Wilson caught red-handed as it were, we saw no reason to pursue that avenue any further. We were supposed to remove the note you saw. Mr. McLeod is a respectable businessman and there's no point to embarrassing the man." Chamberlain pursed his lips as if trying to make certain nothing else leaked out.

Holmes waited for Watson to complete his note-taking, then thanked the policeman for the information, promised to treat it with care, and turned the conversation to another topic. "Captain Chamberlain, I wonder if it would be possible for us to see the prisoner at this time."

The policeman screwed his face to a look of intense concentration, and again accelerated the rate at which he twirled the pencil between his fingers before finally bouncing it back on his desk. "Why not." He looked to the clock that was his only wall decoration. "It's almost three-thirty, and visiting hours ended at two, but you're here all the way from London, England, and you're certainly not the typical visitor. Let's go see Warden Fallon and find out if an exception can't be made this once."

The way to Warden Fallon's office lay across the center hall, requiring that they pass the Sergeant who gave each of them a warm smile that was reciprocated by Watson alone. They stopped at an office whose solid walls reached to the ceiling. On the beveled glass half of its door was written: WARDEN'S OFFICE. Chamberlain knocked and a woman's voice commanded more than invited them to enter.

Her hands still poised above her typewriter, the secretary who had given them license to enter nodded a stern greeting to Holmes and Watson, and looked questioningly to Chamberlain. With an officiousness appropriate to the secretary's demeanor, he stated his wish to introduce the Warden to two distinguished visitors who had arrived from across the Atlantic. She looked skeptically at the allegedly distinguished visitors, but rose to put the matter before the Warden. She emerged from his office moments later to announce his willingness to see them, making it sound an act of extraordinary broad-mindedness on the Warden's part.

The entire contents of Captain Chamberlain's office would have fit in one corner of the Warden's office—if the Warden could have been induced to accept the Captain's decidedly inferior sticks of furniture. The visitors faced a large man behind a massive desk. Low bookcases lined the wall behind him, displaying rows of neatly aligned books and stacked periodicals. Without waiting invitation, Chamberlain took one of the straight-backed chairs facing the Warden, and Holmes and Watson followed suit. The leather covered couches set against the walls to either side were rejected as too distant from the Warden to allow easy conversation. Desk, bookcases and couches were all of mahogany and all contained enough swirls and flourishes to make clear their owner's importance. Above one couch were the pictures of three men unknown to Holmes and Watson, but with the unmistakable glare of public officials, each of them appearing to resent having to share the wall with the other two. Above the couch on the wall opposite, there was hung a framed map of Manhattan as it might have appeared fifty or a hundred years earlier.

Warden Fallon was as big a man as Chamberlain, but lacked the captain's careful attention to his weight and appearance. He had a full head of grizzled hair that lay on his head in tufts, and half-glasses were balanced precariously at the end of a broad nose. He addressed himself to Chamberlain without so much as a glance to the two men with him. "Captain, I understand you wanted to see me."

Chamberlain's wry smile suggested he was accustomed to the Warden's display of hospitality. "Allow me to introduce Mr. Sherlock Holmes and his colleague, Dr. John Watson."

Fallon's blank expression made clear the significance of the meeting was lost on him. Chamberlain was undaunted. "The internationally famous detectives."

Fallon affected a faint smile that left unclear whether he now recognized the celebrity of his visitors or had simply elected to adopt a pretense of manners. All three of his visitors suspected the latter.

"I'm delighted to meet you. And may I ask what brings you here?" He looked from Holmes to Watson in search of a spokesman.

Holmes again described the web of relationships that had brought him finally to the Warden's office. He ended with the same request he had made to Chamberlain a short time earlier, but added a sense of urgency encouraged by the Warden's breezy disinterest.

"Dr. Watson and I have come a very long way, Warden, and I can tell you that our housekeeper is quite upset. Your assistance would be greatly appreciated."

Whether it was Holmes' plea or a wish to rid his office of the three men, Warden Fallon promptly gave his consent for Holmes and Watson to see Wilson on condition they spoke for no more than 20 minutes. With their promise secured, a trustee was called to escort Holmes and Watson to the second tier of the men's prison where Wilson, and all others accused of murder, were held for trial. Chamberlain excused himself, claiming the need to return to his work. He expressed to Holmes and Watson his pleasure on meeting them and his hope he might see them again. He and Fallon shared nods of bare recognition, and each spoke the other's last name by way of taking his leave.

Whether stimulated by the silence, or freed to speak by the absence of the police chief, a wistful smile crossed the Warden's face as he sounded suddenly confidential. "You know, you two aren't the first with an interest in Wilson to come and see me. Caroline Littleberry, Wilson's fiancée, was in here a few days ago. She wanted to bring him a few small comforts for his cell and a change of clothes. It's standard practice for relatives and friends to provide those, but of course I have to approve any change to prisoners' issue. I must say I was struck by how genuinely devoted the woman is to Wilson. And we get plenty of a different kind. They'll come in behind thick veils so no one will recognize them, and pretend affection as long as there's something the prisoner's got that they think they can get to. But not Miss Littleberry. Star-crossed lovers is what Wilson and Miss Littleberry are, if you know your Shakespeare. But of course you would, wouldn't you?" Holmes and Watson adopted soft smiles of acknowledgment. "Right out of *Romeo and Juliet*. She's here every day, and they tell me she always gets as close to him as the bars on his cell will let her—which is allowed as long as the officer can see her hands. It can get noisy and you have to stand close just to be heard, but I've been out on the walkways, and I've seen it's not just getting past the hubbub with that one."

Warden Fallon's reflections were interrupted by his secretary's announcement of the arrival of the trustee who was to take Holmes and Watson to see Wilson. He dismissed them into the prisoner's care with a parting observation. "Star-crossed lovers is what they are. An unhappy story bound to have an unhappy ending."

The trustee led Holmes and Watson up two flights of stairs, each step clanking beneath their feet. They walked beneath an arch on which was engraved TIER IIA and came onto a walkway that admitted only two men walking abreast,

47

one if a man was the size of the Warden. The walkway fronted the twenty cells lining one side of the second tier, mirroring the twenty cells on its opposite side, the two sides joined by bridges at their front, back, and center. William Wilson's cell was next to the last one in his tier. Holmes and Watson had been instructed they would be standing outside the lattice-like arrangement of bars through which visitors could talk to prisoners. The criss-crossing of bars created squares of no more than three inches across the front of the cell, and explained the willingness to allow visitors to stand close to prisoners they could imperfectly see in the windowless cells. One of the two guards assigned to the second level occupied a chair set midway across its center bridge. He eyed Holmes and Watson as if they were planning Wilson's escape, if not the mass exodus of the entire second tier. The trustee who had been their guide called to Wilson that he had visitors, and left before waiting to see if Wilson acknowledged the information, or speaking a single word to Holmes and Watson.

Wilson, too, maintained his reserve. He stood at the back of his cell studying his visitors. Through the shadows of the closely interlaced bars he could be seen as being a few inches above middle height, trim, with a thick mop of light brown hair and flaring moustaches. But for the grim expression that seemed permanently imprinted across his face, he might have been described as a handsome young man.

"Who are you and what do you want with me?"

For the fourth time in less than a half hour Holmes detailed their identities and his somewhat remote relationship to Wilson's fiancée. "What we want with you is simply to understand your view of what happened the morning of the shootings. We are both of an open mind and prepared to be of assistance to you and Miss Littleberry if we can."

There was silence from the other side of the barred door as dark eyes continued their study. When he spoke, Wilson did nothing to hide the distrust he felt. "I've already told the police everything I know and you see what that got me."

"We are not the police and you may know more than you suspect," Holmes replied.

There was another pause and the dark eyes went back to work. Finally, Wilson broke the silence he had created. "What is it you want to know?"

"First, Mr. Wilson, why were you at Mr. Morgan's home the morning of the shooting?"

"That's simple enough. I went to see Miss Littleberry the morning before the team was scheduled to go to Boston. It's something I do—or I did—most all the time. I'd go over to see her most mornings when the team was home—unless of course I was scheduled to pitch. And I always made it a point to see her when we were going out of town, where we wouldn't see each other again for a week or even longer."

"And what happened after you arrived? Please leave nothing out. The smallest detail may be critical. Dr. Watson will be taking notes as you speak. Don't be put off by that. We rely on his careful reporting to unsnarl the tangles that are brought to us."

Wilson gave no sign of concern about the note-taking. "I got to the servants' entrance a little past nine. I knew there was to be a breakfast celebration for Morgan's daughter, Miss Juliet, who'd got married the day before, and it might be difficult for Caroline ... Miss Littleberry ... to get away, but I thought I'd try to catch her between her taking care of Mrs. Morgan and the hoorah that was scheduled. As it turned out, I had to wait even longer than I expected and by the time we got outside, the newspaper people were already setting up their cameras and a crowd was gathering. It didn't take long before there was maybe twenty-five or thirty people picking out spots between the trees and the house where they might have a good view. Can you picture that many people come to gawk at Morgan and his rich friends? Anyway, Caroline and me got over to the street side of the crowd because I knew I'd have to be able to get away to catch my train. Besides, I was there to see Caroline. I didn't care about Morgan; I never have."

"Anyway, Morgan's coach made its way through the crowd and stopped as close to the back entrance as Mr. Ferguson, the coachman, could manage. Somebody I didn't recognize climbed out, and then Morgan started out. That's when I heard two shots, but I can't tell you where they came from, only that they didn't come from me. I'll swear to that, not that anyone will believe me. I did take out my gun, I admit that, but it was like a reflex to protect myself from what was happening. And then everyone was looking at me and pointing to me, so I took off. Of course, that was the worst thing I could have done and I can't tell you why I did it. It's what everyone asks and I got no answer for them. Well anyway, I'm an athlete and could easy outrun everybody coming after me. I had it in mind to get away, seeing as how I was sure by then nobody would believe my side of it, but the police found me before I got to the train station."

Having delivered a report that had garnered skepticism at its every telling, he thought to beat his audience to its inevitable dismissal. "You can see it's hopeless. I appreciate your coming, but there's nothing you're gonna be able to do for me."

Holmes ignored Wilson's rejection of his assistance. "Mr. Wilson, why did you have a pistol on your person, and how do you explain there being two empty chambers in your weapon?"

"It's like I told the police, I carry a gun for protection, and I had no idea it had two empty chambers; I hadn't looked at it for weeks. But what you got to understand is that when you're a ballplayer you can find yourself in some pretty rough neighborhoods when you're traveling, and you never know when you'll run into somebody who's liquored up and looking to blame you for beating his team and losing him money. I'm a pitcher, Mr. Holmes, and it's me they're most likely to blame. So, yes, like a lot of the players, I do have a gun. But I only carry it when I'm gonna be out of town—which is why I had it the day of the shooting. Regardless, I never shot at anybody; I can't imagine I ever would. I only have it to scare away trouble."

"Even with your radical inclinations, Mr. Wilson?" Holmes asked. "You seem to have very strong feelings about the harm men like Mr. Morgan do. We saw the pamphlet that was taken from your room accusing Morgan of buying his way out of the war and of causing the deaths of other young men by selling defective rifles. That's pretty strong stuff, Mr. Wilson. Why shouldn't we believe you schemed to get rid of this man you called your enemy?" Watson looked up from his writing, surprised to find Holmes sounding a good deal more like Wilson's prosecutor than his savior.

Wilson's response was edged with equal fervor. "I don't like the man. I never said I did. And I do regard his class as the enemy. But I don't shoot people just because I don't like them."

Wilson became silent, and for a moment it appeared the exchange with the prisoner was over. But he'd only been gathering himself, and when he spoke again it was in a far more measured tone.

"There is one thing I can't explain. It's all this radical literature that was supposed to have been found in my apartment. I had no literature, Mr. Holmes. I don't know where it would have come from unless the police put it there."

"You *really* think the police would put incriminating material in your flat?" Holmes asked.

"Mr. Morgan is a very important man. I don't know what it's like in London, but over here the police do favors for important men."

While unable to fathom Wilson's charge of police conspiracy, Holmes thought it wise to change the subject rather than argue the point.

"What about the shot taken at Mr. Morgan at his club? Are we to understand that had nothing to do with you?"

51

"I wasn't near his club. It was a day we had a game. I would have gone to see Caroline, and been on the cable car on the way to the ballpark when whoever it was took a shot at Morgan."

"Then you know Morgan's schedule for getting to his club?"

"Sure, I never said I didn't. He gets to the Metropolitan Club, Saturdays at eleven. What's any of that to do with me?"

"It has to do with your knowing where and when to find Morgan. I must be honest with you, Mr. Wilson. Your case is not a strong one. Your gun was drawn at the time the shots were fired, and is missing the same number and caliber of cartridges that were fired at Morgan. You ran from the scene of the crime. You knew where Mr. Morgan would be and when he'd arrive there on the occasion of the earlier attempt on his life. And now you would have us believe that the radical literature found in your flat attacking Mr. Morgan was put there by the police."

Holmes moved closer to Wilson's cell. His voice was soft, but his tone was harsh. "If I am to help you, Mr. Wilson, I must have the truth. If you won't share it with me, I shall have to go down a great many blind alleys to find it, and time is not our ally."

"I've told you everything I can. Believe what you will. There's nothing more I can say."

"Very well, Mr. Wilson. I must proceed using what you have told me, but I promise nothing—not even that we will see each other again." Holmes had already turned to leave when Watson raised a final question.

"On the morning of the shooting, did you recognize anyone in the crowd who was waiting for Mr. Morgan's return?"

"No one. I saw no one."

With that, Watson wished the prisoner good day, and hurried to catch up with Holmes who was already several yards down the narrow gangway. Wilson retreated to the shadows at the back of his cell, left alone to contemplate the fate he saw being readied for him by government officials prepared to do the bidding of their robber baron masters.

3.
Frederick Washington

By the time Mrs. Hudson arrived back at the Waldorf it was too late to find her way to Brooklyn and be back in time to join Holmes and Watson for dinner, especially as she had no idea where Brooklyn was to be found. She spent the remainder of her afternoon correcting that deficiency. Brooklyn, she learned, was a city southeast of New York that could be reached by ferry, or by crossing a bridge that had been built ten years earlier. Her informants were an interchangeable group of bellboys, elevator operators and receptions clerks, who came and went in association with the demands of other guests. In spite of the group's inconstant membership there was broad agreement that Brooklyn's attractions did not merit the considerable effort required to visit them.

With some embarrassment, Mrs. Hudson explained she had a relative living on Snediker Street in Brooklyn she felt obliged to visit. Her revelation led to a massive rethinking of the merits of travel to Brooklyn with a resulting consensus that the presence of a relative in that city justified the rigors of travel. One of her informants, a young bellboy, went so far as to reveal he traveled to Brooklyn from time to time to visit his grandmother who lived on Eastern Parkway a few streets from Snediker. His secret out, he went on to inform Mrs. Hudson she would be taking the Flatbush Avenue cable car, but to remember that across the river they called it a trolley. He had no idea why.

With her route within Brooklyn clarified, the group set about the task of getting Mrs. Hudson to Brooklyn. They had agreed on her taking the Sixth Avenue cable car downtown to the Fulton Ferry, and the Ferry across the East River to Brooklyn until a receptions clerk, joining them after checking in a family from Cherbourg, insisted Mrs. Hudson should take the cable car that ran across the Brooklyn Bridge rather than the ferry that ran beneath it. His thinking was rejected, and his person ridiculed, when it was discovered he had never been on either the cable car or the ferry, and was simply repeating a guest's opinion. The bellboy, having negotiated several successful ferry crossings, was given the last word on choice of transportation. Flushed with victory, he revealed that he had even, on one occasion, taken the ferry and a cable car to Eastern Park to see the Brooklyn Bridegrooms play baseball, adding quickly that he was just curious about the Bridegrooms, and his team remained the New York Giants. With her education complete, Mrs. Hudson thanked her instructors, gave the bellboy a warm smile, and excused herself, reporting a need to rest before dinner.

As they had agreed, the three detectives met in the Waldorf lobby at 6:30 and set off for Delmonico's at Fifth Avenue and 26th Street. Mrs. Hudson suggested it was a fine night for a walk; Holmes and Watson understood that Mrs. Hudson's interest in walking involved as much a reluctance to pay the cost of a four-wheeler as the warm night air. They strolled along Fifth Avenue comparing the homes they passed with homes in England, and found much of what they saw wanting. The small plots of unadorned earth did not compare to English gardens, the brownstones lacked the grandeur of English estates, the streets were devoid of history, and the stores were without the charm of English shoppes. At 26th Street they merged with a group of well-dressed men and women funneling their way through the doors of the broad sweep of Delmonico's Restaurant.

Their plan to take a short break from the work of investigation, and postpone discussion of the day's events until tea and dessert, was abandoned with the placing of their orders. As soon as the waiter had put away his pad and congratulated Holmes on his choices with a last "very good, sir," Watson removed his accounts book together with the sharpened pencil he always had available, and apologized for breaking their agreement with a plea of his need "to stay on top of things." The need he voiced was echoed instantly and enthusiastically by his colleagues. Over soup and mushrooms on toast, Mrs. Hudson reported her meeting with Mrs. Sowder and her curious encounter with the Pinkerton detective. The trip to the Tombs was reported by Holmes during servings of the mains—lamb cutlets to Mrs. Hudson, Maryland terrapin to Holmes and pigeon with peas for Watson. His rapid note-taking between bites of dinner excited curious glances from the neighboring tables, which largely disappeared as onlookers became aware of the English accents that accompanied, and thereby explained the eccentric behavior.

When Holmes had finished his account and Watson had filled in his own observations, Mrs. Hudson laid her fork beside what was left of her lamb cutlet, looking to the meat as though suddenly suspicious of its origins. "Now I find that curious. Why do you suppose that is?" She raised her eyes to direct a question to her colleagues. "Why would this Franklin stay to see the man who fired him unless 'e 'ad it in mind to get even in some way, and if 'e was thinkin' about gettin' even, why let the whole staff know 'e's there, and why bring along toughs with 'im besides. And why did Mr. Wilson deny seein' Franklin? The crowd wasn't so large they were likely to miss each other. I'm thinkin' there's somethin' between the men that bears lookin' into."

"Is the animosity between the two men really significant, Mrs. Hudson?" Holmes asked. "I can't be the only one having a problem reconciling the several parts of Wilson's story. Mind you, I feel badly for your cousin's daughter. She would seem to be an innocent bystander—if not Wilson's dupe—but shouldn't we be all about softening the blow rather than giving her false hope, Mrs. Hudson?

"Certainly, if the 'ope is false, Mr. 'Olmes. But I'm not ready to say that just yet. There's too many loose ends. We 'ave the strange appearance of Mr. Franklin, and then there's Mr.

McIlvaine. Was 'e waitin' in the crowd just to be sociable to the girl who rejected 'im, and to the father 'e blames for gettin' 'im turned down?" Mrs. Hudson brushed her napkin across her mouth although she hadn't taken a bite for several minutes. "But we can wait on the two of them. They're not goin' anyplace."

"For tomorrow, I'll take the cable cars to Brooklyn to visit Caroline. Dr. Watson, I'd like you to go to Eastern Park, where the people with the Brooklyn baseball team work. They're the ones who see Mr. Wilson up close every day. They can tell us what they think of the boy, and just 'ow much of a radical they believe 'e is. Mind you, Doctor, it won't be easy to get them to open up to a stranger."

"Mr. 'Olmes, yours will be a difficult job too. You'll need to see Mr. Morgan and find out what 'e can tell us about that morning, and whether a man in 'is position doesn't 'ave more enemies than just a footman 'e dismissed and a rejected suitor." She looked grimly to Holmes, who acknowledged her request with a nod that was equally grim.

"They 'ave one of those telephones over at the Waldorf that you're always so anxious to 'ave me put into Baker Street. Maybe you can get some practice with it by makin' an appointment to see Mr. Morgan." Without prompting, Watson had already decided to make use of the telephone to arrange for his visit to Eastern Park.

With the state of their investigation clear, and the next day's plans elaborated, they settled back to complete their dinners and conduct a spirited discussion on the quality of Delmonico's cooking. They agreed the food was good, in fact quite good, but felt certain it was not quite up to the measure of the Strand. Mrs. Hudson deferred to their thinking, never having set foot in the Strand.

To provide a fair test before passing final judgment, they made separate selections from the restaurant's dessert menu. After careful study, Mrs. Hudson opted for the charlotte russe, Holmes selected tutti frutti ice cream because, as he explained later, he wanted to hear their very dignified waiter speak its name, and Watson chose Stilton cheese to learn, he said, how well it traveled. All ordered French coffee, not seeing tea on the menu, and not feeling up to Turkish coffee which was Delmonico's only other offering.

When the waiter returned, he was accompanied by a young assistant carrying their desserts on a silver tray. The youngster stood statue-like while the waiter removed and announced each dish as he set it before its recipient. Having served Mrs. Hudson and Watson with proper solemnity, he made effort to lend the same gravity to his announcement of Holmes' dessert, "Tutti frutti ice cream, sir." Holmes sniggered his delight, then pretended he hadn't heard him clearly and asked for a repeat performance. The waiter swallowed once before again attempting to announce Holmes' dessert with a dignity it clearly did not deserve.

The task completed, and his face once more a mask of pompous severity, the waiter asked if he could bring them anything else.

Holmes gave the man a dismissive wave. "Just our coffee, thank you."

The waiter bowed his head and left with his mute assistant.

The three detectives continued their conversation oblivious to the waiter as he set down their coffee, and the check Watson made certain was not shared with Mrs. Hudson. They were oblivious as well to a powerfully built, heavy-browed man sitting alone at a table a good distance from them who had positioned himself to be sitting at Mrs. Hudson's back. He left moments after the three detectives had, trailing them to the Waldorf Hotel before turning on 33rd in the direction of Madison Avenue.

At seven the following morning, they gathered for breakfast and a review of the morning papers. The "assassination attempt," as both papers described it, was still on page one, but was no longer the banner headline. The articles in each paper described Mr. Morgan's resumption of duties and continuing recovery. They indicated that a daughter of the deceased Conrad Wagner had been located in Cleveland, Ohio where Mr. Wagner had lived until his wife died in 1871, and that arrangements were being made to transport the victim's body for internment in the family plot. The papers used identical language in reporting that the cost of transport was being born through "the beneficence of Mr. Morgan." The papers went on to report that the renowned phrenologist, Dr. Bernard Hollander, who was recently arrived in New York on the first leg of a national lecture tour, had volunteered his services to the authorities. Dr. Hollander was to conduct an examination of William Wilson's cranium later that same day. The news of Dr. Hollander's involvement reduced what little appetite Holmes and Watson had for breakfast. They poked disconsolately at their food while Mrs. Hudson ate heartily of eggs, bacon, sausages, and toast.

Shortly after eight, Holmes called JP Morgan's secretary to arrange an appointment, only to be asked the purpose of his visit and a telephone number where he could be reached. Holmes was told he would be called back within the hour. He waited in the lobby of the Waldorf Hotel fully an hour and a half before a bellboy came to fetch him to the phone. Without acknowledging the delay, Morgan's secretary advised Holmes he could see Mr. Morgan at his home at 2:30 that afternoon, and directed Holmes to bring with him a sheet of paper containing Dr. John Watson's signature and a separate sheet containing his own signature. Holmes replied that his housekeeper was traveling with him and wondered if Mr. Morgan wanted her signature as well, but his sarcasm was wasted on the secretary who soberly informed him that it wouldn't be necessary before hanging up.

Watson enjoyed a very different experience with his call. He was immediately connected to Charles Ebbets, an executive with the Bridegrooms, and provided an appointment. When informed of the purpose of his visit, Watson was told two players, who were particular friends of Wilson, would also be made available to speak to him.

After hearing Morgan's request, Watson authored a note on Waldorf Hotel stationery stating his wish to make Mr. Morgan's acquaintance at a later time. He signed it John H Watson, MD with what Holmes regarded as an unnecessary flourish. Taking a second sheet of Waldorf stationery, Holmes wrote a short note extolling the taste, texture, and appearance of tutti frutti ice cream, before scrawling his name with studied unconcern. He folded both sheets into a Waldorf envelope and pronounced America's finances in the hands of lunatics.

The three detectives went their separate ways for the remainder of the morning. Holmes spent much of the time searching out area tobacconists in hopes of locating the pipe tobacco he preferred, but had forgotten to pack; Watson chose to take the time to put his notes in order; and Mrs. Hudson elected to explore the neighborhood around the hotel, rejecting as unnecessary Watson's offer to accompany her. It was a decision she would soon come to question.

She left the Waldorf followed, as she expected, by the Pinkerton companion she had acquired the day before. She was unconcerned about him now; a stroll through the New York streets would reveal nothing of significance. As it turned out, their walk together lasted less than two streets. As Mrs. Hudson turned on 34th in the direction of Sixth Avenue, she came on three boys of 14 or 15 attacking a smaller boy she thought to be about 12. Without hesitation she turned to the Pinkerton a half block behind, called for him to hurry, and began striding toward the site of uneven battle. In another moment it was over. Perhaps it was the sight of a middle-aged woman striding toward them brandishing a furled umbrella; more likely it was the sight of a well-muscled younger man running toward them with a stout club held high above his head. Whichever the cause, the three tormentors took off in the direction of Sixth Avenue where they turned the corner and disappeared. The Pinkerton man tipped the homburg that had somehow remained firmly in place during his short sprint, and said a single word, "Ma'am," in a soft baritone that gave no hint of his recent exertions. Mrs. Hudson smiled her thanks as the Pinkerton man backed away, both of them well aware they would see each other again, and likely soon.

Mrs. Hudson turned her attention to the small boy whose fists were still clenched as he watched the Pinkerton man follow the same path his tormentors had taken. His shirt was torn and there was a small cut on one cheek, but the boy showed concern only about the purse tucked into the waist of his pants. The youngster, unlike his attackers, was black although his complexion was, in fact, like that of Mrs. Sowder's coffee after she had added milk. His long face and prominent cheekbones were accentuated by his thin frame, but it was his eyes that captured Mrs. Hudson's attention. They seemed to belong to someone a great deal older. They didn't leave the man who had come to his rescue until he turned the corner. Only then, the boy turned to Mrs. Hudson and spoke a single word in question, "Policeman?" The voice was eerily calm.

Her response was as terse as the question, "Pinkerton."

The boy gave a low growl of acknowledgment. "Same thing," he said, and followed the path the others had taken up 34th Street.

Ordinarily, Mrs. Hudson was not one to meddle in the affairs of others, but ordinarily Mrs. Hudson was not presented with the affairs of a vulnerable 12 year old.

"I'll walk a way with you."

The boy shrugged his response. "There's no need."

"I'd like to just the same. There's no tellin' whether those boys are waitin' for you. I'm Mrs. 'Udson."

"They won't be." The boy quickened his pace, ignoring the opportunity to introduce himself.

Mrs. Hudson sped up as well, not quite as much as the boy, but she remained not far behind. He led her west across Sixth Avenue to Seventh and then north on Seventh as hotels and elegant restaurants gave way to a steady stream of bars, some nearly elegant, most aspiring to get beyond seedy; shops advertised "games of chance" with pictures of outsize cards and dice whitewashed on their windows; and bordellos were interspersed among the bars and betting parlors, sometimes wearing the mask of dancehalls and sometimes feeling no need of a mask. The population changed with the change in business establishments. The boy who stood out because of his race on Fifth Avenue became indistinguishable on that account on Seventh, and Mrs. Hudson became aware of her increasingly exceptional status. It seemed to her that her exceptionalism was not lost on the young men who lounged on the steps of row houses that sporadically interrupted the stream of area businesses.

Her 12 year old companion took note of the several young men as well, but his eyes came to be fixed on just one of them. He was older than the boy, 15 or 16, seated on the top step of a walk-up, and to all appearances undersized and unimpressive. But when he straightened and flicked the last of a cigarette into the street, the others cleared a path a good deal wider than was needed, and laughed a good deal more heartily at what he said than any brief remark seemed reasonably to justify. He walked with exaggerated care down the few steps before strutting leisurely toward Mrs. Hudson, who prepared herself for the mugging she had been warned was a common occurrence in New York. The boy she had set out to protect was between the two of them and he now moderated his pace, narrowing the distance between himself and Mrs. Hudson. Finally, he stopped altogether and waited for Mrs. Hudson to catch up to him. At that point he took her hand and walked with her past the approaching menace, who gave them as wide a berth as those on the steps had given him.

Mrs. Hudson was rarely mistaken about people. She had spent too much time in their careful study. On this occasion she had been gravely mistaken. She had yielded to her own expectations and ignored the evidence. She had seen a 12 year old boy being roughed up by a group of toughs, and responded to that 12 year old. It was clear there was yet another 12 year old who was now holding her hand. The self-possessed nature that she had seen as bravado in the face of threat, she now recognized as the certain knowledge that, once across Sixth Avenue, his safety was assured. The purse he had wedged inside his pants would contain money or betting slips or both, and identified him as a runner for a gambling organization powerful enough to protect him from toughs like the one they had just passed. Mrs. Hudson now understood she was no longer the protector, and her safety was in the hands of a 12 year old boy whose name she still didn't know. She decided that situation at least could be remedied.

"I thank you for your 'elp. Will you now tell me your name?"

"They call me 'Wash's boy'."

Mrs. Hudson urged him to repeat himself, not certain she had heard correctly. He did, and then added his only attempt at conversation. "You talk funny."

"I'm English."

He made a long face of understanding before again becoming silent.

They went another block and a half before speaking, and then Wash's boy used the same economy of words to give direction. He stopped before a three-story brownstone whose ground floor was a shop. Green shades were drawn across its two broad windows with a sign in the corner of one window reading: OPENS AT 6PM. A foot-wide board above the windows held the message, "FRED WASHINGTON'S" in large block lettering

"This is where I live," Wash's boy said, and releasing her hand, led her up the three steps to a door beside the shop. He withdrew a key from the purse that had been tucked into his waist, unlocked the door and led her through the small entranceway, then up a narrow flight of stairs that opened on a single room spanning the whole of the shop below. An open stairway across from where they stopped led to the floor above. He took her hand again, crossed a short way into the room and waited.

"What have we here?" The question came from a Morris chair at the far end of the room. The chair was turned away from Mrs. Hudson to face windows looking out on the street over which she and Wash's boy had come. A cloud of smoke from a briar pipe was the only visible evidence of the chair's occupant. Nonetheless, Mrs. Hudson knew a good deal about her unseen host.

From the respect accorded his emissary, she already knew him to be a power in his world. She knew, too, he kept a continuing surveillance of that world. The room had a single window running nearly floor to ceiling, and extending more than halfway across the back wall, allowing him to see all that was happening on the street below. The absence of indentations in the thick carpeting indicated the Morris chair was permanently in its place at the window. The constancy of his oversight was apparent from the full ashtray, and a plate containing browned apple cores and stems long since stripped of their grapes that lay on a round table beside his chair. Books stacked on the same table suggested the resident was an educated man. It was clear as well that the decision to reject a more active participation in the world was a voluntary one. There were no crutches, no cane, and no chair to indicate infirmity. A poorly made bed in the corner to her right and dining table to her left indicated the capacity of the room to serve his multiple needs, while the state of the room suggested that housekeeping was entrusted to contemporaries of Wash's boy.

Her companion answered the phantom presence for both of them. His tone and words suggested the morning's adventures were not without precedent. "Some boys were bothering me on Fifth over by the Waldorf and this lady—she's Mrs. Hudson and she's English—chased them, together with a Pink who was there." The boy set the purse on the dining table as the voice from the chair became a person, and the person came forward to welcome her.

"Good afternoon, Mrs. Hudson, my name is Frederick Washington."

Though she prided herself on being well-mannered and respectful, Mrs. Hudson's eyes widened and her mouth came briefly open on seeing Frederick Washington.

The man had kinky hair and features that put Mrs. Hudson in mind of men she'd seen of African descent, but his hair was white, his eyes were blue and his complexion was lighter than any man or woman she had ever known. Mrs. Hudson had never seen an albino before and she could do nothing to hide her surprise at seeing one now.

Frederick Washington was too accustomed to the shock he occasioned to take more than brief notice of it now. He was, in any event, concerned about one aspect of the youngster's report. "Did the Pinkerton take any interest in you?"

"No, sir, I watched him leave, and he never come back or followed us."

"Never *came* back," Washington corrected the boy before complimenting his action, "That was smartly done." He smiled broadly and waved Mrs. Hudson to a part of the room organized to receive guests. A settee, couch, and easy chair were grouped around a low table. Though mismatched, all the pieces were new and well crafted. Mrs. Hudson chose the settee and Washington took the easy chair opposite.

65

"May I get you a cup of coffee, or perhaps you'd prefer tea?"

Mrs. Hudson had every intention of returning to the Waldorf Hotel, wanting only assistance in locating a four-wheeler—this one time acknowledging a need for that extravagance. However, she felt it appropriate to be courteous toward the man, especially after appearing shocked upon first meeting him.

"A cup of tea would be lovely, thank you."

Frederick Washington dispatched Wash's boy to have Rose prepare tea, and to wash up and get himself something to eat. The youngster smiled brightly for the first time, and descended the steps for a kitchen that lay somewhere below the ground floor. Washington mirrored the boy's smile, directing it to his guest.

"I'm sure you've no idea where you are, so let me explain. You've wandered into what's called African Broadway. Which means you're now in a part of New York City filled with people who look like me." He laughed at the line Mrs. Hudson was certain he'd used many times before. "My little joke, you'll have to excuse me. But you should not have come here. It can be a dangerous place for a woman alone." He looked to her with sudden seriousness, then recovered his smile and waved off the threat he'd just spoken. "*You* have no cause for concern however. You meant to do a kindness taking care of the boy and I'll see you get home safely. Indeed, I stand in your debt for your good intentions. If I can do you a kindness in the future, you have only to call." With that he produced a business card showing his name and telephone number, but nothing more. "For now tell me something about yourself. How do you come to be in America?"

As she reported her reason for traveling to New York and the crisis she discovered after arriving, the roguish smile with which Frederick Washington had been regarding her gave way to surprise and finally to concern. When she named her

66

traveling companions and described their intention to investigate the attack on Morgan, he shut his eyes a moment and shook his head the slightest bit from side to side. He waited while a youngster who might have been sister to Wash's boy placed two cups of tea on the low table between Washington and Mrs. Hudson. He nodded satisfaction with her work and smiled her out of the room. When he spoke again, it was slow and deliberate as he searched for the right words to capture his thoughts.

"As you are undoubtedly aware, Mrs. Hudson, the shooting of JP Morgan and the arrest of Brakeman Wilson—as he's commonly known—are the talk of the City, and Wilson is believed by everyone to be guilty. I do mean *everyone*, Mrs. Hudson. Your Mr. Holmes is well known in this country, I'd guess nearly as well known here as in your own country. But even with Mr. Holmes backing him, I must tell you it is nearly impossible to think of Wilson avoiding a long prison sentence, if not the gallows."

"Do you believe the case against 'im is that strong?"

"I think the case is strong; I think the politics are stronger."

Mrs. Hudson took a sip of tea she found tasteless, and smiled a satisfaction she did not feel. "What do you mean by 'politics'?"

"Money is politics in this country, Mrs. Hudson. And Mr. Morgan has a great deal of money. I'm afraid your Mr. Wilson doesn't stand a chance against all those who would like to be in Mr. Morgan's good graces, or better yet have Mr. Morgan feel beholden to them. There's no lawyer anxious to take Wilson's case, while those in the office of the district attorney will compete for the privilege of making certain he is punished to the full extent of the law. There may be a judge capable of ruling fairly—I've known stranger things to happen—but I wouldn't bet on it, Mrs. Hudson, and I'm a betting man. If you'll take some advice, I'd suggest you gather up your little lady and all of you take the next liner back to England. That way you can at least protect her. If you insist on searching for someone else to accuse, you'll get no cooperation from the authorities—quite the reverse. You'll make a great many powerful enemies, and in the end you'll achieve nothing."

"Of course I 'ope you're wrong, Mr. Washington—I mean about achievin' nothin'—but I'm afraid Mr. 'Olmes' mind is made up and there's no chance of turnin' 'im around."

Frederick Washington's face crinkled into a tired smile. "I've already told you what I believe the odds favor. If your Mr. Holmes insists on continuing his investigation, tell him to come see me. I'll give him ten to one against his success, and I'll cover any amount he chooses to wager." He let go a low rumble of laughter before turning serious in response to Mrs. Hudson's tight smile.

"I mean no disrespect for your Mr. Holmes, and I've no wish to sound unfeeling about Brakeman Wilson. Perhaps I've grown too accustomed to the harshness of the world I see from my window." Washington paused as though considering the ferocity of that world, but had another thought to share.

"I will tell you two things that may prove helpful to Mr. Holmes. First, he should watch out for the Pinks. Their reputation is tied to Wilson being found guilty—they're the ones who captured Wilson—and they'll not take kindly to somebody trying to prove them wrong. Second, there's a footman named Franklin Langer who worked for the Morgans. Being a footman isn't his job now, and it wasn't his only job then. He's in a part of the wagering business that does no credit to our profession."

Raised eyebrows made clear Mrs. Hudson's skepticism. Frederick Washington saw the gesture and made a small smile. He made his living reading people, and he made a comfortable living.

"You don't believe there is a respectable side to the wagering business." It was not a question. "I know you don't approve of the way I make my living, Mrs. Hudson, but I assure you my business is conducted every bit as honestly as that of your butcher or greengrocer, although they probably don't have to supplement a constable's wages to remain in business. Regardless, everyone who enters my betting parlor has an honest chance of winning, and that's better odds than most of my customers get with life outside the betting parlor. For as little as a penny, I provide each of them a chance to dream, and every now and again their dreams come true." His point made, Frederick Washington took up the pipe whose fire he had let die. He tipped it slightly in Mrs. Hudson's direction by way of asking permission and relit his tobacco after getting a small nod.

"That's as may be, Mr. Washington. I'm sure it's none of it my business. I'm more interested in learnin' what you know about this Franklin chap. I believe 'e's somebody my Mr. 'Olmes will want to talk to."

Frederick Washington took a long draft on his pipe and watched a trail of smoke follow a snaky path toward the ceiling before it broke apart and slowly disappeared. When he spoke, it was again in the deliberate fashion he reserved to make clear his concern. "Mr. Holmes would do well to take care with Franklin Langer. Mr. Langer works for some very dangerous people, Mrs. Hudson, and you must make certain Mr. Holmes understands that."

Mrs. Hudson would make certain Holmes understood that, but she knew it would make him all the more interested in speaking with Franklin Langer.

"Dangerous in what way, Mr. Washington?"

He took another long draw from his pipe and directed another stream of smoke above their heads. "There's different kinds of gambling, Mrs. Hudson. There's cards and dice, both of which you can find downstairs later in the evening. And there are numbers or policy as it's called where three numbers will be drawn by someone other than myself or anyone who works for me. That will also take place this evening." Washington stopped to drain the last of his tea. His blue eyes held Mrs. Hudson in

their stare. "Everything done here is open to view. *Everything.*
It's why I can say anyone who comes to Frederick Washington's
shop stands a fair chance, and it's why my establishment will be
filled to bursting in a very few hours. The crowd Franklin
Langer runs with operates differently. They'll do cards and dice,
and policy of course, but those aren't their only interests, and
maybe not their main interest. They like taking bets on sporting
events—boxing of course, and horse racing, and now baseball.
Nothing's been proven or probably ever will be, but there's talk
that the people Langer works for wouldn't be above fixing things
to know in advance how games will come out."

Mrs. Hudson gave the sober nod Washington's statement
demanded, waited for a moment to pass, and asked him about
another of his points she found disturbing.

"Who are these Pinkertons you say captured Mr. Wilson?
Isn't that the job of your constables?"

Washington smiled his tolerance of the woman's
pardonable confusion. "It should be. But men like Morgan can
hire the Pinks to do things the police can't or maybe wouldn't
do—although the police are always ready to do a good turn for
the JP Morgans of the world." Frederick Washington stopped for
another deep draft from his briar, and Mrs. Hudson recognized
yet another revelation would be forthcoming.

"To tell you the truth, Mrs. Hudson, the very rich are not
the only people in this city to want protection. There's a history
you wouldn't know that might explain some of the things you'll
see while you're in New York. I'm going back thirty years. I was
just a boy of course, but there are things you don't forget, no
matter how long ago they happened. It had to do with recruiting
for the army in what was called the War Between the States. At
first they only took volunteers for the Union and there was no
trouble. But then they needed more men and they started
drafting people. The problem was that by that time everybody
knew if you went to war there was a good chance you could
come back missing an arm or a leg, or maybe not come back at

70

all. That was bad enough, but what made it even worse was that rich people could buy their way out of the draft. If you had the money you could pay someone to take your place. Well, a lot of white people didn't think it was their war anyway, so when they found out that they would be drafted to do the fighting and maybe the dying, while rich people could stay home and get richer, they got to staging a full blown riot. They set buildings on fire—even the mayor's house—and they captured and roughed up the superintendent of police."

"And after that they came for us. Because of course they saw us as the real cause of their troubles. I hope you never see a lynching, Mrs. Hudson. I don't ever want to see another one. They hunted us for three days, and to this day nobody knows how many men they killed. They even burned the Colored Orphan Asylum a few streets from here. It was just a miracle they got all the children out. Anyway, after the riots there were some who were determined to be ready for a next time. We obey the law, Mrs. Hudson, but we won't allow what happened once to ever happen again."

Frederick Washington straightened in his chair and reprised the smile that had been absent while he recounted the history he had lived. "But enough of the past, Mrs. Hudson. Now it's time to get you back to your hotel, and to prepare my establishment for the evening." With that, he put a whistle to his lips and blew three short bursts. In response, two boys Mrs. Hudson judged to be twelve or thirteen descended the stairs from the floor above. They were dressed in matching uniforms of dark pants and tunic, the tunic buttoned to the neck with epaulets sewn to each shoulder. Their shoes showed evidence of a recent, if not wholly successful effort to make them shine.

"Mrs. Hudson, let me introduce Chester and Sebastian, two young colleagues of mine who will help you find your way home. Don't be put off by the young men's age; I assure you no one will bother you while you're in their company." He smiled benignly to the newly ordained bodyguards whose stony expressions did not change. Frederick Washington rose and extended his hand to Mrs. Hudson. "Let me again offer thanks for your good-hearted gesture, and repeat that I remain in your debt, madam."

Mrs. Hudson shook his hand soberly, thanked him for the tea and hospitality, and promised she would keep his kind offer in mind. She departed for Fifth Avenue and the Waldorf Hotel, her small protectors on either side. Their expressions seemed, like Wash's boy, to be better suited to men closer to her own age. They stared straight ahead, with only an occasional glance to the knots of youngsters gathered in doorways and on the steps of modest brownstones. This time no one came forward to interrupt Mrs. Hudson's progress. They turned left on 33rd Street, and proceeded to a point halfway to Sixth Avenue, where Sebastian stopped and pointed, issuing the only words either boy spoke during their short journey. "That's Fifth Avenue." Their work done, Chester and Sebastian turned and started back to their home on African Broadway.

4.

JP Morgan

Four hours later, after a light lunch and a detailed account of Mrs. Hudson's adventures, all were ready to set out on their afternoon assignments. Mrs. Hudson and Watson left together, while Holmes lingered in the hotel's reception area where he sought directions to the Morgan residence from the ever present Pinkerton. The request took the man by surprise. He tried to excuse himself with a faint smile and the suggestion that Holmes had him confused with someone else. He made effort to maneuver around Holmes and follow Mrs. Hudson and Watson, but an arm round his shoulders locked him in place.

"There's really no hurry. My friends will be back later. You will see them again soon enough. For now, I'm certain you can help me keep my appointment with Mr. Morgan. We both know he is your employer, and I feel certain you can direct me to his home."

The Pinkerton tried to squirm his way out of Holmes' grip which led to Holmes drawing the man more tightly to him. A receptions clerk looked questioningly to the pair; he found Holmes' relaxed smile and attempted a tentative smile of his own. The clerk's attention convinced Holmes it would be wise to move the Pinkerton man and himself to another part of the reception area. Still smiling, he tightened his grip on the man's shoulder and led his grim-faced prisoner to an alcove beyond the lobby's center.

"We'll wait here until my friends are on their way."

The Pinkerton tried once more to jerk away and failed again. "Who the hell do you think you are?"

"I am Sherlock Holmes. You may know the name."

"I know the name. You're one of those amateurs who choose to meddle in things you barely understand. You have an occasional success and become the darling of the popular press. I also know you're trying to exonerate William Wilson. I can tell you that's not going to happen. If you'll release me right now, I'll promise to forget this incident and tell no one about it."

Holmes grunted and maintained his grip. "You can tell whoever you like you were detained by Sherlock Holmes. You might start with Mr. Morgan. I have an appointment with him a little later this afternoon. Perhaps you'd like to accompany me."

There was a fluttering of the smaller man's eyelids. "What is it you plan to discuss with Mr. Morgan?"

"I might want to warn him to think twice about the people to whom he entrusts his safety."

"You can tell Mr. Morgan whatever you choose. He knows the Pinkerton Agency is responsible for capturing the man who threatened him, and that man is now in the Tombs where he belongs. I know all about Mr. Morgan agreeing to see you today—against our advice I don't mind telling you. And I would urge you to leave Mr. Morgan and his household alone in the future. If you don't, the consequences will be on your head."

Having decided that Mrs. Hudson and Watson were well away by now, Holmes released the Pinkerton man and offered his own warning. "I and my colleagues will speak to whomever we choose, and explore whatever areas we find promising. We seek nothing more—or less—than justice, and we will tolerate no interference with our efforts."

In spite of his request to the Pinkerton man, Holmes was well aware of the route to the Morgan home. He reprised on foot the carriage ride taken by Mrs. Hudson. Unlike Mrs. Hudson, he ignored the carriage path and strode directly to the front door of the Morgans' brownstone. The butler welcomed him with professional indifference, led him to Morgan's library, and left him there with the assurance Mr. Morgan would be with him directly. Holmes found himself surrounded by rows of books locked behind leaded glass doors. On one shelf a thick volume had been placed on a stand and opened to a page with the single word "GENESIS" scripted in English, all the rest written in a language unfamiliar to Holmes. Beneath the book a small card identified it as "John Eliot's Indian Bible written in the Algonquin dialect."

"That is the first Bible to be printed in America. It surprises everyone that the first Bible printed in this country was produced for the First People."

From the descriptions he'd read, Holmes was prepared to find Morgan a striking figure. Nonetheless, the reality exceeded his expectations. Greater than six foot and weighing more than 200 pounds, he seemed to tax the limits of the doorway through which he entered. Apart from mere size, however, there was the look of the man. Heavy-browed hazel eyes appeared to study his visitor as if searching for the flaw he would inevitably find. His mouth, tightly drawn beneath a thick walrus moustache, appeared ready to emit a disparaging snarl with the least provocation—or with no provocation at all. The sling supporting his left arm seemed hopelessly out of keeping with the rest of his dynamic figure. With all that, it was the nose that caught Holmes' attention; it was the nose that caught everyone's attention. It was bulbous and deeply purple in its widest part— and of no seeming consequence to Morgan. He swaggered across the room, every bit the master of his domain—and wholly convinced his domain knew no bounds. He was followed by a prematurely balding man of perhaps 35 wearing rimless glasses and an expression of concern bordering on dread, that he never relaxed over the course of their time together. He pressed a notebook tight to his side leading Holmes to wonder what vital information might be hidden on its well guarded pages.

"Welcome to my home, Mr. Holmes. This is Tarkenton, my private secretary. You spoke with him on the phone earlier." He didn't look back to where Tarkenton had stopped a respectful distance from his employer. "I would think a man with your interests might appreciate my copies of Collins' *The Moonstone* and *Woman in White*, both first editions of course."

"I'm afraid I've never developed a taste for mystery fiction. I find it to pale beside crime's reality. But please, allow me to thank you for having me to your home."

Morgan grunted acknowledgment of either Holmes' gratitude for being seen, or his rejection of the Wilkie Collins' collection, and with a broad sweep of his free hand directed his guest to one of the room's well stuffed leather chairs. Tarkenton chose a seat some distance away, loath to intrude on the conversation he nonetheless diligently recorded in his notebook. Morgan settled himself in a chair angled to that of his guest, and after calling for brandy for the two of them, spoke to his own interest in Holmes' visit.

"Do you have the signatures I asked you to bring?"

"I do," said Holmes, withdrawing an envelope from inside his coat. He held it a moment before sharing it with Morgan. "Both Dr. Watson and I wondered why you wanted them." It was a small lie. He had wondered why Morgan wanted Watson's signature; Watson had been unconcerned about Morgan's interest in either signature.

"As you can tell from the shelves around you, Mr. Holmes, I am an avid collector, but not just books. I also collect art, gemstones and the signatures of the famous and the famously obscure. Dr. Watson is one of the latter. While he labors in your shadow, he is important enough to allow me to speculate on his signature. It has limited value now, but that value will increase, perhaps markedly, as your own reputation grows and the scarcity of your colleague's handwriting becomes evident. Many may have the signature of the legendary Sherlock Holmes, few will be able to display signatures of the team of Holmes and Dr. Watson. I urge you to do all you can do to increase the value of my collection. For now, I appreciate your providing me with these. Please thank Dr. Watson for me."

"Ahh, the brandy." Morgan directed his attention to the glasses his butler had poured before backing his way from the room. "I trust you will join me in a glass celebrating your fame and my acquisition." Holmes raised his glass in response.

"Your health, sir."

"And yours, Mr. Holmes." Morgan took a generous swallow; then looked to his glass as though reluctant to part with a dear friend, before setting it finally on the table between them.

The toast reminded Holmes of Morgan's injury. "May I ask how your recovery is progressing?"

"Quite satisfactorily, thank you. The shot missed everything—at least everything in terms of all vital parts. If it wasn't for this confounded sling my physician insists on, I'd have no problems at all. But I must be thankful for so little difficulty in light of poor Wagner. He and I were the same age, Mr. Holmes. We'd seen a lot of the same world." Morgan again raised his glass, this time creasing his face into an expression of pain before downing what remained of the brandy in his glass. Holmes modeled his host's action. While Morgan refilled both their glasses, Holmes began the preamble necessary to his questioning.

"As you may know, Mr. Morgan, I am in New York for a wedding involving a young woman formerly of your household, a Miss Caroline Littleberry, …"

A dismissive wave was followed by Morgan's dismissive speech. "Yes, yes, I'm aware of all that. And I'm aware you're hoping to find some basis for getting this Wilson fellow off. Understand me, Mr. Holmes, that's not going to happen. The man shot me. I intend to see him pay for it."

As Mrs. Hudson could have told Morgan, it was a mistake to challenge Holmes. He did not run from a fight, he embraced it. Now, he found himself seized with a sudden agnosticism about Wilson's guilt, a topic on which he had been a true believer moments before.

"I am here, sir, solely to learn the truth of what happened that awful morning." Holmes tilted his head to look down his aquiline nose to Morgan. "I had been led to believe you were a man unafraid to face all possibilities."

Morgan glared at Holmes and leaned his great bulk toward him, grasping the chair's armrest as he did so. For a moment, Holmes thought the interview was over before it had begun, and he wondered how he would explain it to Mrs. Hudson and Watson. But the moment passed. Morgan relaxed his grip and leaned part way back in his chair, keeping his glower intact even as his body relaxed.

"I'm a busy man with no time to entertain impossibilities. You are, however, a guest in my home, and I will humor your concerns in the hope you will come quickly to see the foolishness of this activity. I warn you, however, my time is limited. Now, tell me what it is you are intent on learning."

"First, I should like to know what you saw the morning of the attack."

"I've already told all that to the police."

Holmes' eyes widened and he remained determinedly silent.

"Alright, if you must hear it from me, I saw very little. Wagner got out of the coach first and when he was hit I started for him, but then I felt this pain in my shoulder and fell back against the door frame. I looked out and I saw Wilson. He had a gun and it was pointed straight at me—which is what I fully intend to say in court when the time comes." He spat the last at Holmes. "After that, I was sort of in and out of consciousness. I was told Wilson ran off, but I didn't see that."

"Did you recognize anyone else in the crowd before you lost consciousness?"

"There were a number of people there, Mr. Holmes, more than I expected, but I wasn't interested in who they were. I just saw people, some together and most by themselves. I will say I was surprised to see a footman I had discharged in the crowd. And before the coach stopped I caught sight of some of my guests who had come outside to greet me, but I only saw one man with a gun pointed at me."

"Might there have been other people you can imagine wanting to harm you? You're a powerful man, Mr. Morgan. Powerful men can make strong and long-lasting enemies. There may be men you've bested in business dealings, men who are jealous of your success, men who resent your wealth, your influence, your control of their lives. Might that describe any of the men present that morning?"

Morgan's response boomed across the short space between the two men. "That would describe nearly all the men present that morning. What of it? It's business. I've bested some and some have bested me—although not more than once and never for long. We take our revenge in boardrooms and on the floor of the Exchange. It's only the radicals who resort to guns to take their revenge, Mr. Holmes." Morgan poured drinks for Holmes and himself, but set his own glass down without drinking. "I'm satisfied we have the right man in jail. I'm sorry it inconveniences you; I'm sorry it causes suffering for your housekeeper, but there it is and everyone will just have to live with it."

"Perhaps Mr. Tarkenton saw something suspicious that morning."

"Tarkenton has reported what he saw to the police and, in any event, saw nothing more than I did."

The subject of the two men's dispute never raised his head from the notebook over which he labored. Holmes decided to take a different tack.

"Would Archibald McLeod have access to boardrooms or the floor of the Exchange to seek his revenge, or would he just have to live with it?"

An impish smile crossed Morgan's face, then disappeared as quickly as it had formed. "Neatly done, Mr. Holmes. Your reputation is well earned. I don't know how you ferreted out information about McLeod, but you're quite right.

He no longer has access to the seats of power he once had—and rightly so given his business practices. And you probably know McLeod tried to contact me within the last few days. I gave instructions I had no wish to see him. Indeed, I've never met the man. My review of his administrative performance convinced me of the need to discharge him from his position in Philadelphia. I admit I have no idea why he wanted to see me, but as for trying to kill me," Morgan snarled, "perhaps if he had shown that sort of initiative with the Philadelphia and Reading, I wouldn't have had to replace him."

Holmes ignored Morgan's view of commendable business initiative to explore another area. Given your ability to see only a portion of the crowd, I wonder, Mr. Morgan, if you'd have objection to my speaking with your coachman. He would have had a good view of the crowd, and greater opportunity to spot anything that looked suspicious."

"He, too, has given a statement to the police, Mr. Holmes, and I'll thank you not to disturb my staff further. I've directed them to have nothing to do with you or your meddling woman on pain of losing their positions. You've already interrogated my housekeeper—for which she has been reprimanded. To answer your question, my staff saw the same things I did: Wilson with a gun; Wilson running off. They came to the same conclusion I did—the same conclusion the police came to, and the same conclusion any rational person would come to. You do know two bullets were missing from his gun, exactly the number of shots fired. I really don't know how much more proof you need."

Holmes sipped from his second glass of brandy; Morgan's glass was still untouched.

"Mr. Morgan, might I ask why you have enlisted the protection of the Pinkerton Detective Agency if you are certain the man who shot you is safely locked away?"

"That should be obvious to a man of your experience. We live in difficult times. This country has been experiencing a great economic upheaval for the past year. So indeed has yours. But in this country we have a radical element intent on stirring things up for their political advantage."

Holmes had little knowledge and even less interest in either politics or economics, but judged that on this occasion it would be well to explore Morgan's obviously strong feelings. "What is it you mean by a radical element, Mr. Morgan?"

"Socialists. Anarchists. The people who mean to use workers' demands to tear down this country. Mind you, I'm not talking about the legitimate demands of workers. There's something to be said for getting youngsters out of the mines and factories, and into school. And there's room to talk about wages and hours. I'm not a Gould or Carnegie; I have no fight with unions as such. Frankly, I believe increased unionization to be inevitable, and I have never found it profitable to stand in the way of the inevitable." Morgan grunted approval of his own broad-mindedness. "But there's unions and unions. You can talk to Gompers, but you take this fellow Debs and his American Railway Union—you can't talk to him; he'll stop the trains to get his way." As if alarmed by his own prediction, Morgan reached for his glass of brandy and downed it in one swallow.

Holmes was about to ask what any of that had to do with Wilson when Morgan answered the nascent question. "You can tell from his nickname Wilson used to be a railroad worker. And I know, because I make it my business to know, that he was active in organizing the Railway Union—very active." Morgan again leaned his body close to Holmes, this time lowering his voice as he did so. "There's no shortage of stories about people being coerced to join his union. I'm not saying I believe them all, but I am saying where there's that much smoke there's bound to be some fire."

Morgan stared at the brandy bottle a moment, stared at his empty glass, and proceeded to remedy the situation. "I don't talk about it, Mr. Holmes, it's nobody's business, but I don't want you to get the wrong idea. There's things I do—a number of things frankly—for the good of the community. Some would call it charity, I don't. It's my opinion that those of us blessed with wealth have a responsibility to our communities. To me that means supporting the cultural and spiritual life of the city. But not just that. In a year, or two at most, there'll be a lying-in hospital for women built on land that was quietly purchased earlier this year. You won't hear anything about it, not about that or any of the institutions I support, certainly not from Wilson's socialist friends, but I guarantee they'll make use of all of them—except maybe the churches."

Morgan shifted position in his chair and waved off any further consideration of his beneficence. "Anyway, my company brought in the Pinkertons because there's reason to believe the radicals have targeted me, and that Wilson's shooting is not an isolated incident. I take it you've seen the pamphlets they're circulating accusing me of being an enemy of the people, and encouraging people to take retribution. They've even stooped to raking up the ancient slander that I profited from selling defective rifles to the government. They don't tell you that the sale occurred while I was out of the country—on my honeymoon in fact—and was carried out by an unsavory character I was happy to get away from. And, of course, they don't mention that I was completely exonerated of any wrongdoing by a committee of the United States Senate."

Holmes resisted the temptation to ask Morgan if he ever returned the profits from the sale to the government, and raised a second charge instead. "The pamphlet also states that you bought your way out of your country's Civil War."

The response came in the now familiar bombastic tones. "Me and many hundreds, probably thousands of others. There was nothing unusual about it. There was work to be done at home to support the war effort. Frankly, Mr. Holmes, I find the implication of that comment insulting, and your understanding of events in this country sadly wanting."

Having ventured far afield of the questions worked out with Mrs. Hudson and Watson, Holmes thought it wise to direct the conversation back to the attempt on Morgan's life."You say there's no one with whom you've done business who would make an attempt on your life. What of your personal life? Is there anyone who might feel so angry or so hurt that they would seek to harm you?"

Morgan growled his rejection of any such possibility. "That's preposterous, Mr. Holmes. The people I know don't settle disputes with sneak attacks on each other. I've already told you it's a political act; it's got nothing to do with business and it's certainly not personal." Morgan fixed Holmes with a stare designed to intimidate the man and end his line of questioning. Morgan did not know his man.

"I have only just begun my investigation, Mr. Morgan, and have already learned of two men who might have strong personal feelings about you. You removed Franklin Langer from your household staff on suspicion of theft, and you encouraged your daughter, Juliet, to reject Clarence McIlvaine, her former suitor. There seems no question these are men you have seriously offended who could have reason to seek revenge. Moreover, they were in the crowd waiting for you. The question is how many others have you offended just as seriously, Mr. Morgan?"

The stare that unfailingly discouraged others having failed with Holmes, Morgan shook his head in mock wonder at the detective's ignorance of the workings of his world. My God, Holmes, at one time or another I've fired I don't know how many people from my household staff and from my company. If all the people I've fired were assassins, I'd have been dead long ago. As for McIlvaine, that milksop probably doesn't know one end of a gun from the other. Wilson is our man. You are aware this isn't the first time he has made an attempt on my life. He took a shot at me outside my club just a few weeks ago."

"Did you see Wilson fire at you?"

"If you mean did I see him aim a revolver at me and pull the trigger, the answer is no. But I'm certain it was Wilson."

"Regardless of whether he was seen?"

Morgan glared at Holmes as though he found him a half-wit and thought the world would be much improved if it possessed one less half-wit. His tone reflected the exasperation he found no reason to hide. "Wilson would know from the young woman formerly on my staff that I arrive at my Club at eleven in the morning every Saturday. He would have no difficulty tracking my movements to get to me. See here, Mr. Holmes, there are issues involved in all of this that you're not considering, issues of which you're likely unaware." Morgan's tone had shifted from annoyed and dismissive to near reasonableness.

"If word gets out that Sherlock Holmes believes the police have the wrong man, and that my assailant is still at large and means to assassinate me, it could have a disastrous effect on the markets. It is not too much to say your efforts—apart from being fruitless—could prove ruinous to this country's recovery, perhaps even its governance. I'm directing you to give this up, Mr. Holmes, in light of the problems you could trigger—problems far beyond your level of understanding."

"I have no wish to appear insensitive to your concern, Mr. Morgan, or to make light of the dangers you suggest. However, I'm afraid I'm only a struggling investigator with a somewhat pedestrian interest in making certain that the right man—or woman—is brought to justice. But I must make clear that my determination in that regard is unyielding."

Morgan rose from his chair without releasing Holmes from his glare. He was prepared to declare the interview at an end when a woman's voice interrupted the two men. "I'm sorry. I should have checked first. I wasn't aware anyone was in here."

The woman in the doorway was a tall, large-boned woman with deep-set sad eyes and thin lips that seemed continuously on the verge of quivering. After brief, but seemingly tortured consideration of her proper course, she apologized again and turned to go, only to be stopped by Morgan.

"Please don't leave, Mrs. Porter. There's someone here I'd like you to meet." He pointed to the chair he had given up, and both Morgan and Holmes stood while the woman took her seat. Morgan continued standing, addressing Holmes in spite of the promised introduction. "Mrs. Cornelia Porter is the daughter of Conrad Wagner, my employee who was killed taking the bullet intended for me. Mrs. Porter is staying with me while her father's body is readied for transport to Cleveland."

His face softened and his voice lowered as he turned back to make the promised introduction. "Mr. Sherlock Holmes is from London where he is a private detective. He is in New York to attend a wedding, and has decided to occupy himself with investigating the death of your father and the attempt on my life. He believes the police may have the wrong man in custody."

"Is that true, Mr. Holmes?" There was a small unsteadiness in her voice, and she straightened in her chair to bring herself under control. "Why would you think so?"

"I am first of all very sorry about your loss, Mrs. Porter. I have no wish to trouble you or cause any further disruption to your life. I am simply here to affirm that Mr. Wilson is the man responsible for taking your father's life and attacking Mr. Morgan. As I have been telling Mr. Morgan, there was a small crowd gathered that morning to greet him on his return home, and in that crowd were several people—we don't yet know how many—who appear to have reason to feel themselves badly used by Mr. Morgan. I want to rule out the possibility that one of them is responsible for your tragedy and Mr. Morgan's injury. In so doing, I promise I will try to add as little to your troubles as possible." Holmes reinforced his statement with what he hoped was a comforting smile.

"I know nothing of these things, Mr. Holmes. My husband and I run a school in Cleveland for orphaned and troubled children. The world Mr. Morgan inhabits and the world my father inhabited are foreign to me. I'm afraid my father and I had grown apart after my mother died. Don't misunderstand me, Mr. Holmes, there was no ill feeling. I was a young married woman and my father was very upset by mother's death. Of course we both were. I stayed in Cleveland; he didn't feel he could. He gave up his business transporting goods across Lake Erie and took a position with the railroad in Philadelphia. We exchanged occasional letters and there were always gifts at Christmas, but we saw each other very little over the years. Still, I'm his only child, and will make the necessary arrangements while Mr. Porter keeps the school running. Mr. Morgan has been kind enough to allow me to stay with him during this time, and has provided a great deal of assistance in organizing things for me, for all of which I'm deeply grateful."

Morgan waved off Cornelia Porter's gratitude. "Your father was with me for more than ten years—which is to say from right after we got the Philadelphia and Reading on its feet. He's been loyal and hard-working, a fine man and I'm happy to do what little I can."

Mrs. Porter smiled at the tribute to her father. She looked from Morgan to the hands in her lap and then to Holmes. "I know you must do what you feel wise, Mr. Holmes, and I appreciate learning of your involvement in this further investigation. I will be leaving in a very few days as I've imposed on Mr. and Mrs. Morgan's hospitality quite long enough. If you need me for anything, Mr. Morgan has my address. Now, if you'll excuse me, I'll leave the two of you to your business." She nodded a relieved smile to Holmes and Morgan, and held it until she was past Tarkenton.

When the door was closed behind Cornelia Porter, Morgan turned to Holmes, glower once again firmly in place.

"That may give you some idea of the difficulties you'll be creating if you continue your hopeless quest. Mrs. Porter has already endured more difficulty than anyone should have to. She is just now beginning to adjust to the tragedy you plan on stirring up again. I will keep her contact information for myself, and thank you not to ask for it. Now, as I told you earlier, I have business to conduct, so I'll declare our interview to be at an end." Morgan walked to a pull cord by the door. "I bid you good day. I see no reason for the two of us to meet again; I thank you for yours and Dr. Watson's autograph." He called to an approaching figure not yet visible to Holmes. "Sachs, please show this gentleman out."

5.
Two for Brooklyn

Mrs. Hudson and Watson joined the small group gathered at the car stop on Sixth Avenue. When the cable car came into view they waited for a queue that never formed. Instead, riders jostled each other in the rush to mount the steps at the back of the car. Mrs. Hudson and Watson shared looks of disgust, and stood aside as travelers clambered on board. As it happened the car was barely half full, and although last into it, they easily found seats together. As instructed by Waldorf staff, they went from the cable car to the ferry across the East River and finally to the Brooklyn cable car, each time electing to step aside while their fellow passengers pushed their way into the waiting conveyance. Once on board, the two of them took turns alerting each other to views along the way, causing those nearby to search in vain for attractions along a route that had long since lost what little novelty it may have once held for them. At Snediker and Pitkin Avenue, Mrs. Hudson left Watson to seek out her cousin's daughter, while the Doctor stayed on board to keep his appointment with Charles Ebbets.

The address she'd been given by Mrs. Sowder turned out to be a three story red brick building that looked to hold six flats—which Mrs. Hudson understood to be called apartments. On either side of the three white steps leading to the entrance, there were two windows, each with cornices made from the same white stone as used for the steps. The pattern of corniced windows on either side of the building's center carried through all three stories. The door bell was answered by a woman whose clothes hung as loosely from her gaunt body as her skin seemed tightly drawn over the bones of her face. Mrs. Hudson judged her to be about her own age, although she gave the appearance of being much older. Hairs of multiple colors clung to the dark wrapper the woman wore indicating the woman lived with multiple cats. The absence of a wedding ring and inattention to her appearance made clear they were her only companions. Her appearance in a wrapper in mid-afternoon and her ashen coloring indicated she was accustomed to being indoors through much if not all the day. Mrs. Hudson observed that her eyes were narrowed although the day was overcast, and she scratched at what appeared a persistent itch on the back of one hand. She noted as well that the woman concentrated her weight on her left leg, while her right leg seemed unnaturally stiff and straight. Chronic use of laudanum explained the squint and frequent scratching, and the injury to her leg explained the laudanum. Recognition of drug use was all too much a part of Mrs. Hudson's experience.

The woman's voice was as unwelcoming as the wary look she gave her visitor. "Is there something I can do for you?"

"I'm lookin' for a Miss Littleberry. I believe she's stayin' with another woman. I'm afraid I don't know that woman's name."

"Are you a relative?"

Mrs. Hudson didn't see that as any of her business, but decided there was nothing to be gained from being disagreeable, especially as she had not yet been allowed to cross the building's threshold. "Indeed I am. 'Er mother is my cousin on my own mother's side, and I'm 'ere because that lady asked me to come."

"And your name is?"

"Mrs. 'Udson, and Miss Littleberry will know about my visit although she won't be expecting me today."

She sniffed her suspicion of Mrs. Hudson's claim, directed her to stay where she was, then shut the door on her. Mrs. Hudson looked to the closed door and wondered whether the landlady was protecting Caroline or simply exercising what limited authority her position permitted.

When the landlady returned a few minutes later, she opened the front door wide, and her expression eased very nearly to a smile, providing Mrs. Hudson the answer to her question. "I do apologize, Mrs. Hudson, but we can't be too careful. The other day we had someone come by pretending to be Miss Littleberry's brother—except she ain't got no brother. You'll find Miss Littleberry on the second floor, the apartment on the left. My apartment is there," she pointed to a room beyond the stairs. "I'm Mrs. Guskin. Knock on my door if you need anything."

Midway up the steps Mrs. Hudson became aware of a fiercely squinting face half hidden behind the barely open door of the flat to which she had been directed. At the top of the landing the door was thrown open and the flat's sentinel transformed herself to a smiling, petite young woman who welcomed Mrs. Hudson with a warm embrace. When they separated, Mrs. Hudson tried with only partial success to hide her concern.

Caroline had been the pretty one in a family whose women were most often described as agreeable looking. The high forehead, large dark eyes, and just slightly weak chin gave her face an innocence and vulnerability that led both women and men to look on her warmly. Now, her face was drawn and there were dark circles beneath her eyes making her look a washed-out 21 years. Those changes would be temporary. Others would not be, and set the woman she now saw apart from the girl who had visited her before leaving for America. She had aged beyond the mere accumulation of years. Her mouth was set in a tight line, her chin seemed to have become firmer, and even with the circles beneath them, her eyes blazed with fires that would not be easily extinguished.

"It's wonderful to see you, Auntie. I'm so happy you're here and so sorry everything seems to have gone wrong." Caroline Littleberry guided her into the apartment where a second woman was holding fast to a frozen smile, waiting for her opportunity to join the two women.

"Auntie, this is my very special friend, Lucy Donaldson, who was kind enough to take me in when I had no place to go. Lucy, this is Mrs. Hudson, my favorite aunt in the whole world."

90

The woman who was Caroline's very special friend was attractive in the fresh-faced way 18 year-old girls are attractive. She wore the white blouse and dark skirt that was the frequent uniform of working women. Mrs. Hudson judged her to be a salesclerk likely employed in one of the shops her cable car passed along Pitkin Avenue. The girl was too young to have been educated as a teacher or bookkeeper, and was home too early to have traveled far. The room's furnishings were more functional than fashionable, reflecting the modest earnings of their owner. A white pine couch and two matching easy chairs provided seating in an area half the size of Mrs. Hudson's parlor. A round table to one side of the couch held a photograph showing a family smiling uncomfortably as they stood before a modest farmhouse. Dressed in their Sunday best, the family revealed the humble origins of Caroline's roommate.

"Auntie, please sit. I know you've a million questions, but first tell me, how did you leave my parents? I know dad hasn't been well and mum says very little about it."

Caroline drew Mrs. Hudson to the couch and sat beside her after first moving the jacket, hat and veil she had not yet put away from her visit to see Wilson. Mrs. Hudson took particular note of the heavy veil, behind which Caroline doubtless felt a need to hide from reporters and a curious public. Lucy had remained standing and now excused herself to put up the tea Caroline told her Mrs. Hudson might like. Mrs. Hudson waited for the door to close before speaking. She told Caroline her mother was fine, her father was unchanged according to the last she had heard, and then she moved the conversation to her own concerns.

"Caroline, I want to talk about the troubles you and your Mr. Wilson are 'avin'. You know I'm 'ere with Mr. 'Olmes and Dr. Watson. Mr. 'Olmes promises 'e'll do all 'e can for your Mr. Wilson, but 'e must know the truth of what 'appened that terrible mornin'. I need you to tell me everythin' you can remember for me to tell Mr. 'Olmes."

91

Caroline grimaced her understanding, then did what she could to comply with Mrs. Hudson's request. At first, her story was no different from Mrs. Sowder's report of events. Caroline and Wilson sought a private moment in the back of the Morgan home only to be overtaken by a crowd of the curious waiting to see Mr. Morgan and his guests. They found themselves pressed to the street side and nearly back to the tree line. When the coach arrived, James, the first footman, went to open its door for Mr. Morgan and Mr. Wagner to climb down. Mr. Wagner started out first. She knew Mr. Wagner from having seen him at the house many times. He had just taken a packet from Mr. Morgan when the first shot sounded. She saw him fall back against Mr. Morgan; then there was a second shot and Mr. Morgan fell back in the coach. After that, everybody started yelling and pushing to get away. Somebody yelled "he's got a gun," and everything seemed to stop just long enough for people to look to William who was holding a revolver. Caroline was certain he hadn't fired it. But then he ran. She was sure it was because he panicked, but she knew his running away made him look guilty.

She paused a moment, furrows lined her forehead as she appeared to consider what else she might reveal. Finally, looking from Mrs. Hudson to the empty wall behind her, she acknowledged the possibility of something more that explained Wilson's behavior. Mrs. Hudson was poised to learn what that was when Lucy returned from the apartment house's communal kitchen with the tea she had promised. Not knowing what Caroline had shared and not shared with her roommate, Mrs. Hudson decided to pursue a safer line of inquiry.

"I was wonderin', Caroline, 'ow you and your Mr. Wilson met?"

Caroline smiled at the memory. "I'm afraid it won't sound very romantic, and you may disapprove, Auntie. We met in Union Square on my day out." She looked to Mrs. Hudson's blank expression. "It's a place in New York that's like Hyde

Park. Anyone can get up and make a speech about anything they want. When I got there, William was making a speech about unions and railroads, but there was hardly anybody listening. It was morning, and there's mostly baby carriages and nursemaids at that hour. Of course, I didn't know it then, but that was almost the only time William could be there because of his playing baseball in the afternoon. I stood and listened, and I thought he was wonderful. Afterward, we talked some more about unions and the railroads, and then we took a lovely walk and talked about ourselves, and it was after that we started seeing each other."

When Caroline finished, both she and Mrs. Hudson were smiling, each stirred by her own memories.

"Why would you think I wouldn't approve?" Mrs. Hudson asked.

"I thought you might think it's not very ladylike to have political interests. I'm sure mum would feel that way."

Mrs. Hudson took a sip of a drink that could in no way be mistaken for tea. "I've no intention of discussin' your private business with your mother. You're a modern woman and entitled to your own ideas. I've no interest in your politics except as they may be important to Mr. Morgan bein' shot. You know there's talk about your Mr. Wilson havin' radical ideas that could explain the shootin'."

Lucy Donaldson, who had been turning from Mrs. Hudson to Caroline as if following a tennis match, felt obliged to make some contribution to the conversation. "It's something I don't understand at all, Mrs. Hudson, I can't see why Caroline wants to be involved with all that mumbo jumbo."

Caroline smiled tolerance of her friend's disapproval. "William's ideas have to do with the changes that are coming, Auntie. Changes that will have working people standing together to demand higher pay and better working conditions. It will take time, but it's coming."

Mrs. Hudson stared blankly at her cousin's child. The ideas were not new to her. The same things were being talked about in England. Her blank stare was a reaction to hearing the ideas from the mouth of the little girl she and Tobias had taken to the amusements in Brighton, the little girl who rode four times on the merry-go-round, and cried when she was finally taken off.

"That's the mumbo jumbo I mean. You can hear it from her and her William both. And her with a good position—or she did have—and him a pitcher with a fine future according to my Candy. Candy's my beau, Mrs. Hudson. Him and William are both on the Bridegrooms. Anyway, that kind of talk used to drive Candy near crazy before he moved into a place of his own. Not that the two of them aren't still great friends and all. In fact, it's because of them being such good friends that Caroline is staying with me, and I'm very glad for that." The smile she gave Caroline was warm and genuine, and it occurred to Mrs. Hudson that the young woman was beyond artifice of her own, and likely an easy target for the artifice of others.

Caroline thought an explanation was needed for names that must sound strange to Mrs. Hudson. "Candy is a nickname, Auntie, like they call William, Brakeman, because of his work on the railroad. Candy's real name is Arthur, Arthur Cochrane, but he's known to everyone as Candy Cochrane. He and William knew each other in Ohio where they first played baseball together, and Arthur—or Candy—sort of helped him get settled when William came to pitch for Brooklyn. It seems as though every ballplayer gets some sort of a nickname."

Lucy nodded vigorous agreement. "That's true, Mrs. Hudson. Even his family calls him Candy. He took me once to see his home in Ohio. We took the train. It was so exciting; I'd never been on a train before. We stopped in Cleveland, and then went on to the station in Bedford where his brothers came to get us and took us to their farm. And everyone, even his mother, called him Candy the whole time we were there. In fact, almost all they talked about was Candy and how well he was doing, and what a great ballplayer he'd always been. And all Candy talked about was the farm. Of course, Caroline's heard almost as much about the farm as I have. The farm and baseball are Candy's two favorite subjects."

Caroline's tolerant smile returned, but seemed a little thinner as her friend continued. "It's a pretty big place, a hundred and sixty acres they said, but you'd think it was a million acres to hear Candy talk about it. And it's got this lovely little stream at its back. They say it's for irrigation—whatever that is. I just thought it looked so nice. Anyway, when Candy talks about it, you can tell it's more than just a farm to him and it's the same for all the family. They even give it a name. They call it Ian's Sod which is for his father, who was mostly a bargeman on Lake Erie, and bought the land and the house and all just before he went off to the War. Which makes it just about the saddest thing you ever heard. After he done all that, Mr. Cochrane never saw the farm again; he died at someplace called Chancellorsville. He never even saw Candy who was born after he left. Of course, he was Arthur then. I think him not knowing his father is a big part of why Candy got close to Brakeman. You know Brakeman never knew his father either. Of course, Brakeman never knew his mother or his father, which is even worse."

Lucy stopped, either having nothing more to say, or having an urgent need to replenish her supply of oxygen. Mrs. Hudson did not wait to learn which. "Thank you, Miss Donaldson. That is very helpful." She forced down the last of her cup. "I do 'ate to impose, but would it be possible to get another cup of tea? I'm that dry from all the excitement."

"Certainly, Mrs. Hudson, I'd be glad to." After Lucy was once again on her way to the kitchen, Mrs. Hudson turned to Caroline to follow up on their earlier conversation.

"You were sayin' before that you thought there might have been somethin' else the day of the shootin' that made Mr.

Wilson run off. Could that 'ave somethin' to do with the footman, Franklin, bein' in the crowd?"

"Yes, but how ....?"

"Never mind, I know about this Franklin and 'is gamblin' ways and about 'ow the people 'e works for sometimes like to get the odds in their favor."

"That's exactly right, Auntie, but how could you know?"

Mrs. Hudson saw the question as an opportunity to instill confidence in the person she wanted Caroline to believe capable of exonerating her fiancé, and thereby deserving of her full disclosure. "Oh, you'd be surprised what you can learn from bein' around Mr. 'Olmes."

"It does have to do with Franklin, Auntie, but it's something not even Mr. Holmes could know. I looked around to see where the shot came from and I saw Franklin turn to look back to us, and there was a gun in Franklin's hand. You couldn't hardly see it. His coat covered almost all of it, but he was right in front of us and I could see it plain and I know William saw it too. There's something more, Auntie. I think Franklin purposely came over to stand near us, and he had some very rough looking people with him that I never saw before. I couldn't say anything about it to the police because Franklin is tied to gamblers like you say, Mrs. Hudson, and William is not supposed to have anything to do with those people. I'm only telling you now because Mr. Holmes already knows about the gamblers."

Mrs. Hudson nodded a solemn appreciation for Caroline's revelation. She maintained her solemn expression to raise question in an area she knew would be difficult."I'm wonderin' about somethin' else, Caroline. I was a lady's maid once. It was just for a week, but I know a lady's maid 'ears things. I'd be curious to know what you might 'ave 'eard that could be important to Mr. Wilson's case. Like whether there were things Mr. Morgan was doin' that could cause 'im to 'ave enemies." Mrs. Hudson paused, hoping silence might force a confidence.

The silence was long, but the outcome was as Mrs. Hudson wished. Allegiance to her fiancé triumphed over allegiance to her former employer. Caroline took a deep breath before sharing the conversations a lady's maid was expected to hold secret.

"There's things Mrs. Morgan told me about Mr. Morgan that I'm sure the master wouldn't want anybody to know." Caroline's voice grew soft as if she feared Morgan's spies might be lurking in the adjoining room or the wardrobe of this one. "Mr. Morgan had quite a lot of lady friends."

Mrs. Hudson gave Caroline a knowing look as if the information came as no surprise to her. She knew the more unimpressed she appeared, the more information Caroline would be willing to share about her employer's indiscretions. "What did Mrs. Morgan say about that?"

"Not a word. She treated his lady friends as though they were just that, and nothing more. But none of the staff saw it that way. Not with the flowers and jewels, and one time even a case of whiskey being sent to one of his lady friends. Of course, none of us would dare say anything about it in front of Mrs. Sowder or Mr. Sachs, but Mr. Ferguson, the coachman, delivered the whiskey, and Mr. Ferguson drove Mr. Morgan to his appointments, and Mr. Ferguson is a talker."

"And Mrs. Morgan did nothin' at all about it?"

"Oh, she never would. You don't understand society, Auntie. She welcomed Mrs. Randolph to her house—Mrs. Edith Randolph was the name of the lady the master was seeing—and she worked with her on church committees. But she knew, and Miss Louisa and Miss Juliet—they're the Morgan daughters—they knew."

"And did Mr. Randolph know?"

"Mr. Randolph died years ago." Caroline looked to Mrs. Hudson with a coy smile. "I know what you're thinking, Auntie, and Mrs. Randolph does have a brother, Fred May, but you have to remember these are the nineties and this is New York. A widow seeing a married man isn't cause for a shooting as long as the two of them don't make a show of it. Besides which, I know that Mr. May wasn't invited to the breakfast. The truth of it is, I'm not even certain Mr. Morgan is still seeing Mrs. Randolph. Mr. Ferguson says he hasn't driven Mr. Morgan to her house for several weeks, and now he's seeing Mrs. Adelaide Douglas who just happens to be a very good friend of Mrs. Randolph."

Caroline adopted her best woman of the world look. "You shouldn't be too shocked by it all, Auntie. There's different rules for people like Mr. Morgan. Anyway that's what William says, and as best as I can see he's right. And before you ask, Mrs. Douglas *does* have a husband, and the Douglases *were* at the breakfast, but Mr. Douglas had an accident playing polo which did something to his brain, and he hasn't been right since. Anyway, that's what Mr. Sachs told us. I mean about Mr. Douglas not being right in the head."

Caroline pursed her lips and her voice sounded gently dismissive. "I appreciate what you're trying to do, Auntie, but I don't think any of this can help William. There's too much against him and too many people—important people. Maybe there's need to find some other way to help."

Mrs. Hudson wondered at Caroline's "other way," but thought it was likely the expression of her understandable frustration, and pressed for the additional information she felt it critical to obtain before Lucy returned with another cup of her insipid tea. "Mr. 'Olmes will want to know about William's gun? Did you ever see it before that morning?"

"I think so. I knew he had a gun. He didn't make a secret of it. The truth is he was hoping he'd never have to use it, and it just being known he had one might be all the protection he'd need."

"When did 'e get the gun?"

"I don't know when exactly, Auntie. I know he's had it ever since we started seeing each other and that's nearly a year."

"What kind of a gun is it?"

98

"It's just an ordinary Colt revolver. They're very popular in America because they're so easy to operate. Lots of people carry them. Candy calls Colt revolvers practically standard issue to all the players."

Mrs. Hudson nodded grimly at Caroline's easy tolerance for an abundance of firearms, and wondered what other foreign ideas she had picked up since coming to America.

"'Ow did it 'appen that there were two empty chambers in the gun, Caroline?"

Caroline shrugged her response. "I don't know, Auntie. Probably William only put four cartridges in the gun. Auntie, it's sounding almost as if you're on their side." She tried to smile at the foolishness of an idea she did not find at all foolish.

"I'm very much on your side, Caroline, but these are questions Mr. 'Olmes will want to 'ave answered if 'e's to get to the bottom of all that 'appened that morning."

Lucy had returned and stood just inside the room's threshold holding a cup rigidly at waist level as though it contained nitroglycerine rather than heavily diluted tea. She looked to each of the women, sensing the tension even before she heard their words, and hesitant to advance further into her own apartment lest she be seen as interfering. Mrs. Hudson smiled her awareness of Lucy's presence, and the young woman took that as sufficient encouragement to come forward. "I'm sorry, Mrs. Hudson, there was quite a crowd in the kitchen and it took a while for me to get a turn."

Mrs. Hudson expressed regret at having put the young woman to so much trouble. Lucy's return made it necessary for Mrs. Hudson's questioning to again become more circumspect and less revealing.

"I wonder if you've thought what you'll be doin' now that you're no longer with the Morgans?"

"I've told Caroline she doesn't have to do anything until she's absolutely ready." Lucy's comment was directed to Mrs.

Hudson, but she looked to Caroline as she spoke, and punctuated her offer with another broad smile.

Caroline shared a muted smile of her own as she responded to Mrs. Hudson's question. "I'll wait to see what happens with William and make my plans after that."

Mrs. Hudson softly grunted acknowledgement of Caroline's words and wondered at their meaning. Her cousin's daughter was not one to go through life without plans; she never had been. It awakened in Mrs. Hudson Caroline's earlier comment about the need to find some other way to free her fiancé, and she wondered what Caroline was not sharing.

Having learned all she could without learning all she wished, Mrs. Hudson decided to return to the hotel to hear what her colleagues had discovered.

"We'll leave it there then. For now, I'd best be gettin' back. I'll share all you've told me with Mr. 'Olmes. I'm at the Waldorf 'Otel, and want you to get to me if there's anythin' more you think of, or if there's ever anythin' I can do. I'll be back to see you with good news I 'ope, but I'll tell you whatever is found out."

Mrs. Hudson pushed hard on the arms of her chair to bring herself to a standing position. It had already been a long day and it wasn't over yet. Caroline came to embrace her, and seemed to linger a few moments longer than was needed for her good-bye. Mrs. Hudson repeated her offer of help, thanked Lucy Donaldson for her hospitality, and went in search of a cable car that would take her the first leg of her journey back to the Waldorf. She took no notice of the scenery this trip, she was too busy sorting through all she had learned and all she had yet to learn.

Watson knew only that his destination was the last cable stop and so waited for the conductor to direct him to disembark. The command came when he was the car's only remaining passenger, and left no doubt he had reached his objective.

"Eastern Park. Everybody out. Last stop."

Instead of a park, Watson found himself on the edge of an overgrown field that served as the terminus and starting point for several lines of the Brooklyn Railroad Company. Four cable cars waited their return to service, and he found himself dodging the movement of a fifth as he started in the direction of two sets of bleachers angling away from the tower that loomed above them. The tower, with a pennant flying from the cone at its top, appeared better suited to housing a lady in distress than the offices of the Brooklyn Bridegrooms baseball team, but Watson guessed that was its purpose. A large open space lay between the diverging bleachers, and Watson took that as his immediate destination. He set out along a narrow path of trampled grass that looked to be a well traveled route to Eastern Park.

As he neared the Park about a dozen men ran onto the open space, all of them dressed alike in short-sleeved white shirts, knickerbocker pants with knee-length socks, and shoes that came to their ankles. Each man wore a single glove a good bit larger than the dress glove a gentleman might wear, and had on small workman caps with short visors. All of them had their backs to Watson and were focused on a man some distance away who held a thick, slightly tapered stick, and was hitting a white ball the size of a tennis ball to each of them in turn. As he came onto the field, the player nearest Watson turned to him, and Watson saw the word "BROOKLYN" printed in an arc across his chest. The man was frantically trying to wave him off the grassy area without letting his eyes stray for long from the man with the stick.

"Can you tell me where I might find Mr. Ebbets?" Watson called to him.

The player pointed to the tower directly ahead, hollered "Second floor," and then instructed Watson to leave the field using words Watson found unnecessarily and inaccurately critical of his lineage. Watson did not see how it was possible to reach the tower while staying off the field, but received shouted instruction for doing so. "Get on the other side of the foul line." This time the man pointed to a white line well to Watson's left. Watson expressed greater appreciation than he felt for the guidance received, and followed the other side of the white line past the man with the stick until he arrived finally at the tower.

On its second floor, he stopped at a door open to a cramped office, where a jowly figure in a tie and stiff-collared white shirt was seated behind a small desk, staring critically at a set of papers. Seeing his visitor, the man put aside his papers and rose in greeting. On standing, his critical expression softened to a salesman's smile, and his prominent jowls were seen to be matched by an equally prominent paunch giving the man a rounded shape that contrasted markedly with the trim athletes on the field below.

"You must be Dr. Watson. Come in, sir. I'm pleased to make your acquaintance. I'm Charles Ebbets." He leaned across the desk and affirmed his welcome with a vigorous handshake, then pointed to the single chair available for his visitors. On the wall behind Ebbets there were 11 pictures from 11 different years, all showing 15-20 men wearing the same uniform as the men on the playing field and all posed in exactly the same way. There were three rows of men, one seated on the ground, one seated on chairs behind them, and the third standing behind the other two. A handful of the athletes were smiling, most looked to the camera as though it might be a lethal instrument.

"Please have a seat and tell me what I can do for you."

"Thank you for making time for me, Mr. Ebbets. I can see you're busy, and I'll try to be as brief as I can. My colleague, Sherlock Holmes, and I have taken an interest in the criminal case involving Mr. William Wilson, and I am here to learn what you can tell me about the young man."

Charles Ebbets took a deep breath and leaned far back in his swivel chair before responding. "And what exactly is your interest in Brakeman Wilson, Doctor?"

Watson described his housekeeper's relation to Wilson's fiancé much as Holmes had done a short time earlier with JP Morgan. Ebbets grunted acceptance of Watson's explanation, but didn't relax the wary expression that had replaced the welcoming smile. "Do you believe Brakeman innocent of the charges?"

"I would have to say we're undecided at this stage. We've only been looking into Mr. Wilson's case for the past two days, and are still in the process of gathering information. Since you employ the man, we were hoping you might give us your thinking about him." Watson withdrew his accounts book and a pencil to record Ebbets' responses.

At the sight of the accounts book, Ebbets raised an eyebrow that for the next few moments appeared to have found a permanent place in his forehead. "Of course, I'll be happy to tell you everything I know—I'd like to do all I can on the young man's behalf. But I should also tell you I barely know Wilson apart from our business dealings."

"From a business standpoint then," Watson responded, "it's my understanding that Mr. Wilson could be a difficult employee. He's been described as something of a rabble-rouser, intent on organizing his co-workers into a union strong enough to make demands on management."

"I know all about Brakeman's reputation. And I'm not saying we didn't have some concerns when we picked him back up from the Players League." Ebbets pursed his lips as if he could taste a disagreeable memory. "Being an Englishman, you wouldn't know about the Players League." Watson's blank expression confirmed the accuracy of Ebbets' judgment. "It was formed by a bunch of ballplayers who decided they could get along without the owners and quickly found out they couldn't. Wilson was one of them, but he wasn't one of the ringleaders, which is why we took him back. That, and the fact that he's left-handed, and has got a near unhittable curve that he can put exactly where he wants to when he's right. You can't have too many left-handed pitchers with a good curve ball. As long as

103

he's throwing strikes and not leading them, he can talk union all he likes. That's all it is with Wilson anyway, just talk."

Watson looked up from his writing, making no effort to hide the puzzlement he felt. "I take it, Mr. Ebbets, you saw nothing of the firebrand about Mr. Wilson."

"I might not feel that way if I was batting against him, but I know what you mean. I'll tell you the truth, Doctor, I came to the conclusion a while back that Wilson was a ballplayer first and foremost. He's got his own way of looking at things, and maybe feels pretty strongly about what he sees as problems, but he'll go out on the ball field when it's his turn to pitch and give it everything he's got. That's firebrand enough for me."

"So you were surprised when you heard he was accused of trying to kill Mr. Morgan?"

"Frankly, Dr. Watson, I was more than surprised. And I wasn't alone. But you're the only person who's seen fit to come to Brooklyn to ask about it. When I was told about your phone call I asked two of our players who know Brakeman real well to make themselves available. One's Brickyard Snyder and the other's Candy Cochrane. Brickyard's our catcher and rooms with Brakeman when we travel; Candy is his friend from their days in Ohio. He roomed with him in Brooklyn and is probably the person he's closest to on the team."

"That will be very helpful, Mr. Ebbets. Thank you."

Ebbets grunted and pushed away from the desk. He walked to the door of his office and called out a name that might have been Packer or Packard or Pickford. When the man of whatever name arrived, he was instructed to find Brickyard and Candy, and bring them to his office.

Resuming his seat, Ebbets told Watson he could use the empty office next door for as long as needed. He grew silent and stared without seeing to the open door behind Watson. When he spoke again it was as if he was choosing his words with great care.

104

"Doctor ... Tell me, do you really believe there is some chance of getting Brakeman off? I know your Mr. Holmes has done some extraordinary things, but the police seem so certain. Is it really possible they've gotten it wrong?"

"I'll just say I've seen Holmes do a great number of surprising things in our time together. It often appears as if he's guided by a superior intelligence."

Ebbets nodded gravely. "I can tell you, Doctor, if anything can be done the team will be very grateful. We would love to have Brakeman back. He could save our season."

Both men sat with their own thoughts until interrupted by a knock on the open door. It was one of the men from the field below wearing the Brooklyn uniform minus its single glove.

"Brickyard, please come in. Dr. Watson, I'd like you to meet Brickyard Snyder, the finest catcher in the National League." The finest catcher in the National League was a rugged-looking, moon-faced young man who showed no response to a compliment spoken too automatically to inspire belief. "Brickyard, this is Dr. Watson. He is here investigating the shooting at Mr. Morgan's home, and believes he and his colleague, Mr. Sherlock Holmes, may be able to help Brakeman. I'd like you to give him every assistance."

"Absolutely." Brickyard Snyder grinned his agreement to Ebbets' request showing brown stained teeth that explained the bulge in his cheek.

"I'll put you both in the office next door and send in Candy when he gets here."

The room next door was an exact replica of Ebbets' office except for an absence of pictures and the addition of a brass cuspidor. Watson took the chair behind the desk; Snyder took the chair facing him, and proceeded to make frequent and impressively accurate use of the room's single adornment.

Before Watson could pose his first question, Snyder, still grinning broadly, offered an opinion about the case against his teammate. "Dr. Watson, I don't know what's goin' on with Mr. Morgan or why people are taking shots at him, but I can tell you Brakeman is a good egg. Whoever done it, it ain't him. And I'd stake my life on that."

"Why do you think so, Mr. Snyder? How can you be so sure with all the evidence there is against him?"

"I'll tell you what I think of the evidence." There was another well-placed stream of tobacco juice which Watson took as the expression of his opinion, but Snyder chose to add a slightly more nuanced comment. "It's all hogwash."

Watson tried again. "I very much want to help Mr. Wilson. Can you tell me why you think the charges against him are what you call hogwash?"

"Do you know Brakeman?" Snyder did not wait for Watson's response. "You room with a guy for two years you get to know him. I'm from Texas. You're English, right?" The accuracy of Snyder's observation won him a bemused smile. "I thought so. You talk like one—at least the way I think an Englishman talks. I never met one before. Anyway, in Texas we got an expression that fits Brakeman. We talk about whether a guy is someone you could go to the well with. See, in the old days if you knew there were Indians around and you had to get water for the house, you had to go to the well with somebody you could count on to stick by you no matter what. Brakeman's a guy you could go to the well with. A man like that don't take pot shots at nobody. He faces him straight on. Besides which, I been hunting with Brakeman and I can tell you he hits what he aims for—with a rifle anyway. But I never seen anyone who was good with a rifle who didn't know his way around all kinds of guns. And Brakeman can outshoot me and Candy both, and the two of us are damn fine shots if I do say so myself."

Brickyard Snyder punctuated his report with a final splash before being joined by another man wearing the uniform of the Brooklyn Bridegrooms. Snyder performed the introductions. "Dr. Watson, this here's Candy Cochrane. He's the only man on this team who knows Brakeman better than me, him bein' a friend from before they was teammates on the Bridegrooms. He can tell you why Brakeman couldn't have took a shot at Morgan. This is Dr. Watson, Candy. Dr. Watson is workin' with a friend of his to get Brakeman sprung." Brickyard Snyder smiled his satisfaction to both men as he stood to cede his chair to the new arrival. He indicated a need to get back, wished Watson well and left without waiting to hear Watson's thanks.

Candy Cochrane was above middle height and trim like all the Bridegrooms. Watson judged him to be about 31 or 32. His sandy brown hair had begun a slow retreat from his forehead, and in combination with his boney face served to make him look older. He nodded a small smile to Watson, but continued standing. The steady look from his watery blue eyes made clear he would pose a different challenge than Brickyard Snyder.

"Mr. Ebbets said you wanted to see me."

"That's right, Mr. Cochrane. Please have a seat."

Cochrane looked to the chair as if deciding whether it could hold his weight before finally deciding to chance it. "He said you were here to help Brakeman." Cochrane's tone was cautious.

"My colleague, Mr. Sherlock Holmes, and I are exploring whether there is reason to believe Mr. Wilson is innocent of the crimes for which he's been arrested. Mr. Ebbets suggested you and Mr. Snyder were particularly close to Mr. Wilson and could be helpful."

Candy Cochrane loosened his grip on the armrest he had been clutching and sat back in his chair. "Then you're not with the police or one of those Pinks."

This time he got a vigorous nod from Watson.

"How can I be of help?"

"First, tell me how you happen to know Mr. Wilson."

Cochrane grinned and traced the bill of the baseball cap he had set in his lap. "Well now, that does go back a way. He was a kid pitcher with the Forest City Robins in Cleveland and I was the second baseman. That would have been eighty-five and we just naturally got together. I'm not sure I could say how it happened, it just did. Anyway, Mr. Nolan—he was the Robins' manager—he had this working agreement with the Bridegrooms except they would have been the Brooklyn Grays back then. So when two infielders from the Grays got hurt crashing into each other when they were going for a fly ball, Mr. Nolan arranged for a couple of guys from the Grays to come watch me play to see if I could fill in for them at second base. Well, I had a real good day. I got two hits, stole a base and turned two double plays so they ended up taking me. But they also got a look at Wilson who was pitching that day, and they liked what they seen. They told Nolan to keep him under wraps; that they'd be back for him after he got some seasoning. So we spent the one season together in eighty-five, then got back together in eighty-seven and we been together ever since, except for ninety of course when some of the guys got together to form what they called the Players' League. I stood with the regular Brooklyn team, but Wilson went with the Brooklyn team in the Players' League. I told Brakeman it wouldn't last, but he said it was the right thing for him to do."

"There's talk of Mr. Wilson being something of a radical. Was that why he joined this renegade league of baseballers?"

Cochrane shifted position a second time. "I wouldn't say that. There were a lot of guys—a whole lot—who decided they might make more money in a league that was under their control. Oh, I know what they say about Brakeman, but he's alright. He reads a lot of stuff and likes to talk about the things he reads, but you get him away from all that and he's a regular guy. If you're thinking he could kill somebody over politics, you can just forget it. I seen him have a hundred arguments with guys about the Brotherhood—that's what they call the union—

and then sit down and play cards with them. Hey, I didn't agree with him about the Brotherhood and we got along just fine."

"Mr. Ebbets said you and Mr. Wilson roomed together. Is that still the case?"

"No, we split up about four or five months ago." Cochrane read the knowing look that crossed Watson's face. "It's not what you think. It had nothing to do with the union or politics." Cochrane made a laugh that came out through both his nose and mouth. "It was about having ladies over to see us. I'd got to keeping company with a young lady who was living with her mother until she passed away a couple of months ago. While Lucy's mother was there it made it hard for us to be alone. You understand. Anyway, it looked to be best for me to move to my own place, which I did with no hard feelings and nothing to do with Brakeman's politics."

Watson nodded his understanding. "What about the gun Mr. Wilson owned? Had you ever seen it?"

Cochrane' lip curled in disgust. "I knew about it, but I never seen it. You got to understand, we go to a lot of cities and a lot of places we don't know anything about, and it's gotten so there's all this low life that hangs around the parks and hotels where we stay. And if you don't know it, Brakeman's a big star, so he's gonna have a lot more of those people tagging after him than someone like me. And I'll tell you something maybe nobody else will, Brakeman's not the only one on the team who carries a gun."

"Does that include you, Mr. Cochrane?"

There was a derisive laugh following the earlier path through both his nose and mouth. "No, I'm not important enough for anybody to want to bother me."

Watson rewarded the young man with the smile his modesty seemed to merit before responding to one of his comments. "Tell me Mr. Cochrane, what do you mean by 'low life'?"

"The cranks mostly. That's what we call the people in the stands. They're most of them fine, but you never know when you're gonna run into one who is just plain crazy. You could have a thousand people sitting out there with nine hundred ninety-nine of them okay, but there's the one who hates you for beating his team or for not beating some other team, or maybe just because you look like his boss or his brother-in-law. Whatever sets him off, he decides to get even with you. But the cranks are just part of it—and they're not the worst part. You also got the gamblers who hang around the hotels, or come over to your table where you're trying to eat a meal, hoping they can learn something from you that will give them an edge. Some of them will even promise to give you a piece of their winnings if what you tell them turns out to be useful. And there's stories—I ain't saying they're true—that if you *really* help them, you can get a really big piece." Cochrane gave Watson an exaggerated wink.

"Were there stories about Mr. Wilson?"

"There's talk about everyone who can control the score of a game. I don't believe any of it when it comes to Brakeman." Cochrane grasped the armrests firmly. "Is there more I can help you with? I really ought to get back on the field."

Watson grunted, but otherwise ignored Cochrane's request. "Did Mr. Wilson ever mention to you anything he heard, anything he suspected about a threat to Mr. Morgan? You know his fiancée was Mrs. Morgan's maid so he was in a position to hear things. Did he ever share anything with you?"

Cochrane frowned, shook his head once slowly, then several more times. "We just didn't talk about that kind of thing, Dr. Watson. We talked baseball—he was always wanting to go through the other team's batting order, or talk about their pitchers or the ballpark if we were out of town, or maybe the umpire, and on the day he was scheduled to pitch he didn't talk at all, at least not until the game was over—and not always then.

If he had a bad outing it could be another day or two before he said a word."

Cochrane brightened at a sudden thought. "We talked about his wedding of course—you know I was to be best man. And any time I got a letter from home we talked about that. When I think about it, we talked about my letters and my family a lot. Sometimes he'd even add little notes to the letters I wrote home. You know he didn't have any family of his own, and I suppose he sort of adopted mine. He wanted to know everything about my family—what my brothers were like, what they did all day; and things about my mother, like what were her favorite things to cook, what preserves she put up, just all kinds of things. Brakeman even asked questions about our dogs. Besides all that, he had to know everything about the farm, what did we grow, when did we plant, when did we harvest, what did we do in between. He said it was exactly what he wanted for himself and Caroline some day. His own piece of land. Of course, Brakeman is city through and through—which I tell him all the time—and farm work isn't the paradise he thinks it is—which I also tell him all the time."

"Anyway, I don't remember him ever mentioning Morgan except to lump him in with Rockefeller and Carnegie and some of them other millionaires to tell me how they were all against the working man, but he knew I wasn't political so like I was saying those conversations never lasted long." Cochrane pressed his hands down on the armrests, but remained seated. "And I really should get back, Dr. Watson, I promised Mr. Foutz—he's our manager—I'd only be a few minutes."

"I won't detain you further," said Watson, rising from his chair to permit Cochrane's escape. "Thank you for meeting with me."

Cochrane stood with Watson and engaged in a prolonged handshake. "Thank you, Dr. Watson. I hope you can help Brakeman shake this awful thing."

Watson watched Cochrane leave before going next door to thank Ebbets for his time and hospitality. Ebbets expressed his own support for Watson's effort, affirming his earlier observation that lefthanders with a good hook were not falling out of the trees. Watson gave fresh assurance that he and Holmes would do everything they could. He carefully skirted the ball field at Eastern Park where the man with the tapered stick was still hitting balls to the other men. Like Mrs. Hudson, Watson ignored the scenery on his return trip. It came as no surprise that Wilson's teammates would speak well of him, and Ebbets' positive comments were obviously colored by his hope that Wilson could rejoin the team if found innocent. On that account, he'd heard nothing to exonerate Wilson, but he'd heard enough to consider the possibility.

6.
Paying Calls

Holmes took the precaution of jotting a few notes describing his visit with Morgan and Cornelia Porter before joining Mrs. Hudson and Watson. He included nothing of his exchange with the Pinkerton. There was no need; that confrontation had been orchestrated by Mrs. Hudson. Watson assembled his usually meticulous notes detailing his meetings at Eastern Park while Mrs. Hudson put down a few keywords covering the highlights of her meeting with Caroline and Lucy. They were to gather together in Mrs. Hudson's parlor suite. Watson pointed out, not for the first time, that her room was the largest, and would therefore best support their meeting. Mrs. Hudson ignored, not for the first time, his reference to the spaciousness of her accommodations while accepting Watson's proposal for a meeting site.

Mrs. Hudson seated herself on the parlor's settee while Holmes and Watson plumped down on two well cushioned easy chairs. A low rectangular table lay between Mrs. Hudson and the two men. The empty table triggered a single thought in all three minds and Watson called to have the space filled with a pot of tea and a basket of scones.

Forty-five minutes later, the pot of tea had been drained and only crumbs remained in a basket that had earlier held three scones. Reports of the afternoon's meetings had been given by each of the detectives, and Mrs. Hudson was ready to make assignments for the next day.

"Regardless of what Mr. Morgan says," she began, "'e's bound to 'ave more than 'is share of enemies. We'll want to talk to as many as could've been waitin' on 'is coach the mornin' of the shootin'. Mr. 'Olmes, you'll be seein' Franklin Langer, the footman Mr. Morgan discharged. We know 'e was in the crowd, and Caroline reports 'e 'ad a gun. You can see what you can learn about that, and why Franklin chose to be in the crowd that mornin'—only keep in mind this Mr. Langer can be a bit of a rough character."

"Dr. Watson, I'd like you to 'ave a talk with Mr. McIlvaine and see whether 'e doesn't, in fact, know one end of a gun from another in spite of what Mr. Morgan says. And I'd like to know why a jilted lover waits around to see the father who got 'im jilted."

"But first off we need to get to Mr. Archibald McLeod. Neither Mr. Langer nor Mr. McIlvaine are goin' anyplace, but Mr. McLeod is a guest of this 'otel and there's no tellin' 'ow long he's plannin' on stayin'. I'm wonderin' why did he want to meet with Mr. Morgan? And after 'e come all this way to have 'is meetin', did 'e really give up on seein' Mr. Morgan, or might 'e 'ave made the short walk to Mr. Morgan's 'ouse." Mrs. Hudson grimaced at the memory of just how short a walk it was. "I suspect our Mr. Langer's work keeps 'im out late at night and in bed most of the morning so, Mr. 'Olmes, you should be able to see 'im after you meet with Mr. McLeod."

Holmes nodded soberly to Mrs. Hudson.

"What about the people affected by Morgan's infidelities? There's …" Watson consulted his notes from Mrs. Hudson's report, "there's Mrs. Edith Randolph and Mrs. Adelaide Douglas, and we can't discount Mrs. Morgan having an irate brother or cousin."

"That's just it, Dr. Watson, Mrs. Morgan doesn't 'ave a brother, irate or otherwise. I can't say about a cousin, but the truth is Mrs. Morgan, to all accounts, 'as made a kind of peace with Mr. Morgan's behavior. I'm told it's what 'er class does." Mrs. Hudson's voice sounded as close to a sneer as either man could remember ever hearing.

"Aren't we discounting Wilson's radical tendencies," Holmes grumbled his objection to the direction the conversation had taken. "Are we truly to believe the police planted all that literature in his room? They're not Scotland Yard, but it's still difficult to swallow."

114

"We'll 'ave to look into that, Mr. 'Olmes. I will say I am impressed with the statement of Mr. Ebbets that Mr. Wilson is more talk than anythin' more serious, and so is Dr. Watson I do believe. Still, you're quite right, Mr. 'Olmes, we need to look into that some more. For now, I suggest we get ourselves ready for dinner. I'm lookin' forward to a pleasant meal without so much as another word about business." Two vigorous nods gave silent approval to that same prospect.

It would be a night of unfulfilled expectations.

The Palm was the Waldorf's premier restaurant. It owed its name to the live palm trees placed at strategic intervals throughout the two-tiered dining room. They had barely been seated when they were approached by a prematurely balding man of perhaps 35 who directed his full attention to the only person at the table he knew.

"Mr. Holmes, I trust you'll remember me. I'm Tarkenton, Mr. Morgan's private secretary. We met earlier today. I beg your forgiveness; I know you are about to dine with your friends. It's just that Mr. Morgan instructed me to see you as soon as possible. Perhaps the two of us could have a word in private. I promise not to detain you more than a very few minutes."

The object of his request stared at Mr. Morgan's private secretary as if he were having trouble placing him. When he spoke, it was as though the memory stirred was not a pleasant one. "You are quite right, Mr. Tarkenton, you are interrupting our dinner. If you are intent on doing so, please be seated and state your business. There is nothing you can say to me you cannot say in front of my colleagues. You have five minutes to do so." Tarkenton seated himself quickly as if fearing the chair might otherwise be snatched away. Holmes stated his colleagues' names by way of introduction, and repeated his request that Tarkenton state his business.

Morgan's private secretary shared a fragment of smile with Watson and Mrs. Hudson, then proceeded to ignore them.

"You're making it rather difficult, Mr. Holmes, as I will be forced to report to Mr. Morgan." He paused, hopeful the threat of displeasing Mr. Morgan would have the chastening effect on Holmes that it had on every other man he'd known. It did not, and he continued with his carefully rehearsed presentation. "I am instructed to inform you, Mr. Holmes, that Mr. Morgan would like to retain your services for the London office of Drexel, Morgan and Company at the rate of ten thousand pounds a year. He will have that office draw up the papers immediately upon your agreement. Mr. Morgan wishes the arrangements to be finalized within the next few days, and for you to assume your London responsibilities immediately thereafter."

Three sets of eyebrows shot up, then returned to their normal positions. If Tarkenton took notice, he didn't show it. He looked around the restaurant, leaned closer to Holmes, and became for the moment his confidant.

"There's no need to make an immediate decision. I can tell Mr. Morgan you need time to consider his offer." Tarkenton set his hands on the arms of his chair prepared to leave after getting Holmes' assurance he would consider Mr. Morgan's proposition. It was the only sensible response and he felt certain it would satisfy Mr. Morgan. No sane man would reject 10,000 pounds out of hand, and no prudent man would agree to a job as vaguely stated as Mr. Morgan had insisted it be put.

Like his employer, Tarkenton had reckoned without a knowledge of his man.

"That's very kind of Mr. Morgan, and I'd like you to thank him for me. You can tell him …." At that precise moment, Holmes felt a sudden pain in his shin as if he'd been kicked—as indeed he had been. Mrs. Hudson, wearing a sweet smile, addressed a question to him.

"Mr. 'Olmes, isn't Mr. Tarkenton the very gentleman you were tellin' us likely 'ad things to say about all that 'appened that dreadful morning, but never got a chance to talk?"

Holmes ignored the need to massage his leg as well as the urge to retaliate. "Quite right, Mrs. Hudson. Good of you to remind me." He turned from the housekeeper's saccharine smile to Tarkenton's worried look. "You won't deny you were outside that morning."

The private secretary leaned far back in his chair. This was not a conversation he wanted. "I was outside. I never said I wasn't. What of it?"

"Only that you might have seen something—or someone—that struck you as out of place or unexpected."

"Mr. Morgan already told you there was nothing unusual—outside of Wilson holding a gun and running off."

"Yes, I heard that from Mr. Morgan, but I didn't hear your version of events."

"There's nothing I can add to what Mr. Morgan already told you."

"Well, Tarkenton, I don't see how I can consider Mr. Morgan's offer until I'm certain I've done all I could here. There are questions to which I must have answers before I would feel comfortable returning to London."

Tarkenton could ill afford to return to Mr. Morgan empty-handed. He'd seen the looks and he'd heard the rumors. Half the staff below stairs already had him out the door.

"What is it you want to know?"

Tarkenton looked to Holmes, but the response to his question came from Watson. "If I might, Mr. Tarkenton, there is one thing that interests me. It concerns this man, McLeod. Since you were outside at the time, is it possible that Mr. McLeod was in the crowd that morning?"

Tarkenton looked to Watson, before again focusing his attention on Holmes. "As Mr. Morgan said, Mr. McLeod had never been to the house so I wouldn't know him if I saw him. I simply can't say whether he was there or not."

Tarkenton's face reddened as he spoke, giving Watson ample reason to pursue the issue. "We will be talking to Mr.

117

McLeod later about his own activities that morning. Everything we learn from him, just as everything we learn from you, will be treated as confidential unless, of course, we run into a conflict between accounts. Then, we might have to raise our concerns to the police and perhaps Mr. Morgan. We already know Mr. McLeod made several calls to Mr. Morgan before the morning of the attack. Those calls would have been referred to you for response. We'll be asking Mr. McLeod what he took from those conversations. In light of that, is there anything you'd like to tell us before we see him?"

Tarkenton pursed his lips and swallowed hard, then swallowed hard again before beginning. "It's possible Mr. McLeod was there—I mean in the crowd that morning. When I talked to him, I could hear how disappointed he was about not being able to meet with Mr. Morgan, and I took pity on the man. It was a weak moment, I know, but he sounded awful. Anybody with half a conscience would've done what I did." Seeing Holmes' cold stare, Tarkenton judged he had somehow managed to find a man lacking half a conscience. Having no other recourse, he returned to the confession he had begun. "I told Mr. McLeod about Mr. Morgan's schedule and Miss Juliet's breakfast, and said that he *might*—I never said more than he might—get a moment with Mr. Morgan if he was at the house when Mr. Morgan arrived. That's all there was to it and I don't know whether he ever came to the house."

Holmes gave Tarkenton a moment to compose himself before posing a second question nearly as discomfiting as the one posed by Watson. "Tell me, Mr. Tarkenton, do you own a gun?"

Tarkenton seemed torn between confusion and outrage. "I beg your pardon, Mr. Holmes. Do you really think I would make an attempt on Mr. Morgan's life—the life of my benefactor?"

"I accuse you of nothing, Mr. Tarkenton. I simply want to know about the availability of guns in the house. Do you own one?"

"I do—for my own protection. The neighborhood west of the residence is a little rough and I don't always have access to a carriage. I can tell you I did not have a gun with me when I went outside. And I did not follow Mr. Morgan to the Metropolitan Club where someone … where Wilson fired at him earlier this month."

"Where do you keep the gun when you're in the 'ouse, Mr. Tarkenton?" It was the woman Dietz had warned him about. Dietz was certain Holmes was using her to worm information out of the staff. He would have ignored her effrontery, except that he still needed a response from Holmes and dared not offend any of these people. He chose being brusque as the next best thing to saying nothing.

"I have an office, madam, and I keep it in my office."

"And do you always lock your office, Mr. Tarkenton?"

He grimaced at the question. The woman's point was something he hadn't considered. "My door is usually left unlocked, but I have the greatest confidence in the integrity of staff." Having given the obligatory statement of support, he made a mental note to check for his revolver when he got back.

"And what type of revolver do you have, Mr. Tarkenton?" His questioner was again Holmes.

"A standard Colt. And I can't tell you the number of cartridges in the chamber. I haven't checked it in some time."

"Do others on staff also own revolvers?"

Tarkenton winced at being grouped with staff. "I really have no idea, Mr. Holmes, it's not something that's discussed, but I would tend to doubt it."

The table again fell silent, and Holmes took note of the waiter who watched them without seeming to, uncertain what to do with the brace of menus he held. Even at the Palm there was a need to turn tables in a timely manner. Holmes looked with

119

widened eyes to his colleagues who answered with small nods of agreement.

"I believe we've kept you long enough, Mr. Tarkenton. I appreciate the time you've given us, and now we would like to proceed with dinner. Please tell Mr. Morgan I deeply appreciate his gracious offer, but for the moment I am unable to accept as there are simply too many loose threads requiring my attention."

Tarkenton gave a low, involuntary groan from behind tightly pursed lips. He stood and expressed a concern that had significance for him alone. "Mr. Morgan will be very disappointed, Mr. Holmes, but I will relay your message." He pivoted with military precision and strode from the restaurant. His place was quickly filled by the waiter who shared the plastic smile he had been waiting to display, and disposed of the menus he had been carrying overlong.

Their plans for a dinner free of business no longer possible, they reviewed the people at the Morgan house who appeared to have reason and opportunity to assassinate the financier, now adding to that list the possibilities created by access to Tarkenton's revolver.

They finished with rich desserts that did nothing to lift their spirits; then set a time for an early breakfast, and wished each other the good night no one of them would enjoy.

The new day brought no easing of their mood as they gathered again for breakfast. Holmes had provided each of the three bellboys with a shiny new dollar, and the promise of another dollar to the one who alerted him to an Archibald McLeod sighting. Watson had purchased a *Tribune* and a *Sun*, and they were relieved to find a day free of articles about Wilson or the shooting. Mrs. Hudson noticed a report that Mr. Mark Twain, "author of several popular books and noted lecturer," was staying at the Chelsea Hotel and would be speaking in Cooper Union's Great Hall the following week. The article went on to say that the famous author's talk was being sponsored in part by a number of prominent businessmen, listing JP Morgan among others. She flirted briefly with the idea of seeing her friend again, before deciding it would require a discussion with Holmes and Watson she had no wish to conduct.

As Holmes accepted a second cup of coffee in his continuing effort to adapt to American tastes, one of the bellboys in his pay approached him, looked hesitantly to the others at the table, and spoke only after receiving assurance from Holmes it was safe to do so.

"Mr. McLeod is taking breakfast in his room. His order is just now on its way up. It's oatmeal plus scrambled eggs and bacon." He delivered the last with a smile of pride in the breadth of his undercover investigation.

Holmes gave him a solemn nod and an additional dollar. The bellboy returned to his post in the reception area with a promise he could be available "for any more detecting." Holmes excused himself and started for Archibald McLeod's room.

Holmes' knock on McLeod's door was answered by a voice garbled by a mouthful of breakfast, "Who is it?"

"Sherlock Holmes. I'd like a moment of your time."

There was a pause, and it was unclear for the moment whether Holmes' request would be honored or ignored. Then there came the click of the door being unlocked, and Holmes was admitted to a room that was a duplicate of his own in everything other than the color of the bedcover.

"How do I know your name?" McLeod asked, waving Holmes to an easy chair across from the one drawn up to a round table holding a partially digested breakfast. He was a slight man with a neatly trimmed moustache, sunken cheeks and a brightly inquisitive expression. "Do you mind?" he asked as he reseated himself, "My food is getting cold."

Holmes smiled his indifference. "Please go ahead. You may know me as a consulting detective from London, England.

121

I'm in America on personal business, but have gotten involved in the investigation of the attempt on Mr. Morgan's life."

McLeod held a forkful of eggs in readiness as he voiced his confusion. "I didn't know there was an investigation. I thought the police were satisfied they had captured Morgan's attacker."

"Mr. Wilson has been taken into custody and is being held for trial. However, not everyone feels certain of Wilson's guilt, and I have pledged to look into the situation to see that all stones are turned." Having no wish to reveal the small number of people constituting the "not everyone" group, Holmes plunged into the task of turning stones.

"Currently, I'm checking on all who had business with Mr. Morgan at the time of the shooting. It's my understanding that you made several attempts to reach Mr. Morgan by telephone."

McLeod had continued with his breakfast throughout Holmes' brief explanation without change in expression or a break in the speed with which food disappeared from his plate. Now, he took a sip of coffee and patted his napkin to his mouth before responding. "There's no secret about that, Mr. Holmes. I called several times, but never got past Morgan's lackey—I believe the man gave his name as Templeton."

"Tarkenton," Holmes corrected. "He reported your phone calls to me, and said he encouraged you to be at Mr. Morgan's home when he got back from the office. You *were* at his home that morning, were you not?"

"I'm not certain I like the tenor of your questions, Mr. Holmes, or see any reason to answer them." McLeod sat back from his breakfast to devote his full attention to staring Holmes into submission. It was a tactic at which he was no more successful than Morgan had been the day before.

"As you wish, Mr. McLeod. I can simply advise the police of my understanding, and encourage them to undertake whatever action they see fit." Holmes gathered himself as if preparing to go without quite leaving his seat. McLeod regarded Holmes with continuing disapproval, but the words he spoke promised cooperation.

"I simply resent the imposition on my time, and the implication that could be drawn from your questions. However, I have nothing to hide and can give you a few more minutes."

Holmes nodded recognition of McLeod's acquiescence. "You *were* at Mr. Morgan's that morning."

"I was, but it soon became apparent I wouldn't be able to see him, what with the crowd that had assembled, so I left about the same time his carriage arrived."

"Was that after the shots were fired?"

"I left before the shots were fired. I was already a good way up 36th Street on my way back to the hotel when I heard them. The line of trees blocked whatever view I might have had of the shooter, and I didn't rush back to learn what had happened and maybe get myself shot. Believe me, I wasn't the only one thinking that way. It looked like everybody was pouring out onto the street from where they'd been standing in back of the house. One man even managed to work his way through the blind of trees to escape the gunfire. And then I saw what must have been Wilson running the other way on 36th with some of the men chasing him although they all gave it up pretty quick when they saw they were never going to catch him. It was about then I stopped watching and went on my way."

"Why were you interested in seeing Mr. Morgan?"

"My reasons were personal; I can't see them as any of your business."

"You visited Mr. Morgan the morning he was shot. We have only your word that you left before the shooting took place, and it's known you were dismissed from your job as head of the Philadelphia Railroad by Mr. Morgan. For the moment I am making it my business. As I've said, there's no doubt in my mind it could be made into police business."

123

"First, it's the Philadelphia and Reading Railroad, not the Philadelphia Railroad," McLeod said, shifting his eggs from one side of the plate to the other before setting down his fork. "My reasons *are* personal and I will trust you to hold them in confidence. You are right, Mr. Holmes, Morgan dismissed me without giving me an explanation. I know he believed the expenditures I authorized were cutting too deeply into company profits, but I could have justified every expense if Morgan had only given me a chance. Instead, he never invited me to New York, and he never came to Philadelphia. Would you believe, to this day we've never met. And of course all the while his little toad, Wagner, was working for me and feeding Morgan lies and half-truths about my operations. I know you should say nothing unkind about the dead, but I'll be hanged if I'm going to be as two-faced as he was." Both men ignored the prophetic suggestion within McLeod's outburst.

"For how long did you know Wagner?" Holmes asked.

"Forever, Mr. Holmes. Anyway, that's how it seemed. He was at the Philadelphia and Reading when I got there and he was there when I left. He was always involved with transport of one kind or another, first with shipping on Lake Erie and later railroads. He came to us from Cleveland where he made something of a reputation getting supplies to Union forces during the War. He left Cleveland after his wife died. I don't know what he was like when she was alive, but when he was with us, work was his life. I heard he had a daughter, but you wouldn't know it from him. I never saw her picture or heard one word about her."

McLeod stood and walked to the wardrobe in a corner of his room. He picked up the cigarette case from its top shelf, removed one and showed the open case to Holmes who shook his refusal. He lit up and inhaled deeply as though only the smoke could give him the strength to continue. "I know what it sounds like, but I'm simply telling you what the situation is. I assure you I had no interest in doing harm to either man. I'd long since forgotten Wagner, and I was hoping to see Morgan to ask if he'd relent and give me a letter of reference, maybe even offer me a job. So you see, I had no reason to harm Morgan. Shooting him might not be the best way to get his recommendation."

Holmes nodded woodenly, purposely dense to McLeod's sarcasm. "I appreciate what you say; I still need to know whether you own a gun, Mr. McLeod."

Unexpectedly, McLeod responded with a throaty laugh. "Of course I own a gun, Mr. Holmes. This is America. Everybody owns a gun."

"So I'm discovering. Tell me, Mr. McLeod, when did you arrive in New York, and how long do you plan on staying?"

"I'll have been in New York a week tomorrow; I have no plans to leave although I doubt I'll be staying at the Waldorf unless I find a satisfactory situation in the near future. You see, Mr. Holmes, I've been spending a considerable part of my dwindling funds to stay at this hotel in order to convince people my funds are not dwindling."

Holmes smiled for the first time since meeting McLeod, and rose to leave. "Thank you for your time, Mr. McLeod. I will let you return to your breakfast. I can tell you I've heard nothing to this point that I see as being of interest to the police, but I would appreciate it if you would keep me advised of your whereabouts until my investigation is complete. I'm staying at the hotel, and you can leave me a note if there is any change in your plans."

The two men nodded their good-byes. McLeod looked mournfully to the remains of his breakfast, and decided to salvage a piece of toast and a half cup of lukewarm coffee from the residue. Holmes took the elevator to Mrs. Hudson's sixth floor suite to report on his meeting with McLeod. When that was done, it was time for Holmes and Watson to leave for their next interviews.

Mrs. Hudson went with them to the lobby where she hung back ostensibly marking their departure. Her focus, however, was not her colleagues, but the staff clustered around the hotel's reception desk. As she watched from beyond the curve of the long desk, one of them, a short paunchy man with glasses that seemed in constant danger of sliding off his nose, frowned a sudden purpose as he watched her colleagues leave. He sidled his way along the desk to the telephone, glanced to his left and right, then lowered his head as he lifted the earpiece and rang the switchboard. From her position behind the desk, Mrs. Hudson watched him shift weight from one leg to the other as he waited for his call to be placed. When he had his party on the line, he huddled still lower over the instrument as he whispered a message to his correspondent. Mrs. Hudson was certain of the correspondent's identify. Knowing the identity of his hotel informant could prove useful at a later time.

Franklin Langer lived downtown on Broome Street not very many streets from the Tombs. Holmes guessed the location might prove a convenient one for both Langer and the authorities. The lodging-house was a two story red brick building that was aging gracelessly. Chunks of brick had fallen away or been hacked away from its walls; its wooden entrance door was pock-marked, and possessed a lock that no longer discouraged entry.

Holmes knocked loudly on the door of Langer's apartment, but got no answer. It was half nine and as Mrs. Hudson had observed, it was more likely Langer was asleep than that he was out. Accordingly, he knocked a second time, more loudly, but with the same result. He waited another minute before giving his best imitation of a hammer striking a blacksmith's anvil. The only response came from across the hall where a door opened a few inches, and a man's pinched face appeared beneath wisps of white hair, and above a tightly wrapped green and white striped robe. He stared his displeasure at Holmes until, satisfied his message had been received, he shut himself away from the intruder to his morning.

126

Holmes was prepared to beat on the door one last time before deciding the situation was hopeless when a voice from within simultaneously acknowledged and rejected Holmes.

"Go away. I don't care to see anybody." The voice was throaty and sleepily indignant.

"This isn't anybody. This is Sherlock Holmes and I assure you, you want to see me."

"And why would I want to see you?"

Holmes called his purpose to the closed door. "If you are innocent of firing at Mr. Morgan and killing a man in the process, I may be able to save your life."

The door across the hall creaked barely ajar, the man in the striped robe now an invisible presence behind it. Holmes suspected doors now stood ajar throughout the lodging-house.

The only door of interest to Holmes opened full and a thickly built man of about 30 looked him inside. With the closing of the door, eavesdropping ended, and the sudden notoriety of their neighbor, together with speculation about his visitor, became the next preoccupation of the building's residents.

"What is this nonsense about murder?"

Franklin Langer's broad face was creased into an ugly sneer, and Holmes recalled Mrs. Hudson's advice that he be wary of Langer. The room was dominated by the unmade bed from which it was apparent Langer had just been roused. He was fully dressed, but the rumpled nature of his clothing indicated it had been his night as well as daytime dress. There was a single basket chair which Holmes was not invited to occupy, and a dresser and washstand. The room's furnishings were completed by a small table distinctive for its combination of cigarette burns, coffee stains, and crumbs from an earlier meal.

"I know you were in the crowd when Morgan was shot and his aide killed. I know you own a gun, and I know you have a grievance with Morgan. That is the nonsense about murder, Mr. Langer."

127

Langer found a crumpled cigarette and matches in a pants pocket, and exhaled a long stream of smoke before responding. "And even if any of that is true, what concern is it of yours?"

Having tired of waiting for an invitation he judged was never to be extended, Holmes removed a jacket from the basket chair and seated himself. "I have chosen to make it my concern. My reasons are my own, but I assure you the authorities in New York will be as interested in what I have to say as the authorities in London have always proven to be."

Langer had turned away from Holmes and now turned back and strode toward him, his jaw jutted and his eyebrows threatening to knit together above a fierce squint. "If you mean to frighten me, it won't work. I have friends just as powerful in their own way as Morgan."

Langer stood over him, his fists balled. Holmes looked up at Langer as though he was an insect not worth flicking away.

"I'll make an agreement with you, Mr. Langer. I will treat you with as much respect as you show me you deserve, and in return you will answer my questions. If you do not wish to answer my questions, I will simply share all that I already know, and all that I suspect, with your police." Holmes wondered how many more times he would feel called upon to threaten people with providing information he didn't possess to officials he didn't know.

In spite of his misgivings, he found the strategy successful a second time. Langer lingered another moment, long enough to let the ash from his cigarette drop at Holmes' feet, before turning and seating himself on the edge of the bed facing his visitor.

"Let's say I was there that morning. So were at least 50 other people."

Holmes chose to ignore Langer's generous view of the crowd's size. "Why were you there, Mr. Langer? Surely not to pay your respects to the man who had released you from his service."

"Morgan?" Langer spat the name as if it might otherwise lodge in his throat. "I wouldn't give the old man the time of day. But Miss Juliet was always nice to me and I wanted to see her; I'm sure you already talked to Sachs and know that."

"I know that was your story, and I know you stood no chance of seeing Morgan's daughter, so why don't you tell me your real reason for being there?"

"Since you know so much, why don't you tell me?"

"If you like." Holmes brushed an imagined thread from the cuff of his jacket. "I could say that you appeared at Morgan's home knowing the time of the breakfast celebration from the newspapers. I could say you were still furious about being discharged, that you knew from your time as a footman at the Morgan residence that a crowd would gather to see Morgan and his guests, and you seized the opportunity to take your revenge."

"Do you really believe that? If I wanted to kill Morgan, couldn't I have found a better opportunity?"

"What better opportunity could there be? All eyes were focused on the coach. A man at the edge of the crowd would go unnoticed. Two quick shots in the midst of the excitement wouldn't be that difficult."

"Except I wasn't the one seen holding a gun, and I didn't go running off after the shooting."

"You didn't run off, but you were seen with a gun. Or are you saying that in your current line of work you don't own a revolver?"

"I don't know who you been talking to, but it don't matter. Even if I own a gun it don't mean anything. There's nothing illegal about having a gun." Langer got up to grind his cigarette into a saucer already cluttered with cigarette stubs. "If you get Wilson off, good for you. But you're not gonna do it by putting me in the frame, and I'm telling you not to try. There's friends of mine wouldn't like it, and *all* of them carry guns.

129

Have you got any more questions because I got to get ready for work?"

"Will your work keep you in New York for the next week?"

"I'm not going anywhere, but that don't mean I'm gonna see you again anytime." Langer was up off the side of the bed, and waiting impatiently for Holmes to leave the basket chair and his room.

Holmes rose slowly, the action seeming to require considerable effort, then stretching to his full height, he stared down at Langer.

"Thank you for your hospitality, Mr. Langer. You *will* see me again. I mean to find the person responsible for the attack on Mr. Morgan and the killing of Mr. Wagner, and you are very definitely suspected of being that person. You may share that information with your friends if you choose." Holmes opened the door for himself, and left a fuming Franklin Langer framed in the doorway as he went to collect the carriage he had left waiting to return him to the Waldorf.

Clarence McIlvaine lived uptown from the Waldorf in an area the doorman alternately described as "the West End" and "a wasteland." He did all he could to argue Watson into taking a hansom, emphasizing the points that reliably struck home with other guests who contemplated similar adventures.

"The trains are dreadfully uncomfortable, sir, with all the rocking back and forth, and stopping and starting, and the element that rides the train can be rough. I recommend against it, sir, recommend most strongly."

Watson had a single question, and when the doorman admitted the train would take about the same time as a hansom to get where he was going, Watson decided on the train. Having found the trip to Eastern Park relatively uncomplicated, Watson was determined to see the city the way a New Yorker might. Besides which, he knew the use of public transportation would be in accord with Mrs. Hudson's wishes, and he thought he owed her something after putting her in an expensive suite in an expensive hotel. The doorman gave a resigned shrug and recommended Watson take the Ninth Avenue train to the 72nd Street station, and then walk east to Central Park West. There, he would find the Dakota Apartments he was seeking.

The train shuddered its way from station to station. Watson remained alert throughout for exposure to the rough element the doorman had promised, but found his fellow passengers no more forbidding than his fellow guests at the Waldorf. Arriving finally at 72nd Street, he followed the directions he'd been given and came to a single building set against an otherwise uninhabited landscape, fulfilling the doorman's description of a wasteland. But it was a wasteland that promised to be short-lived. Steel skeletons cluttered the area, indicating the Dakota Apartments would have considerable competition in the very near future. Nonetheless, no matter what new structures arose, Watson was certain the Dakota Apartments would remain a distinctive presence. The seven-story building looked to have been assembled in sections, some fitted with turrets, some with balconies, some having both, with each of the sections unevenly joined to the others, resulting in their jutting in and out beneath a series of tall gables.

Watson passed beneath the entrance arch on 72nd Street, taking no notice of the Dakota Indian far above who appeared to be searching for members of his tribe who might be camping in downtown New York City. Inside the entry hall a uniformed attendant sat behind a small desk reminding Watson of his experience at the Tombs, except that the Dakota attendant was welcoming and the surroundings were opulent.

"Good day to you, sir. How may I be of help?"

"Good day to you. I wish to visit with Mr. Clarence McIlvaine. My name is Dr. John Watson." Watson handed the man a card confirming his identity.

The attendant's round open face remained welcoming even as his words were designed to hold the stranger at bay.

"Did you have an appointment with Mr. McIlvaine?" His glance to an open book on his desk suggested the answer to his question was already known.

Watson admitted his interloper status. The attendant looked to his phone, promising to learn if Mr. McIlvaine was available. Watson thought it wise to lend direction to his inquiry. "Please inform Mr. McIlvaine that I am here on behalf of Mr. Sherlock Holmes investigating the attack on Mr. J Pierpont Morgan."

The introduction of at least one, if not both names appeared to spark the attendant's interest. He dialed three numbers and stared impatiently at the instrument. When he spoke again, he made clear which name had occasioned his reaction. "Mr. McIlvaine, there's a gentleman here who wishes to see you. He's a Dr. John Watson and he's investigating Mr. Morgan's shooting along with his colleague, a Mr. Shylock Holmes." After a pause, he bobbed his head up and down toward the phone's speaker. "Yes sir, he's quite alone." Another pause, this time followed by a head to toe study of Watson. "Yes sir, I'd say so." And then a vigorous nod of agreement to the telephone speaker. "Very good, sir." He put the ear piece back on the instrument, and confirmed what Watson had already guessed. "Mr. McIlvaine will see you. He's in 514. The elevator is at the end of the corridor and to your left. A very good day, sir."

Watson rapped softly on 514. The door was opened instantly by a bulky man in his mid-thirties with sandy-brown hair and a small moustache, both carefully groomed. With his alert blue eyes and regular features he might have been described as good-looking were it not for his face appearing too broad for its features. In spite of the size of the man, it gave him the soft appearance that had led Morgan to belittle him in speaking to Holmes.

His formal greeting complemented his genteel appearance in frock coat, striped trousers and tie. "Good morning, Dr. Watson, I am Clarence McIlvaine. I don't believe we've met. I am, of course, familiar with the exploits of Mr. Holmes and yourself." As he spoke, Clarence McIlvaine led Watson down the apartment's hallway to a book-lined room Watson guessed he treated as a parlor when he entertained guests, and as a library and study when he was alone. Its solid oak furnishings reflected a concern for durability over aesthetics. He pointed Watson to a velveteen-covered couch and seated himself in a matching chair opposite.

"I might explain that I lived in London for several years. I was associated with the London branch of Harper Brothers, the book publishers. You can see I have a passion for books." He waved an arm across the surrounding walls.

"May I get you anything? I can send down for refreshments and coffee—unless you'd prefer tea. Let me warn you however, it won't be the tea to which you're accustomed."

"Thank you, Mr. McIlvaine, it's very good of you, but I'll try not to interrupt your day any longer than necessary. As the porter indicated, Holmes and I are investigating the attempt on Mr. Morgan's life."

Still absorbed with his responsibilities as host, McIlvaine shook a cigarette case in Watson's direction, only to suffer a second rejection. With nothing else to offer, he turned his full attention to Watson's concern.

"I'm not clear how I might be of assistance to you and Mr. Holmes. It was my understanding that this fellow Wilson had been identified as the assailant. May I ask your interest in this affair, Dr. Watson?"

Once again, Watson detailed the complex of relationships that led to the current investigation. When he had finished, he posed the first of the questions for McIlvaine that had been developed during his breakfast meeting. "It is my understanding you were at the Morgan house that morning. Did you see anything you felt to be suspicious or unexpected—beyond the shooting itself of course?"

McIlvaine's lips puckered and his eyes narrowed to slits in a moment of fierce concentration. The effect was to make his face appear even broader and more empty. "I did go to Morgan's house, I suppose you've talked to Jack Morgan and know about our little fracas. Anyway, I was there when Mr. Morgan was struck, but I don't see how I can add anything to what you already know, Dr. Watson. There was a great deal of confusion after the shots were fired what with everybody running to get away. Fortunately, his footman and Tarkenton kept their heads and went to Morgan's assistance, as did I. Poor Wagner was beyond assisting."

"*You* went to provide assistance?"

"Yes, certainly. Not that I was of any help. By the time I got near I could see Morgan's staff had the situation well in hand."

"May I ask why you chose to stay and be a part of the crowd at Morgan's house that morning?"

Again, his features seemed to converge as he considered the question. "It's a little embarrassing to tell. You see, Mr. Morgan and I had a bit of a falling out a while back. I asked Miss Juliet to be my wife and she declined. I felt it wasn't her decision alone, and I'm afraid I wasn't very gentlemanly about it. Regardless, Mr. Morgan has always been very gracious to mother, and has done me a good turn from time to time, so I wanted to put things right. I wasn't invited to the wedding—I understood that of course—but I thought I might catch Mr. Morgan for a moment before the breakfast, congratulate him, and make clear there were no longer hard feelings on my part. Anyway, Jack Morgan made sure that didn't happen, but I decided to stay to be a part of the welcome to Mr. Morgan as a sort of show of respect, and I guess I hoped he might see me and recognize I wanted to make amends."

McIlvaine looked away from Watson, and appeared to consider the quality of the shoe shine he'd gotten the day before. Watson screwed his face into a display of understanding, and for the moment pursued another line of questioning.

"I take it you are still living the single life, Mr. McIlvaine?"

"You mean have I found someone to take Miss Juliet's place in my affections? No, not yet, but please don't think of me as pining away for lost love. It was two years ago that all this happened and I assure you my life is far from empty."

"I must ask in that regard, Mr. McIlvaine, who are the attractive ladies pictured in the photograph?" Watson pointed to a framed picture on one of the book-lined shelves for which a space had been carefully carved out. It showed two young women in formal gowns, one in profile looking demurely to the ground, the other full-face, prettier, and staring confidently at the camera.

The picture was to his back, but McIlvaine answered without turning. "Those are two of the Morgan daughters, I did think it a striking photograph and yes, one of them—the woman looking straight out—is Juliet. It's a picture I was given before the unpleasantness around my proposal. I've kept it because the people were then, and I believe are still family friends."

McIlvaine looked stoically ahead. Watson supposed appearances were meant to be deceiving. "Mr. McIlvaine, I apologize for raising issues that may be disagreeable, I assure you it's necessary I do so, and I would be harshly criticized if I didn't pose them to you." McIlvaine imagined a severe tongue-lashing from Sherlock Holmes; Watson imagined a disappointed stare from Mrs. Hudson.

"I need to know if you own a revolver."

McIlvaine's mouth opened wide. "Surely you don't suspect ... but I suppose you must suspect everyone, mustn't you. Well, well, well." There was a pause, but he found no new words to express his surprise, "Well, well, well." And then a wry smile coincided with an unexpected invitation. "Come with me, Doctor, if you would."

Watson followed McIlvaine down the hall past a dining room and bedroom, stopping finally at a locked door. McIlvaine extracted a key from his waistcoat and opened the door to reveal an extensive, if largely outdated arsenal. Mounted on one wall was a blunderbuss, two muskets and several muzzle-loading rifles; another wall held a collection of breech loading and revolving rifles; while a third had flintlocks, and a variety of single-action and double-action revolvers. A cabinet with pull-out trays stood against the one bare wall. The only other furniture in the room was a large table in its center on which the parts of a handgun were spread.

"In answer to your question, Dr. Watson, I do own a revolver and numerous other guns as you can see. I'm a bit of a collector. It's not something I talk about a great deal. In fact, you're one of a very few people who've been inside this room. Too many might get the wrong idea, and think because you collect guns you must be violent and irresponsible. I'm only telling you of my hobby because there's a good chance your Mr. Holmes will learn about it anyway. And to answer your next question nearly all of these are working models."

"Thank you for being so forthcoming, Mr. McIlvaine. I must ask, however, do you carry a revolver yourself?"

"I'm sure you've noticed that this is still a rather desolate area. I'm often out quite late so yes, I do carry a revolver. In fact, I'm quite a good shot, Doctor." McIlvaine opened the top tray of the cabinet revealing a careful arrangement of ribbons and medallions. "I've even won a few awards for trap shooting." It struck Watson that McIlvaine was taking great pleasure in the effect he was creating with the revelation of an unexpected side to his life.

"Make no mistake, Doctor, the only targets for my shooting are inanimate. I don't even hunt." McIlvaine replaced the tray, and with a broad smile for Watson, spoke with a forcefulness absent before he entered his armory. "I wonder if I haven't addressed all your issues, Dr. Watson. I should really be getting on with my day."

"Of course. Just one last question, Mr. McIlvaine. May I assume you will be staying in town for the next several days?"

McIlvaine gave vent to a high pitched giggle, yet another unexpected quality in the man. "My rent is paid through the month, Doctor Watson, and I enjoy the location too much to contemplate leaving any time after that." He led them out of the room, taking care to lock the door behind them; then strolled to the entry hall without looking to Watson trailing behind.

"It was good to meet you, Dr. Watson. I doubt we'll be seeing each other again so let me take this opportunity to wish you well during your stay in New York." He opened the front door, shook hands with Watson, and watched him to the elevator before closing the door again. Unlike Holmes, Watson did not assure his interviewee that he'd see him again although he was equally certain he would.

7.
Exiting the Tombs

In the beginning, she had felt certain there would be quick recognition of the error that had been made and William would be released. Then, it appeared the process would take time, but Caroline remained confident justice would be done. Now, she thought herself a fool for ever believing they could get fair treatment. The situation was exactly as William described it. Justice was a commodity to be purchased like any other. And whoever had the most money could buy the justice he desired. Mr. Morgan and his class had a great deal of money, and Mr. Morgan wanted William in prison. He sold the newspapers on the idea of William as a dangerous radical, and the public believed what they read in the newspapers. William already stood convicted in the court of public opinion, the trial would be a formality. William said it all made for a grand diversion. By tying him to the radicals and making him the enemy, Morgan and his ilk would get more sympathy for themselves and less scrutiny for their business practices.

Even the lawyer who had been willing to take William's case had urged him to plead guilty and ask for clemency. Of course, their lawyer didn't appear old enough to shave. William told him he wasn't pleading guilty to anything he didn't do. At which the lawyer said he couldn't be responsible for what was certain to happen and quit.

That's when they decided to take matters into their own hands—theirs and Candy's and Lucy's. For just a moment her aunt's offer to have Sherlock Holmes help them posed a temptation, but the offer came too late and held no guarantee of success. Everything was already in play to act on this day—Sunday—when there would be the largest number of visitors to the Tombs, the courts would be closed, and the police that served them would be gone.

For Caroline, Lucy was the weak link in their plans and before leaving for the Tombs, she asked Lucy to act her part in the pantomime one last time.

"Who are you, ma'am?" Caroline began.

"I'm Mary Chandler. I'm Caroline's American cousin on her father's side."

"Good. I'm sure the officer won't ask you, but just in case it was your grandparents that came to America. That will explain your not having an English accent. And how far along are you?" Caroline stared at the protuberance that covered Lucy's stomach.

"I'm expecting a little bundle in another two months or so." A considerable amount of planning had gone into determining how large the protuberance should be for seven months of pregnancy. Mrs. Guskin had been called in to give her opinion, and the three childless women spent several hours negotiating the proper size of Lucy's artificially swollen stomach.

"What are you to say if you're asked about traveling in your advanced state?"

"I just had to be here for my cousin. And the midwife says it's perfectly safe for me to travel."

"That's fine," Caroline said with undisguised relief. Lucy didn't always seem to appreciate the gravity of the situation, and on this day she was to play a critical role. Indeed, it promised to be a long day for all of them. At this time tomorrow they might all be celebrating William's freedom or be under arrest with him.

Preparation for the emergence of the very pregnant Mary Chandler had begun several days earlier, before anyone imagined there being a Mary Chandler. On her visit to the Tombs that day, William told her that many of the prisoners on the second tier (neither of them called it by its common name, Murderers' Row) furnished their cells to their liking, adding rugs and furniture, with one prisoner even having paintings brought to him. William said you just had to get the Warden's permission, and if it wasn't too much trouble he'd like to get a pillow and blanket. He explained that the pillow he had was "flat as a pancake," and the blanket thin and badly torn. Caroline told him it would be no trouble.

That led to talk about how much she meant to him, followed by how much he meant to her with agreement finally on how much they meant to each other. They talked of the wedding they'd planned and the life they could have together, refusing to acknowledge the finality of the barred door between them. Finally, Caroline could no longer control her feelings, and through the sobs she'd kept to herself all the days of their ordeal, she spoke of how terribly unfair it all was, and how there had to be a way for him to be set free. William stroked her with words and gently made clear the reality he saw daily. Escape was not possible. Even if he could somehow get the key that unlocked the cells on his tier, even if he could somehow overpower the two guards who patrolled the second floor cells, there would still be the police and the guards downstairs, to say nothing of the police who'd be called as soon as word got out about an escape. They agreed finally not to talk about it further. For now, they would do what they could to reduce William's discomfort, maybe later they would find a way to do more.

When visiting hours were over, Caroline lingered behind the others making their way to the street, until she was certain she would have Sergeant Norbert to herself. She approached him with a timidity she was certain he'd appreciate, and made the one word she spoke sound as a question, "Officer?"

"May I help you, ma'am?"

"I hope so, Officer, I wanted to see the Warden if you can arrange that. I was hoping to bring some things to my fiancé who's a prisoner here."

Sergeant Norbert smiled at the familiar request. He was certain Warden Fallon would want to see the woman he recognized as Caroline Littleberry. "I'll be happy to take you to see the Warden, Miss Littleberry." He fumbled through the center drawer of his desk before finding a large ring more than half filled with a collection of keys. He grinned to Caroline. "Never want to be without these."

They strolled across the now deserted center hall with Caroline twice repeating her appreciation for Sergeant Norbert's assistance, and Sergeant Norbert reporting accurately that it was no trouble at all. He knocked on the door marked WARDEN'S OFFICE; then opened it just wide enough to insert his head.

"Miss Littleberry would like to meet with Warden Fallon on a matter of furnishings for a cell."

The woman behind the typewriter looked at Sergeant Norbert as if the door's opening had admitted a disagreeable odor.

"I'll see if Warden Fallon is available."

She knocked softly, then entered and closed his door behind her. When she returned, she resumed her seat behind the typewriter before giving the Sergeant a curt nod. Without so much as a glance to Caroline, the secretary directed a cautionary message to the Sergeant.

"He will see Miss Littleberry, but I need to remind you, Sergeant, the Mayor of Buffalo will be stopping by in a very short time. Mayor Gilroy would like the Warden to see him and his party when they arrive. I'll thank you to notify us."

Sergeant Norbert was well aware of the visit, and gave assurance the Warden would be properly alerted.

As Caroline hesitated at the door to the Warden's office, his secretary gave her instruction without looking up from the typewriter on which she had resumed her work. "You may go in now, Miss Littleberry."

Caroline opened the door and stepped barely inside it. As she did, Warden James Fallon pushed down on his desk and raised himself to his feet. He came nearly erect and gave her nearly a smile before settling himself back in his chair. "Miss Littleberry, please sit. Tell me, what is it I can do for you?"

As had Holmes and Watson before her, Caroline rejected the couches along the side walls and took a chair across the desk from Fallon. She had a sudden fear that William might have misunderstood what people said and she would be requesting something she shouldn't, and might even get William in trouble for making the request. Still, neither Sergeant Norbert nor the Warden's secretary had acted as if there was anything inappropriate about her request.

"I was wondering, sir ... I've been told that prisoners could have some things in their cells if it's alright with you." She looked to Fallon for a sign she was on the right course.

"That's true, Miss Littleberry, we see no reason to make life more difficult for our prisoners than it already is. What is it you were thinking of providing ... you're speaking of Mr. Wilson, I take it?"

"It is William, yes sir. Just a blanket and pillow, if that's alright, and maybe some of his clothes."

"That's very reasonable, Miss Littleberry, and very sensible, if I may say so." There was again the near smile. "You may also want to bring him some food from time to time. The food here is very nourishing of course, but there's nothing like something from home to lift the spirit."

Caroline's own smile was genuine and spoke to the relief she felt. "That's very kind of you, sir, I hadn't thought about food."

Fallon took off his glasses and spoke in a dull flat tone as though he was giving a well practiced set of directions—as indeed he was. "I'm not sure it's been explained to you, Miss Littleberry, but we have to levy a modest charge in association with the additions we allow prisoners. That allows us to record and process the changes, and to dispose of any goods or materials should that prove necessary. In your case the charge is modest because you're asking for very little. Let us say two dollars and fifty cents ... no, let's make it just two." Fallon replaced his glasses, and again let his face approximate a smile.

142

Before Caroline could respond, the door at her back opened and she heard the secretary's voice advising Warden Fallon that the delegation from Buffalo had arrived, and Mayor Gilroy would appreciate it if he'd step out for a moment and address the group. She added that the Mayor had expressed a concern they were running late.

The Warden grunted his understanding of the secretary's admonition. He rose, this time to a fully erect posture, scraped from his desk a ring of keys that had been lost until that moment among stacks of paper, and tossed them in a lower drawer. Caroline stood, thinking she would have to leave. Instead, he invited her to remain in the outer office with his secretary. He never introduced the two women, stopping only long enough to ask his secretary to look after Miss Littleberry until he returned. With that, Fallon went to meet the men from Buffalo. Caroline smiled vaguely to the woman at the typewriter. The woman at the typewriter showed the same warm hospitality she had displayed earlier. There being no chair other than the one occupied by the secretary, Caroline stood beside a file cabinet in a corner of the room attempting and failing to look at ease.

When Fallon returned a long few minutes later, he waved Caroline back to his office. She seated herself, and without further discussion the Warden pressed her for a decision about adding items to Wilson's cell. She agreed to come to his office the next day with a blanket and pillow for William, and two dollars for him. The Warden stood and Caroline followed suit; he thanked her for coming, nodded toward either Caroline or the door behind her, and after seating himself, began thumbing through papers while Caroline made her way out. She turned at the door, mumbled a last "thank you, sir," and left without exchanging her first word with the secretary or any further word with Sergeant Norbert. Once outside the Tombs, she took a deep breath and started for her temporary home in Brooklyn, and as long a bath as she could manage.

That night Lucy cooked dinner for Caroline, Candy and Candy's older brother, Micah, who was staying with Candy for a few days. They formed a marked contrast in mood. Lucy was, as always, in good humor and anxious to see others the same. Candy and Micah were near to bursting with excitement, but intent on exercising appropriate restraint in light of Caroline's low spirits. Candy had had a good day with the Bridegrooms. He'd been moved into the starting line-up for the team's slumping third baseman, had gotten a key hit and made several slick fielding plays. The good fielding was unsurprising; it was the reason he had been able to stick with the club as long as he had. The key hit was a surprise to everyone including Candy who had no illusions about his skills as a batter.

Candy and Lucy encouraged Caroline to share her day in the hope of finding a bright spot she had missed. She sighed her reluctance to review another day spent with William inside the Tombs, and only agreed to speak to give proof of how disheartening her day had been. She became briefly animated in describing her encounter with Fallon. She told of his agreeing to allow her to bring a blanket and pillow to William for a two dollar fee, and of the visit from the Mayor of Buffalo, and watching him scoop up the keys that could have given William his freedom, how near they seemed and how impossibly far away.

When she was done, Candy clapped his hands and shouted, "Wonderful," then repeated himself, and sat smiling to the utter bewilderment of Caroline and Lucy, and the uncomprehending delight of Micah. Candy set down his knife and fork, and announced he knew a way to get Brakeman out of the Tombs. When he had finished sharing his thinking, even Caroline felt some small surge of optimism about the future. The odds were still against them, but they seemed a little shorter after hearing Candy's idea—maybe even more than a little. They spent the rest of the evening elaborating a plan based on Candy's idea. When she finally got to bed, Caroline slept more soundly than she had for days.

A little past sunrise Candy set out for Eastern Park. With the early hour and no game scheduled for the day, he was certain no one else would be at the park. He used his key to gain access to the room that housed both equipment and a small workout area. Some time back, he had told the Bridegrooms manager he needed to be able to exercise regularly to stay game ready since he wasn't playing regularly. He had meant it at the time. Then he met Lucy Donaldson and found other use for his spare time, but he kept the key. Now, he ignored the Indian clubs and medicine balls, and went straight to a high shelf in a corner of the room on which were stacked two catchers' masks, and a variety of gloves that shared the qualities of age and disrepair. They were the gloves players had brought with them when they joined the Bridesgrooms. They had been cast aside, but were too much a part of their owners' lives and careers to be destroyed. Candy was intent on locating the materials used to help create the gloves they now wore. He found what he was looking for farther down the same shelf.

Neatly aligned one on top of another were 12 pieces of wax, each one nearly a foot in length and eight inches in width—somewhat larger than a large man's hand. Indeed, their purpose was to make a mold of a player's hand to allow a new glove to be fashioned.

He returned to Lucy's apartment in time for breakfast, and to make his prize available to Caroline before she started for the Tombs. The two pieces of wax he brought were cut nearly in half. The two larger sections were inserted at the top of a stocking that reached well above Caroline's knee, a small reticule was put in place at the top of her other stocking, both the wax pieces and the reticule were tied around her thighs to guarantee they'd stay in place. The additions to her wardrobe were well hidden beneath her petticoat and a dress that reached nearly to the ground.

At 10AM, Caroline was back inside the Warden's office. Fallon made no pretense of sociability on this occasion. He took from Caroline a blanket, pillow, change of clothes, and two dollars. He promised all but the two dollars would be delivered to Wilson before the day was out.

With visiting hours already well under way, Caroline first explained the reason for her delay to Wilson, then shared with him the plans developed the past evening. He stared at her wide-eyed while she outlined the steps in his escape. When she was done and after he had swallowed several gulps of air, Wilson stammered out a barrage of questions which she answered as best she could, admitting there were some areas still to be worked out. When visiting hours ended at two, they vowed their love as they always did, this time sharing a solemnity their vows hadn't known before. Caroline returned the entry ticket to the admissions officer who had issued it, and wished him a "good evening" as she had every other afternoon.

At 6:20PM, Caroline returned to the now deserted center hall of the Tombs. Her "good evening" to Sergeant Norbert's replacement was now a greeting, and a prelude to the next step in the plan to free William.

"I've done something awful, Sergeant ...," Caroline looked in vain for some indication of the man's name."

"It's Officer, Officer Peterman, and what terrible thing have you done, Miss ...."

"Littleberry. Caroline Littleberry. I'm afraid I've lost my purse, and I think I might have left it here. I mean someplace in the building. I was visiting William Wilson until two, and spent the rest of the day in the City with a friend. I only realized about an hour ago my purse was missing. I went back to where I'd been with my friend, but it wasn't there. That's why I think I must have left my purse here. My keys are in it as well as most all my money so I can't take the cable cars to my apartment, or

146

get inside my apartment even if I could somehow find a way to get home."

"I'm awfully sorry, ma'am, I really am, but if you lost the purse on the cells I can't help you." The officer had been standing behind the desk in the reception hall since Caroline entered the building. He was tall and thin, and to Caroline's thinking, impossibly young. He looked truly pained by Caroline's dilemma.

"Haven't you any friends you could stay with, ma'am? Anyone in town who can take you in?"

"There's no one, I'm afraid. I wonder … Officer Peterman, I wonder if it would be possible …" Caroline pouted her prettiest and most pitiable, "do you think I might get a look inside the Warden's office? You see, before I went to the cells to see my fiancé I met with Warden Fallon in his office. It's just possible I forgot my bag in the Warden's office." Caroline's look turned sheepish. "I was that nervous on meeting with such an important man as the Warden."

Peterman saw the reasonableness of Caroline's request, but saw as well the demands of his position. "I'm sorry, ma'am, I'm not permitted to leave the reception area, anyway not until my replacement shows up, and that's not until midnight. Are you absolutely certain there's no friend or family you could stay with?"

"I only wish there was." Caroline appeared to Officer Peterman to be near to tears. "Couldn't I go look in the office. Just for a minute. I'll come right back out. I promise."

Officer Peterman swallowed hard and shook his head violently at the prospect of such a dereliction of his duties. "I couldn't possibly do that, ma'am. That would be way against my orders." He stiffened his posture to make clear the impossibility of her request, but Caroline's pleading had taken its toll, and while he wasn't prepared to break the rules, he was already considering how he might bend them.

147

"I'll tell you what I can do. If we make it really quick, ma'am, I'll go with you into Warden Fallon's office and we can see if you dropped your purse somewhere. But it has to be quick. I won't be doing this at all except I don't want you walking the streets all night."

Caroline's thanks to Officer Peterman were heartfelt and genuine—as were the renewed feelings of guilt she was suffering for involving a well-meaning bystander in her necessary, but disagreeable deception.

He pulled out the massive key ring she had last seen in Sergeant Norbert's possession and proceeded to the Warden's office, his eyes shifting frequently from side to side as if expecting his superiors to materialize suddenly and wreak the vengeance he feared. One time there was a sound at the front door and he turned to it quickly, prepared to recant this moment of betrayal, but the door stood silently shut and he decided it was only nerves.

Caroline followed a respectful two steps behind. She, too, heard the front door, and she knew it wasn't Officer Peterman's nerves. He opened the door to the outer office, turned on its electric light—an impressive recent addition to the building—and the two of them undertook a search of the secretary's office. Hers was cursory, his thorough. Fearing that his diligence might disrupt their plans, she reported having spent little time with the secretary; she had, she said, only been in her office waiting to see the Warden and would, she was certain, have kept her reticule with her the whole time. Peterman nodded, but seemed reluctant to invade the Warden's office.

When he finally unlocked Fallon's door, the search for the missing reticule became intense on both their parts, but was almost immediately interrupted. Peterman's worst fears were suddenly realized. There was someone in the reception hall he had deserted, and that someone sounded loud, aggressive and very drunk. Peterman looked to Caroline, looked to the noise

148

two doors away, and quickly determined where his first responsibility lay.

"Stay here. Don't touch anything, I'll be right back."

While Peterman went to attend to a boisterous but quite sober Micah Cochrane, Caroline lifted her dress to withdraw two pieces of wax from the top of her stocking, and then opened the right hand bottom drawer of Warden Fallon's massive desk. As if in answer to her silent, but very fervent prayer, the ring of keys was sitting on top of two thick volumes of *Detention Facilities Policies and Procedures*. It occurred to her suddenly that while William had assured her that a single key opened all the cells on his tier, she had no idea how to recognize which key was the prize. It was something they hadn't discussed in all their hours of planning. She fumbled through the ring of keys with fingers gone suddenly stiff, and an awareness that Micah could not detain Officer Peterman for long without risking his own arrest. In spite of all the care taken, everything seemed about to come undone because of this one thing they hadn't considered. This one essential thing.

Caroline was ready to give it up, meet with Candy and the others, tell them things hadn't worked out, and try to come up with another plan for another time—when she suddenly realized the Warden had provided the solution to her problem. He, too, needed a system to distinguish between the many keys on the ring, and when she turned the ring in an opposite direction, she discovered that the gold colored discs, at whose backs she had been staring, separated the sets of keys, and on the sides newly revealed, indicated the areas to which they gave entry. She worked her away around the ring until she came to the disc inscribed TIER IIA, the same identifier as was etched into the arch under which she passed daily to see William. She laid her prize flat against the wax piece she had set at the edge of the desk, then, standing on tiptoes, she pressed a second wax piece over the key and transmitted as much of her weight as she could through her two hands. She became aware the scuffle in the center hall was beginning to subside, and she gave a final push before deciding that the risk of discovery outweighed any further gain to the precision of the impression she was creating. She wiped the keys free of any remaining wax, put them back in the drawer, and put the two pieces of wax back in her stocking, again tying them securely to her leg. She removed the reticule from her other stocking, then kicked the small purse out of sight beneath Warden Fallon's couch as the now heavily breathing Officer Peterman reappeared.

"Was there some difficulty, Officer?"

"Nothing really. Just someone who had a few too many and wandered into the wrong building. Good thing for him the police station here closes at six or he would be spending the night with us. Have you found anything?"

"I didn't see it sitting out anyplace, and I didn't want to move things around before you got back. I should probably retrace my steps from when I was here earlier. I first came to about here." She walked to a spot halfway between the door and the desk. "And then the Warden asked me to sit on that couch." She pointed to the couch under which the reticule now lay.

Peterman grunted. "Let's start there." He looked doubtfully to the tightly meshed cushions, then dropped to his knees and peered beneath the furniture. "Here it is." He pulled out the purse and showed Caroline a broad, if perplexed grin. "It's such a little thing you must have kicked it under while you were speaking with Warden Fallon."

"Oh, I'm sure you're right, I must have done just that. Thank you so much, Officer."

He blushed appreciation for her gratitude, and escorted her back to the entrance hall. "It's been a pleasure meeting you, Miss Littleberry, and I'm glad you were able to find your purse."

Caroline echoed and reechoed her gratitude to Officer Peterman as she bid him good-bye at the door. She turned left on leaving the Tombs, then left again at the corner where Candy and Micah were waiting. She gave the wax impressions to

150

Candy. He would take them to a friend who knew a man who would manufacture the key without questioning its origins or future use.

It took two days and twenty dollars to get the key. It joined a large-size woman's traveling suit, blouse, and hat and veil to make up the bundle that was Mary Chandler's pregnancy. Her child-bearing state established, Mary Chandler made her first visit to the Tombs, and Caroline made what she hoped would be her last.

Once inside the building, Caroline lifted the heavy veil she wore to discourage attention from the press. While press interest had, in fact, nearly disappeared, it was still seen as appropriate for Caroline to protect her privacy. Secretly, most of the correctional staff sympathized with Caroline, none of them having a positive view of the press or its methods.

The officer looked to the enlarged middle of the woman named Mary Chandler, and scraped her admission ticket along his jaw before handing it to her, advising her she would need to return it when she left. All the while his eyes never left the large bulge that held a woman's clothing.

Lucy saw the officer's stare and felt obliged to answer his unstated inquiry. "I know I probably shouldn't be here, but I couldn't very well leave my favorite cousin in the whole world to deal with this terrible situation all by herself, could I?"

The officer shook his head slowly side to side in exaggerated agreement with Mary Chandler. "No, I suppose not."

"And the midwife says it's perfectly safe." Lucy had now delivered all parts of the discussion about her pregnancy she had prepared, and with a less than gentle nudge from Caroline, the two women left the red-faced admissions officer to make their way to William Wilson's cell.

As she did on every visit, Caroline leaned close against the cell's latticework. Her action was not unusual. Simply to see

151

the prisoner through the tight cross-hatching of the bars required putting oneself beside the door; to speak intimately required the visitor to press against it. Caroline smiled her greeting to William and he gave as cheerful a response as he could manage, both of them were intent on making the day appear normal. Caroline reminded him he must certainly remember her cousin, Mary Chandler. William assured her he did. The pantomime was not really necessary. The two officers assigned to the second tier were having the usual busy Sunday. Mary Chandler's advanced state of pregnancy was something of a novelty, but merited only a glance. There were 35 to 40 mothers, wives, sweethearts, friends, sisters and brothers lingering outside 25 to 30 prisoners' cells. The unit was a jumble of sounds—scolding, pleading, apologizing, arguing, mourning. And from every side there sounded pledges of eternal love. Most wouldn't survive the day's visit, some would carry to the grave.

Caroline knew the peak time for visiting was eleven o'clock. The late risers and the church goers arrived by then, and those who timed their visits to be completed before lunch would still be in attendance. It was during that late morning their plans would go into effect. Until that time the two women exchanged the smallest of small talk with William, and he reciprocated in kind.

At exactly eleven fifteen, Mary Chandler collapsed in a heap outside William Wilson's cell. The sight of a very pregnant woman lying prone outside a prisoner's cell elicited shock in some, curiosity in most, and intense activity on the part of one observer. The nearer of the two guards ran to where the woman lay, calling as he drew close for everyone to step back and give her room, although he and Caroline were the only ones who had moved to her side. He bent over to make closer study, at which point Mary Chandler opened her eyes and murmured weakly, "Water, could I please have some water," then closed her eyes again.

"I was afraid the excitement might cause this, but she insisted on coming," Caroline said. "I think she'll be alright if she can just lie down someplace and get some water. I should also loosen her clothes—but not out here. Would it be possible …" Caroline bit her lower lip in a show of desperation. "Could she lie down on William's cot and somebody bring her some water while I undo her garments. Of course, not with William there." Caroline looked to the officer with the same plaintive expression that had once attracted scores of patrons to her parents' pie stand in Brighton.

"I've an idea, Miss. We'll put the young lady on Wilson's cot, and I'll take Wilson with me to get her some water. I won't have her drinking out of his glass. You do what you have to do for her and I'll get back as quick as I can."

"Thank you, officer. I'm sure she'll be fine, but do give me time to …"—the lower lip received another nip—"to do all I have to."

The guard was already gently helping Mary Chandler to her feet. "I understand, Miss, and I'll shoo the crowd from the cell so you can have privacy." He leaned down to Caroline and his voice became suddenly confidential, and so solicitous she again had to remind herself of the necessity for their deception. "I got six of me own at home and there was none of them was easy on the missus, but there's not one of them she'd give back, and your friend will feel the same." He opened the cell door, ordered Wilson into the back corner opposite the bed, and then gently helped Mary Chandler to lie down.

"Wilson, you'll come with me. You're to walk in front of me with my hand on your right shoulder. If you don't feel my hand on your shoulder, you stop dead in your tracks and you don't move until you feel it again." He didn't wait for a response from Wilson, instead turning his attention to the five or six people who had drifted over to Wilson's cell. He responded to a question Caroline could not hear. "The little lady is in good hands and will be just fine. Now, I don't want no congregatin'

153

out here. The ladies have got to do some female things and I don't want them bein' stared at while that's goin' on, so all of you just move back and go about your business."

The officer propelled Wilson down the walkway, the people who had gathered now disbursed, and Caroline was left alone with Lucy in the shadows at the back of William Wilson's cell. Together, they loosened the dress and divested Mary Chandler of her pregnancy. They removed the bag tied around her waist and unrolled the clothing and key inside. They covered the bag's contents with the cell's ragged blanket, then restored Mary Chandler to pregnancy through the use of the pillow and blanket Caroline had brought for Wilson earlier.

The officer returned, still propelling Wilson before him. He announced himself before arriving, calling out his request to enter the cell. Caroline informed him it was safe to enter, and had Lucy sit with her at the edge of William's cot blocking from view the shabby blanket and all it concealed. Mary Chandler drank from the glass offered and, in answer to the officer's question, declared she had no need of a doctor. Caroline suggested instead it would be well to get her cousin home and allow her to rest. Mary Chandler nodded her weary support, and the officer grunted his agreement as he backed his way out to allow the women to leave, and to lock Wilson back in.

In spite of the general agreement about Mary Chandler's need to get home and rest, she and Caroline were stopped from leaving the Tombs by the Tier II admissions officer. In the excitement Mary discovered she had mislaid the admission ticket she was required to hand back before leaving. The women volunteered to go back and look for the ticket, but the admissions officer told them it wouldn't be necessary "this one time," waving them through after Mary staggered briefly and fell against her cousin.

Once outside the two women walked two blocks, found an empty doorway, and the pregnant Mary Chandler was restored to a barren Lucy Donaldson. Caroline walked with

Lucy to the cable car that would take her to the ferry and back to Brooklyn. Caroline was now ready to return to the Tombs for the final act in the drama that was to be William's escape.

She smiled a second greeting to the admissions officer who gave her a second admissions ticket. He asked after Mary Chandler, and Caroline said she was feeling much better and thanked him for his interest. She made her way along the tier's walkway, repeating the message she had given the admissions clerk to the several inquiries she received along the way, before coming finally to the second cell from the last where William waited. It was nearing one o'clock, and the visitors were gone from the last cell as they always were by lunchtime. Caroline again stood close against the bars, positioning herself so that her back was to everyone but William. She remained in that position even when there was the angry voice of a stranger in the admissions area at the far end of the walkway, demanding to know how his pregnant sister could have been allowed on the tier, expressing outrage in colorful terms regarding the lack of judgment, gross insensitivity, and possible blindness of the admissions officer in particular, and the jail management in general. He asserted that the damage done to his sister was indescribable, although he proceeded to describe it in vivid detail. He could only hope the baby didn't appear before its time, that it was not seriously deformed, and that the mother survived the ordeal.

Although unseen, his voice drew the attention of the Tier IIA guards, who moved to the end of the walkway where they would be able to hear more clearly, and of the visitors and prisoners whose conversations quieted lest they miss a single charge the man was leveling at their common adversary. While everyone else gave rapt attention to the disembodied voice, Caroline accepted from William the key that had been placed beneath his blanket. In concert with the speaker's full-throated complaints she worked the key into the lock and turned it to the

155

right. She pulled the door cautiously toward her; then pulled harder, but it stayed stubbornly locked. She felt the perspiration on her body, and became aware their fate depended on the skillfulness of a man none of them had met or knew anything about. William continued to offer soft encouragement through a tightly clenched jaw, but she heard none of it. She took a deep breath and offered her second prayer in the past few days to a God to Whom she hadn't spoken in years, and found the key turning finally to the left. And then, whether the result of the Deity's intercession or the locksmith's skill, there was a click as the key connected inside the lock, and turned slowly, but very surely to the left. She pulled the door to her to be certain it would open, then closed the unlocked door and handed the key back to William through the narrow latticework. Both found themselves exhausted from the effort.

Some distance away, the infuriated visitor could still be heard, but softer now, and silent for brief periods, as though listening to a staff member's ameliorative words. Finally, the visitor called out, "Okay, I'm leaving now," the voice loud again, and then the infuriated visitor was heard no more. Had Officer Peterman been on duty, he would have recognized Mary Chandler's brother as the drunk who wandered into the wrong building some nights before, but Officer Peterman was at home fast asleep, and Mary Chandler's brother was a stranger to Sergeant Norbert.

Caroline had taken her final turn on the detention center stage. She left before the end of visitors' time, indicating a need to get back to Mary Chandler as she returned her admissions ticket to the officer. It was now left to William to give his own farewell performance.

At 1:50, with ten minutes remaining in visiting hours, a large woman in a heavy veil and traveling suit peeked out the slit of the barely open door of William Wilson's cell. Satisfying herself that attention was focused on the clusters of visitors farther down the walkway, she eased her way out of the cell and quickly, and as noiselessly as she could, shut the door behind her. She steeled herself to move slowly along the narrow catwalk, stubbornly resisting the impulse to hurry her way along. Speed, she knew, would create suspicion, and suspicion could undo everything.

The bell sounded at two and the woman eased her way past one cluster of visitors, and lingered behind another. She held tightly to the admissions ticket that had earlier been given to Mary Chandler, and reported as lost in the excitement of her collapse. Her fellow visitors took note of her out of the corners of their eyes—it being impolite to stare—but no one did more than look.

The admissions officer took her ticket as he studied the large woman. He was certain he hadn't seen her before; he would surely have noticed her. She must have come while Finkle was filling in for him when he went to lunch, or maybe when he was on his break. Whatever the case, she had a ticket and he had no reason to detain her. Besides which, there were a number of people behind her anxious to leave the Tombs. He, himself, was hoping to grab a cup of coffee before finishing his shift and heading home. He gave her a non-committal grunt, and turned his attention to the next woman in line who was holding her ticket with outstretched arm as if it was a small torch and she was in a huge cave.

The large woman measured the pace of her exit by the pace of those around her, fighting anew the urge to speed her way to freedom. Finally outside, she turned the corner and, like Caroline before her, she found Candy Cochrane seated atop the carriage he had rented. Micah sat beside him and Caroline was in the seat behind, nearly hidden under the canvas top. They stopped long enough to allow the large woman to climb to a place beside Caroline in a decidedly unladylike manner. The canvas hid the affectionate display between the two women that would have otherwise scandalized passers-by. Candy Cochrane shook the reins of the bay and they were off.

At the Tombs, the admissions officer couldn't shake the image of the large woman from his mind. He decided to forego his coffee, and instead went in search of Finkle to see if he remembered a big woman from the time he filled in for him. Finkle was the newest Tombs guard and so was assigned fill-in jobs. He was told it was in the interest of his career that he experience the various jobs that had to be performed at the detention center. It was what they told all new employees who were given no single assignment, but always seemed to get the least desirable ones.

Finkle had been sent to the kitchen to supervise the youngsters from the Boy's Prison who were to help the cook prepare meals, and clean up the kitchen when the preparations were done. The officer's job was to keep the boys from helping themselves to whatever food they could fit into the small pockets of their uniforms, and to make certain their sweeping went beyond piling the dirt in distant corners or behind the kitchen's fixtures. It wasn't a bad job for the officer during the winter when the kitchen's heat was tolerable if not desirable, but it was spring and New York was having a particularly warm spring.

Pausing only to instruct one Jeremiah Goolsby to transfer the potato he had finished peeling from his pocket to the large pot in which it belonged, Finkle told his questioner that he remembered no such woman, although he was mostly concerned about giving and taking back tickets, and didn't look closely at all the people who passed his station.

Finkle's inability to recollect the woman was enough to send the officer hurrying back to the second tier to conduct a search of the cells. He started down one walkway of Tier IIA, calling each prisoner by name to come forward to be seen. When he got to the next to the last cell and called, "Wilson," he got no response. He opened the lattice door and, on the metal shelf above the sink, he found a straight razor, shaving cream and the remains of Wilson's flaring moustaches. On the cot were Wilson's clothes and a key that was a duplicate of the one the officer carried. He sprinted down the corridor to the office of the Deputy Warden whose bulk prohibited anything beyond a spirited walk to the office of the Warden. By 3:15 the New York City Police force had been alerted, and for good measure the assistance of the Pinkerton agency had been requested. The search for William Wilson was on again, this time with the information that he was likely traveling with Caroline Littleberry, and that he could be disguised as a woman.

The escapee and his co-conspirators hoped his absence from the Tombs won't be detected until dinner. That would give them time to be on the train out of town before anyone would know to search for them. They went first to a quiet section of Battery Park that Candy knew, where Caroline climbed down from the carriage and waited while Wilson changed his clothing and gender. In addition to bringing him his clothes, Candy had obtained a gray wig that William fit as best he could over his hair. Candy hadn't thought to bring charcoal to provide the lines in Wilson's face consistent with the character created. The disguise would not have won Holmes' approval, but might still work if no one looked too closely. Candy had thought to bring a revolver which he insisted Wilson carry "to be protected against whatever might come."

They arrived at the Grand Central Depot at 3:40 in plenty of time to catch the 4:10 New York Central to Buffalo with connections to Cleveland, but found the station surrounded by uniformed police, as well as men in frock coats and soft homburgs holding newspapers they let go limp from time to time as their eyes swept the crowd around them. Candy drove the carriage past the station as slowly as he could without arousing suspicion. No words were spoken, but all were agreed

159

the situation was impossible. Caroline would surely be recognized, and some sharp-eyed officer or Pinkerton would likely spot Wilson, grey wig notwithstanding.

Candy went a street beyond the station and pulled the carriage to the curb.

"They must have discovered Brakeman's escape. We need to figure something else out, but for now it's time for you to go back home, Micah."

Micah offered vigorous protest, but Caroline and William joined his brother in urging him to catch the train to Buffalo.

"You're what they call an accessory, Micah," William said, "and after they figure out about the drunk the other night and Mary Chandler's brother today, they'll be looking for you too. So far nobody knows who you are and we need to keep it that way."

Candy added his own reasoned argument. "Get going, Micah. Now."

As Micah started on his way to the station, Candy turned to his remaining passengers. "Any ideas?"

Caroline had been holding in readiness the answer to that question. "Take us to the Waldorf Hotel. A back entrance if you can find one."

8.
Sanctuary

Having received reports of the morning's interrogations from Holmes and Watson, Mrs. Hudson settled herself in the deepest easy chair in her parlor and began a leisurely review of Dr. Watson's meticulous notes and Holmes' informative, but rather less detailed account. An opinion was forming as to Morgan's attacker, but she wasn't one to rush things. Nor was she feeling any pressure to do so. Wilson was safely, if uncomfortably confined in New York's detention facility, giving her time to consider at length all those who could be seen as suspects. She had read as far as McIlvaine's arms collection when there was a rapid knocking on her door. It was too loud to be Holmes and too frenzied to be Watson. It came a second time before she had worked her way out of her easy chair, and a third time before she had crossed the room. By the time she reached the door she knew who stood on its other side. The frequency of the staccato pounding signaled an emergency, and there was only one person in New York she had encouraged to contact her in case of emergency. Opening the door, she was unsurprised to see that person; the man in the ill-fitting grey wig *was* a surprise—and an unwelcome one.

They hurried inside, Wilson searching the room as if satisfying himself none of their pursuers had preceded them. Caroline embraced Mrs. Hudson, clinging to her with relief as much as affection. She stepped back finally to make the proper, if unnecessary introduction.

"Auntie, this is William Wilson who I've been telling you about." The baseball pitcher managed a tentative smile. Mrs. Hudson nodded her own cautious greeting.

"I'm sorry, Auntie. We had nowhere else to go. William escaped from jail less than an hour ago. Of course, you know he's innocent." It was the fundamental truth Caroline saw as justifying their presence in Mrs. Hudson's hotel room. "We planned to take the train to get away, but there were police all around the station." Caroline looked her most pitiable. "Can you help us, Auntie?"

Mrs. Hudson was aware they had already gotten help. Someone had transported them first to the station and then to the hotel; that person had undoubtedly provided him the weapon causing the bulge in his jacket pocket. And Mrs. Hudson had a good idea who that person was.

"Of course, I'll do what I can. Tell me first, 'ow did you know which room was mine?"

"I asked at the reception desk."

"And was the clerk a short, heavy-set man wearin' rimless glasses that kept slidin' down 'is nose?"

"That's him, Auntie, that's the man exactly."

"Then we've no time to lose. We must go see Mr. 'Olmes at once."

Caroline and William assumed that Mrs. Hudson felt the need to call on the great detective to extricate them from their situation. In fact, Mrs. Hudson felt the need to leave her suite before her Pinkerton shadow arrived in response to the call his hotel informer would have made to him. Before leaving she gathered up one of the black formless dresses that had been her wardrobe before coming to New York; then hurried her visitors to the stairs and the two flights down to where Holmes and Watson had their rooms. She dared not make use of an elevator whose operator would be obliged to make known their whereabouts when questioned.

She was relieved to find there were no witnesses to their flight along the sixth floor corridor or their arrival on the fourth. She came to Watson's room first and knocked softly three times. Watson opened the door as promptly as she'd hoped, then stepped back on seeing the visitors accompanying Mrs. Hudson. Holmes came away from where he had been sitting by the window, the relaxing hour he had planned to spend with a pipe and his friend no longer a possibility.

162

Mrs. Hudson provided brief introductions although in fact all were familiar with each other. Holmes and Watson nodded in the general direction of Wilson and Caroline, and looked to Mrs. Hudson for explanation.

She recounted what she knew of the two fugitives' travels, then stated the problem that had led to her hurrying to see them.

"They got directions to my room from the clerk downstairs—the one you know is supplyin' information to the Pinkertons." Until that moment, Holmes had known nothing of a clerk supplying information to the Pinkertons, but he brushed past that small gap in knowledge.

"Then we'll need to move quickly to protect our young friends," Holmes said. "They will certainly come to mine and Watson's rooms when they get no answer at yours, Mrs. Hudson."

"They'll need disguises, Mr. 'Olmes. It's a good thing you thought to bring the make-up and costumes." Mrs. Hudson looked properly in awe of Holmes' good judgment, and Holmes allowed himself an indulgent smile.

"Yes, well, one never knows, Mrs. Hudson." Holmes looked disapprovingly at the gray wig, judging it a poor match to a face made suddenly boyish by the absence of its moustaches. "I'm certain we can improve on the disguise for Mr. Wilson. Miss Littleberry may prove more difficult, but we will still be left with a problem of where to take them since we have no allies in the City."

The "them" had settled hand in hand on Watson's settee, looking alternatively to Holmes and Mrs. Hudson as the two plotted their well-being. At the mention of locating a suitable refuge, Wilson joined the discussion. "I have friends on the Bridegrooms, Mr. Holmes, several of them with apartments in town; I'm sure we could find one willing to put us up."

Watson had been standing at the window watching the street for any sign of impending doom, and came away for the moment to join the conversation. He first answered Holmes' inquiring stare. "There's no sign of anything unusual on the street, Holmes. Still, I think we would all agree there's no time to contact Mr. Wilson's friends. Besides which, after the authorities get done with us, Mr. Wilson's friends would almost certainly be the next people contacted."

"Exactly right, Watson, but then who is there?" Holmes tapped his chin and looked to the ceiling for guidance while Watson returned to his station at the window.

Mrs. Hudson provided a welcome antidote to the gloom that had descended on the room. "There's something I plain forgot to tell you, Mr. 'Olmes, and I do apologize. You remember I made the acquaintance of a Mr. Washington after bringin' the young boy who works for 'im to where the two of them live. Mr. Washington said at the time 'e was in my debt— in fact, 'e made a great point of it. I'm sure 'e didn't 'ave anythin' like this in mind, but I'm sure as well 'e's a man of 'is word."

"And with this Mr. Washington there'd be no connection to Mr. Wilson or Miss Littleberry," Watson added, this time without leaving his post.

"It's an inspired suggestion, Mrs. Hudson," Holmes said, "although I do wish you had shared the information earlier." Mrs. Hudson's eyes widened for a long moment. She was willing to defer to Holmes' alleged good judgment to maintain the fictitious nature of their relationship; she was not inclined to suffer Holmes' criticism of her alleged poor judgment. Her back was to everyone but Holmes, making her displeasure visible to him alone, although the significance of her suddenly straightened shoulders was not lost on Watson.

Holmes elected to focus on the information revealed. "We should take steps to organize our disguises for the trip to see your Mr. Washington."

"We've not much time, Holmes. Our Pinkerton friend is just arriving. He appears to be alone." Watson's report

164

reestablished the gloom the discussion of refuge had briefly dispelled.

Mrs. Hudson spoke as though uncertain about her words. "We might 'ave a little bit of time. If the Pinkerton man is alone, 'e'll 'ave to guard the downstairs to make sure nobody gets away. 'E likely won't come up to the rooms until 'is colleagues get 'ere."

Holmes grunted agreement and went with Mrs. Hudson to his room to explore the contents of his trunk. When they returned it was with disguises and a detailed plan of action.

Mrs. Hudson stood with Watson at the window while Holmes set costumes and his makeup kit on Watson's bed, and gave directions. "We'll leave in two groups. They'll be looking for a man and a woman, maybe two women—one of them rather distinctive—so we'll provide two men leaving together, and later a woman leaving alone. We'll become men of the cloth—at least Mr. Wilson and I will—we'll be two brothers who have stopped at the hotel for light refreshments after attending mass at St. Patrick's Cathedral and taking a short constitutional. I'll be wearing a priest's habit and collar, and should be addressed as Father Lestrade. Mr. Wilson, who will be known as Brother Michael, will be wearing the robes of a Capuchin friar. I regret I did not bring a Jesuit habit which would be a great deal less conspicuous, although lacking the drama of the Capuchin robes. Mr. Wilson, you will take care to have the robes hide from view the revolver if you insist on carrying it. An armed Capuchin monk might create talk. We will, of course, have to shave a good part of the back of your head in light of the Order you are joining."

Wilson looked to Holmes in disbelief. Caroline gathered herself more quickly. "And what of me, Mr. Holmes? How do you propose I leave the hotel?"

"You will leave the hotel as a maid, Miss Littleberry, and exit through the staff's entrance. No doubt it will be under observation as well, but you will be in uniform. Between that, and the sheer number of hotel staff, as well as some few changes to your appearance, I feel certain we can be successful. Watson, you'll have to take charge here. As soon as I and Mr. Wilson have transformed ourselves, you'll need to talk one of the maids out of her uniform."

"I beg your pardon, Holmes." Watson looked incredulous while Mrs. Hudson glowered.

"It only sounds scandalous, Watson. I want you to locate one of the maids on this floor. You'll tell her you'd like to exchange the dress Mrs. Hudson has thoughtfully brought with her for her maid's outfit. You can explain that it's a bit of a joke you want to play on your wife back in London; you can say she accuses you of treating her like a maid, and you want to bring her a maid's outfit as a gift from the States. Offer her whatever seems a fair price."

"Miss Littleberry, you will then use the stairs and take care that no one sees you leave this floor. If anyone speaks to you, tell them you're Miss Noel, you're new and you're leaving early because you're not feeling well. You are to walk to the Holland House, take a cab at the back of the line of carriages there, and have the driver take you to St. Patrick's Cathedral where you will join Mr. Wilson and myself. If the coachman seems to wonder about a maid taking a carriage, tell him you just left work and need to be at the church for a baptism."

"Mr. Holmes, why are we going to St. Patrick's Cathedral once we're clear of the hotel? Why don't we go directly to this Mr. Washington?" Wilson was recovered sufficiently to ask about the strategy he took to be the product of Holmes' thinking.

Holmes smiled his confidence in the plan he had heard elaborated moments earlier. "It seems to me certain the Waldorf doorman will be questioned about people he's put into carriages and their destinations. It will not appear out of the ordinary for him to have put two men of the cloth into a carriage going to St. Patrick's Cathedral, whereas it might appear peculiar if the destination was a gambling den. Besides, we'll need Mrs. Hudson to be with us when we visit Mr. Washington, and her route to St. Patrick's will be rather more circuitous."

Having found his voice, William Wilson spoke his cooperation. "I'm ready to get started." Caroline slipped her hand into his, and all were now allied on a plan to elude the Pinkertons.

Holmes added a grizzled wig, graying moustache and beard to his own priest's costume; then added the lines and shading that furthered his appearance as an aging cleric. Finally, he assumed a posture appropriate to the weight he bore in caring for the many souls that were his responsibility.

Having lost a brief argument to wear the hood that was part of his robes, Wilson suffered with only brief complaint Mrs. Hudson's careful fashioning of a bald spot at the back of his head, and Holmes' addition of a somewhat unruly beard and moustache. Holmes stepped back to admire his work and decided the disguise was still incomplete. He dug deep into his trunk and came up with a pair of rimless round-lensed glasses that added a dimension of studiousness Holmes felt appropriate. Although not entirely satisfied with his creation, Holmes yielded to Watson's admonition that they needed to hurry things along. While the priest and his disciple strode to the stairs in the empty corridor, Watson went in search of a hotel maid roughly the size and shape of Mrs. Hudson.

Holmes and Wilson waited in a vestibule on the mezzanine level a few doors from the English Tea Room until certain the path they would follow was safe. When confident that it was, they hurried past the alcove leading to the door of the restaurant, before assuming a leisurely pace as they approached the center staircase descending to the reception area. Holmes' voice took on a somewhat nasal quality, a high pitch, and his best effort at an American accent as he extolled the quality of the tea and scones he pretended having just eaten.

"That was a delightful repast, wouldn't you agree, Brother Michael. Fit for a bishop I'd say."

Brother Michael looked up to his companion as though meeting him for the first time as, in a very real sense, he was.

"It was pretty good," he mumbled.

Holmes was about to take steps to improve Wilson's delivery, which he felt lacked appropriate gravity and any hint of sincerity, when he was interrupted by the respectful greetings of a middle-aged couple on the stairs.

"Good afternoon, Father, Brother."

Holmes nodded deeply to the two of them as Mrs. Hudson had recommended, but wondered if his first instinct to make the sign of the cross above them might not have been more largely appreciated.

The priest and the brother arrived on the first floor without further incident. They waded through tourists who had come to gawk at the Waldorf's marble floor and columns, its huge tapestries, the many electric lit chandeliers dangling from its timbered ceiling, and above all at the streams of people coming and going from its long curved reception desk. Any one of them could be a foreign dignitary or an American millionaire. They stared, too, at the middle-aged men huddling together in straight-backed chairs who might be planning the takeover of unsuspecting industries, or negotiating the framework of international agreements, the details of which would only become known weeks or months later—if they became known at all. The tourists provided a ready audience for a talented actor, and Holmes made no effort to resist a turn on the stage.

He adopted an ingratiating smile tinged with a modicum of the gravity he had found lacking in Wilson's delivery, and showered it on all in his path as he edged his way to the door. Brother Michael walked a few paces behind, unsuccessfully trying to achieve a degree of anonymity for himself. Now and again he'd come forward to join the good Father, a frosty smile affixed to his own face. Father Lestrade was nearing the door when he only just avoided crashing into a heavy-browed stocky man in a soft homburg and frock coat who had risen from his chair to greet a body of men, all of whom shared a dark intensity that identified them as engaged in either crime or law enforcement.

"I am so sorry, my son, I trust you are alright?" The smile seemed insincere and the voice sounded vaguely familiar to the heavy-browed stocky man, but he had no time to reflect; his newly arrived colleagues had to be immediately assigned to their posts.

The short, rotund clerk behind the receptions desk had also taken note of Father Lestrade and Brother Michael. He hadn't seen either man enter from the hotel's main entrance on 33rd Street, although there were several side entrances visitors often used. There was something about the two that made him suspicious, and he was paid to alert Dietz when he saw something suspicious. He was paid well in fact, but not well enough to risk losing his job. And falsely accusing members of the clergy of being charlatans would definitely cost him his job. He had already decided on blindness to the events in the reception area when he was approached by a German couple inquiring about their reservation. Assuming the practiced smile of reception clerks, headwaiters and salesmen everywhere, the members of the clergy who might not be members of the clergy were dismissed from thought as he greeted the guests in one of the several languages in which he was expected to be fluent, "Guten tag. Willkommen zu der Waldorf."

Having taken note of the arrival of the Pinkerton reinforcements, Holmes decided that Father Lestrade had dispensed sufficient blessing on those at the Waldorf Hotel, and gathered up Brother Michael to make the trip to St. Patrick's Cathedral.

Mrs. Hudson also observed the arrival of six Pinkerton men to the hotel, and urged Caroline to finish her preparations. The maid Watson had selected had already departed wearing a

169

black dress that was at least one size too small for her. (Watson had rejected one maid as too tall, and a second as too broad, before approaching the maid who seemed the best available in the short time he could allot to the selection process.) In accord with Watson's instructions, while still in uniform, the maid confided to a co-worker she was feeling feverish and had to leave, asking her to tell their supervisor of her illness and promising to be in the next day. The woman left after informing Caroline and Watson about the location of the staff elevator, and talking Watson into parting with $12.50, $10 for her and $2.50 for the uniform, which she would tell the supervisor was badly scorched in its ironing, and which she would replace at her own expense.

The maid's outfit was large on Caroline, but no one expected a maid to be fashionably dressed, and she drew only a dismissive glance from the Pinkerton exiting the elevator she entered. The Pinkerton newly installed at the service entrance was somewhat more inquisitive, but waved her on when Caroline asked him not to get close to her as she was highly contagious. Caroline proceeded along Fifth Avenue, drawing little attention until she climbed into a cab at the end of the line waiting outside the Holland House. She drew hostile stares from the other coachmen, and a curious look from her own driver, who quickly decided that while she wasn't playing by the rules, a fare was a fare and it had been her decision not his. She explained she had a baptism to attend, and ten minutes later she joined Father Lestrade and Brother Michael in the chapel of St. Patrick's. Fortunately, there were few parishioners present to witness the warm embrace of a hotel maid by a Capuchin monk.

After winning grudging approval from Mrs. Hudson to inspect her suite, Dietz received an even less enthusiastic response from Watson to look through the rooms occupied by Holmes and himself. All evidence of their visitors had been removed, allowing Watson to express outrage over the indignity

170

of the Pinkerton man's search. An increasingly red-faced Dietz expressed his own outrage over the disappearance of people he was certain had been in those rooms moments earlier. After he had fumed his way back to his post in the reception area, Mrs. Hudson began her own afternoon adventure.

She had no need of disguise or stealth. Her strategy for getting to St. Patrick's Cathedral would be no less devious than that of her colleagues, but would be open to view.

She proceeded to the nearest elevator, got off at the reception area, caught sight of herself in a beveled glass mirror wearing her russet brown traveling suit, and was surprised to find the image smiling its approval back to her. As expected, Dietz was waiting for her. There was no longer a need or capacity for him to pretend he was doing anything other than trailing her, or for Mrs. Hudson to pretend ignorance of being trailed. Both now played their parts, one with gusto, the other with resignation.

Mrs. Hudson decided to take Dietz to Ladies Mile, a downtown area with several department stores, nearly all of them with a special emphasis on women's clothing according to her bellboy informant. She directed the coachman to take her to B. Altman's Dry Goods Store.

Dietz climbed into the carriage behind and directed the driver to follow her cab. His job now was to be dogged, ready to pounce on the slip which he had found inevitable in earlier investigations, but which he had come to believe far less likely in this one. His arrival at B. Altman's did nothing to reduce his foreboding. The department store was four stories tall and extended a distance down 19th Street from its entrance on Sixth Avenue. It provided ample opportunity for Mrs. Hudson to lead him a less than merry chase through the displays of women's merchandise.

Mrs. Hudson made her way across the building's first floor which was devoted almost entirely to the display of fabrics. She stopped periodically to finger silks from France,

171

cashmere from England, wools from Australia and Peru, Irish linen, and cottons from Egypt and America. At each stop, her Pinkerton companion developed an interest in the ceiling plaster, the store's broad windows or, if necessary, whatever fabric was nearest where he stood. Finding a lift (having learned to look for the word "elevator"), she went to the second floor where she was again joined by Dietz who had mounted the nearby stairs.

She examined purses, hats, and footwear, before purchasing a pair of gloves and having them boxed. She took pity on her shadow and lingered only briefly at counters displaying an assortment of undergarments and nightclothes, before taking the elevator to the third floor where coats, and dresses for all occasions were on display. She believed it certain her colleagues would be at St. Patrick's Cathedral by now, and the time had come for her to join them. She patrolled the section of tea dresses and evening wear, before moving to day dresses and selecting a gold and beige cotton print. A tall angular woman, one of several brightly smiling saleswomen, accompanied her to the changing area. Before Dietz disappeared from view, Mrs. Hudson caught sight of the Pinkerton man pretending interest in the collection of bridal gowns. She set the cotton print down in the cubicle to which she was directed, and turned to the saleswoman with a look of utter desperation.

"Miss, you can be of great assistance to me. May I assume you have people on staff responsible for security?"

"Yes, certainly we do."

"Oh thank goodness! It's been such a time. Let me sit for a moment." Mrs. Hudson collapsed more than lowered herself into the well cushioned chair designed to make evident B. Altman's recognition of the need for occasional respite from the rigors of shopping. "There's a man who's been followin' me from the time I left the Morgan residence and all through your store." Mrs. Hudson shook her head vigorously and groaned her frustration. "I'm sorry. 'E's gotten me so upset I'm not explainin' myself properly. You see I work for Miss Juliet 'Amilton who

172

was formerly Miss Juliet Morgan. I was sent to pick up the gloves Miss Juliet 'ad ordered." Mrs. Hudson raised the B. Altman box containing the evidence of her assignment. "And that man is a newspaper reporter who's been after me to tell 'im where to find Miss Juliet. You know 'ow reporters are (Mrs. Hudson was certain the saleswoman had no idea how reporters are); they'll do anythin' to get one of their stories. I think they call them scoops. First, 'e tried to bribe me, but I'm not about to betray my family, or lose my position come to that. Now, 'e's followin' me everyplace, thinkin' I might lead 'im to Miss Juliet. I'm afraid to leave the store with 'im behind me. Can you be of any assistance, Miss? I'd be ever so grateful."

The professional smile the saleswoman had been wearing had disappeared, and would not return for the remainder of their exchange. She couldn't ignore the concerns of a woman claiming association with such an important customer, but wondered if this woman's judgment was to be trusted. Certainly, her strange way of speaking did nothing to inspire confidence.

"Are you sure you're not just imagining all this? You know how the mind can play tricks on you. I remember one time when I thought this man was winking at me when I was on the horse-car, and it turned out he wasn't doing anything of the kind. He just had this dreadful tic, and he couldn't keep himself from winking when he looked at you."

"Oh, it's nothin' like that, Miss. You go to the door and just sort of peek out. You'll see 'im standin' in the middle of women's clothes where only a man who's up to no good would be. You just go and look. 'E'll be a medium tall, sort of stocky man with dark hair and bushy eyebrows wearin' a soft homburg, and a brown-checked frock coat."

The saleswoman peeked out from the door she had opened a crack and found a medium tall, sort of stocky man with dark hair and bushy eyebrows wearing a soft homburg, and brown checked frock coat pacing among the bridal gowns, and looking to the changing rooms every now and again. The man existed, that much was clear.

"Have you contacted the police? Surely they can help if the man is proving such a nuisance."

"That's just it, Miss. 'E is a nuisance—a very great nuisance, but e's done nothin' that's strictly speakin' against the law. Their 'ands are tied. That's why I've come to you. If there was a way to keep 'im away from me for just for a little while, I could get a carriage back to the Morgans and I'd be safe. 'E won't dare bother me there."

The saleswoman still had doubts, but the man the customer described was clearly out there, and he had no conceivable reason to be looking at bridal gowns. Besides which, she could be in serious trouble if she didn't act on behalf of a member of the Morgans' staff, which was to say the Morgan family. There would no such penalty attached to alerting security about a man acting suspiciously among women's fashions.

"You stay here, ma'am, I'll get security and they can question him. I'm sure it's all some sort of misunderstanding, but we'll let the officers sort it out. While security is questioning the man, you can get back to the Morgans."

"I'm forever in your debt, Miss, and I won't forget it." Mrs. Hudson pursed her lips and looked to be in some pain. "There's just one thing you might want to share with the security people. The way 'e works, and I'm told a lot of these newspaper people do, is to flash a made up identification card or badge so people will think they're somethin' they ain't. I heard tell of a reporter who 'ad cards and badges to show 'e was a fire fighter, policeman, army officer and even a doctor. That's just 'ow under'anded these people can be." Mrs. Hudson had, in fact, once heard such a story although she had dismissed it at the time as nonsense.

The saleswoman nodded, anxious now to give security the problem and be rid of this woman. "I'll be sure to tell them."

174

She returned a few minutes later leading two bulky men who appeared intent on making themselves appear still bulkier. They parted company with the saleswoman, and from right and left flanks advanced on the Pinkerton who had transferred his interest in bridal dresses to a fascination with evening gowns. Provided with uninvited support under each arm, Dietz was spirited to a more secluded location for interrogation while Mrs. Hudson made for the elevator, the exit, and a four-wheeler to St. Patrick's Cathedral.

Holmes, Wilson and Caroline, still in disguise, went their separate ways within the cathedral in the hope of bringing as little attention to themselves as possible. Their efforts were only moderately successful. Holmes was asked by three parishioners to hear their confessions, and came close to agreeing to hear a particularly insistent older woman in widow's weeds. No one requested Wilson to perform any such service, but a Capuchin monk was sufficiently a novelty that he drew curious glances from every visitor—glances that grew into stares from several of them. A young priest joined Wilson at one point intending to question him about his experience in the Capuchin Order, but found the monk intent on his prayers and unable to respond. The same priest asked Caroline if he could be of any assistance to her as she wandered from one part of the cathedral to another and suffered a second, if somewhat more gracious rejection. When the three of them spotted Mrs. Hudson, they traveled by separate paths to a point below the south transept where she had paused after entering the Cathedral's 50th Street entrance. The priest, who had expressed interest in all three as individuals, now wondered at their meeting as a group with the new arrival who neither made use of the Holy Water Font on her arrival, nor crossed herself before joining the others.

He was about to try for a third time to learn if he could be of assistance, although aware that on this occasion his request would be motivated as much by secular curiosity as by Christian duty, when the group broke ranks and its tall bearded priest approached him.

"Father, might I have a word?"

"Certainly, Father."

"The woman who just entered the Cathedral bears a terrible burden. I have come from my parish upstate to be here at the request of the young lady you see in her work uniform. She is the daughter of the older woman's cousin. Brother Michael, who is with us, has known the family for some time." Holmes looked beyond the priest to the carved wooden image of the crucified Christ, swallowed hard and hoped for Divine forgiveness. "She has information about a terrible crime that has been committed. Their perpetrator is not known to the authorities. She has come here wanting to contact the authorities from within the safety of the Church. I feel it is urgent we give her that opportunity. There is a telephone somewhere in the Church offices, is there not, Father?"

"Yes, of course, more than one, but I could have Officer Hawkins here in a jiffy. He'll be happy to take the woman's statement."

Holmes was unclear whether a jiffy referred to a time frame or one of New York's conveyances, but neither was acceptable. "I'm afraid she'll not talk to anyone face to face, not even in the church. Father, you can't imagine what it's been like to get her to come this far. If I could just take her to a telephone."

The young priest's brow furrowed, and he started edging away from Holmes. "I really should speak to my superior."

"Father, there is so little time. I don't know how long she can maintain her resolve. Just look at her, you can see she is already having second thoughts." In fact, Mrs. Hudson looked exactly the same as when she entered the Cathedral. Still, it was hard to know what second thoughts looked like, and Holmes believed the cleric's imagination might do what his eyes alone would not.

"I suppose there's no harm. Have her follow me. I am Father Kiernan."

"Thank you, Father; I'll fetch her. I am Father Lestrade."

Moments later, after pleading a need for privacy, Mrs. Hudson sat alone in a small office whose only adornment was a crucifix, to which she nodded apology before turning away to make her telephone call.

When she was done, she expressed profound thanks to the priest who had conducted her to the office. He accepted her gratitude with a courteous smile and commented that she wasn't a native New Yorker.

"Goodness no, I've only recently come to America."

"May I ask if you're a Catholic, ma'am."

"I'm not, Your Worship, but I 'eard so many good things about your religion that I knew I'd be safe 'ere. Is there a poor box where I can leave a little somethin'?"

The priest indicated where the box for contributions could be found. "And were you able to make the arrangements you wanted?"

"I was. I'm certain the proper man will be in custody before the week is out."

"Then I will pray for you both."

Mrs. Hudson turned at the door and bowed her head toward Father Kiernan. "Thank you, Father. Thank you for that kindness."

A short time later clerics and parishioners were in the carriage Frederick Washington had sent in response to Mrs. Hudson's call. Mrs. Hudson had told Washington she needed to see him and would be bringing guests. Stating as little of her intended business as possible, she left to their arrival an explanation of the favor she was asking.

It was six o'clock and day was just giving way to night when they arrived at their destination. Wilson and Caroline, but not Holmes, drew attention from those on streets just beginning

177

to come alive. A clergyman hoping to harvest souls was not a novelty on African Broadway, a Capuchin monk and white maid were. They were a novelty to Wash's boy as well. He critically assessed all but Mrs. Hudson as he admitted them to the small foyer. "I'll take you to Mr. Washington, but he may not like this, Mrs. Hudson. He's already been saved—several times."

"Then once more won't hurt," Holmes observed.

Wash's boy shrugged and led them upstairs.

As Mrs. Hudson knew would be the case, Frederick Washington had watched them arrive. He regarded his guests with amused tolerance as he waved them to chairs and waited an explanation. Other than Mrs. Hudson, none of the guests were prepared for Washington, and they stared at him with the disbelief to which he was well accustomed.

"Thank you for 'avin' us, Mr. Washington. Let me explain why we've come to you." Mrs. Hudson paused while the girl who had served her on her earlier visit brought in five tumblers and a pitcher of ice water. The youngster looked to Washington for instruction, and he smilingly pointed to the low table between the chairs on which her burden was to be set, then raised a hand excusing her from the room, correctly guessing Mrs. Hudson's wish for privacy.

"First, let me introduce Mr. Sherlock 'Olmes (Father Lestrade nodded), William Wilson (Brother Michael nodded), and Caroline Littleberry (the Waldorf maid nodded). You once told me if ever I needed anythin' I could look to you. I know this is a good deal more than either of us was thinkin' about at the time, but things I never expected 'ave 'appened. Most particularly, Mr. Wilson 'as left the Detention Center without permission as it were, and is needin' a place to stay for a few days. I thought you might be able to 'elp us out."

Frederick Washington let out a soft whistle. For a while it was his only response. He rose and left the cluster of chairs to look from his window to the street below. He watched for a while, before returning to his waiting guests and pouring glasses of water for each.

"It doesn't appear you were followed. I don't want to know how you escaped, Mr. Wilson, perhaps another time, but I do want to know whether anyone who's not here was involved in your escape.

"Two people. A teammate of mine and his girl friend. They're the only ones, and they're totally trustworthy."

"And I have the word of a monk for that," Washington observed drily. "You've come here from St. Patrick's Cathedral. I've never been." His eyes fell on Holmes as he spoke.

"It's quite impressive, Mr. Washington."

"Which you no doubt appreciated, Father. But why the church?"

"We followed a devious route to throw pursuers off our trail," Holmes said.

Washington drank nearly half a glass of water, and turned the glass one way, then the other as he considered the situation. At last he set the glass back on the low table. "How long do you propose my hiding Brakeman, and I assume Miss Littleberry, if I agree to take them?"

It wasn't something they'd discussed. "Mr. 'Olmes isn't one to boast, but I know 'e's thinkin' it wouldn't be much over a week before 'e'll 'ave the whole case wrapped up."

"Meaning you're certain of Mr. Wilson's innocence?" Washington did nothing to hide his incredulity. "Forgive me, Mr. Holmes, it isn't that I don't have a high regard for the judgment of the clergy, I'm simply thinking about the evidence against Mr. Wilson."

Holmes bowed his head in acknowledgment of Washington's understandable skepticism and elected not to challenge it. "It would be a blessing if you would house these unfortunates while I go about my business."

A broad grin stole slowly across Washington's face, as he favored Holmes with a reverential nod. No sooner was the grin complete then he turned serious again, his tone reminding Mrs. Hudson of that used days earlier to describe the New York riots.

"Mr. Holmes, the penalty for harboring a fugitive is significant. I am, it is true, well protected under normal circumstances, but these would not be normal circumstances. Moreover, I have a business to run, and have people going in and out all the time. My own people are entirely trustworthy, but I can't speak to the others. I did make a promise, and I fully intend to honor it, but under the circumstances I can only agree to five days—and that's stretching things. In addition, Mr. Wilson and Miss Littleberry must agree to abide by my rules with no questions asked." He turned to the two of them. "That will mean staying completely out of sight, and that will mean a confinement, Mr. Wilson, that may lead you to feel nostalgia for your time in the Tombs."

In the end, there was little choice other than to accede to Washington's terms. They agreed further that Holmes and Mrs. Hudson would have no contact with Wilson and Caroline during the five days on the assumption that both would be under constant surveillance. On the morning of the sixth day, if Holmes had been unable to establish Wilson's innocence, Washington would drop Wilson and Caroline at the Fulton Ferry with whatever disguise they chose to employ. If captured, Wilson and Caroline would refuse to divulge where they had been for the five days, and Washington and his staff would deny any knowledge of them.

There were formal handshakes all around, after which Wilson was given opportunity to change from his monk's robes to a shirt and pants provided by Washington, and Caroline to change from the maid's uniform to a dress Washington was also able to provide from a source no one sought to identify. Holmes removed the wig he'd been wearing and made a small ceremony of presenting it to Wilson "just in case things did not turn out well." After a last round of thanks and good wishes, Wilson and

Caroline went to inspect their new living arrangements, and Washington recruited a young man and light-skinned black woman to wear the monk's robes and the maid's uniform for the carriage ride to the Waldorf. Their leaving, together with Father Lestrade and Mrs. Hudson, would make clear to prying eyes that the same number who had come to visit Frederick Washington were now leaving him. The man drew the hood over his head and shrank as best he could into his robes. The woman held a handkerchief to her face as she hurried to the waiting coach. Holmes was given a shirt to wear beneath his priestly garments, and the two recruits similarly wore street clothes beneath their disguises that would allow them to transform themselves for the return trip.

Holmes and Mrs. Hudson exited the carriage two streets from the Waldorf Hotel, Holmes clearly uncomfortable without his frock coat and hat. He nonetheless greeted Dietz with enthusiasm when he spotted him in the hotel's reception area. Before the Pinkerton could ask the first of his many questions, Holmes apologized for his rudeness, explained his need to dress for dinner, and sweeping Mrs. Hudson before him, made the elevator their refuge. Holmes volunteered to inform Watson about the day's events, while Mrs. Hudson went to her room to rest. Later that evening they gathered in Mrs. Hudson's suite and ordered dinner through the room service the Waldorf boasted, sharing at last a relaxing meal without the threat of the interruptions that had frustrated each earlier attempt.

9.
Setting the Trap

With the intrigues of a long day behind them, morning brought a need to take stock of the effect of Wilson's escape on their investigation. Two things were obviously and importantly changed. Wilson would now be the focus of a city-wide manhunt—indeed, a manhunt that could stretch beyond the city—and Wilson's guilt would now be even more firmly fixed in the public mind. It was widely believed, and frequently stated, that an innocent man has nothing to fear from the justice system. To Mrs. Hudson's thinking that went against any proper understanding of the justice system. Whereas the guilty man will receive the punishment he deserves or be rewarded with the freedom he doesn't; the innocent man risks receiving a punishment he doesn't deserve unless given the freedom he does. With the prospect of injustice real and its consequences considerable, Wilson's escape made perfect sense; only the unlikelihood of its success argued against it. Now, with Wilson having opted to defy the odds, and Frederick Washington having set limits on his hospitality, she would have to move quickly to identify Morgan's attacker before Wilson and Caroline were put out on the street—assuming they were not first discovered by the police or the Pinkertons.

There was still one piece of information she deemed significant if not critical, and it had to be gotten from the State of Ohio. She had prepared two telegrams, one in Holmes' name to be sent to the appropriate government bureau, and a second to be sent by cable to her cousin in Brighton. She stuffed both drafts in her purse and strolled through the hotel's reception area, making certain that a young man with sandy hair and a troubled expression took notice of her. He sat too erect and looked too furtively at those entering and exiting for him not to be new to the task of surveillance, and she had no wish for him to fail on her account. She knew the Pinkertons no longer believed

William Wilson was being sheltered in the hotel, but did believe Mrs. Hudson and her colleagues knew where he was. She was certain as well the Pinkertons no longer believed she or her colleagues would lead them to where Wilson was in hiding—not after the escapade at B. Altman—and so had assigned a junior investigator to the task of surveillance.

She asked the route to the nearest post office, directing her question to a plump receptions clerk whose glasses kept slipping down his nose, and spoke loudly enough to draw the attention of a couple checking into the hotel half the counter away. At the post office she copied out two telegrams while her young man stood outside pretending to study his pocket watch and the traffic as if waiting for someone, only to ruin the effect by glancing frequently in her direction. She put the drafts of the two telegrams one atop the other, so they would appear as one to her shadow. She tossed one of the drafts in the waste basket while she was being watched, and stuffed the other into her reticule when she wasn't. She waited while the clerk tapped out her messages, paid what she owed, and left after collecting the receipt for payment. Moments after she exited, the young Pinkerton entered. He made straight for the waste basket where he pulled out the balled up paper he had seen her deposit. He learned that Mrs. Hudson's cousin was not to worry, that she would be late getting back due to some little difficulty that was delaying Caroline's wedding. He pocketed his dubious treasure, and hurried from the premises under the bemused scrutiny of the telegraph clerk and the post office's two patrons.

If sending the telegrams proved relatively uncomplicated, Mrs. Hudson's second task promised to be far more complex. She had a list of people she needed JP Morgan to invite to his home at the behest of Sherlock Holmes, and Morgan had made clear he wanted no further association with Sherlock Holmes. If that wasn't enough, there was one person on her list whom Morgan viewed with even greater repugnance than Holmes. If Morgan was to proffer the desired invitations to his home, he would have to be enticed into doing so. And Mrs. Hudson thought she had a way of enticing him.

First, however, it was time to reveal to Holmes and Watson the identity of Morgan's assailant. They met in the sitting room of her suite, their exchange following a familiar pattern. Mrs. Hudson put forward a name. Holmes rejected it, Watson was incredulous. Point by point, she set forth the reasoning that led inevitably to the person she had named. There followed a storm of questions, some sounding as challenges, some as stunned surprise, and some as simple curiosity. The last of the questions led to a prolonged silence as each man struggled to incorporate all that he had heard. At last, the silence gave way to acceptance, grudging by Holmes, awe-struck by Watson.

The quarry identified, Mrs. Hudson set forth her rationale for using Morgan's home to expose the gunman, and her strategy for winning his cooperation.

"We need to find a place big enough to bring together everyone we've been talkin' to, a place where Mr. 'Olmes can announce to them who it was attacked Mr. Morgan. Besides which, we need someone to do the invitin' that nobody will turn down. The long and the short of it is we need to use Mr. Morgan's 'ome for our meetin', and we need to get 'im to do the invitin' of the people we want there. And I think I know a way to do that." She swallowed hard before continuing, knowing she would soon regret the necessity of sharing with them word about the friend she had made on their voyage.

"While we were travelin' to New York, I made the acquaintance of Mr. Samuel Clemens, or Mr. Mark Twain as 'e is also known. Mr. Clemens is to give a talk at Cooper Union later this week. One of the sponsors for that talk is Mr. Morgan. I believe Mr. Clemens may be able to 'elp us convince Mr. Morgan to send out the invitations. According to the newspaper, Mr. Clemens is stayin' at the Chelsea 'Otel and I plan on payin' 'im a little visit."

She sat back against the chair's cushion and waited the inevitable banter at her expense.

"Is there anything further you wish to share, Mrs. Hudson?" Watson asked. "You're not carrying a secret message from the Queen to President Cleveland?"

"Watson, I believe there is more to this *chance* encounter with Mr. Clemens than Mrs. Hudson is willing to share," Holmes said.

"Good point, Holmes. Perhaps we should explore this further."

"I 'aven't the time to indulge the fantasies of middle-aged juveniles. Remember, there's a life at stake 'ere, and a marriage to see gets done."

The two men were little chastised. Her disclosure was too tantalizing to set aside without further comment. While she sipped tea and feigned deafness, they speculated about "the real reason" for her new outfits, wondered if they shouldn't return to England on separate ships so as to stay out of the way of her future friendships, and urged her to let Mr. Clemens down gently if she had grown tired of his company. When they had run out of scenarios for Mrs. Hudson's secret life, she resumed outlining the activities to be undertaken during the remainder of that day and all of the next. She told Holmes of the telegram expected from Ohio, and warned him about the sandy-haired young man lounging in the Waldorf reception area. Holmes grunted his understanding. His effort to appear soberly attentive competing unsuccessfully with the opportunity to enjoy a rare light moment.

At twelve stories the red brick Chelsea Hotel easily stood out from its surroundings. Once, it had been the tallest building in New York, but height wasn't its sole distinction. The balconies of its apartments were bounded by railings holding within them four-foot tall cast iron flowers, making them an object of wonder and curiosity for passers-by. Mrs. Hudson, however, took no notice of either the building's ornamental railings, or its dominance of the New York skyline as she strode purposefully to the hotel's check-in counter. A bored registration clerk looked up from his paper to report that a Mr. Clemens was a guest of the hotel and was in 508. In answer to her second question he gave her a sour look, and pushing off the counter that had appeared essential to his remaining upright, checked the case of cubbyholes behind him for the contents of the one marked 508. Finding it empty he told her that Mr. Clemens was likely in, but called a warning to her back that guests didn't always remember to leave him their keys when they went out. On the street outside, a sandy-haired young man struck up a conversation with the Chelsea doorman before going inside to strike up a conversation with the registration clerk.

Clemens was in shirtsleeves and looking even more unkempt than usual when he opened the door to Mrs. Hudson. He took her hand and gave it a warm squeeze that coincided with a broad grin. The combination banished her fear that she might not be remembered.

"My friend, who shares my enthusiasm for fingerprints. I had hoped to see you again, but had no way to find you."

Mrs. Hudson blushed a pretty rose color providing a good match for her purple dress. "And I am delighted to see you again, Mr. Clemens, but I look to 'ave come at an awkward time. You're at work on your talk for the Cooper Union." She looked beyond Clemens to the foolscap scattered on and around the table serving as his desk.

"Nonsense. I've been working on this for nearly a week, and it should never take more than two days to develop an impromptu speech." He waved away her concern, and indicated a well stuffed easy chair in the same motion. "Can I offer you something to drink? I can get you coffee, but no tea I'm afraid."

"Thank you, Mr. Clemens, a glass of water would be most welcome."

186

Her host left to get water for them both, sinking into a chair opposite Mrs. Hudson on his return.

"I've read of the troubles your niece and her fiancé are experiencing, and I'm dreadfully sorry about the way things have turned out. I fear it's made life very difficult for you." Clemens took a sip of water and his voice became suddenly confidential. "Does the fact that you're still in New York suggest you're staying to support your niece?"

Mrs. Hudson chose to ignore Clemens' characterization of Caroline as her niece recalling his refusal to calculate their true relationship. "You could say that, but probably not the way you mean, Mr. Clemens. You see, Mr. 'Olmes is not convinced Mr. Wilson is the man who took a shot at Mr. Morgan. 'E's been givin' some fresh thought to that."

"I see. And what is Mr. Holmes' thinking?"

"That's not for me to say, Mr. Clemens. Mr. 'Olmes' thinkin' 'as always been some ways beyond me. But I do know Mr. 'Olmes is fixin' to tell what 'e knows about Mr. Morgan's attacker, only 'e wants to do it in front of Mr. Morgan and all the others who've 'ad somethin' to say about Mr. Wilson and the attack on Mr. Morgan."

A smile began to form that never got far beyond its beginnings, but for much of the rest of their conversation, never quite disappeared. "That sounds likely to be a far more dramatic performance than my poor effort at Cooper Union could ever hope to be, Mrs. Hudson, but I feel certain you haven't interrupted your schedule, and come all the way to the Chelsea to inform me about it."

"Indeed, you're right about that, Mr. Clemens. You see there's a bit of a problem for Mr. 'Olmes in organizin' 'is meetin', and you could be a big 'elp if you would." Clemens grunted, drew back in his chair, and waited to hear what his friend from the transatlantic voyage would ask of him.

"Mr. 'Olmes wants the meetin' to be called by Mr. Morgan. The people Mr. 'Olmes wants there are people who would feel obliged to come if Mr. Morgan asked them."

"What's the problem then?"

"I'm afraid Mr. 'Olmes is not on the best of terms with Mr. Morgan. They 'ad a meeting two days ago and there was some unpleasantness between them."

"What kind of unpleasantness, Mrs. Hudson?"

"Mr. Morgan told Mr. 'Olmes 'e never wanted to see 'im again."

Clemens' near smile transformed to a broad grin and then became a low roar of laughter. "I see you believe in never wasting a whole truth if half of one will do just as well."

Mrs. Hudson blushed a second time, but maintained her sober demeanor to which Clemens at length responded.

"You think I might be able to influence Morgan to drop his objections."

"I think the whole world puts great stock in Mark Twain's suggestions."

"Mrs. Hudson, you have a honeyed tongue ... but it hides a brackish mind." A soft chuckle removed any question of his continuing good feeling. "I will help you on one condition. I must be counted among the invitees. I'm not about to miss a chance to see Mr. Holmes in action."

And with that a bargain was struck. Clemens would get in touch with Morgan to schedule an appointment for himself and Holmes for the following day or evening, at which they would argue for the meeting Mrs. Hudson had in mind. He would get word to Holmes of the time he should appear. Clemens promised to arrive first to prepare Morgan for the ensuing discussion.

Their business concluded, Clemens turned to an issue he knew to be of interest to them both. "Mrs. Hudson, I wonder what you think of my idea that typewriters may be very nearly as distinctive as fingerprints."

At the end of a pleasant hour plotting the future of criminal investigation, Clemens saw Mrs. Hudson to a carriage. Her sandy-haired shadow listened for the doorman's instructions to the driver, then accepted his offer of a second carriage. When Mrs. Hudson got back to the Waldorf, she found Mrs. Guskin, the landlady for Caroline and Lucy, studying the chandeliers in the reception area while waiting for her return. Mrs. Guskin somehow managed to appear even more ashen and drawn in the Waldorf lobby than she had on Snedecker Street. She wore a formless dress and no hat, and appeared so out of place she was approached three times by staff asking if they could be of assistance. She shook off each of her would-be helpers without a word or even a glance in their direction.

On seeing Mrs. Hudson enter, she rose and opened tightly pursed lips to speak, only to be stopped by Mrs. Hudson's pressing a finger to her own lips. She led Mrs. Guskin to the elevator where she stymied the woman's urge to speak a second time. When they were safely inside Mrs. Hudson's rooms, the woman was finally allowed to deliver the message she had been at pains to hold in check.

"I thought you should know, Mrs. Hudson, Lucy's gone. It must have happened early this morning. I spoke to her last night and she told me all about Caroline, and how she wouldn't be coming back to the apartment. But she didn't say a word about herself. I just thought you should know." With that her lips again clamped tightly together.

"Please 'ave a seat, Mrs. Guskin. Mrs. Hudson saw her visitor into an easy chair on whose front edge she remained poised throughout nearly all their conversation. "Tell me, did Lucy leave a note?"

"There was no note, I looked. She did take some of her clothes though. I just thought you should know because of you being a relative of Caroline's, and because of all that happened yesterday." She squinted at Mrs. Hudson. "You do know what happened yesterday?"

"I know."

"Well then, you understand the problem."

Mrs. Hudson understood the problem, but wasn't sure Mrs. Guskin did.

She shared with her yet another of the half truths Mr. Clemens had so admired. "It's natural Lucy would want to get away from where there's going to be an investigation. With Caroline gone, they'll want to talk to 'er roommate. By gettin' away she avoids all that. If she told you where she was goin', you'd be obliged to tell it to the police when they come around. This way you can truthfully say you don't know where she's gone off to."

A weight removed, Mrs. Guskin's back momentarily threatened the cushion behind her. "You think that's all there is to it, Mrs. Hudson."

"I do, but you've got to think what you're goin' to say, Mrs. Guskin. The police will ask you what you know about Mr. Wilson's escapin' from the Tombs. You'd best decide what you know."

It hadn't occurred to Mrs. Guskin that anyone would be interested in what she knew about Wilson's escape. "What should I say, Mrs. Hudson?"

"Why, the truth of course, Mrs. Guskin. You're the landlady and you don't intrude on the private lives of your tenants. You knew Miss Donaldson 'ad taken in Miss Littleberry, but you don't know anythin' more than that."

"Will they believe me, Mrs. Hudson?"

"Isn't it the truth, Mrs. Guskin?"

"It is absolutely, Mrs. Hudson."

"Then just you say it and they'll 'ave to believe you."

"Thank you, ma'am, and thank you for seeing me.

A less anxious Mrs. Guskin took leave of a more anxious Mrs. Hudson, who had grave concerns about the truth as regards Lucy Donaldson.

That evening and morning of the next day passed without incident, leading to a shared but unspoken feeling of being caught in a very temporary calm before a rapidly approaching storm. Holmes would absorb the early brunt of that storm in his effort to gain the financier's cooperation.

At exactly three o'clock, as had been negotiated by Clemens, Holmes was admitted to Morgan's study. Clemens, having preceded him, came forward to shake his hand. Morgan stood behind the sea of desk where he had positioned himself, acknowledging Holmes with a curt nod before reseating himself. Clemens assumed the host duties Morgan was obviously at pains to avoid.

"Mr. Holmes, this is indeed a pleasure. Your reputation precedes you."

"As does yours, Mr. Twain. I am delighted to make your acquaintance. And may I say, Mr. Morgan, I appreciate the opportunity to see you again." His experiment with civility won Holmes a grunt and a second nod before gaining a more concrete display of hospitality.

"If you'll have a seat, Mr. Holmes, I'll ring for refreshments."

Holmes looked to the remaining chairs, and chose one that was straight-backed and some distance from his host.

The three men formed a triangle with the desk the visible evidence of the barrier still to be overcome. Clemens took on the task of mediation—a task he hoped would be facilitated by the timely arrival of the butler carrying a decanter of brandy and three glasses. Sachs poured drinks for the men and withdrew. Clemens raised his glass high, "To good health and continuing friendship between our two great nations." Holmes smiled, Morgan grunted, and all three drank heartily.

"Holmes, I have asked for this meeting to demonstrate we are not at cross purposes in wanting to see justice done. It serves no one's interest for it to appear that your investigation is being hampered. At the same time, it serves no one's interest to draw out that investigation any longer than is absolutely necessary. It is in that spirit Mr. Morgan has made time available to hear you out. You must know you stand alone in questioning Wilson's guilt. I will say that given the company one suffers when standing with the majority, standing alone can have its advantages. But tell us, Holmes, what is the action you propose to determine Wilson's guilt or innocence?"

"I want to have a meeting involving all those we know to have been in the crowd the morning of the shooting, together with some few others who can shed light on areas significant to the investigation. However, I have nowhere to put the dozen or so people needed, nor would they be likely to attend based solely on my invitation even if I somehow found the space for them. Mr. Morgan's home and his invitation however ...." Holmes meant for his voice to trail off with dramatic portent. However, the pause he was counting on never developed.

"Absurd! Patently absurd! Use my home as the staging area for your ill-conceived theatrical. Absurd! Twain, I agreed we could look into this further, but there has to be another way."

Clemens ran a finger around the rim of his glass. "Morgan, think how many theatricals you've seen, with none of them having the dramatic value, not to say personal interest, of the one that can be staged in your own home. I wouldn't dismiss the opportunity lightly."

"It may strike you as an amusing evening, Twain. I can't say it offers me the same level of entertainment. Who is it you propose inviting to my home, Mr. Holmes?"

Holmes attempted to build slowly to the crescendo he saw as inevitable. "Ourselves of course, Mr. Sachs and Mr. Tarkenton from your staff, and Dr. Watson and Mrs. Hudson from mine. Also, Mr. McIlvaine and Mr. McLeod."

"Archibald McLeod? You think he would take a shot at me. I don't believe it. And McIlvaine," Morgan sputtered."We've discussed this. It's utter nonsense."

"We'll see. I will also want to have present Mr. Cochrane and Mr. Snyder, two baseball players who know Mr. Wilson better than anyone else, and have given valuable information to my colleague, Dr. Watson. Mr. Dietz will need to be present of course, as well as your former footman, Mr. Langer."

"That tears it,' Morgan barked. "I'll not have Franklin Langer inside my house and that's final. I'd be content to humor this burlesque for your sake, Twain. But this goes too far. I am asked to invite a man I dismissed from my service for thievery. And it's not as if I believe for an instant that justice is being denied. Wilson is guilty—I, at least, feel it a certainty. His running off a second time makes it clear, if nothing else does. An innocent man doesn't fear his day in court." Morgan glared to Holmes, daring him to disagree. "You ask too much, Mr. Holmes—at any rate you ask more than I am willing to give."

Morgan stood, his face florid, his moustache quivering, and his hand poised to ring for Sachs and see his guests escorted to the front door, one of them for the eternity he thought he had achieved earlier. Clemens again assumed the role of mediator.

"I wonder if I might have another half glass of this wonderful brandy before we go."

Morgan wavered between his duties as host, and his desire to bring an unpleasant episode to a close. For the moment his duties as host won out.

"A half glass then and a different topic."

Clemens accepted the brandy, but rejected Morgan's condition. A smile meant to mollify the financier lit up his face, and Morgan's moustache slowly ceased its quivering.

"Perhaps we can all take a step back. Holmes, I take it you're proposing a short meeting with no thought of this being a social gathering."

Holmes gave a vigorous nod.

"Morgan, I think we can safely say that none of these people can be construed to be guests in your home. I've enjoyed your hospitality and can't remember a single evening when one of your guests was to be accused of trying to murder you. That may, of course, suggest a need for you to gather a more spirited group of acquaintances. Regardless, the evening Holmes proposes should prove informative, if only to make Wilson's guilt more abundantly clear. And as you've mentioned more than once, it won't be helpful for it be reported that Sherlock Holmes has doubts about Wilson's guilt."

Clemens looked hard to Morgan lest there be anything unclear about his statement before again turning the mood light—or trying to. "If we were to bring these people together, we would, of course, forgo finger sandwiches and keep hidden this excellent brandy." Clemens took a healthy swallow and looked to his glass appreciatively. "And just think, Morgan, if Holmes is right and someone other than Wilson is your assailant, not only will you have rooted out the real threat to your life, you will be celebrated as someone unafraid to face down a murderer, even in your own home. To say nothing of the fact that you will provide me with a wonderfully entertaining hour in New York, and additional material for my lecture."

Both men looked to Morgan, and were relieved to see the glower had melted into a look of concentration. "Holmes, can you promise this farce will take no more than an hour?" A firm nod. "And are the names you reported the whole of the list of people you want to see invited?" A second nod, not quite as firm.

"It may be necessary to call on a colleague to encourage one of the people to attend. Langer is certain to be no more enthused about seeing you than you are to see him. I guarantee, however, the person we ask to escort Mr. Langer will not prove an embarrassment to you or to this house."

Morgan studied Holmes a moment before speaking. "I trust neither of us will regret this. I still regard it as a thoroughgoing waste of time. However, if it will finally end your meddling in this business, it may yet have some value. For now, I want to keep this as contained as possible. As Clemens has said, I am concerned about the effect a continuing investigation could have on the markets; simply discovering the scheduling of this meeting could have a negative effect. I'll rely on the two of you to keep word of this exercise in confidence. I will ask Tarkenton to develop invitations as vague to purpose as possible with no one being told the names of his fellow visitors. You may hold a one hour meeting two days from now to begin at precisely ten in the morning. That will allow you to conclude your business without my losing opportunity to monitor the markets, and make whatever corrections may prove necessary. I will see to the delivery of invitations and confirm acceptances for all but Langer. I leave that to you, Mr. Holmes, and your colleague."

Morgan paused, but there was no response from Holmes.

"It's agreed then," Morgan said. "I will call together these people, you will use my home for a brief meeting, and then we will have an end to this." He rose and rang for Sachs. Smiling for the first time, he turned to the renowned author. "Twain, I look forward to your lecture when all this is finally behind us. Indeed, all New York is looking forward to your lecture."

Clemens gave a little bow. "Thank you, Morgan. I will do my best not to disappoint you or any of the rest of New York." They sat silent a few moments avoiding eye contact until Sachs arrived to escort them to the front door. On the top step they took leave of each other, Clemens asking to be remembered to his "remarkable housekeeper," and Holmes mumbling a promise to do so. Each then expressed satisfaction with the accomplishments of the day before going their separate ways.

Mrs. Hudson was satisfied as well and heaped rare praise on Holmes. She deferred discussion about the upcoming meeting in Morgan's home to await arrival of the telegram from Ohio. Declaring there was nothing to do for the time being, Mrs. Hudson suggested her colleagues spend the day seeing something of New York beyond its detention facilities.

Both men embraced Mrs. Hudson's proposal, Watson asking only for assurance she was content to remain in the hotel.

"Oh, I might take a bit of a walk, but I'm well satisfied to stay back."

Holmes sprang from Mrs. Hudson's settee energized by a sudden inspiration.

"Watson, if you'll be so good as to join me, I should very much like to visit the city's art museum—I believe it's called the Metropolitan—to learn if they have any oils painted by Horace Vernet, my great-uncle on my mother's side. I'm sure you've heard me speak of him. He was quite accomplished, and if the art museum is as comprehensive as the hotel's literature states, some of his work will surely be on exhibit.

"I would be delighted to join you, Holmes, and to make a day of it by also visiting their Museum of Natural History. From what I've read they've done some important work in the field of paleontology, and if it won't bore you to tears, Holmes, I'd like to see what they have on display."

Holmes believed it most assuredly would bore him to tears, but counted it a fair exchange for his friend's company and readily agreed to the second excursion. Mrs. Hudson wished them well and returned to Francis Galton, on whom she depended for her own stimulation, while she waited for the State of Ohio to provide the final piece to the puzzle she had painstakingly assembled.

The day proved as great a success as both men wished, and as much of a disappointment as Mrs. Hudson feared. The Metropolitan Museum of Art held no less than three Vernets, and while one was a portrait neither man found of particular interest, Holmes went on at length about the vibrancy of his great-uncle's *Start of the Race of the Riderless Horses*, and the emotional power of his *Stormy Coast Scene after a Shipwreck*. Watson found both paintings workmanlike and nothing more, but said nothing. He, on the other hand, was quite taken with the murals of life in the Jurassic Age and the sculptures of its prehistoric creatures, which Holmes regarded as excessively theatrical, but he too said nothing. Mrs. Hudson pretended interest in their accounts, but was concerned that day was now turning to evening, and the prospect of receiving the hoped for telegram was fading with the ebbing daylight.

At breakfast the following day, her spirits were raised briefly with the delivery of a note confirming that all those Morgan had invited to Holmes' meeting would be in attendance. The note contained a reminder that Holmes was responsible for getting Franklin Langer to the meeting. Mrs. Hudson had already made those arrangements. Later that day they would plan and rehearse the presentation for tomorrow's meeting, hopefully with the much awaited telegram in hand. For now, Mrs. Hudson was envisioning a long day if Holmes and Watson remained underfoot. A diversion was in order and one presented itself in the morning's *New York Tribune*.

"There's nothin' to be gained by us all sittin' around 'ere starin' at each other. I can wait on the telegram, and you can explore what the paper describes as 'an important scientific advance' on display just a short distance from 'ere." Both men looked to her, waiting to be steered in the direction she had chosen for them.

"It's at a place called the Holland Brothers' Kinetoscope Parlor. What they 'ave there, accordin' to the newspaper is the first ever exhibit of pictures that actually move. I'm not sure I believe it myself, but it sounds to be somethin' worth seein,' especially with the interest the two of you 'ave in scientific discoveries." She opened her eyes wide in a mock display of enthusiasm which they reciprocated with a mock display of interest. They agreed to be back by four to prepare for the next morning's meeting.

Mrs. Hudson took a short walk along Fifth Avenue, but houses, shops and passers-by that would have excited curiosity another day were largely ignored on this one. As she feared, no telegram awaited her when she got back. At one o'clock, she decided she should get something to eat, if only to keep up her strength. She had barely been seated in the English Rose Room when she found herself joined by an old acquaintance. Dietz greeted her with a smile too broad for Mrs. Hudson's comfort.

"Forgive the intrusion, Mrs. Hudson or whatever your name is, but it's so difficult to catch you alone. And please don't let me keep you from ordering. I won't be staying, but I don't want to keep you from lunch. I understand the omelets are excellent."

Mrs. Hudson had, in fact, lost what little appetite she had immediately on being joined by her uninvited guest. She ignored his recommendation, which seemed to neither surprise or trouble him, and ordered a raspberry scone and pot of chamomile tea.

After a glance to the departing waiter, Dietz turned again to Mrs. Hudson, his smile improbably broadening. "I'm on to you, you know."

Mrs. Hudson took the napkin from her plate, unfurled it with a small ceremony, and set it on her lap before meeting the gaze of the Pinkerton.

"And what is it you're on to me about, Mr. Dietz?"

"We don't have to play games do we, Mrs. Hudson? You can fool the others, but we're both professionals and can be honest with each other." Dietz's smile was in danger of becoming a smirk.

"I'm afraid I don't know 'ow to take your meanin', Mr. Dietz."

"There you go. That's the tip-off. 'I don't know 'ow to take your meanin','" he parroted her words to exaggerated effect. "Nobody talks like that. It's one of the things you should work on if you're going to stay in this business. I know it worked well enough with Morgan's staff, and the story of your being some distant relative of Miss Littleberry was truly inspired. You made the relationship so remote no one could possibly check it out."

"But you made a mistake—I'm not being critical, mind you. Just one professional to another. You shouldn't have let me

198

know you saw me following you the day you visited the Morgan residence. Of course, if I had known then you were an investigator yourself, I would have been more careful. But when I saw you were on to me, it was a dead give-away."

"Tell me, are you part of Mr. Holmes' London agency or did he just hire you here? With that phony English accent, I'm thinking you're from the stage, not the New York stage where someone might recognize you, but out of town—probably Philadelphia or maybe Boston. It doesn't matter really. Whatever tricks your Mr. Holmes has up his sleeve won't work this time. If there was anybody in New York who had any doubt about Wilson's guilt up to now, his attempt to escape will convince them otherwise. I'm just hoping it's not Mr. Holmes' handiwork; we take that kind of thing very seriously in this country. I'm not accusing anybody of anything mind you, but I believe you know Wilson's location, and I'm suggesting you tell it to me or the police. Because we'll find him. I guarantee you that, and it would be best if we don't find out you've been hiding him."

"I thank you for the warn*ing*, Mr. Dietz." Mrs. Hudson laid heavy emphasis on the "g" she carefully inserted.

"Like I say we're in the same business, madam." Dietz rose and put his napkin and some coins on the table. "Allow me to buy you the lunch I've interrupted. I must get back now. Mind what I said about Wilson, and do work on that accent. I'll see you and your Mr. Holmes tomorrow." He turned away from Mrs. Hudson, and without looking back, gave his best imitation of a relaxed saunter as he made his exit.

"Excuse me, madam."

A new and far more welcome figure replaced Dietz at her table. It was the same bellboy who had given her detailed instructions for finding Snediker Street in Brooklyn.

"I've a telegram for Mr. Holmes. I was told it should be given to you if he's not in the hotel."

Mrs. Hudson thanked him, gave him five cents for his troubles, and tore open the envelope. After reading its brief message she was confident Dietz and everybody in New York would shortly have their doubts about Wilson's guilt regardless of his attempt to escape.

At four o'clock, Holmes and Watson were again in Mrs. Hudson's parlor. They had seen moving pictures of a man being shaved, a horse being shoed, two chickens fighting, and a strongman flexing various muscle groups. They thought the invention amusing, but believed moving pictures to have limited cultural significance. In contrast, the telegram Mrs. Hudson shared had them exhilarated.

They spent the next two hours in rehearsal for Holmes' performance. In accord with the outline developed, and under his colleagues' critical eye, Holmes set forth and then refined his delivery. When that was completed to everyone's satisfaction, Mrs. Hudson and Watson fired questions and challenges to prepare Holmes for every contingency. Finally, Mrs. Hudson declared a need for all to rest. She went in search of Galton, while Holmes and Watson left to relax with a pipe. The late dinner they shared was more convivial than any since they'd left London.

10.
The Trap Sprung

Morgan allotted the drawing room to Holmes' meeting. Extending the whole of the west side of the mansion, it contained a generous scattering of elegantly carved small tables, and well cushioned rosewood chairs and settees. The haphazard arrangement of furniture combined with displays of delicate Japanese embroideries, and paintings that could have graced the walls of any major museum, gave the room the appearance of an extravagantly furnished hallway. It would easily accommodate the twelve people scheduled to attend without forcing intimacy or even acquaintance among them. At Holmes' request, one of the two doors permitting entry and exit had been shut and locked. The concern was with exit not entry. Having concluded the work of identifying Morgan's attacker, the three detectives were determined to guard against that person's untimely departure.

Holmes, Watson and Mrs. Hudson arrived at a quarter to five, and were the first to be shown to the drawing room. Sachs informed them that Mr. Clemens had arrived earlier and was with Mr. Morgan. Moments later, Morgan, now freed of his sling, entered the room with Clemens. If one squinted hard, Mrs. Hudson thought, they could almost be mistaken for brothers. Both were in their late 50's, both were large powerful-looking men, and both had great bushy eyebrows and full drooping moustaches, leading both to look slightly unkempt regardless of the care taken in grooming. Without the squint there came an awareness of the bulbous roseate Morgan nose that overrode all similarities. Morgan nodded grimly to Holmes, accepted introductions to Watson and Mrs. Hudson, and muttered his need to speak to Dietz, who had just entered the drawing room. Clemens greeted Holmes with a sly grin as if they shared a secret understanding. He took Mrs. Hudson's hand and gently squeezed it, and greeted Watson as though he was an old friend when Holmes introduced the two men to each other.

Excusing himself from the small island of good feeling, Holmes strolled to the fireplace at the center of the far wall, allowing him to face down the length of the room and see, and be seen, by everyone in it. Watson and Mrs. Hudson took seats at the back beyond the room's side entrance where they could watch guests enter and, if necessary, Watson could block one guest's departure. Clemens found a seat opposite them by the windows, on the other side of an imaginary center aisle that all later arrivals proceeded to honor. Watson and Clemens pulled pads and pencils from their jackets, each to record from his own perspective, events as they unfolded.

The first of the invited guests to arrive was McIlvaine. He paused on the room's threshold, taking stock of a room with which he was wholly familiar, and of the people, with most of whom he was wholly unfamiliar. He wandered to the room's center and pretended an interest in the Japanese embroidery he had studiously ignored on prior visits.

Next to enter were Cochrane and Snyder. The two ballplayers tread cautiously across the room's carpet as if fearful of leaving footprints. They came forward nearly to where McIlvaine was standing, their attention flitting from furniture to artwork to silk brocade curtains to the coved ceiling painted to appear a mosaic. They found chairs together and as close to the wall as they could get, then continued their awed and silent cataloging of the room's treasures.

McLeod followed closely on Cochrane and Snyder, the small man appearing nearly frail compared to the ballplayers. He looked to Morgan, but made no effort to get his attention, glanced briefly past those already seated, finally giving a tentative nod to McIlvaine who appeared the nearest he could find to a kindred spirit. McIlvaine returned the acknowledgment with the hint of a smile, and a relationship was forged between the two men based on their mutual discomfort.

At ten o'clock all were assembled except Tarkenton and Sachs who were elsewhere in the mansion, and Franklin Langer whose whereabouts were unknown. Morgan remained at the back of the room, talking to Dietz but looking to Holmes, and doing nothing to hide his impatience. Finally, unable to contain his displeasure any longer, he dispatched Dietz to learn from Holmes his plans for the morning, and to remind him he had one hour to make his case. As Dietz finished his whispered conversation with Homes, the financier waved a thick Cuban cigar in the direction of the grandfather clock on the mantle above the fireplace. Holmes did his best to look unconcerned even as others, although unaware of Morgan's gesture, were also becoming restive and beginning a low grumbling.

And then, just as discontent seemed at risk of flaming into rebellion, four men entered the room, and the small thunder of protest was replaced by a suddenly profound silence. Two of the men occasioned nothing more than a quick glance. Tarkenton and Sachs had been flitting in and out of the room continuously; their return was expected and thereby as inconsequential as the men themselves. All eyes followed a glowering Franklin Langer and the expressionless albino black man who held him firmly by the arm as they found seats near to where Holmes stood watch over the final additions to his audience.

He nodded his appreciation to the one of the two men he had last seen when a member of the clergy. "Everyone is now here. Some of you know Mr. Langer who was formerly a footman in Mr. Morgan's employ. Allow me to introduce my friend, Frederick Washington, who has been kind enough to escort Mr. Langer to our meeting."

The introduction freed all assembled from the embarrassment of continuously stealing glances at the new addition to the group, and allowed for long stares at a man whose like they had never seen before. Brickyard Snyder alone broke into a broad grin, and called out a single word in greeting, "Gladtomeetcha."

"If everyone will please be seated we can begin," Holmes said by way of summoning the group's attention to himself.

In fact, all but Dietz and Sachs had already taken seats, and both would remain standing, taking positions along the far back wall in accord with Morgan's directive they keep a close watch on Langer. Cigar firmly in place, Morgan had taken a seat beside Clemens, and now offered the author the cigar he had brought for him. While Clemens puffed contentedly, the financier blew frequent clouds of smoke that suggested the fire he was barely containing.

McLeod yielded to his own fire, directing a question to Holmes that unintentionally put into words the question held by nearly all those in attendance. "We can begin exactly what, Mr. Holmes. We've been summoned here for what purpose?"

Holmes straightened his slender frame to its full height, and looked down to McLeod and the rest of his audience from the hilltop he felt himself to have ascended. These were the moments he most enjoyed, striding center stage, leading an engrossed audience through a thicket of misunderstandings, of signs misread and signs unread, to surprise them finally with the identification of the guilty party seated amongst them. It mattered not that he had been led through the same thicket, and had had the signs revealed and interpreted for him less than a day earlier; the path to the clearing was now his to describe.

"Each of you is here because he has something to contribute to the unraveling of the crime that's been committed. You, Mr. McLeod, like several gathered here, were present at the time of the assault on Mr. Morgan. Others of you can speak to the character and activities of our prime suspect, Mr. Wilson. It is, of course impossible for us to have Mr. Wilson himself join us. As Mr. Dietz can confirm, his arrival would have necessitated the police being summoned to restore him to his former lodgings. Isn't that correct, Mr. Dietz?

"Quite right, Mr. Holmes. And as you have been informed, those who know his location and do not share that information with the authorities are violating the law and can be punished as well." As he spoke, he looked to the backs of heads whose fronts stared resolutely forward.

"Thank you for that clarification, Mr. Dietz. It is in light of that difficulty that I have invited his colleagues, Mr. Cochrane and Mr. Snyder, to join us." Holmes pointed with an open palm to the two ballplayers, sharing the ghost of a smile with the two men. Cochrane reciprocated with a small nod while Brickyard Snyder grinned back to him.

"Let me introduce our other guests and explain why each of you is here today. Mr. McLeod, the gentleman who wondered why you have been invited, was until several years ago a successful railroad executive, the president, in fact, of the Philadelphia and Reading Railroad. He was relieved of all such responsibilities at Mr. Morgan's insistence, and as a condition for his financing the railroad's continued operation. Mr. Morgan felt Mr. McLeod's excessive spending was limiting the Railroad's profitability. However, as McLeod reported to me, Mr. Morgan acted without hearing from him or even meeting with him. In the intervening period, Mr. McLeod has been unable to secure a position appropriate to his talents. That would seem ample reason to hold hard feelings for Mr. Morgan. And although he denied to the police being at the Morgan home the morning of the attack, he later admitted he was there and was carrying a concealed revolver, which, he assured me, is one of your quaint American customs. He said he left the area before the shooting, but since no one was present who could identify Mr. McLeod, we have only his word for that."

"Mr. McLeod was, of course, not the only person in the crowd that day who had reason to harbor hard feelings toward Mr. Morgan. Mr. McIlvaine (Holmes nodded in his direction) hoped to win Juliet Morgan's hand in marriage, but the young lady was discouraged from taking that step by Mr. Morgan—or so McIlvaine believes—depriving him of both the woman he loved, and the fortune to which she is heir."

"I beg your pardon!"

"How dare you, Holmes!"

Two voices rang out, and two men leaped to their feet. One shook a fist at Holmes, the other an angry cigar.

Holmes' voice sounded the promise of still waters. "I share only the way these events might appear. I hold no brief one way or the other. It is enough to know that Mr. McIlvaine, like Mr. McLeod, had reason for being unhappy with Mr. Morgan, and was also in the crowd at Morgan's house. I have learned, as well, that Mr. McIlvaine is an excellent marksman."

The two men worked their way slowly back into their chairs, Morgan little mollified by Holmes' claim to a concern with appearances, and McIlvaine unnerved at being identified before Morgan and a group of strangers as a suspect in his attack.

We come next to Mr. Langer. As I believe everyone knows, Mr. Langer was dismissed from Mr. Morgan's service on suspicion of having treated his employer's possessions rather cavalierly."

"If you mean stealing, nothing was ever proved. I was never even taken down." Langer barked his dismissal of Holmes' charge without leaving his chair.

"All the more reason for your holding a grievance against Mr. Morgan. You were discharged without a reference, and could be expected to find it difficult to obtain honest employment. You were at the house when Mr. Morgan was shot and you were seen to have a gun drawn. Moreover, you have a particular understanding of Mr. Morgan's schedule. You would know when he was to be at his club, and you could be the one who fired a shot at him several weeks ago."

"Well, I'm not the only one who knows Mr. Morgan's schedule. Tarkenton there knows his every move, and Tarkenton has good reason to get back some of his own. He could tell you about it if he wasn't such a jellyfish. Tarkenton was on his way out. Mr. Morgan wasn't happy with his work, and was fixing to sack him. Mr. Sachs can back me up on that. The whole of the staff can say as much if they're honest about it."

The butler searched for something of interest in the ceiling, while Tarkenton looked to Langer as if the one-time footman had poisoned his dog and he couldn't decide whether to weep or fight. Morgan was experiencing no such conflict.

"Now you can see just how much of a scoundrel this man is. Tarkenton is, in fact, a valued employee for whom I have great regard."

It was lost on no one that Morgan had not denied the essence of Langer's charge. Tarkenton set his jaw and looked straight ahead, determined to appear untroubled by a conversation that deeply troubled him.

"Aren't you conveniently forgetting Wilson?" Dietz could contain himself no longer. He took several steps from the back wall voicing his accusation with greater volume than even the room's great size demanded. "Wilson was at the shooting and was seen with a gun—a gun with two cartridges fired, the same number as was fired that morning—and he ran away. He could easily get Mr. Morgan's schedule from Miss Littleberry and be the shooter at Mr. Morgan's club. Besides all that, he's the only one who's tied to the radicals that have targeted business leaders like Mr. Morgan. You know he had all that bomb thrower literature in his apartment—right there on his nightstand, and with all the parts about Mr. Morgan underlined. This stuff you're going on about today just muddies everything up. We've got our man. Or anyway we did until he somehow got free. Now, if you'd just turn him over from wherever you've got him hid, we can all go on about our business." He looked again to the backs of heads that never turned in his direction.

Holmes remained unruffled by the points he had expected to be offered although not in such strident tones. "Since the issue has been raised, let us look at the case against Mr. Wilson. He is seen, as Mr. Dietz so colorfully describes, to be part of a radical element bent on nothing less than the overthrow of the country's political and economic institutions. There's little question that the assassination of Mr. Morgan would severely disrupt the financial markets, and might even threaten the stability of the government. And we have seen two attacks on Mr. Morgan in a single month preceded by violent acts against other business leaders. But is there reason to expect such a level of violence from Mr. Wilson?"

Holmes looked to the only members of his audience he felt likely to speak in favor of Wilson's peaceful intent. "Both Mr. Cochrane and Mr. Snyder told Dr. Watson that he talked about the need for organizing a baseball union, but confined himself to talk. Would that be right, gentlemen?"

Cochrane nodded thoughtfully while Snyder offered a vigorous affirmation, "Absolutely, that's right. Like I told your Dr. Watson, this is all hogwash. I know Brakeman better than any man here—except for Candy of course—and he wouldn't no more shoot somebody than I would." There was a brief pause. "And I wouldn't neither."

"Thank you. These gentlemen are his colleagues and might be expected to speak in his favor, but his employer, Mr. Ebbets, said essentially the same thing. Ebbets reported Wilson was in favor of the union, and encouraged organizing as a general principle, but he also said that Wilson stopped well short of stirring the men to act against management, much less himself engaging in violent protest. And as his employer, we can be assured Ebbets would be alert to such behaviors. Nonetheless, we can't entirely dismiss Mr. Dietz's concern. As he has said, we know Wilson was devoted to radical change, had incendiary literature in his flat and was seen with a gun—a gun with two cartridges missing—and that he can be presumed to have been aware of Mr. Morgan's schedule through Miss Littleberry."

"And there's his running away from the house after that, and his breaking out of the Tombs," Dietz added, insistent that every piece of evidence against Wilson be surfaced.

"All true," Holmes agreed, "but for the moment I ask you to indulge me in considering something about the shooting that has concerned me from the beginning. Mr. Wilson was seen with his gun drawn. That much is clear, but no one reported seeing him fire the gun. It would seem possible that Wilson, hearing the shots, immediately drew his gun to face Langer who was a few yards in front of him and whom he viewed as a threat. Langer appears with us today accompanied by Mr. Washington, a local businessman. Normally however, Langer appears in the company of one or more goons who are his business acquaintances. It seems that Langer operates in one of the shadier enterprises in the city. His employer's interest lies in taking bets and himself wagering on sporting events, especially your sport of baseball. Mr. Langer's employer also likes to remove the element of chance from his business." Holmes paused to allow his audience to digest ideas belonging to a world alien to many of them. "I am told that in baseball the critical player is called the pitcher, and that he exerts enormous influence over the outcome of contests. I am also told that Mr. Wilson is an excellent proponent of the art and skill of pitching, and that his team is likely to prove victorious on the days he is assigned to do the throwing. Is that correct, Mr. Snyder?"

"If ya mean, the Brakeman is a good bet to win his games, what with him having the best curve in the business, you'd be right as rain, Mr. Holmes—but you know we're not supposed to bet on our games."

"But people do bet on your games."

"Oh yeah, it goes on all the time."

"In that regard, we know Langer had a job additional to that of under-footman at the Morgan residence. He was acting on behalf of an employer who sought to be guaranteed a handsome profit on the days of Wilson's games. Langer no doubt promised he could arrange for Wilson' cooperation based on their frequent contact. However, Wilson proved remarkably resistant to his efforts. Langer's presence at Mr. Morgan's arrival was not to honor Miss Juliet as he reported, but to further menace Wilson. He'd brought his toughs with him, and thought to be able to make clear the danger Wilson would face if he continued to be uncooperative. That was the reason Wilson drew his gun when he heard gunshots, and why no one saw him fire the gun. He feared retribution from Langer and his crowd, and was prepared to defend himself."

"Why wouldn't Wilson go to the police if he was being threatened or go to his team's owners?" Morgan bellowed his disbelief.

"These are dangerous people, Mr. Morgan, and I've been told some of your police may receive an incentive to look the other way when it comes to gambling. Wilson couldn't be sure what reception he'd get from the police; he could, however, be sure Langer's people would feel it necessary to make an example of him if he didn't cooperate, and to make an especially unpleasant example of him if he went to the authorities—either the police or his team's management. Wilson found himself on the horns of a dilemma. He would not ally with the gamblers, and he could not go to the police or his employer. Indeed, going to his employer posed the additional risk of exposing that he was the target of gamblers, and that could add to the owners' already cautious view of Wilson, perhaps lessening their interest in retaining his services. Is that not correct, Mr. Cochrane?"

"We're under orders to keep away from gamblers, Mr. Holmes, though it can be hard to do when they're practically in your lap half the time."

"If this is another try at making me the fall guy, you can just forget it." Langer had been dragged to Morgan's house, by a black man no less, or anyway by somebody who was supposed to be black, and had sat fuming through Holmes' presentation. "I work for a respectable businessman. The police got nothing on him or me. There's plenty others who make a living from gambling—just ask your friend over there." Langer jerked his head toward Washington who sat impassively beside him.

"I have no interest in how you make your living. My concern is with Mr. Wilson, and the shots fired the morning you and the others were at the Morgan home. Our evidence indicates that Mr. Wilson was more orator than murderer. But if Mr. Wilson did not fire at Mr. Morgan, who did? It was Mr. McLeod who provided me the answer. He reported walking a distance up 36th Street when he heard gunshots and turned back to look. He saw a man squeezing himself out of the thick stand of evergreens at the back of the house. Mr. McLeod quite reasonably thought he saw a man trying to escape from a gunman somewhere in the crowd; what he saw was the gunman himself. He had worked his way into the blind of trees in back of the crowd where he could fire two quick shots in succession without being seen. I've been informed the day was quite windy, and with the gunman located behind a crowd whose attention was focused on Mr. Morgan, the smoke from the revolver would have cleared before anyone could notice. The surrounding noise would have made it impossible to pinpoint the location of the gunfire without a visual cue. Seeing the gun in Wilson's hand it would be natural to assume he had fired the shots. His running away corroborated that assumption. The effort to escape, and the resulting chase after Wilson, also guaranteed the gunman could slip away in the opposite direction."

Morgan's face was creased into a mask of fierce concentration. He wasn't ready to concede anything yet, but neither could he outright dismiss Holmes' version of the events of that morning. "Alright then, Mr. Holmes, if you don't believe it was Wilson, who do you believe tried to kill me?"

Holmes gave Morgan a small nod in recognition of his unexpected display of open-mindedness, and the opportunity he provided to move a step closer to naming Morgan's assailant.

"It had to be someone slender and athletic enough to work his way into and out of the blind of trees, someone who would know Mr. Morgan's schedule, who would have access to Wilson's flat, and who was a good shot. Someone like Wilson's trusted friend, Candy Cochrane."

Holmes waited for all eyes to be fixed on Cochrane before continuing. Only Mrs. Hudson looked elsewhere. She turned to concentrate her attention on Dietz, willing him finally to glance her way. She tapped her shoulder and made a curt nod, which he understood well enough to unbutton his frock coat giving him ready access to his revolver.

"Cochrane and Wilson were, to all appearances, good friends. They had known each other for years. They confided in each other; they knew each other's habits. Cochrane knew that Wilson went to the Morgan residence to visit with Miss Littleberry most mornings when the team was in town, and every morning before they left town. He knew as well that Wilson had a Colt revolver that he carried when the team went out of town, and he would know where Wilson stored it when the team was in town. The two men had, after all, roomed together until four or five months ago according to Cochrane himself. At some point before turning his key over to Wilson he would have had a duplicate made—if he ever did turn his key over to Wilson. It would be an easy matter then to wait for Wilson to leave his flat one morning when he would be seeing Miss Littleberry, slip inside and empty two cartridges from the gun. He knew, because Wilson made no secret of it, that the weapon's only use to him was for show to ward off danger, and he wouldn't be likely to count the number of cartridges in its chamber. In this way, Cochrane was assured that Wilson would be carrying a revolver with two empty chambers for the trip to Boston the morning of the attack on Mr. Morgan. Cochrane would, meanwhile, have supplied himself with the same caliber weapon, and we know from Mr. Snyder's report to Dr. Watson that Cochrane was quite a good shot."

"Leaving incendiary literature in Wilson's flat was only a slightly more difficult task for Cochrane. The pamphlets were easy enough to come by. They could be obtained at any Union Square rally. But Cochrane did not have the same leisure to plant the literature as he had to remove the cartridges from Wilson's revolver. The pamphlets had to be left at a time when he could be certain Wilson would not find them, but the authorities would. It could only be done the morning of the attack. Cochrane went to Wilson's flat after the shooting, left the literature on his nightstand after first underlining the appropriate passage, then joined the team for the ride to Boston. He could expect Wilson to be arrested as a suspect in light of his presence on the scene and known antipathy to Morgan. Finding that he had a gun of the caliber used in the shooting with two cartridges missing would be damning; finding literature on his nightstand preaching revolution and identifying Morgan as the enemy would, he felt certain, seal Wilson's fate. And helped by Wilson's running away, Cochrane very nearly achieved his goal."

"In short, Cochrane was implicating Wilson while pretending to be his friend. Indeed, Cochrane was such a good friend he even helped orchestrate Wilson's escape. Of course, Wilson's escape set up two attractive possibilities for Cochrane. His absconding would make it still more likely that a jury would find him guilty if he was captured. Even better from Cochrane's standpoint, it would make it more justifiable for the police to forego the unnecessary risk of trying to capture him alive. To make Wilson's death at the hands of the police more certain, Cochrane took the further step of providing Wilson with a revolver to encourage a shootout—which I believe is the term you use in America."

Cochrane appeared to speak almost without opening his mouth, so tightly were his teeth clenched. "Tell me, Mr. Holmes, why in the world would I want to shoot Mr. Morgan? Morgan is nothing to me."

Holmes showed a faint smile as he prepared to draw the net tight. "I could not agree with you more, Mr. Cochrane. Mr. Morgan was never, in fact, your target. He could, however, be made to appear Wilson's target, and Wilson would take the blame for your crime. I suppose you got the idea when Wilson began courting Miss Littleberry. You had a perfect foil. Wilson had known radical inclinations. The robber barons, as they're called, were his villains. It was easy enough to make Morgan appear first among Wilson's villains. We've already talked about the carefully placed literature, but before that there was the shot at Morgan—a purposely wild shot—from somewhere in Central Park as Morgan entered his club. On the morning of the wedding breakfast you were somewhat more accurate in firing at Morgan. Your second shot was aimed at his shoulder making certain that, in the context of all that had gone before, Morgan would appear the gunman's target, and Wilson would appear the gunman. In truth, that was the morning you killed the man who was your intended target from the first. That was the morning you killed Conrad Wagner."

Holmes scanned the now silent room to revel in the looks of astonishment his audience directed to him. Having been alerted by Mrs. Hudson, Dietz alone concentrated his focus on Cochrane, waiting any suspicious movement.

"Quite by accident, my housekeeper, Mrs. Hudson, became aware of Cochrane's history as it bears on Wagner's murder. She went to visit Miss Littleberry, her cousin's daughter, in Brooklyn where she was living with a Lucy Donaldson after leaving Morgan's service. Miss Donaldson has been keeping company with Cochrane much as Miss Littleberry has been keeping company with Wilson. It was Miss Donaldson

214

who revealed to Mrs. Hudson much of what we know about Cochrane."

"We learned that Cochrane grew up on a farm in Bedford, Ohio, a village just outside Cleveland. His family named the farm Ian's Sod, in honor of his father who bought the land before going off to fight in your War Between the States. Until then, Ian Cochrane worked as a bargeman on Lake Erie. It's an honorable trade, but not one that generates a large income. And Mr. Cochrane had to feed, and keep a roof over the heads of a wife and two children, with a third on the way. How then does a bargeman acquire enough money to buy a hundred sixty acre farm? The fact that Ian Cochrane bought the land just before going off to fight answers our question. Ian Cochrane volunteered to be a substitute soldier. He was paid by another man to serve in his place." Holmes took a step toward Cochrane and stared down at him, his eyes narrowed, his gaze unblinking.

"Conrad Wagner was that man. While visiting here on an earlier occasion, Mr. Morgan introduced me to Mrs. Cornelia Porter, Mr. Wagner's daughter. She revealed that her father was involved in transporting goods across Lake Erie before getting into railroads. Undoubtedly, he would have come to know Ian Cochrane, a bargemen on the Lake, and to have opportunity to offer him a proposition."

Holmes paused, but this time the room was only silent for a moment. "It's a reasonable enough story, Holmes, but that's all it is, a story, unless you have some corroborating evidence." Heads turned to the unexpected spokesman. Not yet willing to let Wilson wriggle away, Dietz posed his objection to Holmes' account, while leaving his coat open to admit of other possibilities.

"And here is the corroborating evidence you very appropriately call for, Mr. Dietz." Holmes removed a paper from his pocket and waved it above his head. "I received a telegram only yesterday from the Veterans Branch of the Ohio Bureau of Vital Statistics in response to my request for information. It

215

states they have on record a report from the Conscription Services of the City of Cleveland stating that Mr. Ian Cochrane's service in the Seventh Ohio Infantry was purchased by Mr. Conrad Wagner. It does not report the sum received by Cochrane, but we can assume it to be substantial. As things turned out, Wagner stayed in Cleveland where he continued to work in transport, profiting handsomely for his part in supporting the North's war effort. Ian Cochrane died at Chancellorsville before his youngest son, Arthur, or Candy as we know him, was born. It is not too much to say Conrad Wagner was the boy's enemy from birth, and that vengeance was bred into him for nearly as long. Candy Cochrane fulfilled a life-long obligation on behalf of his family, an act for which he will very likely hang."

For several seconds, the only sound in the room was the ticking of the grandfather's clock. Unnoticed moments before, it now sounded a drumbeat demanding Cochrane's response. At last, Brickyard Snyder had had enough. His words sounded as though they had been forced painfully from him. "That can't be right, Candy. Straighten him out, wouldya."

But Candy ignored his teammate; there was nothing for him to straighten out. He rose from his seat against the wall waving a revolver he had removed from his coat pocket. "Very impressive, Mr. Holmes. Very impressive." Cochrane turned to flash the gun in the direction of Watson who had started out of his chair. "Everybody stay just as you are. As Mr. Holmes has said, I am a very good shot. And now, thanks to Mr. Holmes, I have nothing more to lose."

Cochrane started for the room's center, his eyes and his revolver sweeping the room as he moved. But the man beside him cared nothing about Cochrane's threat, and with a loud guttural roar he sprang like the animal he sounded at the man he had believed his friend. Cochrane's pistol sounded and Brickyard Snyder fell at his feet, clutching his side and writhing. Mrs. Hudson clawed at Watson to keep him from going instantly to the ballplayer's assistance. There was no need for her concern. Snyder's attack had provided the diversion necessary to allow Dietz to draw his own revolver. Cochrane saw the gun, but too late. Dietz's shot tore through his chest while his own shot did nothing more than disturb the painted mosaic on the drawing room's ceiling. As Cochrane fell, the others, who had been obedient to the gunman's request, now sprang to action. Sachs went to summon an ambulance and the police. Tarkenton went to reassure Mrs. Morgan who would have surely heard the gunfire. Langer made a move to leave the room, but found his way blocked by Dietz still brandishing his revolver. While Watson went to minister to Snyder as best he could, Holmes hurried to Cochrane who was still alive, but sounding as though every breath could be his last.

"Cochrane, will you do one good thing before you die. Tell us, where is Lucy Donaldson?"

A spiteful smile seemed to sap nearly all the dying man's strength. "Maybe Heaven, maybe Hell." There was a pause and two heavy breaths before he labored to continue. "But you're wrong, Holmes, I've already done my one good ...." There was a gurgling noise from deep in his throat, but not another word. Candy Cochrane was dead.

The room quieted once again. Only Watson could be heard speaking soft, calming words to Snyder as he made effort to stem his bleeding. He sent Sachs, back from his phone calls, for hot water and strips of material to be used as bandages. An ashen faced Morgan offered to move Snyder to a more comfortable place, but Watson wouldn't allow it, fearful that such action could trigger greater damage. McLeod and McIlvaine stood together grimacing and shaking their heads, unable to help the situation and unable to leave it. Washington stood apart from the others, showing no sign of shock or even surprise; his concern was now with the impending arrival of the police. It was true the two people he was hiding were no longer fugitives, but he doubted the police would take a sufficiently broad view of the situation to ignore his shielding an escaped prisoner and the prisoner's accomplice. Clemens alone continued in place, grim-faced, filling one page after another for a purpose he alone could have told.

The ambulance arrived first, announcing its presence with a great clanging of bells. The driver and two residents from Bellevue Hospital did their best to pretend to business-like efficiency, but their glances to all parts of the room made clear their curiosity about a house whose splendor they had never before encountered, and were unlikely ever to encounter again. They gently lifted Brickyard Snyder onto a stretcher, and bore the Bridegrooms' catcher out to the ambulance amid a confusion of voices all wishing him a speedy recovery. With considerably less care they hoisted the shrouded body of Candy Cochrane onto a second stretcher, promising Morgan the body would be sent to the morgue and the police alerted. No one ventured near the second stretcher, although every eye measured its progress exiting the room.

Holmes waited until the second stretcher was gone before once more addressing the group. "Mr. Morgan, I thank you again for making your home available. I regret the disturbance created; I'm afraid the course of these events is somewhat unpredictable. I want to thank all of you for participating in this unfortunate, but I think you'll agree, necessary exercise. I see no reason to detain you any longer. Mr. Morgan, I will need to impose on you and Mr. Dietz one last time. Either or both of you will be unimpeachable witnesses to the events of the morning, and I'd ask you to give your accounts to the police when they arrive. Mr. Washington, if you'd be good enough to stay another moment, I'd like to thank you properly as I know would my colleagues. Washington reluctantly agreed to stay, placing an emphasis on the "moment" portion of Holmes' request as he did so.

Morgan volunteered Dietz to describe events to the police, and Dietz grimaced agreement, then smiled at a sudden thought. He excused himself from Morgan and Holmes, and crossed the room to where Morgan's invitees were sharing their astonishment as they made their way slowly to the door. He clamped a hand on Franklin Langer's shoulder and steered the onetime footman back to the center of the drawing room.

"Mr. Langer can stay as well and give the police his view of events."

"You don't need me for that, and besides I'll be late to work." Langer's tone was more whine than request.

Dietz's tone was cold and emphatic. "Don't worry about that, Langer. I'll make certain your employer understands that you were unavoidably detained giving evidence to the police." Dietz turned to the butler. "Sachs, take this man to servants' hall and don't let him out of your sight."

Alerted by the gunshots, James, the first footman, had stolen quietly into the room, his face a mask of bland attentiveness as if the discharge of firearms was a customary occurrence in the Morgan household. With the afternoon's theatrics now complete, Sachs asked James to unlock the second door leading into the drawing room, and to join him in escorting Franklin to servants' hall. James and Sachs took the precaution of arming themselves with the two heavy candlesticks that had been doing duty as decoration on the mantle above the fireplace, before walking Langer to servants' hall.

With all tasks completed and the morning's guests departed, Morgan clasped Holmes' hand between his two and sounded another man in addressing him. "I am fully aware of all you've done, Holmes, and am deeply in your debt. You saved me from sending an innocent man to the gallows. I don't know how much longer you and your associates plan to be in New York, but I should like you to consider being my guests for as long as you choose to stay."

"Thank you, Mr. Morgan. That is most kind."

The two men might have exchanged further pleasantries marking their new found harmony were it not for the sudden appearance of a black youngster, who appeared to be twelve going on forty, being chased by Charles, Morgan's under-footman. Charles attempted to explain to his employer the cause for their inopportune appearance.

"I'm sorry, Mr. Morgan. The boy ran by me before I could grab a hold of him. He said something about having to see a Mr. Washington. If you gentlemen will just help me catch him, I'll put him out the service entrance where he come from." Charles took a step to make good his threat, but Morgan raised a hand.

"That's alright, Charles, it's been a day for the unexpected. You can return to your duties." Morgan gave his bemused attention to the young intruder. "What is it you want, young man?"

Wash's boy ignored Morgan; he glanced to Mrs. Hudson, acknowledging her without changing expression, before giving his full attention to his employer.

"The two of them done a runner, Mr. Washington. They're both of them gone."

While all but the Baker Street trio and Frederick Washington were trying to puzzle out who this new actor was, who "they" were, and why their disappearance was of concern, Tarkenton, having successfully reassured Mrs. Morgan about the disturbance to her home, now reappeared leading two men in police uniforms and a third in civilian clothes. Just as quickly as Wash's boy had commanded their rapt attention, he now receded to the background as the more senior of the two uniformed officers strode purposefully across the length of the drawing room, offering a hand to Morgan as he came near.

"Mr. Morgan, I'm Captain Phillip Emsinger of the Tenth Police Precinct. This is Lieutenant Lewin and I'm sure you already know Commissioner Frederick Grant." He gestured to the two men who had been struggling to keep up with the Captain. Morgan did indeed know the former president's eldest son, who himself had had a distinguished military and foreign service career before becoming a member of New York City's Board of Commissioners. Morgan greeted Grant warmly, and Lieutenant Lewin correctly. He proceeded to introduce all those present, pausing when he came to Mrs. Hudson, and after a sidelong glance to Dietz, describing her as Holmes' colleague. He introduced Washington as "one of our local businessmen" and Wash's boy as his associate, then stared down any urge his audience might have felt to raise question. Indeed, having been introduced to Sherlock Holmes and Mark Twain, the three men were prepared to accept, without comment, any guest of Morgan's. As it turned out, Grant and Clemens were old acquaintances dating back to the time the author published the autobiography of the Commissioner's father in an otherwise ill-fated business undertaking of Clemens.

The social requirements out of the way, the Captain returned to the business-like approach he believed appropriate. "I regret our late arrival, Mr. Morgan. I was off duty when we were informed of the tragedy at your home. I, of course, felt it appropriate to be here to attend to things, and I asked Commissioner Grant to join us. He was good enough to leave the meeting he was attending to do so. Your secretary, Mr. Tarkenton, has already made us aware of the disturbance in your home, and of the identification of this man, Cochrane, as your attacker and the murderer of Mr. Wagner. We will be as brief as we can in gathering the additional information we need."

Morgan felt it time to take charge of proceedings in his own house. "The Lieutenant can take statements from Mr. Dietz and Franklin Langer in the servants' hall. Langer was my footman at one time, and was witness to the events that took place earlier. Mr. Dietz can explain that situation to the Lieutenant." Dietz nodded importantly, and started for the servants' hall with Lieutenant Lewin trailing close behind.

Morgan looked to those remaining, his face set in fierce concentration, "Mr. Washington's young associate was about to share something before we interrupted him. I believe it had to do with Mr. Wilson and Miss Littleberry. I want to remind everyone that Mr. Washington and the young man are guests in my house. It is my understanding they played a significant role in making certain that no harm came to the two young people whom we now know to be innocent. In that spirit, I regard whatever they share to be privileged, in that it will not be used in any way that would penalize them." Morgan looked to the Captain and Grant to be certain his meaning was understood.

The Commissioner cleared his throat noisily to signal to Captain Emsinger he would respond to Morgan for both of them. He stroked his neatly trimmed beard as he spoke, a trick he'd learned to convince his audience of the seriousness with which he took their request and his own response. "I know I speak for the Captain in saying there is no wish to take any action that would jeopardize the well-being of the innocent, or cause difficulty for any who acted with good will, provided they did no harm to others."

Morgan was satisfied; Washington was less certain, but recognized he was not in a strong negotiating position.

Morgan looked to Wash's boy. "Now, what was it you had to say?"

All eyes were now fixed on Wash's boy, but his eyes saw only Frederick Washington. With a small nod to the boy and to the inevitable, he allowed the youngster to set forth his story.

"They wasn't at breakfast, Mr. Washington."

"Weren't, Edward," his employer corrected.

"Weren't at breakfast, but nobody took notice—at least not right away. They skipped breakfast pretty regular, but this time they wasn't—weren't—any place in the building. Old Peter said he seen a carriage at the top of the street in the middle of the night that looked to be waiting for someone, but he didn't stick around long enough to see who. And there's stuff missing from the house. There's some of Sebastian's clothes that's gone and that one's wig besides." Wash's boy crooked a finger in the direction of Holmes.

Having been identified as Washington's partner in crime, Holmes transferred an indulgent smile from the youngster to the others in the group before speaking. "As I suspect everyone is aware, the people who have done a runner, as Edward describes it, are Wilson and Miss Littleberry. I and my colleagues prevailed upon Mr. Washington to take them in because we were certain of Wilson's innocence. Mr. Washington was kind-hearted enough to accommodate our request. It seems clear, however, that Wilson and Miss Littleberry, having fled from Mr. Washington's care, now believe themselves fugitives who must disguise themselves from the police. They will, no doubt, attempt to reach the Cochranes' farm since they believe Cochrane and his family to be their only reliable friends."

"But that's a dreadful state of affairs." Clemens' face was contorted into an expression of pain matching his words.

"What are you suggesting, Twain?" Morgan demanded.

"I'm suggesting we have a crisis on our hands. Mr. Holmes has already made clear it was Cochrane's plan to sacrifice Wilson to avoid punishment for his own crimes. As Holmes described it, Wilson's escape fixed his guilt in the public mind, assuring his death either by a policeman's bullet or the rope. His exoneration leaves Wilson no less vulnerable, it simply transfers the source of danger. When Cochrane's guilt becomes known, Wilson and Caroline are bound to recognize the involvement of the Cochrane family, and Cochrane's family is bound to feel the need to remove those people who can tie them to Wagner's murder. That's quite apart from the vengeance they may wish to exact for the killing of their son and brother. Wilson, even with the gun he's carrying, will be no match for the Cochranes. I'd say we have only a small window within which to rescue Wilson and Caroline. There is a need to move and to move quickly. Wouldn't you agree, Holmes?"

The logic of Clemens' argument, and Mrs. Hudson's vigorous nodding at its end, led to Holmes' emphatic response.

"Exactly my thinking, Clemens. We can't afford any delay in getting to the young couple."

"I'll send a telegram to the Cleveland police. They'll be able to apprehend Wilson as soon as he leaves the train," Captain Emsinger volunteered.

"That won't do." Frederick Grant's authoritative voice stifled further discussion for all but one member of the group.

"Why not, Commissioner?," asked Morgan.

"The man is armed and believes himself facing death if caught. If anyone attempts to detain him—especially anyone in uniform—there could be a bloodbath. I'll not have that on the hands of the New York City police force. Nor can we allow the young couple we have helped victimize face death at the hands of a family bent on homicide. Wilson and this woman have a bit of a head start on us, but not a great one. Morgan, will you work with me to keep this out of the papers for as long as possible? The family, at least, may be slower to act if they don't learn of Cochrane's death." Morgan provided a judicious nod, not yet certain where Grant was taking them. Grant, having exchanged the diplomat's caution for the general's daring, was now again the Indian fighter leading troops into battle.

"Good! Holmes, you're the man for this job. I'm asking you to catch the earliest possible train leaving for Cleveland. Take whomever you like with you, but not a large force or you'll trigger suspicion and risk a counterattack. Are you prepared to leave immediately?"

"I need only Watson with me and we can both leave at once."

"I should like to be a party to this as well." Dietz had reentered the room, having given his statement to Lewin and seen Langer trundled off to the Tenth Precinct. He'd heard enough to know there would be more action in Ohio than he could hope to see on Madison Avenue.

"I'll not have it, Dietz," said Morgan. "There are too many crazies out there for me to give up your services just yet."

224

Dietz groaned his frustration, but said nothing. His place at the detectives' side was quickly assumed by Clemens. "I will plan to join Holmes and Watson in this adventure. I promise, Morgan, I will include its high points in my Cooper Union address, each one suitably embroidered to make certain reality is never given opportunity to ruin a good story."

Morgan grunted Clemens the approval the author never sought, then turned his attention to the task ahead. "Tarkenton, call Mr. Depew. Apologize for interrupting his day, and tell him it's urgent that we talk. Let me know as soon as you have him on the wire." While Tarkenton went to make the urgent phone call, Morgan explained to his guests that Mr. Depew was Chauncey Depew, president of the New York Central Railroad, and that by the time the two men had concluded their conversation, Holmes and his colleagues would have a sleeper and dining car at their disposal as well as a clear track to Cleveland, and arrangements for a train from the Cleveland & Pittsburgh line to take them from Cleveland to Bedford. Morgan had Sachs summon his coach to take them immediately to the train station.

Frederick Washington had waited silently while arrangements were made to intercept the escapees, and now was anxious to return home. Before leaving, he felt obliged to share a last comment. "You do know that even if Mr. Wilson can be rescued in Ohio, he will still be in danger here."

"What exactly does that mean?," Dietz asked.

"Through no fault of his own, Mr. Wilson has gotten himself mixed up with some very dangerous men. They will not take kindly to him refusing a proposition they see as capable of making a great deal of money for them. More importantly, they are in a very competitive business. If word gets around that someone can refuse them without penalty, they risk having others think they're weak, and that would leave them vulnerable to what you people," he looked to Morgan, "call a hostile takeover. If you want to save Mr. Wilson, you will have to do something about Helmut Fleischer, Langer's boss."

Having delivered his small bombshell, Washington gathered up Wash's boy and followed Sachs to the carriage the butler announced was waiting at the back entrance. Before attention could be paid to Washington's admonition, a second carriage arrived to take Holmes, Watson and Clemens to Grand Central Depot and the waiting train Chauncey Depew had agreed to provide. Morgan was ready for a long delayed brandy, over which to consider the newly revealed threat to Wilson, when he took notice there was need of a third carriage.

"Mrs. Hudson, I do believe we've kept you overlong. May I have Sachs arrange for your travel back to the Waldorf, or perhaps you'd like to take some tea in servants' hall before returning to your hotel. I could have Mrs. Sowder arrange that."

"That's most kind, Mr. Morgan. I do appreciate your interest. Maybe, if it's alright with you, I'll just rest a bit with you gentlemen before I go on. But don't let me interrupt your discussion." She smiled her gratitude to Morgan, and he forced a smile in return.

"There is just one thing," Mrs. Hudson began, her brow deeply furrowed, her mouth a tight line as she appeared to struggle with an idea she found it difficult to share. "I can't say just why, but this new business of protectin' Mr. Wilson from Langer's people puts me in mind of what 'appened on the London docks about five years ago. It probably was no big deal over 'ere, but I can tell you it was quite somethin' in London, and the whole of England come to that.'

"I remember it," Morgan's voice held only a veneer of patience. "It was a strike, and the workers ultimately forced their employers to give them higher wages. Raised prices for everyone was all it accomplished."

"The workers did get their way as you say, Mr. Morgan. But it's the way they done it that I can't get out of my 'ead. Do you remember that, Mr. Morgan?"

"I do, Mrs. ... Hudson, is it?" Commissioner Grant interrupted. "We made a study of the way your police handled striking workers. It was a good deal different from the activities of many of our police forces, and very different from the actions of our private police forces." Grant looked hard at Dietz lest there be any confusion about his meaning. There was none.

"I'm sorry, I don't see how any of that relates to the problem at hand," Morgan, unable to wait longer, lit a cigar, then tore it from his mouth before continuing. "If we know who this man is, why can't we just put him out of business, or arrest him for trying to force Wilson to lose his baseball games."

"It's maybe what should be, Mr. Morgan, but it's not the way it is." Captain Emsinger explained. "There's no hard evidence of this Helmut Fleischer fixing baseball games, and there's been no one willing to come forward to talk about it. It's pretty much the same thing with his business operation. The police haven't been able to get anything on him that would allow them to make an arrest." The Captain did not explain that the business in question lay within the 29th precinct, and that a large number of the police of the 29th precinct received handsome reimbursements for turning a blind eye to the many businesses in their area that promised the possibility of sudden wealth or the certainty of an affectionate companion. It was, Emsinger knew, the reason patrolmen were willing to pay a third of their salary to be assigned to the area New Yorkers called "the Tenderloin."

Grant knew it too, and was as affronted and frustrated by it as was Emsinger. He turned from a discussion he found distasteful to ideas the diminutive English woman had awakened in him.

"You may not realize it, Mrs. Hudson, but I believe you've hit on something. I feel certain the reason you were reminded of the dockworkers was because they faced the same problem we do—how to force concessions from a business owner who feels no need to grant concessions. Given the dockworkers' success, it makes sense for us to examine the tactics they employed. As I said, we made quite a study of the events of the confrontation because of our interest in police methods. But even then I was struck by the dockworkers' strategy. You see, they employed a modified siege technique. Of course they didn't call it that, not being military men, but that's what it was regardless." The Commissioner's eyes blazed as he envisioned a regiment of dockworkers, outfitted in the uniform of workmen's dress, holding at bay a cargo ship anchored at the pier they occupied.

"They first prevented goods from being loaded on ships. That is, the ship's owners couldn't take on materials for transport. Then, when that was accomplished, they got the stevedores on board the ships to block goods from being off-loaded onto the docks. Nothing could go in, nothing could come out. Not a shot was fired, and the owners had to capitulate." The president's son cocked his head and raised an eyebrow to make clear the significance he found in his own analysis. "The question, then, is whether there isn't something about those tactics that has relevance for our situation."

As the men puzzled out the problem posed by Grant, Mrs. Hudson pronounced herself sufficiently refreshed to return to her hotel. While Sachs summoned her cab, she replayed in her mind the image of a police chief, a president's son, and the world's foremost international banker jointly devising a strategy based on the actions of striking London dockworkers.

11.
Helmut Fleischer

Escaping Frederick Washington's home and place of business posed none of the risk and proved a good deal less difficult than escaping the Tombs. No one supervised the movements of Wilson and Caroline, supervision being unnecessary. If discovered, Wilson would go back to jail, and this time Caroline would accompany him. But Wilson was mindful of the deadline Washington had placed on their stay, and lacked the confidence of others in Holmes' powers.

To prepare for their escape, Wilson first made a study of the movements of people in the house. He learned that Washington went downstairs to his place of business promptly at six, and didn't return until one in the morning at the earliest. After Washington left the apartment, two of his child caretakers entered to clear dishes, make up his bed, and tidy the room. They never stayed past nine. It was Washington's strict rule that his young people get a good night's sleep.

Accordingly, at eleven o'clock on their third night on African Broadway, Wilson stole down the open stairway to Washington's living quarters, and used his telephone to ring up the hall phone of the apartment house where Cochrane was staying. He held his breath through every ring of the unanswered phone, imagining each one echoing throughout the building. When the landlady finally answered, she first informed Wilson of the hour, then advised him that working people lived in the building's apartments, after which she questioned his sobriety, and only when assured his call was not alcohol induced, agreed to rouse Cochrane for reasons she was certain did not merit her action. Wilson sat in the dark listening for any sound that might signal his impending discovery, while he waited for Candy to come on the line. When he did, Candy provided Wilson instant reassurance. He would, of course, come to get him. They agreed on an hour well before dawn the next morning. This time, Candy said, he would see to it Wilson and Caroline made it to Ian's Sod where, he added, they would join Lucy.

Shortly before dawn, Wilson fitted the grey wig left behind by Holmes over his own straight dark hair, put on a jacket that was several sizes too big for him, and adopted the slouch of an older, heavier version of himself. Caroline stuffed her hair under a workman's cap and dressed herself in clothing she had taken from Sebastian's wardrobe—Sebastian being the tallest of the boys who worked for Washington. The two emerged as an older man and his son making their way along deserted streets to the carriage Candy Cochrane once more held in readiness for them.

This time there were no waiting police or Pinkertons as they approached Grand Central Depot, and no interference with their boarding the early morning train. Nor was there any sign of law enforcement personnel when they changed trains in Cleveland. They reached the Bedford, Ohio station nearly twenty four hours from when their journey began, where they were reacquainted with Micah and introduced to Luke, the third Cochrane brother, who waved greeting from atop the dog cart that was to take them to their final destination.

Well before Wilson and Caroline disembarked, a second train with only three passengers aboard was speeding its way west across the State of New York. Two of those passengers stared without seeing at the countryside they passed, desperate for a plan to rescue Wilson and Caroline, and equally desperate to keep from Clemens the absence of any such plan. They believed themselves to have at most forty-eight hours for a strategy to emerge before the events of the morning would find their way into newspapers across the country. McIlvaine and McLeod had no reason to share what they had seen with the press, and Langer was effectively neutralized, but the absence of Brickyard Snyder and Candy Cochrane would be noticed in two days when the Bridegrooms had their next scheduled game, and that would lead to questions. The answers to those questions would surely become headlines in dailies across the country, and would just as surely find their way to Ian's Sod. The news of Candy Cochrane's death would speed the Cochranes' action to rid the world of two people they knew to be capable of linking them to the death of Conrad Wagner. Holmes and Watson looked to the scalloped hills of the Adirondack range, and waited the inspiration that would prove theirs and their young friends' salvation.

At 10AM, Helmut Fleischer was in his office on the third floor of the building he owned at the corner of 26th Street and Broadway. Fleischer's office rivaled Frederick Washington's in size, but appeared larger by virtue of its sparse furnishings. The room's decor consisted of a secondhand desk, two secondhand chairs, a filing cabinet that had long since seen secondhand come and go, and a large safe in one corner, distinctive as the room's only firsthand acquisition. A stranger would have thought it the office of a businessman struggling to survive, or a businessman who had given up all hope of survival—and would have been wrong on both counts. Helmut Fleischer had, in fact, already risen far beyond his most optimistic expectations when he crossed the Atlantic as a young man in search of a better life. He was long out of the sweat shop where he had gotten a job within days of his boat's docking. At first, the degrading conditions under which he labored made him wonder about the decision to emigrate to America; weeks later he discovered the job would pave the way to his achieving his own version of the American dream.

It began with the discovery that his coworkers had needs he could satisfy, and weaknesses he could exploit. Someone was being intimidated and had no recourse; Fleischer was big enough and ruthless enough to provide a recourse. Someone had lent money to a friend, but the friend had conveniently forgotten the loan; Fleischer could jog the friend's memory. Someone

231

wanted a woman; Fleischer came to know women too destitute to refuse the money promised. And nearly everyone wanted to get rich, and to get rich quick. Gambling provided people the prospect of sudden wealth, while giving Fleischer its reality. He established a life that seemed to fulfill his most extravagant earlier ambitions, but Fleischer's ambitions had grown with his fortune. He wanted something beyond wealth, he wanted to be recognized as a major figure within New York's gambling community. And with baseball he had a way to do just that.

Fleischer came to see that nearly all his customers not only followed the sport, but believed themselves expert about it. At the same time, those same men felt strong loyalty to the two hometown teams. Their hearts often overcame their already suspect reason, allowing Fleischer to reap considerable profit from his customers' rush to misjudgment. There was, however, a way to insure even greater profits, and to establish himself as a kingpin in the gambling community.

Baseball players were typically low paid relative to the revenue they generated for owners, and they were under the tight control of those owners. Their services were reserved for the team with which they first signed, and they could not compete for jobs with other teams. Some day there would be a flood of protest against that practice, but that day was far off. For now, it was a situation ready-made for anyone willing to be unscrupulous. Fleischer was a good deal more than willing. His plan was to entice players through bribes—or perhaps a mix of bribes and threats—to lose games they were expected to win.

Not every game, of course. That would arouse suspicion and ultimately backfire. And not just any players. It had to be a key player, one whose contribution—or lack of contribution— could spell the difference between winning and losing games. Chief among key players, Fleischer had learned, was the pitcher. His hunt narrowed to a pitcher with one of the two local teams, There were two the odds favored to win every time they walked onto the field. He would have liked to have gotten Amos Rusie of the Giants—there were clearly more Giants' than Bridegrooms' fans among his clientele—but he chose to pursue the Bridegrooms' curve ball artist, Brakeman Wilson, for two reasons. One was Franklin Langer.

The Morgan's footman had successfully recruited some of the household staff to make use of Fleischer's services, and when approached by Fleischer had pledged his ability to recruit Wilson as well. Fleischer knew Wilson was seeing a woman on Morgan's staff, and that would give Langer plenty of opportunity to convince Wilson of the wisdom of accepting his offer.

The second reason was Wilson's seeming readiness to accept a proposition. He had made clear his contempt for business leaders he saw as profiting unfairly from the labor of their workers. Fleischer would reward Wilson for his labors, though not near as handsomely as he would reward himself.

But Langer had proven a colossal failure, and Wilson had proven to have unexpected scruples. Now, with Wilson's arrest, Fleischer was back to square one—except for some unfinished business. His police informant had reported that Langer was now in custody and being questioned by the police. That made Langer more than a disappointment, it made him a liability. When he was released, that liability would have to be removed.

For now, he needed to prepare for the new day. His runners would be clocking in soon. He needed to review the last day's receipts, and set aside the payouts they would make to those few who had beaten the odds. He never begrudged the winners—as long as they stayed few in number. Winners gave the losers false hope, and the winners false confidence. And they all came back to try again.

His review of the day's take was interrupted by one of his lieutenants who stood in the doorway of Fleischer's office and noisily cleared his throat.

"Well?" Fleischer asked.

The lieutenant had been with Fleischer long enough not to be put off by a less than cordial greeting. "You need to look out your window. There's something happening. It's something you should see."

Fleischer walked to the nearest of the office's two windows to survey the street below. He found a sidewalk filled with men neatly dressed in frock coats and soft derbies. He counted at least twenty, and more were gathering. Each man seemed oblivious to the existence of any of the others although they stood at measured distances one from another.

"Pinkertons," Fleischer growled, "what do they want with us?"

"Watch." The lieutenant had come into the room, but remained a respectful distance from his leader.

Fleischer grunted and watched. He recognized one of his runners returning with the wagers he'd taken from the night crews at Bellevue Hospital and the area hotels. As he approached the building, three Pinkertons came together in a small but determined phalanx at its entrance. Assuming a ferocious scowl, the runner tried to force his way past the three men. When that failed, he assumed a pained expression, suggesting to Fleischer he was now trying to gain entry through a combination of pleading and reasoning, with a somewhat greater emphasis on pleading. When that also failed, he tried a second rush at the three men, but found it no more successful than the first. Looking either to the Heavens or the third floor window where Fleischer stood, the man acknowledged defeat and slowly made his way down the street. Fleischer left the window to call the police precinct and demand service for the money he was paying them, while a single Pinkerton, clean-shaven and heavy browed, gave quiet thanks to a group of London dockworkers before nodding his satisfaction at the figure departing the third floor window.

"Message received," he murmured.

Fleischer was told that Captain Dodson was not available to speak to him; the officer who did speak to him knew nothing about Pinkertons in the area. Fleischer hung up, knowing he was in trouble without knowing why or from whom. If runners couldn't get back in the building, they couldn't collect payouts to winners or get back on their routes. Nothing would kill his business more quickly than failing to pay off winners. A day's delay in his runners getting out and making payments could be understood. Things happen, and his customers knew it. A sudden clamp down because of a high level visitor, or because an official was demanding a bigger cut of the pie. A stoppage beyond two days would be damaging, maybe even fatal. He'd seen it happen to others who fell out of favor with the authorities. But those people had done things to make the authorities sore. He'd done nothing, at least nothing he knew about. He had to find out why this was happening to him, and more importantly, he had to put a stop to it.

Had he been witness to Fleischer's discomfort, Dietz might have again declared, "Message received."

As their train raced toward the approaching sunset, Clemens interrupted the silence that had taken firm hold of their compartment to announce his need to get something to eat. Noting that none of them had eaten since breakfast, he invited Holmes and Watson to join him. The two demurred, claiming a need to let their stomachs settle from the day's excitement.

Clemens' departure did not prove a stimulant to conversation between the men he left behind. As they looked to the world outside their window, forest and farmland gave way to a town, the station they roared past proclaiming it to be Kingston. At the town's outskirts, a carriage had caught in a roadside ditch and overturned. The two men who would have been its passengers stood beside it, staring forlornly down a long and empty road. The scene was passed in a moment, but it lingered in the minds of its two observers. An accident on a lonely road would leave those affected in need of assistance from someone living nearby. Everything pointed to the Cochrane farm lying along a lonely road where an overturned carriage would demand attention from helpful neighbors. It was nothing more than the ghost of a plan, but it was a good deal more than they had at the beginning of their travels, and they had the better part of a day to build on it. For now, they found themselves suddenly aware they were ravenously hungry, and eager to join Clemens in the dining car.

Helmut Fleischer spent the night in his office, sleeping fitfully in his chair when he slept at all. His lieutenants slept even more uncomfortably on the hardwood floor outside his office. He couldn't chance anyone leaving; he couldn't be certain they could get back in. Through the afternoon he had watched one after another of his runners turned away. In one instance three of his men had joined together, hoping numbers might accomplish what their individual efforts had not. They never got close to the building's door. Men in frock coats and homburgs who had stayed at a distance when individuals sought entry to the building now joined with the men in frock coats and homburgs who had been turning away those individuals. It was clear to Fleischer that his runners, even if they somehow became a united force, would be unequal to the efforts of the better organized and possibly better armed Pinkerton force.

If Helmut Fleischer was confused about why his business was under attack, he nevertheless knew what to do about it. By ten the next morning, Dietz and the twenty of his Pinkerton colleagues on duty found themselves outnumbered nearly two to one by enforcers Fleischer had recruited through the night. Some were his own men, some were borrowed from organizations that owed him a favor, and a few were mercenaries who'd heard about the prospect of battle, and would look to exact money or favors from Fleischer in return for their participation. The reinforcements came as neither a surprise or a concern to Dietz. He was ready to put in place the second part of the plan hatched the day before, the part about goods never leaving the boat. He gave a whispered message to the man beside him who gave him a sharp nod before pulling down on both sides of his homburg and striding quickly to a waiting carriage.

While Fleischer and Dietz watched, their two armies kept just enough distance from each other to avoid the casual jostle—or more than casual jostle—that could provoke open warfare between them. Fleischer's runners had also assembled, and now began drifting into the office building weaving their way past the men who were there to protect them, while nervously eyeing the men who had blocked their entry one day earlier. By eleven, all of Fleischer's runners were in the building. Fleischer was content that in calling out the troops, he had taken the steps necessary to save his operation. His self-satisfaction lasted for the time it took him to walk to his office window.

The corner of 26th Street and Broadway had undergone a substantial transformation. There were now only about ten or fifteen Pinkertons, but they had been joined by nearly forty New York City policemen, none of whom he recognized, and two of whom sat atop a police wagon parked in front of his building. The appearance of the police, and of a wagon used to transport arrestees, occasioned the leisurely, but steady withdrawal of the men who had gathered at Fleischer's behest. The Pinkerton dispatched earlier by Dietz had summoned Captain Emsinger and forces from the 10th Precinct rather than the more obliging 29th. With police officers stationed at the building's entrance and the last of Fleischer's enforcers now fully a half block distant, Dietz entered the building with Emsinger, and the two of them proceeded to Fleischer's office. Their expressions would have made the Grim Reaper appear amiable as they brushed past Fleischer's several employees to enter their boss' office, and introduce themselves to the would-be kingpin. Rather than compete for the single chair available, they stood and instead competed with each other in staring sullenly at Helmut Fleischer.

Fleischer guessed correctly he had no need to give his name, and expressed no interest in theirs. He looked from one man to the other as he questioned the authority of both.

"What do you want with me?"

Emsinger spoke with equal cordiality."We're putting this building and everybody in it under quarantine. Nobody is to leave until everyone can be examined for cholera."

Fleischer bolted from his chair, and for a moment appeared ready to demonstrate that at least one person was prepared to leave the building. He made no move for the door, however, choosing instead to lean across the desk and thunder his displeasure. "What kind of trick is this? There's no cholera here."

Emsinger answered in a voice as composed as Fleischer's was overwrought. "Don't you read the papers? Cholera has been found among immigrants entering New York harbor. It's our job to protect the city from an outbreak that could lead to the deaths of its citizens."

"And what in God's name has any of that got to do with me? Do I look like I just got off the boat?"

"We have the report of a man fleeing a ship on which cholera was suspected, and believe he may have sought refuge here, maybe with somebody who works for you. We'll need to conduct a thorough search of the building, and talk with anyone who might have come into contact with the man. You can consider yourself officially under quarantine. No one will be allowed to leave until we are satisfied none of your people pose a danger to public health. You should prepare yourself and your people. I expect our investigation will take a while."

Confusion competed with fury within Fleischer with no clear winner.

"The only people been able to get in the building have been my workers," he stormed. "You took care of that." He

238

jerked a thumb in the direction of Dietz, then turned back to Emsinger. "What's really going on here? What will it take to get you off my back?"

Emsinger sounded hurt. "'Off your back?' I don't think I understand. We have a sworn duty to protect the City's health and safety." The police captain looked around Fleischer's office as if searching for the appearance of any offending microbes. Apparently finding none, he resumed speaking."Maybe we should get started with the interviewing. That way, if we don't find a problem, we might be able to get your people out by nightfall. I'm not making any promises, but we'll do what we can. I think you should know, however, there may be a problem with your fire escapes. We might need to have the fire department do an inspection before letting your men back in once we clear them to leave. I need to warn you the fire department has quite a backlog of inspections, and it may be a while before they'll be able to get to you."

Fleischer sank into the chair he had deserted at the beginning of their exchange. The glare he directed at the men standing over him seemed to fall short of its mark.

"Mr. Fleischer, I will be leaving now," Emsinger said. "Several of my men will be stationed outside to make certain the quarantine is respected. As I'm sure you understand, the police have a range of responsibilities, and I have asked Mr. Dietz to carry out the remainder of the health and safety investigation on my behalf." Emsinger nodded to Dietz, ignored Fleischer, and turning on his heel, left the room.

Dietz spoke for the first time.

"I expect it's clear to you by now we have the capacity to lock your men in or to lock your men out just as we wish. In a word, we have the capacity to shut you down."

Fleischer kept his lips tight together. He sensed he was about to learn why he had been singled out for punishment and how much it would cost him. He was certain money was their object, although he had no idea why they went about it in such a roundabout way—except that maybe by working it this way the cop could deny any knowledge about the payoff worked out with the Pink, while still taking his cut.

Without invitation, Dietz took the chair across the desk from Fleischer. "There is a way to avoid any further interference with your business."

Fleischer had never mastered the art of subtle negotiation; he had never had to. "How much will it cost me?"

Dietz grinned in spite of himself. Fleischer was so deliciously corrupt, it was impossible to resist needling him. "How much what?"

"Money, of course! How much money? What do I have to pay you and Captain ... whatever his name is? I know that story about somebody jumping ship is the bunk, and so is this stuff about fire escapes. What'll it cost me for you to lay off and let me get back in business?"

"How much is it worth to you?"

Fleischer was ready with a figure. "Fifty a week, but that's as much as I can do." He could, in fact, do a hundred, but it wouldn't be necessary. Cops were lousy at bargaining.

"That's twenty-five hundred dollars a year you'd be willing to pay." Dietz paused as if considering Fleischer's offer. When he spoke again, his voice was soft, but it seemed nearly to echo in the stillness of the empty office. "What I want will cost you nothing."

"What are you talking about?"

"I know you've been trying to get Brakeman Wilson to cooperate with your business. He won't, and you might feel it necessary to make an example of him for that reason. I work for a gentleman who would be very upset if anything was to happen to Wilson."

Fleischer slouched in his chair wide-eyed. With what seemed his last bit of energy, he fluttered a hand toward the window. "Are you telling me all this is about Brakeman Wilson?"

"No, all this is about JP Morgan."

"What are you talking about? I'm nothing to JP Morgan."

"Which is why he can squash you like the bug you are if you choose to be uncooperative. You're up against power, Fleischer, real power, not your penny ante kind. You've been shut down a day on Mr. Morgan's word. You can be shut down permanently on his word. But you've got a choice. You leave Brakeman Wilson alone and everything goes back the way it was, or you can go after him, and everything you've built up will be destroyed."

Fleischer had no trouble reaching a decision, but couldn't keep from stating his confusion before answering Dietz. "I don't get it. Wilson's in jail. He tried to kill Morgan."

"He's not in jail at the moment, and Mr. Morgan is a most forgiving man—except when it comes to scum like you. Now, do we have an understanding?"

The Pink's answer triggered more questions, but Fleischer did not feel it prudent to delay further his agreement to Dietz's proposal. "Sure. I swear to you, and to Mr. Morgan, I don't know Wilson anymore. Hand to God." Fleischer raised his hand in the general direction of where he thought The Deity might be found, but received no answer.

Dietz stood, set his palms flat on Fleischer's desk and leaned across it, letting his stare register before speaking. "See that you don't forget it. Keep in mind, anything happens to Wilson—anything all—we're gonna assume you're responsible, and we're gonna make you pay."

"Hey, just a minute. I'll lay off. I give you my word on that, but I can't account for what else might happen. Wilson could get hit by a cable car, he could get hit by lightning, he could get caught in a fire—there's a million things could happen that's got nothing to do with me."

Dietz had straightened, but not yet released Fleischer from his stare. "Like I said, anything happens you're gonna pay." With that Dietz went to the door, but he turned before leaving to share a final thought with Fleischer. "All of life's a gamble. See what you can do to get the odds to work in Wilson's favor."

Five minutes later the corner of 26th Street and Broadway was deserted.

12.
Ian's Sod

Within hours of Dietz concluding his business with Helmut Fleischer, Holmes, Watson and Clemens were approaching Ian's Sod in a rented carriage. They'd been told to look for the farm's name set in an arched entrance, and to follow the path beneath it to the farmhouse. The directions conjured up images of wooden posts thick as tree trunks supporting a crown with the farm's name carved into it. Instead, they found two sets of slender sticks bound together and set 15 feet apart to support an equally rudimentary overhang that held the words "IAN SOD" fashioned by joining straight sticks of nearly equal size within the overhang's frame. A rutted carriage path ran beneath the rude structure to a farmhouse about 60 yards distant, then curved away to end at a stable angled another 40 yards left of the house. There looked to be corn growing on the side away from the stable, and something green and indistinguishable in the fields beyond the house and stable. They slowed the carriage as much as they dared before continuing on to a forested area out of sight of the farmhouse, where they put the first part of their plan into operation.

The three of them pitched over the carriage, making it appear to have overturned when the driver strayed from the roadway and struck tree roots that lay just right of the path. With a nod to his co-conspirators, Holmes left for the Cochrane farm to get help. Watson and Clemens then disappeared into the thicket beyond the fallen carriage, to search out fallen branches of a heft that would allow an appropriate welcome to the Cochrane brothers with whom Holmes would be returning.

Holmes was well aware of the challenge confronting him. It had been the subject of continuing discussion from Bedford station to Ian's Sod. Beyond getting the Cochranes to join him in righting the carriage, he would need to discover where the Cochranes were holding Wilson and Caroline, and learn enough about conditions at Ian's Sod to effect their escape. To accomplish all that, he would follow a procedure that had been described to him many times over the past several years. He would first take careful note of everything in evidence around him, then determine what was present that shouldn't be, and finally determine what was not present that should be.

The two-story stone farmhouse he approached was shaded front and sides by a mix of elms and oaks that had been left standing when the land was cleared. Other than the flower beds of multi-colored pansies lining much of the path, there was little to distinguish it from the dozen or so other farmhouses they'd passed after leaving the station. As Holmes neared the house, he was greeted by persistent barking from the stable beyond. He could tell there were two dogs, and from their low growls decided they were good sized. In response to the alarm they raised, a woman's face appeared at a farmhouse window, caught a glimpse of Holmes, and promptly disappeared. In another instant Holmes' attention was drawn to the source of the low growls. Two dogs, that were obviously the product of a single litter, staked out the ground outside the stable to loudly challenge Holmes' presence. He judged them to be part Newfoundland and part wolf, with the wolf part predominating. They appeared reluctant to leave the area around the stable, allowing Holmes to proceed cautiously, but steadily along the path to the farmhouse. As he neared his destination, the back of a dog cart became visible behind the stable. It seemed to Holmes the likely vehicle for transporting Wilson and Caroline from the train station. Its position at the stable, and the presence of the dogs standing guard nearby, suggested to Holmes he had found the place the Cochranes were holding their hostages.

He climbed the three steps that led to a broad porch, and rapped twice on the farmhouse door. A stout woman of more than 50 years answered his knock and opened the door part way. She was the woman whose face he had seen at the window. She wore a full apron over a flowered dress and the aroma of fresh

244

baking trailed behind her. Holmes could as easily imagine Mrs. Hudson a murderer as this woman—actually, more easily.

"Can I help you, young man?" Her smile and her voice were more cautious than welcoming.

"Thank you, madam, I'm hoping you can. My name is Calvin Tyler; my carriage turned over a short way down the road. I was hoping there might be men on your farm who could help me get it straight. Two men would do I think, perhaps your husband and another man might be available."

The door now came fully ajar. "I lost my husband some time ago—in the War. I do have two sons. They'll be back shortly, they're just now putting up the horses. You're welcome to wait. Perhaps you'd like a lemonade. It's freshly made and you must be warm from your walk." Having accepted Holmes' story of a not uncommon accident, Mrs. Cochrane assumed the responsibility expected of country people to assist a stranded traveler.

She led Holmes into a room cluttered with oaken furniture that looked to have been crafted by the same inexperienced hands that had fashioned the arch Holmes had passed beneath earlier. Three chairs and a couch did what little they could to form an inviting cluster before a stone fireplace. A small table set beside the couch held two photographs. One showed two young men who seemed to regard the photographer with suspiciousness if not outright hostility. They would be the two sons Holmes would soon meet. The second photograph was of another young man smiling broadly for the camera. He was dressed in the uniform of the Brooklyn Bridegrooms, and Holmes took note that the picture was without the black border the knowledge of his death would have required. He took note, as well, of two empty hooks over the fireplace where a shotgun should have been.

"A lemonade would be very nice, thank you, ma'am." Holmes followed the woman into the kitchen without waiting to be asked. "Allow me to help with the drinks," he said by way of explanation. Mrs. Cochrane wondered what assistance was needed to carry two glasses, but put it down to his being foreign—English, judging by his fancy way of talking—and this was probably good manners where he came from.

While Mrs. Cochrane searched her icebox for lemonade, Holmes searched the kitchen for things out of place. In the end it was his hostess who provided the clue. She apologized to him for not having a clean glass and gave him a teacup of lemonade. Looking to the tub of dishes yet to be washed, Holmes detected five glasses although he saw only three plates in the same tub. It was not damning evidence, but suggested Wilson and Caroline had prevailed upon their captors for water, even as they were denied food, and lent further weight to his conclusion that Wilson and Caroline were alive and were prisoners in the nearby stable.

"The lemonade is delicious, Mrs. Cochrane, thank you again."

"You're not from around here, are you, Mr. Tyler?"

"No, I've come here from the East."

"You're from further away than that. I can tell that from your voice. You're one of those English gents, ain't you?"

Holmes bowed to the inevitable and answered the question he felt certain would follow his admission. "That's right, Mrs. Cochrane, from London. I've decided to see as much as I could of your lovely country while I'm here, but I wanted to see the real America, not just the places the tourists see. That's how I happen to be in Ohio, although I hadn't planned on my carriage overturning."

Mrs. Cochrane smiled her sympathy with Holmes' plight, assuring him of her sons' assistance before ushering him back to the room of rough hewn furniture. "Please have a seat. My boys should be here directly. They've just finished the last of the spring planting."

She had no sooner spoken than Holmes heard the side door to the kitchen open and loudly close. That was followed by excited voices talking over each other, making it impossible for him to grasp any part of the conversation. Mrs. Cochrane pushed herself from her chair, urged Holmes to keep his seat, and fixed a dim smile on her face as she hurried from the room, explaining she would "just let the boys know you're here."

He heard her tremulous soprano above the male torrent and the single word "visitor", followed by a lengthy period of silence, after which all three came into the room. They were preceded by one of the mongrels, which, having barked its suspicions of Holmes earlier, now came forward to sniff its greetings, apparently having decided that if the stranger could be admitted to the farmhouse, he must be an acceptable addition to the household. The animal took the measure of several parts of Holmes' body, and after deciding it had obtained a comprehensive understanding of the man, lost any further interest, and left to stretch its body across the hooked rug that lay before the fireplace. The brothers crossed the room to provide Holmes their own greeting which was briefer and less intrusive than that shown by their dog. They each shook Holmes' hand, calling him by his surname, "Mr. Clayton," before volunteering their own given names, "Micah", "Lucas." The one who introduced himself as Micah carried the missing shotgun which he now replaced over the fireplace. Holmes regarded the replacement of the shotgun as both a good and an ominous sign.

While they showed little resemblance to Candy, no one could mistake the two men being brothers. Both had dark thick hair, brooding blue eyes and thin lips, and both were muscular enough to appear capable of maintaining a 160 acre farm with only each other to rely on. Holmes' attention was drawn to the men's clothing rather than their faces. There was something present that shouldn't have been. Although the day was clear and the ground dry, their boots showed traces of mud where they hadn't been wiped thoroughly. There were streaks of mud across their overalls as well, suggesting they had been working in a marshy area, likely the bottomland adjoining the river that Lucy

247

had described to Mrs. Hudson as being at the back of the Cochrane farm.

Having replaced the shotgun, Micah assumed the role of group spokesman. "I understand you ran into some trouble on the road?"

"Quite right. I'm afraid I've toppled my carriage. I'll need help getting it right side up. Fortunately, the horse wasn't hurt, so if I can trouble you and your brother for assistance I can be on my way."

To Holmes' surprise, his request caused both men to abandon their icy reserve and break into hearty laughter.

"You look to be healthy enough, Mr. Tyler. You don't need the two of us to get one measly carriage set to rights. Besides, I got things to do around here; Lucas can help you get yourself straightened out."

"It's a rather large carriage. I needed something sizeable to carry my luggage."

Micah curled his lip disdainfully as he waved off Holmes' concern. "Can't be all that big. And Lucas only looks like a weakling." He gave his brother a playful shove, and received a somewhat less than playful punch in return.

This was not going the way Holmes had hoped. He needed both brothers to come to his rescue. Capturing Lucas alone would not simply be inadequate, it would be counter-productive. Micah and his mother would be alerted to a problem, and that could further threaten the survival of the people they had come to rescue. Holmes recognized that the plan enthusiastically adopted hours before would have to be scrapped. Moreover, his two collaborators would have to grasp the changed situation instantly to avoid revealing themselves, and jeopardizing the success of any later effort. Their quick grasp of the situation would depend on Holmes' ability to alert them without also alerting Lucas.

While Lucas went to ready the dog cart for their short journey, Micah plied Holmes with questions about life in

England. He first wondered if all Englishmen carried umbrellas; then, if London was always stuck in fog; then, whether all Englishman drank their beer warm; and finally, how Englishmen felt about being bossed by a woman—adding with a prideful smile that nothing like that could happen in America. Mercifully, Lucas came to collect Holmes before he had to explain the nature of constitutional monarchy.

When they arrived at the overturned carriage, Holmes was relieved to find no sign of Watson and Clemens. As he climbed down from the dog cart, Holmes announced to the woods beyond his wish that they had brought Micah with them. Acting as though Lucas was both hard of hearing and had difficulty comprehending the English language, Holmes went on to state his concern that Lucas alone was not sufficient for the action to be successful. Lucas' response lacked Holmes' volume and precise diction, but made clear his disagreement. Holmes shook his head, taking vigorous exception to Lucas' words, but did so while looking to a shaggy-haired man with bushy eyebrows and a drooping moustache peeking from behind a large pin oak.

They got the carriage righted with as little effort as Micah had foretold, which Lucas pointed out several times before finally climbing back atop the dog cart and disappearing around a turn in the road. Only then did Holmes feel it safe to call his two colleagues out of the woods, promising the detailed explanation their querulous looks demanded.

While Clemens urged the small roan to put distance between them and the Cochranes, Holmes described his difficulty in getting both brothers to help him, for the moment saying nothing about their muddy clothing. The troubled expressions of his companions unclouded the merest bit as he stated his certainty that Wilson and Caroline were alive and being held in the stable, only to fully cloud again as Watson pointed out the distinction between knowing the location of those to be rescued and rescuing them.

Clemens was determined to discover the makings of a silver lining in that cloud. His confidence in the abilities of his fellow travelers undimmed, he announced they needed only a little time to rethink their strategy in a venue suited to such deliberation.

"It seems to me we have a three beer problem. I suggest we find a tavern well away from the Cochranes where we can employ alcohol to clear our minds."

Clemens' proposal won instant support, and was promptly put into action. They drove to Macedonia, the next town south, passing two public houses before selecting the Macedonia Road Inn and Tavern, which they reasoned to be at least one tavern beyond any the Cochrane brothers might choose. They were shown to a corner table by the landlord of the house, and offered dinner and drinks with all the forced joviality his position demanded. They declined dinner and ordered beers all around.

Holmes tested the beer set before him, found it surprisingly palatable, and took a larger sip before stating the dilemma he saw. "The danger is clear, but we don't dare put off getting into the stable beyond tonight. There's every reason to believe our young friends are still alive, and no reason to believe they will be much longer. To reach them, we will need to cross unfamiliar territory in the dark, and be prepared to brave the Cochrane dogs, and at least a shotgun for repelling trespassers." Holmes' face was drawn, but there was no mistaking the fire in his eyes as the beer, and the challenge that lay ahead combined to energize him. "Regardless, I see no other route for us to take."

"Nor do I, Holmes," Watson said. "It can't be much longer before Candy Cochrane's death is made public, and then our efforts will almost certainly come too late. At least we know the lay of the land thanks to you, Holmes."

Clemens again found the half full glass. "There will be some things in our favor. There'll be little moon so while we'll be covering unfamiliar ground in the dark, we'll also be less likely to be seen. Of course, I'm not forgetting the dogs in all that." In fact, none of them were forgetting the dogs. All were aware that two huge dogs could wake everyone in the house, if not tear them apart before they ever got to the stable.

Watson pulled from his waistcoat the ever present accounts book and number 2 Eagle pencil. "I suggest we make a list of the obstacles to be overcome if we are to succeed, and then determine how to do deal with each." Watson allowed himself a fleeting wish Mrs. Hudson was there to guide them, Holmes felt no such loss.

There followed a discussion about the need to cover 100 yards of rough, but level ground in the dark; a sharing of largely fruitless suggestions for holding at bay mongrel dogs, whose size grew exponentially with each suggestion; a review of the weaponry likely available to farmers concerned with protecting crops from deer and rabbits; speculation about the state in which they might find Wilson and Caroline; and the difficulty of escaping from the stable in the event they successfully overcame the problems of the dark, the dogs and the guns. Their talk was accompanied by the draining of beers that provided neither comfort nor fresh insight.

At Clemens' urging they ordered a second round of beers. It was Clemens' firm opinion that it took one beer to give them the courage to confront their problems, a second beer to free them to consider even outlandish strategies for overcoming those problems, and a third beer to give them the confidence to make use of whatever strategies, outlandish or otherwise, they devised. A fourth beer, he cautioned, would lead to either overconfidence and misjudgment, or depression and misgivings. And indeed, while finishing the second beer a plan was developed which, while initially seen as having deficiencies, a third beer revealed as certain of success.

In accord with that plan, they first obtained a room for the night, then purchased two slabs of venison which led the landlord to look at them over the tops of his half-glasses with eyebrows in ascendance. He opened his mouth to question their judgment, then closed it again as Holmes offered payment that was twice the market price for the meat. Afterward, Clemens went to their room to record a history of their travels, certain to find its way into his Cooper Union address, should he survive to deliver it. Holmes went for a walk "to consider all possibilities," and Watson drove their carriage to an apothecary in Macedonia where he purchased two vials of laudanum, each made up with a larger than standard proportion of opium he explained as necessary to treat the pain associated with a colleague's advanced state of gout.

At six, they regrouped to share a dinner of chicken fricassee and boiled potatoes delivered to their table by the broadly smiling landlord. He set the plates down with a flourish, sniffing the air as he did so as if hoping to steal a small sample of the extraordinary delicacy he was bringing them. Their plan to attack Ian's Sod now established, they agreed there would be no further discussion of the task ahead. As a result, there was virtually no discussion at all. Even Clemens appeared chastened by the task that lay ahead and was uncharacteristically somber. Their appetite was a match for their conversation, and they returned nearly full plates of fricassee and potatoes to the landlord, who was no longer smiling, and now sniffed the air to signal his displeasure as he contemplated returning the dishes to the kitchen, and to his wife, the inn's chef.

By seven thirty they had finished cigars provided by Clemens from a supply that seemed nearly as limitless as that of Morgan's. An hour later, Watson and Clemens took the two beds in the room, prepared to sleep until three AM, at which time Holmes, who claimed he neither needed nor cared to sleep, would wake them, and all would start for Ian's Sod. There was a good deal of turning, twisting and groaning, but none of the sleep from which they were to be wakened. At a little past two, Watson and Clemens gave up any further hope of sleep, and all three men made ready to retrace the path they had taken hours earlier. A half hour later they pulled the carriage to a stop at a bend in the road not far from where they had overturned it earlier. A break in the trees allowed them to pull the coach well off the road and tie their horse out of sight of any unlikely passer-by. All three had come armed with thick clubs, and Watson also carried a bag containing the two slabs of venison purchased at the inn and now marinated in laudanum, as they proceeded on foot to Ian's Sod and whatever fate awaited them.

As Clemens had commented, there was little moon, and even with the near cloudless night they were well hidden from the house. That was the extent of advantage the night provided. The dark also kept hidden large stones and small holes as they stumbled their way along a route well away from the house in the hope of letting sleeping dogs lie. They advanced in a line toward the stable, communicating with each through rare whispered comments and more frequent nudges, occasionally losing contact until a groan revealed a man who had lost, then regained his balance. Holmes fell heavily at one point, briefly fearing he had sprained his ankle. His club went flying as he hit the ground, but he had no time to search for it. He straightened, working his leg to be certain there was no serious injury, and rejoined his colleagues as they made slow progress toward their objective. All stayed quiet until they began to edge their way past the farmhouse. It was then the barking started. It sounded first from the stable, then from the house with the two dogs seeming to call and answer each other before joining finally in a bedlam of alarm.

The barking gave warning to those in the farmhouse that their land was being invaded; it signaled to those outside the farmhouse they were at risk of imminent attack from large dogs and armed men. Having been so alerted, the three men abandoned the deliberate course they had been pursuing, and ran heedless of the dangers they could only barely see, to avoid the dangers they could clearly imagine. Watson fell once and holding fast to his club, groped for the bag of meat he had dropped. He couldn't find it in front of him where he thought it should of landed, and looked frantically to either side. The venison was essential to their plans. He stepped back straining to see over a larger distance, and nearly fell a second time as his foot caught the corner of the elusive bag. Watson snatched it and, began a headlong dash to join Clemens and Holmes just as lamps were being lit in two rooms on the farmhouse's second landing. Holmes grunted acknowledgement of Watson's late arrival and, pointing to the door, informed Watson in a hoarse whisper to prepare himself. Holmes raised the bar from its latch as slowly as he dared, intent on containing the threat they could plainly hear on the door's other side. He opened the door a few inches, then together with Clemens struggled to hold it firm against the mongrel's excited leaps as Watson dangled one of the two slabs of meat inside the crack in the door. He felt the dog tear the venison from his hand, and all heard the animal bound away to devour its meal undisturbed. In another moment, the three men swung the door wide and entered the stable.

Holmes latched the door from the inside shutting out what little light had existed for them. They listened for any sound beside the slobbering noises of the dog feasting on the venison Watson had spiked with three-quarters of a vial of opiate-concentrated laudanum. He had feared using more lest he kill the animal. They could now make out the sound of horses— more than one, probably three—whinnying and stamping their unhappiness at the disturbance to their night. Finally, they could make out a moaning different from the animal noises, and as their eyes became better accustomed to the dark, they saw the outlines of two figures propped up in a sitting position against the side of the nearest horse stall.

Wilson and Caroline were bound hand and foot, and had cloth gags stuffed in their mouths. Lucy Donaldson was nowhere to be seen, a fact all three men noted, and about which all three remained silent, lest they acknowledge what no one wanted to believe. Holmes stayed by the door while Watson and Clemens tore off the gags and pulled at the knots to free the hostages they had come to rescue. With their gags removed, Wilson and Caroline let loose a flurry of questions ("how did you get here?" "how did you know about us?" "how many are you?"). Before anyone could answer, they gushed their gratitude to the men who had saved their lives ("thank God you came," "we thought for sure we were goners"). It was then the guard dog, its feast consumed, reappeared.

A low growl announced its emergence from the recesses of the stable. The dog took a position confronting the intruders, their beneficence in providing a late night snack clearly forgotten. The dog's piercing eyes, white against its black coat and the darkness beyond, appeared to consider each of them before choosing Holmes as its primary target. The hound's low growl grew into a guttural roar as it bared its teeth and started across the ten feet that stood between animal and man. Holmes set a forearm in front of his face, readying himself to take the weight of its spring when the dog suddenly staggered and fell to its knees. It tried to wobble itself erect, but instead collapsed panting on the stable floor, no longer able to move.

Even as Watson and Clemens dragged the now harmless animal up the alley that ran in front of what could be seen as three horse stalls, the sound of the second dog could be heard bounding its way toward the stable. Freed of their bonds, Wilson and Caroline scrambled up the ladder beyond the first of the three stalls, and climbed into the hay loft above. As they made for their hiding place, Wilson snatched two apples from the half dozen in a burlap bag set outside the first stall. Once in the loft, they slithered on knees and elbows to a point overlooking the entryway, then lay flat in the hay, their eyes fixed on the door below.

Watson and Clemens, meanwhile, having dragged the animal to the stable's rear wall, rushed back to their positions right of the door as planned, their clubs in hand, while Holmes took a stand left of the door. All were barely in place when there came the scratching and growling of the second mongrel at the stable's door. The whinnying and stomping of the horses had never stopped, and now intensified as the animals anticipated a second invasion of their home. Lifting the bar from its catch on the wall, Holmes opened the door wide enough to dangle the second slab of venison within the dog's reach.

The animal growled an enthusiastic acceptance of Holmes' offering, leaping to rip the meat from his hand as Holmes swept dog and venison through the opening, closing the door behind, and replacing the latch as he caught a glimpse of Micah and Lucas framed against the farmhouse lights. He was certain, as well, he saw the shotgun once more in Micah's hand. The dog appeared to sense the danger of its isolation from human allies. It dropped the meat at its feet, and for a second time Holmes had reason to eye a beast warily. By now, Holmes' eyes had grown sufficiently accustomed to the dark to have made out a shovel leaning against the wall behind him, and he slowly reached back and grasped its wooden shaft as he again prepared for attack. But no attack came. Perhaps he had happened on the dog that had earlier found his presence acceptable, perhaps the animal found the venison too tempting a treat to ignore. Whatever the cause, the animal cut short its threat, and picking up the meat, carried its tainted prize to a deserted corner where it could feast undisturbed.

Holmes maintained his position by the door, still holding the shovel while he waited for the brothers' attack. He didn't have long to wait. There was a crash against the door, then a grunt, followed by a second crash and a second grunt in a different voice. A brief pause, then the process repeated itself. It was apparent the brothers were taking turns hurtling themselves against the stable door, groaning their frustration, and resting a moment before trying again.

Holmes was poised, ready for the crash that would prove successful. He raised the shovel high above his shoulder, and was surprised to have pieces of mud fall from it onto his coat. The sight of the muck on his clothing put him in mind of the brothers' work clothes and their muddy boots. His thinking about the significance of that connection was interrupted by an awareness that the sounds from outside had stopped. At first he thought it was a moment of rest before the brothers gathered themselves for a fresh assault.

But no fresh assault came. Instead, there was an exchange of voices and then a low rumble, the voices and the rumble gradually fading into the noises of the night. All became quiet inside the stable as well. Unable to sense the tension that belied the sudden calm, the horses' whinnied complaint ceased, and their hooves no longer beat against the stable floor. The dark corner that had sounded with the contented growls that accompanied devouring the venison treat had ceased as well. Holmes shared with the others the hope that the silence signaled that the second animal had met the same fate as the first, but no one thought it wise to investigate.

And then the rumble sounded again, distant at first, then nearer, and nearer still, until it finally became a roar drowning out the renewed frenzy of the horses inside the stable. Peering through a crack in the door, Holmes caught a glimpse of the source of the thundering menace. He hollered his discovery to the others.

"It's the dog cart. They mean to crash the stable door."

Within seconds of his shout, the cart, turned battering ram, cracked against the stable door, knocking it from its bottom hinge, leaving it dangling off to one side and open to the night. The action left Holmes exposed while blocking Watson and Clemens from seeing anything of the entryway. Holmes hugged the wall, and as much of the dark as he could gather around him, as the brothers made their way slowly through the opening they had created, and around the dog cart that had come to rest halfway into the stable. The path they followed brought them within a few feet of Holmes who held tight to the shovel for what protection it might afford against his armed adversaries.

Like their earlier effort with the overturned coach, the plan carefully framed over three beers was no longer viable. As had been the case with that earlier plan, Holmes was to divert the brothers' attention, allowing Watson and Clemens to attack them from behind while he swung his club at their front. But Holmes' club lay somewhere on the expanse of lawn outside, and Watson and Clemens were blocked by the hanging door from even seeing the brothers, and would, in any event, have been unable to get past the dog cart to attack them. It was suddenly all on Holmes. And the task was no longer rescue, but survival—his own, and that of the others in the stable.

The brothers advanced nearly to the end of the cart they had exploded through the stable door, each of them staring at the empty place where they had left Wilson and Caroline. They called to their dogs in low tones, as if by doing so only the animals might hear them; then shared a stony glance when their calls went unheeded. Without a word they turned away from each other to begin the search for their hostages, and to confront whatever threat existed in the shadowy reaches of the stable.

Micah raised his shotgun to a position parallel to the ground, and Lucas cocked the revolver he drew from where it had been stuffed inside his shirt. Micah was the nearer to him, and Holmes decided it made no sense to wait to be discovered by a man carrying a shotgun. He raised the shovel high overhead, took two long strides and brought his weapon across the side of Micah's head. The blow lacked the force Holmes intended as the armed man pulled back at the last moment on catching sight of Holmes, but the impact was sufficient to send Micah to his knees. He looked up at Holmes as if confused by his presence, then collapsed in a sprawl along the stable floor. The shotgun slipped from his hands, landing at the feet of Lucas, who grasped it without taking his eyes from Holmes or turning his revolver from its focus on the center of Holmes' body.

Holmes still held the shovel, but was too far from Lucas for it to be of any use. Suddenly, neither escape nor resistance was possible.

Responding to the clatter of Micah's shotgun across the stable floor, Watson and Clemens worked their way around the hanging door. They saw Lucas with his revolver trained on Holmes, and confronted the impossibility of getting past the dog cart in time to save him. They hurled their clubs, but they proved unwieldy as projectiles and landed harmlessly a distance from their target. The action served only to alert Lucas to the location of two additional adversaries, and the certainty they were unarmed. He lowered the revolver and took a long step back, looking to where Watson and Clemens stood revealed, unconcerned with their own safety as they watched in horror the tragedy about to unfold.

"First you, Mr. Tyler, or whatever your name is. Then your friends. Then I will find Wilson and the girl. I'll have all of you dead by morning."

Lucas again trained the muzzle at Holmes' heart and fired at the same instant he was struck in the temple by an apple thrown with great force and just the hint of a curve. The gun sounded a small explosion and Holmes reeled back, relying on the stable's wall to keep him erect. Lucas' shot had gone high, cracking Holmes' collarbone, leaving him incapacitated and in pain, but very much alive. Lucas went down, but never lost his grip on the gun, and from his knees he prepared to finish what he started, when he was struck just above the bridge of the nose by a second apple causing him to fall to a sitting position, dazed and motionless, and no longer a threat to anyone.

The next 15 minutes saw a flurry of activity. Watson rushed to Holmes' side to do all he could to stench the bleeding. Clemens and Watson bound the barely conscious Micah, and the stunned Lucas with rope they found coiled on the floor of the stable close to where they had been hiding. All the men except Holmes then joined in pushing the dog cart back out of the

259

stable. Watson led a Morgan horse from its stall, and with help from Clemens hitched it to the cart. In the midst of their labors Mrs. Cochrane appeared, a wrapper over her nightclothes, her grey hair hanging in unkempt strands beyond her shoulders. She made no move to interrupt their labors, contenting herself with showering the intruders with epithets that sounded far better practiced than any of them would have expected from a middle-aged countrywoman.

Under Watson's careful attention, Holmes was set gently on the floor of the cart, and the well trussed Cochrane brothers were placed as far from him as could be managed. Watson seated Mrs. Cochrane beside him on one side of the cart while Wilson and Caroline took seats opposite. Clemens urged the Morgan horse down the road to Bedford, remembering that farming town as larger than Macedonia, and more likely to offer medical care for Holmes, and secure facilities for the Cochranes. There was a medley of disparate sounds as they rode, Clemens calling encouragement to the small horse, Watson giving reassurance to a non-complaining Holmes, and Mrs. Cochrane colorfully disparaging everyone in the cart other than her two sons, who were both too groggy to appreciate the distinction being made on their behalf.

It took repeated knocking on the door of the one room wood-framed building marked "POLICE" to rouse the young constable entrusted with maintaining law and order throughout the Bedford night. He directed Watson to the office of Dr. Damankos, assuring him repeatedly of the physician's ability to help his friend. Clemens then requested the Cochranes be placed in the room's single cell, justifying his plea with a dramatic detailing of the evening's events. The constable made no effort to hide his bewilderment at each revelation Clemens shared, turning frequently to the still bound, but now fully conscious Cochranes for confirmation of Clemens' report. Their strenuous disagreement with the charges did nothing to relieve his bewilderment. He knew the Cochranes, and didn't know the man who called himself Clemens, or why the man who had left had called him Twain, but he did know to be suspicious of anyone with two names. Besides which, he was certain that at least one, and probably both of the two men who had gone to see Dr. Damankos were foreign, and that was cause for suspicion as well.

He did know Brakeman Wilson, or anyway he knew who Brakeman Wilson was; he played for the Bridegrooms—just like Bedford's own Candy Cochrane. It was Brakeman Wilson saying the story told by the man with two names was true that led the constable finally to take the unpleasant step of waking his superior. With an apology to Mrs. Cochrane for the inconvenience, and an embarrassed glance to the Cochrane brothers, he left, promising to return with his Chief, who he was certain would get things straightened out. At Clemens' urging, he also promised to recover their carriage from where they had left it near the Cochrane farm, and to see to the Cochranes' dogs, which the man with two names believed would be waking sometime later in the evening.

Watson's experience with Dr. Damankos was considerably different than Clemens' ordeal. The physician was very familiar with the name, Sherlock Holmes, and expressed his good fortune at meeting Dr. John Watson as well. When he learned that Mark Twain was at the police station, he gave a low whistle, and appeared on the verge of abandoning his patient to go meet the man he described as his favorite author. He was content, for the moment, to win Watson's promise he would meet the great man before he left Bedford. The two physicians, together with the doctor's wife, who was also his nurse, labored over an anesthetized Holmes in Damankos' examining room, removing the bullet, cleaning the wound, and determining the shot had resulted in a clean break of the clavicle, before setting the bone and bandaging the area. The Damankos' indicated they would keep Holmes with them for the next several days, and offered to house Watson as well. Watson declined, saying he needed to rejoin his colleagues, and left after thanking them profusely on behalf of himself and his peacefully sleeping colleague.

By the following day Holmes was weak but alert, and asking to see the Bedford police chief. Bedford's chief of police was equally anxious to see Holmes. Unlike his constable, Chief Weissman was well aware of the reputation of Dr. Damankos' patient. He had also proven more accepting of the story related by Clemens, and had arranged for the Cochranes to be transported to the more secure facilities of the Cleveland jail, and to be charged for their parts in the murder of Conrad Wagner, the attack on JP Morgan, and the kidnapping of Wilson and Caroline. Weissman felt it unnecessary to reveal that, as a precaution, he had contacted the New York Police to confirm the story he had been told. (Clemens was, after all, as he later explained to Mrs. Weissman, a renowned storyteller.) One day later, the news of Candy Cochrane's death, his family's participation in murder, and the roles played by JP Morgan, Mark Twain, and Sherlock Holmes would be the talk of every household in Bedford, and most of those anywhere there was access to a newspaper.

The Chief was accompanied by Watson and Clemens on his visit to see Holmes and all three were joined by Damankos and his wife. Propping himself against a pillow with the help of Mrs. Damankos, he shared with Weissman the discovery he had made in the Cochranes' stable.

"There is an additional assignment I must ask of you, Chief Weissman. Somewhere along the stream that runs at the back of the Cochrane property you will find an area of freshly turned earth large enough to be a grave. In it you will find the remains of Lucy Donaldson."

"How do you know that, Holmes?" Watson's question reflected greater surprise than he wished, and a hint of disbelief he hoped would go unnoticed. Nonetheless, his words echoed the thoughts of all those at Holmes' bedside.

Holmes responded with the certitude that had been one of the traits that first commended him to Mrs. Hudson. "While in the stable I came across a shovel whose blade was covered with mud. Had I greater opportunity to examine it, I am certain I would have found it a match in color and consistency with the mud I saw on the Cochrane brothers' shoes and clothing earlier in the day. When we didn't find Miss Donaldson in the stable, it seemed apparent to me what use had been made of the shovel. The farm provides limitless territory for hiding Miss Donaldson's body, but the dry hard ground made the softer area along the bank of the stream by far the best choice."

Watson expressed great praise for Holmes and his "inspired reasoning"; Clemens, Damankos and Weissman regarded his analysis as nothing more than was to be expected. The later discovery of Lucy's body was regarded as anti-climactic by all but Watson, who viewed it as something akin to Lazarus' rising.

Three days later, Clemens returned to the Damankos' to take his leave of Holmes and Watson, citing his need to get back to New York to appear at Cooper Union. The three men exchanged addresses and pledges to see each other before too much time passed. Clemens was certain he'd be back to London "before long," and Holmes and Watson looked forward to seeing Hartford, while having no idea where Hartford was to be found. They shared drinks from Clemens' flask of Irish whiskey that he promised would put hair on their chests and blarney on their tongues. Toasts were drunk to each other, to Wilson and Caroline, and at Clemens' urging "to Mrs. Hudson, a most remarkable woman." When the toasts were all done, and the last hand had been shaken, Clemens was gone, and the room seemed suddenly increased in size and diminished in spirit.

13.
Home to Baker Street

A week later, with sling in place and repeated cautions to keep the area stable, Holmes was deemed sufficiently recovered to make the trip to City Hospital in Cleveland, and in the space of a week the Bedford township had gained and lost the two most prominent people ever to visit its community. Mrs. Hudson joined her colleagues in Cleveland, she and Watson taking rooms at the Hollenden Hotel. In Holmes' hospital room, Mrs. Hudson reported Dietz's visit to Helmut Fleischer, then listened intently to the account Holmes and Watson shared of their visit to Ian's Sod. Mrs. Hudson was so effusive in her praise for Holmes, he later asked Watson if he'd heard correctly or was experiencing a reaction to the medication he was still receiving.

Wilson and Caroline also came to see Holmes shortly after his arrival in Cleveland. Through Morgan's intercession, they were staying at the home of his friend, Francis Glidden, owner of the Glidden Varnish Company. Wilson heaped gratitude on Holmes, Watson and the absent Clemens while Caroline nodded her vigorous agreement. Watson shrugged off the accolades, reminding Wilson that all three of them would almost certainly be dead if it hadn't been for his strong and accurate throwing arm. Wilson grinned sheepishly and claimed he was just lucky, an opinion no one in the room shared. His expression turned solemn as Mrs. Hudson reported for a second time the visit Dietz and Police Chief Emsinger had made to Helmut Fleischer. This time she added information Dietz had given her before she left New York.

"I'm told it's not likely you'll be 'earin' from Franklin Langer again. Mr. Dietz says Mr. Langer 'as disappeared from New York. No one seems to know to where, and no one is expectin' 'im back any time soon."

Wilson nodded his grim understanding.

"And what of your plans, Mr. Wilson?" Watson asked. "Will you be returning to Brooklyn to throw for the Bridegrooms anytime in the future?"

"I expect to, Dr. Watson. I've been working out with the Cleveland Spiders at their League Park thanks to Mr. Ebbets' arrangements. I'm looking forward to things getting back to normal real soon."

"All this is your doing, Auntie." Caroline's broad smile lit the room, coaxing a tentative smile from Mrs. Hudson and puzzled looks from Holmes and Watson, all three wondering what it was Caroline had in mind. In another moment she made that clear.

"If you hadn't come all the way across the ocean to be with William and me, Mr. Holmes would not have been here to save our lives and prove William's innocence."

Holmes smiled acknowledgment of Caroline's tribute, and Watson grunted what was taken to be his agreement with it. Talk of the ocean voyage reminded Mrs. Hudson of unfinished business.

"I 'ave indeed come three thousand miles to be at a weddin', and I'm not goin' 'ome to face your mother without there bein' one."

And so it was arranged. Francis Glidden volunteered his home for the ceremony, but Wilson and Caroline had insisted that Holmes be at their wedding, and since Holmes couldn't be moved from the hospital, the wedding was scheduled to take place at Cleveland's City Hospital.

Never before and never again would a hospital room at City Hospital take on such a festive air. The room was awash with garlands of roses—red, yellow, pink and white with cymbidium orchids scattered amongst them. The flowers were the gift of JP Morgan who regretted his inability to join them, tactfully overlooking the fact that he hadn't been invited. In truth, the one person whose absence they regretted, apart from family in England, was Brickyard Snyder who was confined to his own hospital bed, but was expected to make a full recovery and rejoin the Bridegrooms the following season.

A newspaper account of the wedding would have stated that "the bride, Miss Caroline Littleberry, looked stunning in a floor length ivory colored silk gown. She wore no veil and carried a bouquet of apple blossoms. Miss Littleberry was given away by Dr. John Watson substituting for the bride's father, who was unable to attend for reasons of health. The well-known detective, Mr. Sherlock Holmes, served as Mr. William (Brakeman) Wilson's best man although confined to a hospital bed. Mr. Wilson's formal dress was a gift of the management of the Brooklyn Bridegrooms, the groom's employer. The Reverend Sylvester Perlmutter officiated. Among those attending was Mrs. Hudson, a cousin of the bride's mother, as well as several of the nursing staff of City Hospital."

There was, however, no newspaper account of the ceremony, and no photograph to preserve its image. Nonetheless, no one who witnessed the wedding at City Hospital would soon forget it.

"Mr. 'Olmes, I do believe it's time for us to be gettin' back to Baker Street." It was eight days from the time Holmes had been discharged from the hospital. They had returned to New York, again taking rooms at the Waldorf after declining with gratitude Morgan's offer to have them as house guests. In the eight days they managed to see every site recommended by an obliging hotel staff, took an additional meal at Delmonico's, this one with Mr. and Mrs. William Wilson after seeing Wilson defeat the Chicago Colts with a shutout (as they were told a score of nil was properly described), and attended a party given in their honor by JP Morgan. They took that opportunity to say their good-byes to the financier and to Dietz. Morgan made a small show of presenting Mrs. Hudson an opal pendant with a sterling silver chain, insisting he be allowed to place it around her neck, much to her embarrassment, and to the delight of Holmes and Watson. In a private moment between the two men, Holmes thanked Morgan for his offer of employment and reiterated his need to refuse it. Morgan accepted the refusal he had expected in a spirit that suggested bitter disappointment, but a willingness to soldier on.

Both their work and sight-seeing now complete, Holmes and Watson agreed it was time to return to Baker Street. No one was prepared to admit it, but the truth was all three were homesick. Holmes was missing his beakers and test tubes, Watson could visualize Lancets stacking up at the door, and Mrs. Hudson had gone longer than she ever had without a visit to St. Marylebone Cemetery. One task remained. There was need to find a suitable gift for Inspector Lestrade. It took them another two days, but they were agreed it was worth it.

The voyage from New York to London involved neither phrenologists or world renowned authors. Nonetheless, Mrs. Hudson once again did not lack for companionship. The first night out, upon learning her widowed status, the middle-aged couple beside her at dinner declared she would never suffer through a lonely meal while they were on board. Ordinarily, Mrs. Hudson would have embraced her solitude, not viewing it as loneliness; however, the woman who introduced herself as Mrs. Michele Hastings proved so charmingly unaffected that Mrs. Hudson found it impossible not to be drawn to her. Nor was Mrs. Hudson alone in her appreciation. Mr. Hastings appeared thoroughly captivated by his wife's recital, smiling and nodding his way through her history of their life together.

"I wouldn't say we was poor as church mice. That would be goin' too far. My Henry has always provided for his family as handsomely as any man could, but we had my parents to care for and the children—there were five—not that there's a one of them I'd trade for a pot of gold—but all of them with healthy appetites, and every year growing out of last year's clothes, and out of shoes so fast we never did see the cobbler. They're all of them out of the house now, with families of their own—well, almost all—there's Sylvan of course, who never will find anyone he thinks is good enough for him. And what do you think. Out of the blue, Henry's aunt in Sheffield—who we haven't seen in fifteen years—did I say fifteen, probably more like twenty, isn't that right, Henry?" Without waiting for Henry to register his choice of time frames, Mrs. Hastings forged ahead. "Well, the old darling passes away in her sleep, as peaceful as a newborn babe from all what we've been told. And you'd never guess what happened then, or maybe you would because these things are always in the paper happening to other people. Anyway, that dear woman, who all this time had everyone thinkin' she hadn't a shilling in the world—I mean to where Henry and me sent her tins of food every Christmas—turns out to have a fortune hid under her floorboards. And she leaves every cent of it to Henry, and to Henry's brother, the two of them being her only living relatives."

Mrs. Hastings stopped long enough to sample the carrot soup that had been set before her. She swallowed a half spoonful, wrinkled her nose, and returned to her story. "Well, here's Henry retired from the Metropolitan Police not six months ago, and the both of us thinking the time to enjoy the money is now, and the thing to do is to travel while the both of us can make our way up a gangplank. And all our children say the same. Of course, we put a good bit of the money aside for them to get after we're gone. Anyway, that's how we come to be in America for two weeks, and now it's back to London, but we're already thinking about the Continent after we get a little rest."

With that, Mrs. Hastings pushed the soup away from her place as she spied the waiter working his way along the table with a tray containing sweetbreads. Mrs. Hudson, having scraped the last spoonful of soup from her bowl, turned her attention to Mr. Hastings.

"Did I understand you to 'ave retired from the Metropolitan Force?

Mr. Hastings spoke with an economy of words that nicely complemented his wife's more generous reporting. "After twenty-eight years of service, ma'am."

"I wonder did you know my 'usband, Constable Tobias 'Udson?"

Mr. Hastings' eyes widened and he took a long breath as he summoned the right words for his response. "A policeman's policeman is what your Constable Hudson was, ma'am. A policeman's policeman. I never had the privilege of serving with him, but I knew about him alright. In those days there wouldn't have been many who didn't."

Mrs. Hudson spent the rest of the voyage in the frequent company of the Hastings couple. She endured tales of children and grandchildren in exchange for the bittersweet pleasure of sharing memories of Tobias and the work of the Metropolitan Police with Henry Hastings. It had been a long time, and she was surprised by her difficulty at times in distinguishing between the memories she knew to be true and those that only might have been, deciding finally that the distinction hardly mattered. Each of the memories had its own integrity, and their total reflected accurately hers and Tobias' life together. By the end of the voyage, Mrs. Hudson felt a melancholy she found strangely welcome.

While Mrs. Hudson found unexpected comfort in the company of strangers, Holmes and Watson reveled in the absence of companions, an absence aided by Holmes' decision to once again become Calvin Tyler, adding to his assumed identity the job of chemist which sparked instant disinterest from his fellow travelers. They endured small talk during meals, then retired to the smoking salon, sometimes reviewing their experiences in New York, sometimes laying plans for their return to London, sometimes sharing a quiet pipe together.

Mrs. Hudson spent only a day at Baker Street before going to visit her cousin in Brighton. She recounted the events in New York, giving Holmes and Watson full marks for capturing the Cochranes, while describing at length Wilson's heroics in protecting Caroline and saving Holmes' life. The stories of jailbreak, kidnapping and murder kept her audience spellbound and stimulated a myriad of questions. When the last question had been answered and the final expression of astonishment sounded, Mrs. Hudson spoke at length of Caroline's wedding after first giving her cousin flowers from the spray of apple blossoms the bride carried. She provided her cousin assurances of Wilson's capacity to support her daughter based on the report of no less an authority than Samuel Clemens. With her association to the author revealed, a new round of questions and expressions of astonishment was begun.

After two days of reminiscing over breakfasts and dinners, and during long walks along the Brighton pier, Mrs. Hudson declared her need to get back to London and her lodgers. Her announcement was greeted with sober nods of understanding, and expressions of disappointment that she'd been with them such a short time, but without a request she reconsider her decision. Pie sales had suffered while Mrs. Hudson transported them from Brighton to America and a life they would never know. It was time for the Littleberrys to get back to Brighton and the life they knew.

With Mrs. Hudson gone, Holmes began work on a new scientific investigation. The shooting at the Morgan mansion had inspired Holmes to make a study of the extent to which spent bullets fired from different revolvers might show different markings, even where the gun type was the same. He had purchased two 1889 Webley revolvers and proceeded to fire each into several of Mrs. Hudson's pillows from whose scattered feathers he extracted the bullets for examination under his microscope. Only at Watson's insistence that they retain pillows for sleeping were three salvaged for use by the residents of 221B Baker Street. While Holmes conducted his scientific investigation, Watson divided time between review of the articles in the three Lancets that had accumulated during his absence, and recording for posterity their experiences in New York, pausing every now and again to recoil from the sound of gunshots fired less than fifteen feet from where he was working.

Even before she unpacked from her visit to Brighton, Mrs. Hudson had scones baking in the oven and had taken tea to the sitting room Holmes and Watson shared. A raised eyebrow was her only acknowledgment of the havoc Holmes had created. History told her that protest was pointless and outrage counterproductive. The jackknife that held Holmes' correspondence in place at the mantelpiece was proof of that. It had only become a permanent fixture after Mrs. Hudson's observation that Holmes might find an alternative filing system.

But the relationship between herself and Holmes had become newly complicated by something more than Holmes' frequent obstinacy. She knew it, and she was certain Holmes did as well. At Ian's Sod, Holmes had displayed a proficiency in the use of her own methods that came as a revelation to both of them, although it would be acknowledged by neither. Holmes would now feel justified in exercising greater independence, and Mrs. Hudson was forced to acknowledge he now merited a wider latitude of responsibility. Working out an accommodation between Holmes' view of a future of limitless horizons, and Mrs. Hudson's more bounded view, promised to be a lengthy and sometimes contentious process. Immediately, it reinforced her view that arguing about the loss of a few pillows would not be a fruitful exercise. There was, too, a more pressing issue to be addressed at 221B. Lestrade was due shortly, having invited himself to welcome them home, and to share with Holmes "a bit of a problem that's come up at the Yard."

Mrs. Hudson had not been downstairs long when the doorbell rang, and she soon found herself staring into the grim face of Inspector Lestrade. He spoke her name and experimented with a smile, achieving only modest success. She urged him to go right up, that Mr. Holmes and the Doctor were expecting him. Once more the housekeeper, Mrs. Hudson followed soon after carrying scones fresh from her oven. The scones gained her entry to the room, but could not delay her departure. She set down her dish after a brief search for an empty place to put it, and reluctantly started for the door when she was stopped by Watson.

"We were just about to describe our adventures in New York, Mrs. Hudson. I'm certain you can deliver a far better account of the wedding we attended than we poor men."

Lestrade's somber look had softened in response to the welcome appearance of raisin-filled scones, and he joined Watson in support of their creator. "By all means, Mrs. Hudson, please stay. And, Holmes, I do want to hear about your adventures on the other side. In truth, there has been no shortage of stories in the papers, and there'll be no shortage of people back at the Yard who'll have questions for me when they learn I've been to see you. I do need to talk to you about that bit of a problem I mentioned, but we can get to it later. Tell me about America."

For the next half hour Lestrade did what he could to reduce the pile of scones Mrs. Hudson had provided, while Holmes and Watson took turns describing JP Morgan and his home (Lestrade shook his head in wonder), the Pinkerton private police force (Lestrade's eyes rolled back in his head), Wilson's escape from the Tombs (Lestrade snickered), Cochrane revealed as the murderer only to be killed moments later (Lestrade pursed his lips and groaned), the arrest of the Cochrane family (Lestrade nodded his satisfaction), and Caroline's wedding to Wilson. The last was told by Mrs. Hudson, with detailed reports of Watson giving away the bride, and Holmes acting as best man. Lestrade smiled broadly for the first time in his visit, and voiced regret at not being there "to see the show."

When they were done, Watson went to a drawer in his desk and pulled out the gift they had purchased in New York. Holmes and Mrs. Hudson joined him, and all three stood together as they presented it to Lestrade. When he saw the gift, the broad smile turned to roars of laughter as he held the present at arms' length to get its full effect.

"I'll put this up in my office and I guarantee every officer in the Yard will come around to see it." The gift that promised to attract the attention of every officer in the Yard was a large framed photograph they had taken in New York. It showed Holmes, Watson and Mrs. Hudson standing on the steps of a building and smiling at the camera. Etched into the gray stone of the building behind them were the words "New York City Detention Facilities." Carefully printed in the space below the three detectives were the words "Wish You Were Here."

Laughter was still in his voice as he thundered his appreciation, "I'll treasure this, I can tell you." Then, the laughter softened again to a smile, and his voice sounded little above a whisper, "I'll treasure this always." The smile still lingered as he turned to the dilemma that was his other reason for coming to 221B.

"Mr. Holmes, we've run into something at the Yard I think will interest you."

Holmes steepled his fingers and peered over them to the Inspector. Watson pulled his accounts book from his waistcoat together with his number two Eagle pencil. Mrs. Hudson gathered up the dishes on her tray, and left the men to their discussion. She'd put up another pot of tea in her kitchen in preparation for learning from Holmes and Watson what it was that had stumped Scotland Yard. She closed the door as Lestrade began his narrative.

"Mr. Holmes, how much do you know about Siamese twins?"

Also from MX Publishing

MX Publishing is the world's largest specialist Sherlock Holmes publisher, with over a hundred titles and fifty authors creating the latest in Sherlock Holmes fiction and non-fiction.

From traditional short stories and novels to travel guides and quiz books, MX Publishing cater for all Holmes fans.

The collection includes leading titles such as *Benedict Cumberbatch In Transition* and *The Norwood Author* which won the 2011 Howlett Award (Sherlock Holmes Book of the Year).

MX Publishing also has one of the largest communities of Holmes fans on Facebook with regular contributions from dozens of authors.

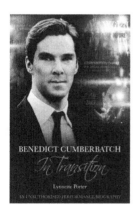

www.mxpublishing.com

Also from MX Publishing

Sherlock Holmes Short Story Collections

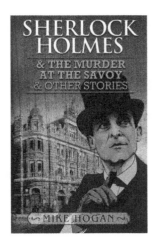 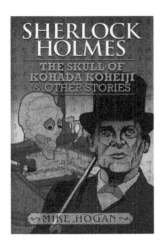

Sherlock Holmes and the Murder at the Savoy

Sherlock Holmes and the Skull of Kohada Koheiji

Look out for the new novel from Mike Hogan
– *The Scottish Question.*

www.mxpublishing.com

Also from MX Publishing

  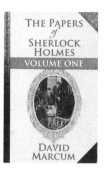

Our bestselling books are our short story collections;

'Lost Stories of Sherlock Holmes' , 'The Outstanding Mysteries of Sherlock Holmes', The Papers of Sherlock Holmes Volume 1 and 2, 'Untold Adventures of Sherlock Holmes' (and the sequel 'Studies in Legacy) and 'Sherlock Holmes in Pursuit', 'The Cotswold Werewolf and Other Stories of Sherlock Holmes' – and many more......

  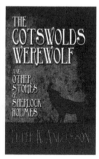

www.mxpublishing.com

Also from MX Publishing

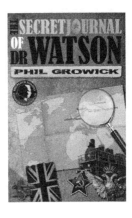

"Phil Growick's, 'The Secret Journal of Dr Watson', is an adventure which takes place in the latter part of Holmes and Watson's lives. They are entrusted by HM Government (although not officially) and the King no less to undertake a rescue mission to save the Romanovs, Russia's Royal family from a grisly end at the hand of the Bolsheviks. There is a wealth of detail in the story but not so much as would detract us from the enjoyment of the story. Espionage, counter-espionage, the ace of spies himself, double-agents, double-crossers...all these flit across the pages in a realistic and exciting way. All the characters are extremely well-drawn and Mr Growick, most importantly, does not falter with a very good ear for Holmesian dialogue indeed. Highly recommended. A five-star effort."
The Baker Street Society

www.mxpublishing.com

Links

MX Publishing are proud to support the Save Undershaw campaign – the campaign to save and restore Sir Arthur Conan Doyle's former home. Undershaw is where he brought Sherlock Holmes back to life, and should be preserved for future generations of Holmes fans.

SaveUndershaw
www.saveundershaw.com

Sherlockology
www.sherlockology.com

MX Publishing
www.mxpublishing.com

You can read more about Sir Arthur Conan Doyle and Undershaw in Alistair Duncan's book (share of royalties to the Undershaw Preservation Trust) – *An Entirely New Country* and in the amazing compilations *Sherlock's Home – The Empty House* and the new book *Two, To One, Be* (all royalties to the Trust).

Lightning Source UK Ltd.
Milton Keynes UK
UKOW06f1152061015

259961UK00001B/9/P